FROM THE PAGES OF
DEAD SOULS

A rather pretty little chaise on springs, such as bachelors, half-pay officers, staff captains, landowners with about a hundred serfs—in short, all such as are spoken of as "gentlemen of the middling sort"—drive about in, rolled in at the gates of the hotel of the provincial town of N.
(page 5)

In the end the fat man, after serving God and his Tsar and winning universal respect, leaves the service, moves away and becomes a landowner, a hearty hospitable Russian gentleman,—he gets on, and indeed gets on very well. And when he has gone, his thin heirs in accordance with the Russian tradition make ducks and drakes of all their father's property. I cannot disguise the fact that such were the reflections which occupied Tchitchikov's mind while he was scrutinising the company and the result was that he finally joined the fat ones, among whom he found all the personages he knew: the public prosecutor with very black thick eyebrows and with the left eye given to winking slightly as though to say: "Come into the next room, my boy, I have something to tell you," though he was a serious and taciturn man; the postmaster, a short man who was a wit and a philosopher; the president of the court, a very sagacious and polite man,—all of whom welcomed him as an old acquaintance while Tchitchikov responded to their civilities by profuse bows a little to one side but no less agreeable for that.
(page 14)

"I say, my good man, how many of our peasants have died since the census was taken?"
(page 32)

Such was Nozdryov! Perhaps he will be called a hackneyed character, and it will be said that there are no Nozdryovs now. Alas! those who say so are wrong. It will be many long years before the Nozdryovs are extinct. They are everywhere among us, and the only difference perhaps is that they are wearing a different cut of coat; but people are carelessly unobservant and a man in a different coat seems to them a different man.
(page 72)

A word aptly uttered or written cannot be cut away by an axe.

(page 109)

Another thing I must mention about the ladies of N. is that, like many Petersburg ladies, they were distinguished by great niceness and propriety in their choice of words and expressions. They never said: "I blew my nose, I got into a sweat, I spat," but used instead some such expression as: "I made use of my handkerchief."   (page 161)

And now the officials asked themselves the question which they ought to have asked themselves in the first chapter of my poem. It was decided to make inquiries of the persons from whom the dead souls had been bought, so as to find out at least what sort of transaction it was, and what was to be understood by dead souls.   (page 198)

Scratching the head signifies all manner of things among the Russian people.   (page 218)

Russia! Russia! I behold thee, from my lovely faraway paradise, I behold thee! It is poor, neglected and comfortless in thee, no insolent marvels of nature crowned by insolent marvels of art, no towns with many-windowed lofty palaces piled in precipitous heights, no picturesque trees, no ivy-clad houses in the roar and everlasting spray of waterfalls rejoice the eye or strike awe into the heart; the head is not turned to gaze at the rocks piled up on the heights above it; no everlasting lines of shining mountains rising into the silvery pure skies gleam in the distance through dark arches, scattered one upon the other in a tangle of vines, ivy and wild roses beyond number. In thee all is open, desolate, flat; thy lowly towns lie scattered like dots, like specks unseen among thy plains; there is nothing to allure or captivate the eye. But what mysterious inexplicable force draws one to thee? Why does the mournful song that floats all over the length and breadth of thee from sea to sea echo unceasingly in the ear? What is in it, in that song? What is it that calls and sobs and clutches at my heart? What are these strains that so poignantly greet me, that go straight to my soul, that throb about my heart? Russia! what wouldst thou of me? What is the mysterious hidden bond between us? Why dost thou gaze at me thus, and why is everything within thee turning upon me eyes full of expectation?   (page 223)

Sandee
Kelso

DEAD SOULS

Nikolai Gogol

TRANSLATED BY CONSTANCE GARNETT

WITH AN INTRODUCTION AND NOTES
BY JEFFREY MEYERS

GEORGE STADE
CONSULTING EDITORIAL DIRECTOR

BARNES & NOBLE CLASSICS
NEW YORK

JB

BARNES & NOBLE CLASSICS

NEW YORK

Published by Barnes & Noble Books
122 Fifth Avenue
New York, NY 10011

www.barnesandnoble.com/classics

The first part of *Dead Souls* was published in Russia in 1842. The surviving five
chapters of the second part were not published until after Gogol's death.
Constance Garnett's English translation first appeared in 1922.

Published in 2005 by Barnes & Noble Classics with new Introduction, Notes,
Biography, Chronology, Inspired By, Comments & Questions,
and For Further Reading.

Introduction, Notes, and For Further Reading
Copyright © 2005 by Jeffrey Meyers.

Note on Nikolai Gogol, The World of Nikolai Gogol and *Dead Souls*,
Inspired by *Dead Souls*, Comments & Questions, and For Further Reading
Copyright © 2005 by Barnes & Noble, Inc.

Dead Souls
ISBN-13: 978-1-59308-092-1
ISBN-10: 1-59308-092-1
LC Control Number 2004116677

Produced and published in conjunction with:
Fine Creative Media, Inc.
322 Eighth Avenue
New York, NY 10001

Michael J. Fine, President and Publisher

Printed in the United States of America

QM

3 5 7 9 10 8 6 4

NIKOLAI GOGOL

The Russian intelligentsia was surprised when the great and famously aloof poet Alexander Pushkin welcomed the young writer Gogol into his circle. Few suspected that Gogol would quickly rise to such literary heights. He was, after all, from a small village in Ukraine and had no aristocratic standing or great wealth to speed his career. But ambition, flexibility, luck, and a heady dose of confidence thrust him into stardom and a life of brief but legendary intensity.

Born on April 1, 1809, Nikolai Vasilyevich Gogol grew up on his family's estate in Sorochinsty, Ukraine. His father, who died when Nikolai was sixteen, was a minor landowner and an amateur poet and playwright who acted in the plays he wrote and directed. Nikolai received his brief education at a boarding school in Nezhin, where he was schooled in the classics and German Romanticism. At school he first became involved in theater and writing, performing in amateur productions and contributing frequently to the literary magazine.

After graduating, Gogol moved to Russia's capital, St. Petersburg, and worked for a time as a government clerk. His real ambitions, however, were creative and literary. After auditioning and being rejected by the Imperial Theater, he turned his energies to writing. In 1829 he self-published the long Romantic poem *Hanz Küchelgarten*; it was a failure, excoriated by the few critics who bothered to read it, and Gogol bought back and burned every copy he could find. A few years later he published the first of two volumes of tales set in his native Ukraine, *Evenings on a Farm Near Dikanka*. These works won the hearts of Pushkin as well as of most Russian readers.

Over the next several years, Gogol worked briefly (and unsuccessfully) as an assistant professor of history at St. Petersburg University and published several new works, all well received, including *Arabesques*, a collection of fiction, essays, and criticism; *Mirgorod*, another collection of tales; and *The Government Inspector*, a dramatic comedy.

In 1836 Gogol left Russia and traveled in Germany, Switzerland, and France before settling in Rome, where he wrote his masterpiece,

Dead Souls. The novel secured Gogol's status as the father of Russian realism and influenced generations of writers, including Dostoevsky, Kafka, and Nabokov.

After living abroad for twelve years, Gogol returned to Russia in 1848. The remaining years of his life were marked by spiritual upheavals and nervous disorders. He turned to extreme religious beliefs and came under the influence thereafter of fanatical Russian monks. Shortly before he died, Gogol destroyed part II of *Dead Souls* (five chapters were later found). He stopped eating soon afterward and died on March 4, 1852.

TABLE OF CONTENTS

THE WORLD OF NIKOLAI GOGOL
AND *DEAD SOULS*

1809 Nikolai Vasilyevich Gogol is born on April 1 on his family's estate in the village of Sorochintsy, Ukraine (then called Little Russia). His father runs the estate and is an amateur poet and playwright.

1812 In June Napoléon I of France invades Russia; his retreat and the humiliating defeat of his Grand Army later that year ruin his campaign of conquest.

1819 St. Petersburg University is founded.

1821 Nikolai is sent to a boarding school in Nezhin. His years at this school will serve as his only formal education. An unremarkable student, Nikolai nevertheless tries out his creative talents by writing poetry and prose for the school literary journal. Russian novelist Fyodor Dostoevsky is born.

1825 Nikolai's father dies. Nicholas I becomes czar of Russia, setting off the short-lived Decembrist uprising (Decembrists were members of a secret revolutionary society), which he crushes on the first day of his reign.

1828 Gogol graduates from school. He moves to the Russian capital of St. Petersburg, ostensibly to pursue a career in civil service, and takes a position as a government clerk. He unsuccessfully auditions for the Imperial Theater.

1829 He publishes, at his own expense and under a pseudonym, a long poem entitled *Hanz Küchelgarten*. The poem receives such scathing reviews that the impulsive author buys back and burns all the copies he can find.

1830 Gogol begins writing stories about his native Ukraine. A Polish nationalist uprising against the czar begins; it is defeated in 1831, when the Russians reenter Warsaw.

1831 The first part of a collection of Gogol's Ukrainian tales, *Evenings on a Farm Near Dikanka*, is published to overwhelming success. Gogol meets Russian poet Alexander Pushkin, who helps establish his reputation as a brilliant new writer.

1832   The second part of *Evenings on a Farm Near Dikanka* is published.

1834   Through connections, Gogol becomes an assistant professor of history at St. Petersburg University. With only a high school education, however, he is ill-prepared for the position. Kiev University (in Ukraine's capital city) is founded.

1835   Gogol's *Mirgorod* (a collection of tales) and *Arabesques* (essays, fiction, and criticism) are published. Despite mixed and sometimes negative reviews, Gogol becomes one of the best known of the Russian literati. He leaves his professorship and devotes full attention to his writing.

1836   His dramatic comedy *The Government Inspector* debuts in Moscow and St. Petersburg. By now immensely popular in Russia, Gogol leaves to travel in Germany, Switzerland, France, and Italy.

1837   He settles in Rome, where he will live for most of the next twelve years. Pushkin is killed in a duel.

1838   The first Russian railroad is built.

1840   Mikhail Lermontov's novel *A Hero of Our Time* is published.

1842   Gogol's masterpiece, *Dead Souls*, is published to rave reviews. The novel will inspire generations of novelists and earn Gogol a reputation as the father of Russian realism.

1847   Gogol publishes a collection of essays, *Selected Passages from Correspondence with Friends*. Long heralded as a political radical, he reveals conservative, czarist views that dismay many of his loyal readers. Literary critic Vissarion Belinsky writes his famous "Letter to Gogol," in which he denounces Gogol's defense of the czarist regime.

1848   Gogol journeys to Palestine. He returns to Russia, living in several cities, for the final years of his life. More and more taken with extreme religious beliefs, Gogol falls under the influence of fanatical priests.

1849   Dostoevsky is condemned to forced labor in Siberia for conspiring against Czar Nicholas I.

1852   In a fit of rage, Gogol burns the manuscript of his sequel to *Dead Souls* (a version of five chapters is later found). Fasting and illness lead to his death on March 4. Gogol is buried in Moscow.

INTRODUCTION

I

Nikolai Gogol was born on April 1, 1809, in the Ukrainian village of Sorochintsy, about 150 miles east of Kiev, the eldest of twelve children, of whom six survived. Three years later, in a traumatic historical event that overshadowed Russian life, Napoléon invaded Russia and suffered a disastrous defeat. Gogol, whose surname means "golden-eye duck," grew up on his parents' 3,000-acre estate, Vasilievka, where the family lived comfortably on the toil of their 200 serfs. His father, an amateur playwright, died when Nikolai was sixteen. In his early childhood his somewhat unbalanced mother frightened him with visions of Hell. "You depicted the eternal torment of the sinners in such a vivid and terrifying manner," he later told her, "that I was shaken and responded with my entire sensitivity."[1] She doted on her son, and later credited him with the invention of steamships and railroads. The nightmarish visions she inspired would recur when he suffered from religious mania at the end of his life.

In 1821, at the age of twelve, Gogol was sent to boarding school in Nezhin, about 70 miles northeast of Kiev. Apart from visits to his family during holidays, he spent the next seven years at this school. The biographical critic Simon Karlinsky described Gogol as a slovenly, ill-mannered, and decidedly unattractive schoolboy: "His long blond hair, elongated face, and abnormally long nose gave him the appearance of a young fox. His neck was covered with messy-looking sores caused by scrofula. . . . Another chronic ailment caused an unpleasant liquid to ooze out of his ears."[2] To protect himself from hostility he developed a satirical tongue and caustic wit.

After completing his studies, Gogol moved to St. Petersburg. Like many young men from a small provincial town, he suddenly felt isolated, alienated, and insignificant in the Russian capital. Desperate for cash, he reluctantly accepted a humble position as clerk in a government office that registered sales of land—and made good use of this bureaucratic experience in his fiction. As aspiring poet, in 1829 he published, at his own expense and under the pseudonym "V. Alov," the long verse idyll *Hanz Küchelgarten*. He received blistering reviews and burned all the copies he could find.

He then used the money his mother had sent to pay off a mortgage to finance a brief trip to Hamburg and Lübeck (what else are mothers for?). Returning to St. Petersburg, he tried a variety of occupations. He enrolled in art school, auditioned as a professional actor, and got a tedious office job. For a while he became a history teacher in a private school for aristocratic girls. In *Dead Souls* he wrote ironically of its limited curriculum: "in boarding-schools, as we all know, three principal subjects lay the foundation of all human virtues: the French language . . . the pianoforte . . . and finally domestic training" (p. 25). Gogol became a writer after notable failures in several professions—including writing.

Russia and Austria controlled Poland. The Ukraine was then part of Russia and Gogol had been educated in the Russian language. If he wanted to establish a serious (as opposed to a merely provincial) reputation, he had to write in Russian rather than in Ukrainian. Like black and southern writers in America, or Jewish and Sicilian writers in Italy, Gogol was an outsider by his background, and he took advantage of this. When he began to write professionally in the 1830s, local color and folk tales were fashionable, and readers were eager for authentic Ukrainian material. Ukrainian peasants ate unusual food, wore colorful costumes, and had their own songs, dances, and musical instruments. Gogol portrayed this local color in his first book of stories, based on a town near his birthplace, *Evenings on a Farm near Dikanka* (1831–1832). It was praised by the Russian poet Alexander Pushkin, who became his friend and patron.

Gogol had a miraculous year in 1834. He published *Taras Bulba*, a Homerically inspired glorification of violence, war, and death, which romanticized the life of the Ukrainian Cossacks, as Mikhail Lermontov in *A Hero of Our Time* (1840) and Leo Tolstoy in *The Cossacks* (1862) would later do for the brigands of the Caucasus. He finished the Mirgorod tales (including the supernatural "Viy"), began the St. Petersburg stories (including "Nevsky Prospect" and "The Diary of a Madman"), and started to write two comedies. Up to "Viy," he had set all his fiction in the Ukraine; after that story, he set all his work in Russia.

That year Gogol also used his connections to become an assistant professor of history at the University of St. Petersburg. His plans were ambitious, but he had no qualifications for the job, was appallingly unprepared, and lacked talent for teaching. As he wrote of the hopelessly blocked project of Tyentyetnikov in *Dead Souls*: "the universal history of man [was] conceived on such a vast scale that the professor only succeeded in treating of the introduction" (p. 262). Ivan Turgenev, the future novelist, happened to attend Gogol's lectures and described the classroom fiasco: "In the first place, Gogol usually missed two lectures out of three; secondly, even when he appeared in the lecture room, he did not so much speak as whisper something incoherently and showed us small engravings of views of Palestine and other Eastern countries, looking terribly embarrassed all the time. We were all convinced that he knew nothing of history. . . . I can still see, as though it were today, his thin, long-nosed face with the two ends of the black silk handkerchief sticking out like two huge ears."[3]

Gogol, out of touch with reality—except for the fictional reality he himself created—complained to a friend about the empty seats in the lecture hall: "Do you know what it means to find no sympathy, what it means to find no response? I lecture in solitude, in utter solitude at the university here. No one listens to me, I have never noticed anyone who seemed to be struck by a blinding truth."[4] After he'd been forced to resign, Gogol angrily claimed that he'd regained his traditional freedom—and then admitted that it had all been a terrible mistake: "The university and I have spat in each other's faces and a month from now I'll be a free Cossack again. . . . General opinion holds that I undertook something that I had no business undertaking."[5]

Like Edgar Allan Poe, born the same year, Gogol suffered from poverty and had grandiose literary ambitions. They came from different countries, had different languages and cultures, and probably never heard of each other, but they were surprisingly similar. Like Poe, Gogol moved restlessly from place to place, shamelessly sponged off family and friends, read his works aloud with dramatic effect, used several pseudonyms (including the cryptic "0000"), was interested in fashionable clothing and interior décor, allowed cats to play intriguing parts in his tales, failed to finish major projects, poached from obscure sources, claimed knowledge he didn't have, suffered delusions of grandeur, and was driven by suicidal impulses. Poe drank himself to death; Gogol starved himself to death.

Like Poe, Gogol was strongly influenced by the German writer E. T. A. Hoffmann, who depicted pathological states and criminal impulses, and he created a disturbing atmosphere by combining factual reality with grotesque fantasies. Both Poe and Gogol had a strong element of sadomasochism in their lives and their imaginations, and wrote tortuous and often outrageous books with "Arabesque" in the titles. They had a haunted, hallucinatory vision, with idealized dead women rising from the grave to harm the living and the Devil himself making a menacing appearance. Both used caricature and melodrama, emphasized the eccentric and bizarre aspects of human experience, and portrayed the lower depths of society. Both described incest and violent retribution, the nightmare of urban isolation, the power of the supernatural, and the horrific as well as the precarious instability, psychological disintegration, and mental collapse of their self-destructive heroes. Gogol's tale "The Diary of a Madman" describes the sort of unbalanced first-person narrator who appears in many of Poe's stories.

Gogol's appearance and character matched his weird behavior. An actor portrayed him as both foppish and slovenly: "Of medium height, blond, with a huge wig, wearing gold-rimmed spectacles on his long, birdlike nose, with squinting little eyes, and firmly compressed, as if bit-together, lips."[6] Turgenev, who hadn't seen Gogol for fifteen years, met him in Moscow in 1851 and, with a novelist's eye, deduced his character from his unattractive, vulpine (rather than birdlike) appearance:

His fair hair, which fell straight from the temples, as is usual with Cossacks, still preserved its youthful tint, but had thinned noticeably; his smooth, retreating white forehead conveyed, as before, the impression of great intelligence. His small brown eyes sparkled with gaiety at times—yes, gaiety and not sarcasm; but mostly they looked tired. Gogol's long, pointed nose gave his face a sort of cunning, fox-like expression; his puffy, soft lips under the clipped moustache also produced an unfavourable impression; in their indefinite contours—so at least it seemed to me—the dark sides of his character found expression. When he spoke, they opened unpleasantly, showing a row of bad teeth. His small chin disappeared into his wide, black velvet cravat.[7]

Another friend, who unexpectedly called on Gogol when he was writing, was astonished by his exotic, theatrical dress: "Before me stood Gogol in the following fantastic get-up: in place of boots— long Russian woolen stockings, which reached above the knee; instead of a jacket—a velvet spencer [short, double-breasted overcoat] over a flannel camisole, with a large, bright-colored scarf wrapped around his neck and a raspberry-colored, velvet kokoshnik, embroidered in gold, on his head, quite similar to the headdress of Finnish tribeswomen."[8]

Gogol's comportment could be as peculiar as his costume. He would relate a funny story to a family in mourning, tell a new acquaintance about his intestinal problems, squirm awkwardly during conversation with women, and fall asleep at the dinner table. Joseph Frank perceptively summarized his peculiarly paradoxical character:

> Gogol was at once a provincial from the Ukraine who never felt at home in Petersburg; a mythomaniac convinced from his earliest years that he had been sent by God to fulfill a great moral mission; a sponger who shamelessly exploited his wealthy admirers while preaching the virtues of poverty to his mother and sisters whenever they asked him for money; a sensual glutton who apparently never touched a woman; a moralist who proclaimed that the highest Christian virtues could only be realized in serf-ridden Russia; a writer whose very success filled him with despair because his best work was interpreted as an exposure of the moral-social monstrosity of Russian life rather than as a call to individual moral regeneration.[9]

Torn by these insoluble paradoxes, Gogol wrote masterpieces in three genres: his play *The Government Inspector* (1836), his story "The Overcoat," and his novel *Dead Souls* (both 1842). A famous statement—"We have all come out of Gogol's 'Overcoat' "—incorrectly attributed to Dostoyevsky but actually made by the French literary historian Melchior de Vogüé in his *Le Roman russe* (*The Russian Novel*, 1886), expressed the belief that Gogol's story had inspired all Russian realism.[10] After Pushkin was killed in a duel in 1837, Gogol was widely recognized as the greatest living Russian writer.

Following the success of his satiric play, which the czar himself saw and applauded, Gogol left for Europe and spent most of the next twelve years wandering through many cities and spas before finally settling in Rome. He returned to Russia for seven months in 1839–1840 and again at the end of 1841, when he'd completed part I of *Dead Souls*. Unlike most travelers, he did not visit European towns for their cultural advantages or intellectual atmosphere, but chose his destinations for their salubrious climate, their esteemed doctors, and their Russian communities. Gogol's imagination was stimulated by distance from rather than proximity to his subjects. He'd written his Ukrainian tales while living in St. Petersburg and wrote most of *Dead Souls* during his reclusive life in Rome. That ancient city, he claimed, provided the perfect "distant vantage point" from which he could write about the vastness and essence of Russia. In Rome, Russia seemed to him an exciting mixture of memory, myth, and mirage. As he rapturously exclaimed in the novel: "Russia! Russia! I behold thee, from my lovely far-away paradise" (p. 223).

. Gogol had a thoroughly perverse character. Toward the end of his life, still chronically melancholic, he turned to mysticism, came under the influence of fanatical monks, and was overcome by religious mania. The Devil was a constant threat and intimate presence; God became a distant, unreachable figure at the end of his spiritual quest. Gogol believed that his divine mission was to save sinful Russia and lead it to moral regeneration. During his pilgrimage to the Holy Land in 1848 he attended Easter service in the Church of the Holy Sepulcher, but could not focus on religion and felt the spirit of grace had failed to descend upon him. Nevertheless, he thought the long-promised and long-awaited part II of *Dead Souls* might still be the instrument of his country's salvation. While working on the sequel in 1845, he confessed: "I have tortured myself, forced myself to write, suffered severe pains when I saw my impotence . . . everything came out forced and inferior." Victor Erlich emphasized "the pain and futility of working against his creative grain, of inhibiting his bent for the grotesquely satirical for the sake of a homiletic . . . reconciliation with reality."[11]

A friend recalled his profound disappointment, and unwillingness to discourage Gogol with the truth, when the author read aloud from the beginning of part II: "I will never forget the deep and oppressive impression that Gogol made on Aleksei Khomyakov and me one evening when he read us the first two chapters of the second volume. After the reading he asked us: 'Tell me just one thing, in all honesty: isn't it worse than the first part?' We exchanged glances, and neither he nor I had the courage to tell him what both of us thought and felt."[12] Another literary friend used a striking religious metaphor to describe Gogol's hopeless attempt to complete part II: "*Dead Souls* was the hermit's cell in which he struggled and suffered until he was carried lifeless out of it."[13]

As didacticism overwhelmed Gogol's imaginative impulse, he lost his creative drive and lapsed into preaching. "God has bidden us [to] bear our burdens without repining," he leadenly wrote, "and pray when we are unhappy, and not rebel or take matters into our own hands" (p. 363). According to the Russian novelist Vladimir Nabokov, Gogol finally realized that his "spiritual message" had ruined ten years of labor and that the "book was untrue to his genius."[14]

Gogol ended his literary career, as he had begun it, by burning his work. He consigned one version to the flames in 1845 and another ten days before his death. Erlich recounted that "in the middle of the night of February 11–12, [1852], Gogol got up from his couch, had his servant fetch him a batch of notebooks and tossed them into the fire. When the manuscripts turned to ashes, he crossed himself, kissed the boy, laid on the couch and broke into sobs." According to another version of the story—and contradictions are endemic in Gogol—the *auto-da-fé* was not deliberate, but directly inspired by the Devil. As he told his host, Count Alexander Tolstoy: "Imagine how powerful is the Fiend! I wanted to burn papers which were long earmarked for destruction and burned the chapters of *Dead Souls* which I meant to leave my friends as a keepsake."[15]

The first five chapters of part II, with some passages missing, managed to survive the conflagration. All critics agree that they contain some lively characters and vivid incidents, but are distinctly inferior to part I. The Irish short-story writer Frank O'Connor called these fragmentary drafts "an insult to the memory of a great perfectionist."[16] Many editors draconically omit them from the text; this edition includes the disappointing but illuminating final chapters.

Gogol's death in 1852 was even more fantastic than his life. He'd complained of severe nervous disorders and spiritual distress, claimed that his head had a peculiar structure and his stomach was abnormally placed. "From February 6 on," Karlinsky wrote, "Gogol reduced his food intake to several spoonfuls of watery oatmeal soup or of sauerkraut brine per day, occasionally supplemented with a few drops of wine taken in a cup of water. He spent most of his nights in prayer, allowing not more than two or three hours for sleep."[17]

The doctors hastened his death by bathing him in clear broth and pouring spirits over him, by pressing hot loaves and a corrosive mustard plaster onto his emaciated body. Nabokov described how they plunged their patient "into a warm bath where his head was soused with cold water after which he was put to bed with half-a-dozen plump leeches affixed to his nose. He had groaned and cried and weakly struggled while his wretched body (you could feel the spine through the stomach) was carried to the deep wooden bath; he shivered as he lay naked in bed and kept pleading to have the leeches removed: they were dangling from his nose and getting into his mouth."[18] Gogol thought he was already in Hell and suffering the torments of the damned. The words carved on his tombstone—"For I will laugh with my bitter speech"—echoed Pushkin's famous description of Gogol's art: "laughter through tears of sadness and tender emotion."[19]

II

Emphasizing the difficulty of understanding *Dead Souls*, which has intrigued and baffled readers for more than 160 years, James Woodward called the novel "the most perplexing work of fiction in the Russian language—a work that appears to owe no significant debt to any literary tradition, to elude every attempt at all-embracing interpretation, to be explicable only as the bizarre creation of a bizarre personality."[20] The book has been variously and contradictorily called realistic and symbolic, humorous and tragic; defined as a novel, poem, drama, epic, allegory, and picaresque travelogue. The comically grotesque characters resemble those in *Los Caprichos*, the satirical etchings by Gogol's older contemporary and soul mate, Francisco Goya.

Gogol's idiosyncratic language intensifies the difficulty for both reader and translator. As Karlinsky noted in his valuable essay on this subject, Gogol "made use of almost the entire lexical range of spoken and written Russian of his time, from the most elevated philosophical and theological vocabulary rooted in Old Church Slavic to the most vulgar and crude slang he could find, not to mention the rich admixture of Ukrainian in his early stories."[21] On several occasions, Gogol alludes to expressions used by his characters that are too coarse to quote in his book.

Pushkin came up with the idea of *Dead Souls*, and Gogol began to write it in the fall of 1835. It took six years to complete and was written mostly in Switzerland, Paris, and Rome. Gogol wanted to show all of Russia and, as he explained in "Confession of the Author," the "subject of *Dead Souls* suited me so well because it gives complete freedom to travel all through Russia with the hero and introduce a multitude of the most varied characters."[22] At first, he plunged into the work without careful preparation. "I was going to begin writing," he recalled, "without setting myself any detailed plan, without having taken into account what, precisely, the hero himself should be. I simply thought the humorous project that Chichikov [Tchitchikov in this edition] undertakes would in itself lead me to varied persons and characters and that the very desire to laugh, originating within me, would itself create a multitude of humorous phenomena, which I intended to blend with touching ones."[23] But he finally decided that he needed a firm plan to organize the sprawling novel.

Gogol did, in fact, give a vivid though satirical sense of contemporary Russian life: its coach travel and country inns, hospitality and food, gluttony and drunkenness, dress and manners, conversation and gossip, hierarchy and servility, ignorance and indolence, bureaucracy and corruption, philistine provinciality and slavish imitation of fashionable Petersburg and Paris. In doing so, he makes the amusingly absurd social distinction between the limited character of "the simply agreeable lady" and the more affected "lady agreeable in every respect," who was "fond of poetry, . . . could hold her head pensively" and "certainly spared no effort to be obliging in the extreme" (p. 182). After reading an early draft, Pushkin exclaimed: "God, how dreary is our Russia."

Gogol, predictably enough, ran into difficulties with the strict czarist censors, who immediately objected to the puzzling and paradoxical title. Since church dogma decreed that the soul was immortal, they accused Gogol of attacking a basic theological doctrine.

When he pointed out that "souls" was a synonym for serfs or peasants, they changed tack and objected to his attack on serfdom, a form
of slavery that was not abolished in Russia until 1861. Gogol alludes
to the dispute and mocks the censors when a foolish character in the
novel criticizes Tchitchikov for using "the expression 'dead souls,'
while every one who has completed a course of humane studies,
knows for a fact that the soul is immortal" (p. 320).

After considerable maneuvering, Gogol was forced to change the
title to *Tchitchikov's Adventures; or, Dead Souls: A Poem* and tone down the tale
of Captain Kopeykin, the maimed war hero turned outlaw, told in
part I, chapter 10. "The word 'poem,' " a Russian critic explained, "set
apart [on the original title page] from the rest of the title, testifies not
only to the wide-ranging scope of the work, but also to a renuncia-
tion of the traditional novelistic conventions."[24] Gogol's "poem in
prose" seemed to complement Pushkin's "novel in verse," *Eugene
Onegin* (1833).

In *Dead Souls*, as in *The Government Inspector* (the idea for which also
came from the fertile mind of Pushkin), an agreeable stranger arrives
unexpectedly, excites a provincial town, and is mistaken for someone
different from his real self. Like the heroes in this genre from Her-
man Melville's *The Confidence-Man* (1857) to Thomas Mann's *Confessions
of Felix Krull: Confidence Man* (1954) and V. S. Naipaul's *The Mystic Masseur*
(1957), Gogol's characters are con men and swindlers who survive
and succeed by imposture and trickery, deceit and fraud.

Tchitchikov's scheme, not explained until the end of part I, depends on his ability to buy dead souls. Serfs were attached to the master's land and usually paid their rent with part of their produce. Some
craftsmen, especially in winter, could get a passport to practice their
trade in town and pay the master a share of their earnings in cash.
The government required landowners to take their own census every
ten years of their male serfs (females and children didn't count), and
a decree of 1824 allowed the owners to mortgage the serfs on their
list for 200 rubles per soul. Since the owners had to pay a tax on the
dead souls until the next census, Tchitchikov is able to exploit their
abstract existence. Though some of the souls on the official list have
died since the last census, they seem, in his cunning scheme, to be as
immortal as the immortal souls of the dead.

Tchitchikov's fiendish two-part scheme works because the dead souls are still officially alive. First, he persuades the puzzled masters to sell their dead souls, which relieves them of the tax burden and is perfectly legal. Then, he mortgages the nonexistent souls, which is perfectly fraudulent. As he finally explains, in an aside to himself late in the novel: "suppose I buy all who are dead, before the new census lists are sent out, if I get, let us say, a thousand of them, and suppose the [government] Trustee Committee gives me two hundred roubles a soul: why there's a fortune of two hundred thousand!" (p. 243). In fact, he starts with only two souls, his personal servants, acquires nearly four hundred more, and makes close to 80,000 rubles.

The location of the town of N. and the chronology of the action are, like almost everything else in *Dead Souls*, puzzling and problematic. Russian critics (with no firm evidence) seemed to think that N. is located somewhere between Moscow and St. Petersburg. Richard Pevear maintained that the novel takes place over a time span of eighteen years, "set in the period between the seventh official census of 1815 and the eighth, taken in 1833."[25] Gogol specifically states that "all this happened very shortly after the glorious expulsion of the French" from Russia in 1812 (p. 208). Yet the townsmen, inflamed by wild rumors, claim that Napoléon, who was confined to St. Helena from 1815 until his death in 1821, has escaped from the remote South Atlantic island and "now here he was wandering about Russia got up as Tchitchikov" (p. 208). However, these early dates are contradicted by the portraits, hanging in the house of Sobakevitch, of the heroes of the Greek War of Independence, who finally defeated the Turks in 1829. So the possible date of the action does indeed range from shortly after 1812, in the middle of the reign of Alexander I (1801–1825), to the early years of the more autocratic Nicholas I (1825–1855).

The structure of part I of this apparently loose, episodic novel is carefully wrought. In chapter 1 Tchitchikov mysteriously arrives in town and calls on the high-ranking officials. In the next five chapters he visits five very different landowners in order to purchase their souls. Gogol has great fun describing how the masters respond in their idiosyncratic ways to his bizarre and baffling proposition. Manilov, a foolish sentimentalist, gives away the serfs for nothing. Korobotchka, a stupid and suspicious widow in an entirely female household, makes Tchitchikov pay 15 rubles for them. Nozdryov, a hedonistic bully with a hearty manner, is always ready to do a friend a bad turn. He refuses to sell his souls and instead proposes all sorts of disadvantageous deals. He persuades his guest to gamble, tries to cheat him, and, when Tchitchikov objects, orders the servants to beat him. Our hero is rescued by the unexpected arrival of the police, who've come to arrest Nozdryov for assaulting another victim. Sobakevitch, a strong, silent, bear-like glutton, bargains mercilessly for his souls and forces Tchitchikov to pay 2 1/2 rubles for each one. The manic miser Plyushkin, whose house serfs take turns wearing the only pair of oversized boots, manages to extract 32 kopecks per soul.

The characters of the masters are partly defined by the hospitality they are obliged to offer the stranger who suddenly turns up at their door. This ranges from the gargantuan, stomach-expanding, and sometimes stomach-turning dinners provided by the insatiable Sobakevitch to the minimal sustenance—moldy old cake and fly-filled liqueur—grudgingly offered by Plyushkin. In part II the master's dog Yarb ("Heat") enters the room jingling its copper collar. After everyone has dined beyond repletion, the dog walks sluggishly: "he too, had over-eaten himself" (p. 309).

In the first six chapters of part I Tchitchikov usually controls the townsfolk and landowners; in the last five chapters his plans become unraveled and they control him. In chapter 7 he contentedly muses over his newly acquired souls and officially registers the deeds of purchase. In chapter 8 Nozdryov exposes Tchitchikov's scheme at the governor's ball. In chapter 9 Korobotchka, afraid that she's somehow been cheated, arrives in town to unmask him. Chapter 10 relates the sad, digressive story of the mutilated war hero Captain Kopeykin, who vainly seeks a government pension and eventually becomes a robber. This story inspires the postmaster's wild rumors that Tchitchikov is actually Kopeykin. When the police chief points out that Tchitchikov, unlike Kopeykin, has all his limbs, "the postmaster cried out, slapped himself on the forehead and called himself a calf publicly before them all. He could not understand how the circumstance had not occurred to him at the beginning of the story" (p. 207). Nozdryov then calls Tchitchikov a spy and forger who's planning to abduct the governor's daughter. He's also compared to the demonic Antichrist and to the demonized Napoléon.

Chapter 11, which forms a frame with chapter 1, belatedly discloses Tchitchikov's shady background: his obscure origins and schooling, delicate nerves and self-denial, agreeable manners and willingness to please, work in the justice department, and ability to adapt himself to any squeamish situation as well as his ferocity at sniffing out contraband after moving to the customs office. When he's caught taking bribes in a smuggling fraud, he escapes criminal charges and portrays himself as a victim of injustice. His dead souls scheme is merely the latest in a series of swindles and he survives this one as he survived all the others. He deftly manages to escape from N. and leaves the town (and the novel) in the same carriage he'd used to enter it.

In early-nineteenth-century Russia society was still feudal and people averaged 8 miles an hour in carriages and carts that traveled over the endless expanse of rural roads or in sledges that slowly crunched through the snow. In *Dead Souls* the rough logs of a bridge "hop up and down like the keys of a piano" (p. 112), causing the traveler to bump the back of his head and bruise his forehead. Tchitchikov is relieved when he passes from the hard cobblestones of the town to the soft earthen roads of the countryside. Despite all the hardships and accidents, Gogol exclaims that Russians love rapid driving.

His praise of travel was probably influenced by Henry Fielding's *Tom Jones* (1749). Commenting on the constricted space, Fielding amusingly wrote: "in stagecoaches, where passengers are properly considered as so much luggage, the ingenious coachman stows half a dozen with perfect ease into the place of four . . . it being the nature of guts, when well squeezed, to give way, and lie in a narrow compass." Fielding also compared the congenial journey to the relationship of the novelist and his readers: "let us behave to one another like fellow-travellers in a stage-coach, who have passed several days in the company of each other; and who, notwithstanding any bickerings or little animosities which may have occurred on the road, generally make up all at last and mount, for the last time, into their vehicle with cheerfulness and good-humour."[26]

Gogol also structures the novel with a series of absurd motifs. Tchitchikov's thick-lipped valet Petrushka "read[s] everything with equal attention" and takes childish delight in "the fact that the letters continually made up a word and the devil knows what it might sometimes mean" (p. 18–19). Tchitchikov tears a poster off a pole and also reads every trivial detail. And Manilov leaves a book he's been reading for the last two years perpetually open on page 14. Tchitchikov's clothes are soiled by mud and then by an incontinent baby. A coach is described as a melon, a man as a pumpkin. There are two balls and two carriage accidents (Tchitchikov's carriage first overturns in the mud and then collides with another coach), two meetings with the governor's beautiful daughter (at the collision and again at the governor's ball). Tchitchikov is exposed first by Nozdryov and then by Korobotchka, and there are two blocked love affairs: Tchitchikov's and Tyentyetnikov's in part II.

The beautiful daughter's face has the transparent whiteness of a newly laid egg and "her delicate ears were also transparent [or at least, in contrast to the hero's opacity, translucent] and flushed crimson by the light that penetrated through them" (p. 90). The physical perfection of the girl provides a striking contrast to the picture in Tchitchikov's hotel room of a huge nymph "with a bosom more immense than the reader has probably ever seen" (p. 7) and of the portrait in Sobakevitch's house of the gigantic "Greek heroine Bobelina whose leg seemed stouter than the whole body of a dandy" (p. 95). There's also a witty contrast between the innocent, idealized governor's daughter and the old gentlemen, "excited by ballet," who've acquired a lubricious taste for nude pictures. The young girl's lack of a name and strange silence make her all the more distant and unattainable.

In two of the most brilliant scenes of the novel, both Sobakevitch and Tchitchikov, through the power of memory and imagination, lyrically describe their serfs and make them more vivid when dead than when they were alive. Sobakevitch, partly to enhance their value, recalls his first-class craftsmen: the wheelwright, the carpenter, the boot maker and the prosperous trader in Moscow. Tchitchikov, who of course never knew them, recreates their often violent deaths with details that "gave a peculiar air of freshness" (p. 137). One of Korobotchka's serfs had burnt himself to death. Another, undoubtedly drunk, was crushed by a wagon while "asleep in the middle of the road" (p. 137). And the carrier, "Grigory-never-get-there!," also surely drunk, fell through "a hole in the ice, and vanished for ever!" (p. 138).

Sobakevitch idealizes his souls; Tchitchikov brings them down (and into the earth).

Though Gogol was a defender of what he considered the "divinely ordained" serfdom, nineteenth-century Russian liberals read his novel as a merciless attack on that oppressive institution. But Gogol's portrayal of serfs (the members of impolite rather than polite society), like everything else in the novel, is ambiguous. Tchitchikov's serf-coachman, Selifan, has a cruel streak and lashes at a beggar on the way out of town. He also understands exactly how each of the three horses pulls the carriage, how they prefer oats to hay, and even how they "talk" to each other. Like the sly, gray trace-horse, who only makes a show of pulling, Selifan merely pretends to drive. He gives the horses free rein when drowsy or drunk and, counter to Tchitchikov's orders, drives in any direction that moves him. He even influences his master's emotional life by colliding with the carriage that contains the governor's daughter. When he tips the coach over and Tchitchikov threatens to thrash him, Selifan disarms his master by immediately accepting, even encouraging, the punishment: " 'That is as your honour thinks best,' answered Selifan, ready to agree to anything, 'if it's to be a thrashing, a thrashing let it be; I have nothing against it. Why not a thrashing, if it's deserved? That's what you are master for' " (p. 42).

Gogol portrays a Russia that Thomas Mann later synthesized as "wolves of the steppes, snow, vodka, the knout."[27] Susanne Fusso agreed that cruelty was endemic in the novel and that "the pathos and misery of the serfs' lives [are] glimpsed at every turn: begging orphans; deaths through fire, epidemic illness and starvation; persecution of the poorest serfs by an unscrupulous steward; serfs being forced by a sadistic, miserly master to walk barefoot on frosty ground; the rape of a peasant woman by a police inspector."[28] The negative side of serfdom is clearly there. But in *Dead Souls* there is no positive portrayal of the serfs themselves. The novel does not have the redemptive folk wisdom and simple spirituality of Tolstoy's idealized peasants. Gogol's serfs—drunken, unreliable, superstitious, deceitful, dishonest, and wicked—are the objects of well-deserved abuse. Runaways inevitably come to a bad end and wind up as robbers or convicts. With fine irony, Gogol writes that only Tchitchikov's dead souls, who supposedly have to be transported over vast distances to more fertile land in the south, "were of an exemplarily docile character, and were themselves favourably disposed to migration, and that there could not possibly be a mutiny among them" (p. 158).

Though the themes of Dead Souls are serious, Gogol constantly startles and surprises the reader with extremely funny scenes. Manilov describes the town officials as "all excellent persons" (p. 27). Sobakevitch, by contrast, emphatically exclaims that the very same men are all scoundrels, rascals, and ruffians. Manilov's conjugal kiss was "so prolonged and languishing, that a small cigar might easily have been smoked while it lasted" (p. 25). After the doting Manilov brags that his little son has heard of Petersburg and Paris and prompts him to say he wants to become an ambassador, the boy is ludicrously elevated to that position—and barely escapes humiliation: "At that moment the footman standing behind his chair wiped the ambassador's nose, and he did well as something very unpleasant might else have dropped into the soup" (p. 30). In similarly degrading incidents, Plyushkin fails to notice that "a piece of snuff of the colour of coffee grounds was peeping out of his nose in a most unpicturesque way, and that the skirts of his dressing-gown had flown apart and were displaying undergarments not at all suitable for exhibition" (p. 124). When Tchitchikov climbs into bed in Korobotchka's house, after refusing her seductive offer to tickle his heels as she once did to put her late husband to sleep, "it sank almost to the floor under his weight, and the feathers squeezed out of the cover flew into every corner of the room" (p. 46).

Gogol's elaborately exact yet absurd similes, instead of glorifying the characters as in Homer, comically exalt or degrade them. He compares the barking dogs that greet Tchitchikov at Korobotchka's estate to the tenors and basses of a church choir. The hotel features "black beetles peeping out of every corner like prunes" (p. 6). The black-coated guests at the governor's party "flitted about, one by one or in groups, here and there, like flies flitting about a sparkling sugar-loaf on a hot July day" (p. 12). Plyushkin's little eyes are like mice "poking their sharp noses out of their dark holes" (p. 117).

The comedy is intensified by a cast of characters who, for all their gluttonous gorging and vivid solidity, are curiously elusive and almost cinematically surreal. The Chaplinesque waiter at the hotel is "so brisk and rapid in his movements that it was impossible to distinguish his countenance" (p. 5). The man selling spiced drinks in a nearby shop has "a face as red as his samovar, so that from a distance one might have imagined that there were two samovars in the window, if one of them had not had a beard as black as pitch" (p. 6). When Plyushkin first appears, Tchitchikov can't tell if he's a woman or a man, steward or master. In the distorting, crepuscular light, the very features of a character may appear to shift—Picasso-like—around his face. The "moustache of the soldier, standing on sentry duty, seemed to be on his forehead and a long way above his eyes, while his nose had disappeared entirely" (p. 132).

Gogol's ladies are always remote and unreachable. In part II the general's daughter, Ulinka, is "a strange unique creature . . . more like a fantastic apparition than a woman" (p. 272). At the end of the novel Tchitchikov is reduced to a pair of impressive eyebrows. And his absentminded valet, Petrushka, "at times completely forgot that he had a face at all" (p. 297). Tchitchikov finds it easy to operate in this constantly shifting and deceptively mutable world, for nobody is able to determine what kind of man he really is. Officials can't find out "whether he was the sort of person who was to be seized and detained as a suspicious character, or whether he was the sort of person who might seize and detain all of them as suspicious characters" (p. 199).

Toward the end of part II, Tchitchikov finally reveals what he intends to do with his ill-gotten money. The con man, ironically enough, has become weary of restlessly passing through life like a phantom gypsy. Dealing with the unreal, he longs to be real. He wants to be a respectable man with ample land and with children who will perpetuate his name. This is doubly ironic, for the children in the novel are portrayed negatively. Manilov's children are hopelessly coddled boobies and Plyushkin has disinherited the ungrateful children who dared to disobey him.

Nevertheless, Tchitchikov "began to think seriously of obtaining not an imaginary but a real estate. He at once determined with the money he would get by mortgaging the imaginary souls to obtain an estate that would not be imaginary" (p. 330). Though the souls of the "souls" were separated from their bodies when they died, Tchitchikov brings them back to life in a kind of ironic resurrection. The metaphorical acquisition of corpses in Dead Souls and the transformation of human beings into property—one landowner asks if

Tchitchikov intends to dig them up—became quite literal, later on, in Robert Louis Stevenson's story "The Body Snatcher" (1884). As Edward Young wrote in his morbid poem *Night Thoughts*, published in 1742–1745 and mentioned in the novel: "How populous, how vital, is the grave!"

Part I of the novel ends with the famous, vertiginous image of Russia

> flying onwards like a spirited troika that nothing can overtake. . . .
> The troika rushes on, full of divine inspiration. . . . Russia, whither
> flyest thou? . . . The ringing of the bells melts into music; the air, torn
> to shreds, whirs and rushes like the wind, everything there is on earth
> is flying by, and the other states and nations, with looks askance, make
> way for her and draw aside (pp. 250–251).

Unfortunately, this paean to progress is flatly contradicted by the hopelessly debased condition of Russia that Gogol has just portrayed in his book. Tchitchikov and the rest of the characters, like the figures in T. S. Eliot's poem "The Hollow Men" (1925), are empty, unsubstantial, and without spiritual awareness:

> We are the hollow men
> We are the stuffed men. . . .
> Our dried voices, when
> We whisper together
> Are quiet and meaningless.

Gogol's dead souls are, paradoxically, more alive than the living ones.

III

The connection between parts I and II of *Dead Souls* is rather tenuous, and Tchitchikov does not turn up for the first thirty pages of the fragmentary second part. There's more description than action in part II, and our hero's scheme, revealed yet again as he appears at several more estates, becomes tediously familiar. In part II Gogol intended to show, through the influence of virtuous men, the purification and redemption of the roguish Tchitchikov. Pevear wrote that we find in part II "a series of nonpareils—the perfect young lady, the perfect landowner, the perfect wealthy muzhik [peasant], the perfect prince, and also, since nonpareils need not be moral ideals, the perfect ruined nobleman, the perfect Germanizer, the perfect do-nothing—all of them verging on the grotesque."[29]

But these characters are not quite as peerless and perfect as they seem. Richard Peace effectively undermined the traditional interpretation by arguing that the tax-collector Murazov and the landowner Skudronzhoglo (who has Turkish as well as Russian blood) are as acquisitive and materialistic as Tchitchikov. The landowner Tyentyetnikov foolishly sacrifices his love for Ulinka because he feels he has been patronized by her father, General Betrishtchev. Pyetuh ruins himself through lavish hospitality. Koshkaryov runs his estate in mindless imitation of St. Petersburg's stultified bureaucracy.[30]

In the last, biographical chapter of part II, which recapitulates the last chapter of part I, Tchitchikov is tossed about by the "mutability of destiny" (p. 276)—a major theme of the novel. He continues to buy dead souls, borrows money he does not intend to repay, and is caught and imprisoned for forging a will. The governor-general condemns him by exclaiming: "Every farthing you have gained has been gained in some dishonest way, by thieving and dishonesty that deserves the knout and Siberia!" and by comparing him to "a hideous insect which he cannot bring himself to stamp upon" (p. 368). Though the ever-resourceful Tchitchikov bribes his way to freedom, his crime and punishment reveal that he's still very far from the long-expected atonement and moral regeneration. This crucial contradiction explains why Gogol could not complete his novel and felt compelled to burn his manuscript. Nabokov perceived the thematic clash between Gogol's didactic intention and unregenerate hero: "Chichikov's swindles are but the phantoms and parodies of crime, so that no 'real' retribution is possible without a distortion of the whole idea."[31]

In a letter of June 1943 about *Dead Souls*, the magisterial critic Edmund Wilson, who knew Russian, described the greatness of Gogol's novel: its idiosyncratic method, vivid similes, studied unreality, rich poetic scenes, and creepy, Poe-like atmosphere:

I began by thinking the Russians overrated it, but ended by being very much impressed by it. He did well to call it a poem, however: it doesn't have the solid reality and clear atmosphere that one expects in Russian fiction. It is really all a monologue by Gogol in which the similes are just as real as the incidents because the incidents, too, are images that represent emotions and impressions of Gogol's and take form and dissolve in his mind. The houses and the people that Chichikov visits are not really known and created as the Rostovs and Bolkonskys [in *War and Peace*]. . . . He is certainly a very strange man. *Mertvye Dushi* [*Dead Souls*] has given me the creeps; but it is magnificent just the same. Some passages—troika, Chichikov imagining his dead serfs, the picture of Russian revelry against the dark background of the forest that figures Russia in the scene at Plyushkin's house—have a dense and sustained poetry.[32]

Jeffrey Meyers, Fellow of the Royal Society of Literature, has published biographies of Katherine Mansfield, Wyndham Lewis, Ernest Hemingway, Robert Lowell and his circle, D. H. Lawrence, Joseph Conrad, Edgar Allan Poe, F. Scott Fitzgerald, Edmund Wilson, Robert Frost, Humphrey Bogart, Gary Cooper, George Orwell, Errol and Sean Flynn, and Somerset Maugham.

Notes

1. Quoted in Simon Karlinsky, *The Sexual Labyrinth of Nikolai Gogol* (Cambridge, MA: Harvard University Press, 1976), p. 11.

2. Karlinsky, *Sexual Labyrinth*, p. 13.

3. Ivan Turgenev, "Gogol," in *Literary Reminiscences and Autobiographical Fragments* (1869), translated with an introduction by David Magarshack and an essay on Turgenev by Edmund Wilson (New York: Grove Press, 1959), p. 171.

4. Quoted in Vsevolod Setchkarev, *Gogol: His Life and Works*, translated by Robert Kramer (1953; New York: New York University Press, 1965), p. 42.

5. Quoted in Karlinsky, *Sexual Labyrinth*, p. 53.

6. Quoted in Setchkarev, *Life and Works*, p. 46.

7.   Turgenev, "Gogol," in *Literary Reminiscences*, p. 161.

8.   Quoted in Setchkarev, *Life and Works*, p. 60.

9.   Joseph Frank, "From Gogol to the Gulag," in *Through the Russian Prism: Essays on Literature and Culture* (Princeton, NJ: Princeton University Press, 1990), p. 90.

10. Ernest Hemingway may have recalled this statement when in *Green Hills of Africa* (New York: Scribner, 1935), p. 22, he insisted, with comparable simplification: "All modern American literature comes from one book by Mark Twain called *Huckleberry Finn*."

11. Victor Erlich, *Gogol* (New Haven, CT: Yale University Press, 1969), p. 203.

12. Quoted in Robert Maguire, *Exploring Gogol* (Stanford, CA: Stanford University Press, 1994), p. 324.

13. Quoted in Richard Freeborn, "*Dead Souls*," in *The Rise of the Russian Novel: Studies in the Russian Novel from "Eugene Onegin" to "War and Peace"* (Cambridge, England: Cambridge University Press, 1973), p. 74.

14. Vladimir Nabokov, *Nikolai Gogol* (1944; New York: New Directions, 1961), pp. 161, 137.

15. Erlich, *Gogol*, pp. 206–207.

16. Frank O'Connor, "Introduction" to *Dead Souls*, translated by Andrew MacAndrew (New York: Signet, 1961), p. x.

17. Karlinsky, *Sexual Labyrinth*, p. 276.

18. Nabokov, *Nikolai Gogol*, p. 2.

19. In *Dead Souls*, Gogol includes two variants of Pushkin's perceptive phrase. In part I, chapter 7 the narrator comments that he is destined to gaze upon life "through laughter seen by the world and tears unseen and unknown by it" (p. 135). In part II, chapter 2, Tchitchikov tells General Betrishtchev: "Your Excellency, what makes you laugh costs me tears" (p. 294).

20. James Woodward, *Gogol's "Dead Souls"* (Princeton, NJ: Princeton University Press, 1978), p. vii.

21. Simon Karlinsky, "Portrait of Gogol as a Word Glutton" (1970), in George Gibian, ed., *"Dead Souls": The Reavey Translation, Backgrounds and Sources, Essays in Criticism* (New York: W. W. Norton, 1985), p. 550.

22. Quoted in Setchkarev, *Life and Works*, p. 182.

23. Quoted in V. V. Gippius, "An Introduction to *Dead Souls*" (1966), in Gibian, ed., *"Dead Souls,"* p. 490. Chichikov, the common spelling in later translations, contains the French word *chichi* (meaning "pretentiously elegant") and emphasizes the character's affected manners.

24. Victor Shklovsky, "The Literary Genre of *Dead Souls*" (1966), in Gibian, ed., *"Dead Souls,"* p. 566.

25. Richard Pevear, "Introduction" to *Dead Souls*, translated by Richard Pevear and Larissa Volokhonsky (New York: Pantheon, 1996), p. xxiii.

26. Henry Fielding, *The History of Tom Jones*, edited by R. P. C. Mutter (1749; London: Penguin, 1966), pp. 543, 813.

27. Thomas Mann, *The Magic Mountain*, translated by H. T. Lowe-Porter (1924; London: Secker and Warburg, 1957), p. 241.

28. Susanne Fusso, *Designing "Dead Souls": An Anatomy of Disorder in Gogol* (Stanford, CA: Stanford University Press, 1993), p. 93.

29. Pevear, "Introduction," pp. xiv–xv.

30. See Richard Peace, *The Enigma of Gogol: An Examination of the Writings of N.V. Gogol and Their Place in the Russian Literary Tradition* (Cambridge, England: Cambridge University Press, 1981), pp. 242–243.

31. Nabokov, *Nikolai Gogol*, p. 137.

32. Edmund Wilson, *Letters on Literature and Politics, 1912–1972*, edited by Elena Wilson (New York: Farrar, Straus and Giroux, 1977), p. 379.

DEAD SOULS

a poem

PART I

CHAPTER 1

A rather pretty little chaise on springs, such as bachelors, half-pay officers, staff captains, landowners with about a hundred serfs*—in short, all such as are spoken of as "gentlemen of the middling sort"—drive about in, rolled in at the gates of the hotel of the provincial town of N. In the chaise sat a gentleman, not handsome but not bad-looking, not too stout and not too thin; it could not be said that he was old, neither could he be described as extremely young. His arrival in the town created no sensation whatever and was not accompanied by anything remarkable. Only two Russian peasants standing at the door of the tavern facing the hotel made some observations, with reference, however, rather to the carriage than to its occupant. "My eye," said one to the other, "isn't that a wheel! What do you think? Would that wheel, if so it chanced, get to Moscow or would it never get there?" "It would," answered the other. "But to Kazan† now, I don't think it would get there?" "It wouldn't get to Kazan," answered the other. With that the conversation ended. Moreover, just as the chaise drove up to the hotel it was met by a young man in extremely short and narrow white canvas trousers, in a coat with fashionable cut-away tails and a shirt-front fastened with a Tula‡ breastpin adorned with a bronze pistol. The young man turned round, stared at the chaise, holding his cap which was almost flying off in the wind, and went on his way.

When the chaise drove into the yard the gentleman was met by a hotel servant—waiter as they are called in the restaurants—a fellow so brisk and rapid in his movements that it was impossible to distinguish his countenance. He ran out nimbly with a dinner napkin in his hand, a long figure wearing a long frock-coat made of some cotton mixture with the waist almost up to the nape of his neck, tossed his locks and nimbly led the gentleman upstairs along the whole

---

*Slaves attached to their master's land and sold along with it.
†City about 450 miles east of Moscow, near the Volga River.
‡City about 100 miles south of Moscow.

length of a wooden gallery to show the guest to the room Providence
had sent him. The room was of the familiar type, but the hotel, too,
was of the familiar type—that is, it was precisely like the hotels in
provincial towns where for two roubles* a day travelers get a quiet
room with black beetles peeping out of every corner like prunes, and
a door, always barricaded with a chest of drawers, into the next apartment, of which the occupant, a quiet and taciturn but excessively inquisitive person, is interested in finding out every detail relating to
the new-comer. The outer façade of the hotel corresponded with its
internal peculiarities: it was a very long building of two storeys; the
lower storey had not been stuccoed but left dark-red brick, which
had become darker still from the violent changes of the weather, and
also somewhat dirty; the upper storey had been painted the invariable yellow tint; in the basement there were shops with horse-collars,
ropes, and bread-rings.† In the corner of one of these shops, or rather
in the window of it, there was a man who sold hot spiced drinks,
with a samovar‡ of red copper and a face as red as his samovar, so that
from a distance one might have imagined that there were two
samovars in the window, if one of them had not had a beard as black
as pitch.

   While the new-comer was inspecting his room, his luggage was
carried up: first of all, a portmanteau of white leather, somewhat
worn and evidently not on its first journey. The portmanteau was
brought in by his coachman Selifan, a little man in sheepskin, and his
footman Petrushka, a fellow of thirty, somewhat sullen looking, with
very thick lips and nose, wearing a rather shabby loose frock-coat that
had evidently been his master's. After the portmanteau they carried
up a small mahogany chest inlaid with hard birch, a pair of boot-
trees, and a roast fowl wrapped up in blue paper. When all this had
been brought in, the coachman Selifan went to the stables to look
after the horses, while the footman Petrushka proceeded to instal
himself in a little lobby, a very dark little cupboard, into which he
had already conveyed his overcoat and with it his own peculiar odour

---

*Russian currency (also spelled rubles), one rouble was worth about half a dollar
under the czars; there were 100 kopecks in a rouble.
†Hard-baked bread shaped in rings.
‡Metal urn used for heating water to make tea.

which was communicated also to the sack containing various articles for his flunkey toilet, which he brought up next. In this cupboard he put up against the wall a narrow three-legged bedstead, covering it with a small travesty of a mattress, crushed as flat as a pancake, and perhaps as greasy, too, which he had succeeded in begging from the hotel-keeper.

While the servants were busy arranging things, their master went to the common room. Every traveller knows very well what these common rooms are like. There were the usual painted walls, blackened above by smoke from the chimney, and glossy below from the backs of travellers of all sorts and more particularly of merchants of the district, for on market days merchants used to come here, in parties of six or seven, to drink their regular two cups of tea; there was the usual grimy ceiling, the usual smutty chandelier with a multitude of little hanging glass lustres* which danced and tinkled every time the waiter ran over the shabby oilcloth, briskly flourishing a tray with as many teacups perched on it as birds on the seashore; there were the usual pictures, painted in oil, all over the walls; in short everything was the same as it is everywhere, the only difference was that in one of the pictures a nymph was portrayed with a bosom more immense than the reader has probably ever seen. Such freaks of nature, however, occur in all sorts of historical pictures which have been imported into Russia, there is no knowing at what date, from what place or by whom, though sometimes they are brought us by our grand gentlemen, lovers of the arts, who have purchased them in Italy on the advice of their couriers.

The gentleman removed his cap and unwound from his neck a woollen shawl of rainbow hues such as married men are provided with by their wives, who add to those gifts suitable exhortations about wrapping themselves up. Who does the same for bachelors I cannot say for certain, God only knows: I have never worn such a shawl myself. When he had removed the shawl the gentleman ordered dinner. While they were serving him with various dishes usual in restaurants, such as cabbage soup with little pies of puff paste purposely kept for weeks in readiness for visitors, brains with peas, sausages with cabbage, roast pullet, salt cucumbers, and the eternal sweet puffs which

---

*Cut-glass pendants of a chandelier.

are always at one's service; while all these things were being set before
him, some warmed up and some cold, he made the servant, or waiter,
tell him all sorts of foolish things, such as who used to keep the hotel
and who kept it now, and whether it was profitable and whether his
master were a great rascal, to which the waiter made the usual answer:
"Oh, he is a great swindler, sir!" Both in enlightened Europe and in
enlightened Russia there are nowadays many worthy persons who
cannot eat in a restaurant without talking to waiters and sometimes
even making amusing jokes at their expense. The questions put by the
traveller were however not altogether foolish. He inquired with
marked particularity who was the governor, who was president of the
court of justice, who was the public prosecutor, in short he did not
omit to inquire about a single one of the more important local officials, and with even greater particularity, even with marked interest he
inquired about all the country gentlemen of consequence: how many
souls of peasants* each owned, how far from the town he lived, what
were his characteristics and how often he visited the town. He made
careful inquiries concerning the health of the countryside, whether
there were any complaints in the province—such as epidemics, fevers,
small-pox and such like, and all this with a preciseness which betrayed
more than simple curiosity. The gentleman had something solid and
respectable in his manners and he blew his nose extremely loud. I cannot say how he did it, but his nose resounded like a trumpet. This apparently innocent merit gained him much respect from the waiter, for
every time he heard the sound he shook his locks, drew himself up
more respectfully, and bending his head inquired whether he wanted
anything. After dinner the gentleman drank a cup of coffee and sat on
the sofa, propping his back against one of those cushions which in
Russian hotels are stuffed not with supple wool but with something
extraordinarily like bricks and pebbles. At this point he began to yawn
and bade the waiter take him to his room, where he lay down and
slept for a couple of hours. When he had rested he wrote, at the request of the waiter, on a slip of paper, his rank in the service,† his
Christian name, and his surname to be presented in due course to the

---

*That is, serfs.

†Reference to the Table of Ranks, fourteen levels of civil service and military ranks established by Peter the Great (Peter I) in 1722.

police. As he went downstairs the waiter spelled out as follows: "Pavel Ivanovitch Tchitchikov, collegiate councillor* and landowner, travelling on his private business."

While the waiter was still engaged in spelling this out, Pavel Ivanovitch Tchitchikov went off to look at the town, with which he was, it appears, satisfied, for he considered that it was in no way inferior to other provincial towns: the yellow paint on the brick houses was extremely glaring, while the wood houses were a modest dark grey. The houses were of one storey, of two storeys, and of one and a half storeys with the everlasting mezzanine which provincial architects think so beautiful. In some parts these houses looked lost in the midst of a street as wide as a field and unending wooden fences; in other places they were all crowded together, and here more life and movement were noticeable. There were shop signboards with bread-rings or boots on them, almost effaced by the rain, with here and there a picture of blue trousers and the name of some tailor; in one place was a shop with caps, and the inscription: "Vassily Fyodorov, foreigner"; in another place there was depicted a billiard table with two players in dress coats such as are worn in our theatres by the visitors who come on to the stage in the last act. The players were represented taking aim with the cue, their arms a little drawn back and their legs crooked as though they had just made an *entrechat*† in the air. Under all this was inscribed: "And here is the establishment." Here and there, tables covered with nuts, soap, and cakes that looked like soap, stood simply in the street; and here and there was an eating-house with a fat fish and a fork stuck in it on the signboard. More often than anything he observed, somewhat darkened by age, the two-headed imperial eagle‡ which is nowadays replaced by the laconic inscription: "Beer and spirits." The pavement was everywhere in a bad state. He glanced too into the town park which consisted of skimpy and drooping trees, supported by props put in triangles and very handsomely painted green. Though these trees were no higher than a reed, yet in describing some illumina-

---

*Sixth rank of the civil service, equivalent in the military ranking to army colonel or navy captain.
†In ballet, a leap from the floor while repeatedly crossing the legs (French).
‡Russian imperial emblem.

tions the newspapers had said of them that: "Our town has, thanks to the care of the municipal authorities, been adorned with a park of spreading shady trees that provide welcome coolness on a sultry day," and that "it was extremely touching to observe how the hearts of the townspeople were quivering with tears in recognition of what they owed to his worship the Mayor." After minutely questioning a policeman as to the nearest way to the cathedral, to the government offices and to the governor's, he went to have a look at the river which flowed through the middle of the town; on the way he tore off a poster affixed to a pole in order to read it carefully on returning home, stared at a lady of prepossessing exterior who was walking along the wooden side-walk, followed by a boy in military livery with a parcel in his hand, and after once more scrutinising it all as though to remember precisely the position of everything, he went home and straight up to his hotel room, slightly assisted up the staircase by the waiter. After drinking tea he sat down before his table, ordered a candle, took the poster out of his pocket, held it to the light, and began to read it, slightly screwing up his right eye. There was little of interest in the poster however: a play of Kotzebue's* was being performed with Poplyovin in the part of Rolla and Mademoiselle Zyablov in that of Cora, and the other performers were even less noteworthy; he read through all their names, however, and even went on to the price of the orchestra stalls, and learned that the poster had been printed at the printing press of the government department of the province. Then he turned it over to find out if there was anything of interest on the other side, but, finding nothing, rubbed his eyes, folded it up neatly and put it in his chest, in which he had the habit of stowing away everything that turned up. The day was I believe concluded by a plateful of cold veal, a pint of sour cabbage soup, and a sound sleep, with every tap turned on, as the expression is in some parts of the spacious Russian empire.

The whole of the following day was devoted to visits. The newcomer set off to make calls upon all the dignitaries of the town. He paid his respects to the governor who, as it turned out, was like

---

*August von Kotzebue (1761–1819), German dramatist; the play is *Die Spanier in Peru; oder, Rollas Tod* (*The Spaniards in Peru; or, Rolla's Death*).

Tchitchikov himself, neither stout nor thin; he had the Anna on his neck,* and was even said to have been recommended for a star. He was, however, a very simple and good-natured fellow, and sometimes actually embroidered on net. Then he went to the deputy-governor's, then visited the public prosecutor, the president of the court of justice, the police-master, the spirit tax contractor, the superintendent of the government factories. . . . I am sorry to say it is rather difficult to recall all the great ones of this world; but it is sufficient to say that the new-comer displayed an extraordinary activity in paying visits, he even called to show his regard for the inspector of the medical board and the town architect. And he sat for a good while afterwards in his chaise, wondering whether there was any one else he could visit, but it seemed there were no more officials in the town. In conversation with these potentates he very skilfully managed to flatter every one of them. To the governor he hinted, as it were casually, that one travelled in his province as in Paradise, that the roads were everywhere like velvet, and that the governments which appointed wise rulers were worthy of the greatest praise. To the police-master he said something very flattering about the town police; while in conversation with the deputy-governor and the president of the court, who were still only civil councillors, he twice said by mistake, "your Excellency," which greatly gratified them. The consequence of this was that the governor gave him an invitation to an evening-party in his house that very day, and the other officials, too, invited him, one to dinner, another to a game of boston,† another to a cup of tea.

The new-comer, as it seemed, avoided saying much about himself; if he did speak of himself it was in generalities, with conspicuous modesty, and his speech on such occasions took somewhat a bookish turn, such as: that he was only an insignificant worm, and did not deserve to be the object of attention, that he had passed through many experiences in his time, had suffered for the cause of justice, had many enemies who had even attempted his life, and that now, desirous of living in peace, he was looking out to find a place for his permanent residence and that being in the town he thought it

---

*Order of Saint Anna, a decoration established in 1735 and awarded for deeds of civil service and labor.
†Card game.

his bounden duty to show his respect for its leading dignitaries. That was all that was learned in the town about this new personage who very shortly afterwards did not fail to put in an appearance at the governor's evening-party. The preparations for this evening-party occupied him over two hours, and on this occasion he exhibited a greater attention to his toilet than is commonly seen. After a brief after-dinner nap he asked for soap and water and spent an extremely long time scrubbing his cheeks with soap, putting his tongue into them to make them stand out; then, taking a towel off the shoulder of the waiter, wiped his face in all directions, beginning from behind his ears, first giving two snorts right in the face of the waiter; then he put on his shirt-front before the looking-glass, tweaked out two hairs that were protruding from his nose, and immediately after that attired himself in a short cranberry-coloured dress coat. Having thus arrayed himself he drove in his own carriage through the immensely wide streets, illuminated by the faint light that came from the windows glimmering here and there. The governor's house, however, was illuminated as though for a ball; there were carriages with lamps, two mounted policemen before the entrance, shouting postillions in the distance—in fact everything as it should be.

On entering the room Tchitchikov had for a moment to screw up his eyes, for the glare of the candles, the lamps, and the ladies' dresses was terrific. It was all flooded with light. Black coats flitted about, one by one or in groups, here and there, like flies flitting about a sparkling sugar-loaf on a hot July day when the old housekeeper breaks and splits it up into glistening lumps before the open window: the children all look on, gathered round her, watching with interest her rough hands lifting the hammer while airy squadrons of flies, floating on the breeze, fly in boldly as though the house belonged to them and, taking advantage of the old woman's dim sight and the sunshine that dazzles her eyes, cover the dainty morsels, here in scattered groups, and there in dense crowds. Sated by the wealth of summer which spreads dainties for them at every step, they fly in, not for food but to display themselves, to parade up and down over the heap of sugar, to rub their hind legs or their front legs one against the other, or to scratch themselves under their wings, or stretching out both front legs to brush their heads with them, to turn and fly out again and to fly in once more in new persistent squadrons.

Tchitchikov had hardly time to look about him when the governor took him by the arm and at once presented him to his wife. The new-comer did not lose his head, but paid her some compliments extremely suitable for a man of his age, who is of a rank in the service neither exalted nor very humble. When the couples of dancers taking their places pressed every one back to the wall, he gazed at them very attentively for two or three minutes with his hands behind him. Many of the ladies were well and fashionably dressed. Others were dressed in whatever Providence was pleased to send them in a provincial town. The men here as everywhere were of two kinds; first, the thin who were always hanging about the ladies; some of them could hardly be distinguished from Petersburgers:* they had the same elaborately and tastefully combed whiskers and the same pleasing, smoothly shaven, oval faces, they seated themselves beside the ladies in the same casual way, spoke French and diverted the ladies just like gentlemen from Petersburg. The second class consisted of the stout or those like Tchitchikov, who, though not extremely stout, were certainly not thin. These, on the contrary, looked askance at the ladies and held aloof from them, while they gazed about to see whether the governor's servants had yet set the table for whist.† Their faces were round and full, some of them even had warts, some of them even were pock-marked; they did not wear their hair either in a top-knot or in curls, nor *à la diable m'emporte*‡ as the French call it; their hair was either cropped short or plastered to their heads, and their features inclined rather to the round and solid. These were the more dignified officials of the town. Alas! the stout know better how to manage their affairs in this world than the thin. The thin serve rather on special commissions or are mere supernumeraries, sent here and there. Their existence is somehow too light and airy and not to be depended upon. The stout never go by by-paths but always keep to the main road, and if they seat themselves anywhere they sit firmly and reliably, so that their seat is more likely to give way under them than they are to be dislodged from it. They are not fond of external display. Their coats are not so

---

*Residents of St. Petersburg, capital of Russia from 1712 to 1917.
†Card game.
‡In a devil-may-care manner (French).

smartly cut as the thin man's; their wardrobe is better stocked however. The thin man will in three years' time not have a single serf left
unmortgaged: while if you take a quiet look round, the fat man has
a house at the end of the town bought in the name of his wife; later
on, at the other end of the town, another one, then a little village
near the town, then an estate with all the conveniences. In the end
the fat man, after serving God and his Tsar and winning universal respect, leaves the service, moves away and becomes a landowner, a
hearty hospitable Russian gentleman,—he gets on, and indeed gets
on very well. And when he has gone, his thin heirs in accordance
with the Russian tradition make ducks and drakes* of all their father's property. I cannot disguise the fact that such were the reflections which occupied Tchitchikov's mind while he was scrutinising
the company and the result was that he finally joined the fat ones,
among whom he found all the personages he knew: the public prosecutor with very black thick eyebrows and with the left eye given to
winking slightly as though to say: "Come into the next room, my
boy, I have something to tell you," though he was a serious and taciturn man; the postmaster, a short man who was a wit and a philosopher; the president of the court, a very sagacious and polite
man,—all of whom welcomed him as an old acquaintance while
Tchitchikov responded to their civilities by profuse bows a little to
one side but no less agreeable for that. Then he made the acquaintance of a very civil and affable landowner called Manilov, and another, somewhat clumsy-looking, called Sobakevitch who to begin
with trod on his foot, saying, "I beg your pardon." Then they thrust
upon him a card for whist, which he accepted with the same polite
bow. They sat down to a green table and did not get up before supper. All conversation ceased entirely, as is always the case when people give themselves up to an important occupation. Though the
postmaster was a very talkative person, yet as soon as he took up his
cards his face at once became expressive of thought, while his upper
lip was drawn down over the lower one and remained so all the time
he was playing. When he played a court card, he would strike the
table violently with his hand, saying if it were a queen, "Away with

---

*Literally, a child's game of skimming a flat stone over the water; here, fooling
around.

you, old priest's wife," if it were a king, "Away with you, Tambov*
peasant!"—while the president would say, "I'll pull his whiskers, I'll
pull her whiskers!" Sometimes as cards were slapped down on the
table, comments burst out, "Ah, come what may! there's nothing
else, so play a diamond!" or the suits were called by various endearing nicknames with which they had rechristened them. At the end
of the game they disputed rather loudly, as is usual. Our hero disputed, but so extremely skilfully, that every one could see that
though he was arguing, he was arguing agreeably. He never said,
"You led," but "You were pleased to lead; I had the honour to cover
your two," and so on. To propitiate his opponents still further he invariably offered them his silver enamelled snuff-box, at the bottom
of which they noticed two violets put there for the sake of the scent.
The new-comer's attention was particularly engaged by Manilov and
Sobakevitch, the landowners above mentioned. He immediately
drew the president and the postmaster a little aside and made inquiries concerning them. Several of the questions put by him
showed not only a love of knowledge but also solid sense in the visitor, for he first of all inquired how many souls of peasants each of
them possessed and in what condition their estates were, and only
afterwards inquired their Christian name and father's name. Before
long he had succeeded in completely fascinating them. Manilov, a
man who had hardly reached middle-age, with eyes as sweet as
sugar which he screwed up every time he laughed, was enchanted
with him. He pressed his hand very warmly and begged him
earnestly to do him the honour of a visit to his country place which
in his words was only ten miles from the town gate; to which
Tchitchikov, with a very polite inclination of the head and cordial
pressure of the hand, replied that he was not only extremely eager
to do so, but would positively regard it as a sacred duty. Sobakevitch
too said somewhat laconically, "And I invite you too," with a scrape
of his foot, shod in a boot of such gigantic proportions that it would
be hard to find a foot to fit it, particularly nowadays when even in
Russia giants are beginning to die out.

Next day Tchitchikov went to dinner and to spend the evening at
the police-master's, where after dinner they sat down to whist at

*City about 260 miles southeast of Moscow.

three o'clock and played till two o'clock in the morning. There he made the acquaintance, among others, of a landowner called Nozdryov, a man of thirty, a jolly good fellow who from the first three or four words began to address him familiarly. With the police-master and public prosecutor Nozdryov was on equally friendly and familiar terms; but when they sat down to play for high stakes, both the gentlemen kept an extremely careful watch on the tricks he took and noted almost every card he played. Next day Tchitchikov spent the evening with the president of the court, who received his visitors in his somewhat greasy dressing-gown, and in the company of two somewhat dubious ladies. Then he spent an evening at the deputy-governor's, went to a big dinner at the spirit tax contractor's, and to a little dinner at the public prosecutor's which was however as good as a big one; he went also to a lunch after mass, given by the mayor of the town, which was as good as a dinner,—in short he had not to spend a single hour at home and returned to the hotel only to sleep. The new-comer was quite at his ease on every occasion and showed himself an experienced man of the world. Whatever the subject of conversation he could always keep it up: were horse-breeding discussed, he talked about horse-breeding; if they conversed about the best dogs, on that subject too he made very apt observations; if they touched on a case inquired into by the court of justice, he showed that he was not ignorant of court procedure; if the topic were a game of billiards, he was not at sea in billiards either; if the conversation turned upon virtue, he made excellent reflections upon virtue and even with tears in his eyes; upon the preparation of hot punch, he was an authority on punch too; upon overseers of customs and excise officers, he discoursed about them too as though he had been himself an excise officer or overseer of the customs. But it was noteworthy that he succeeded in accompanying all this with a certain sedateness, and knew very well how to behave. He spoke neither too loud nor too low, but exactly as he ought. Take him how you would, he was a thoroughly gentlemanly man. All the government officials were pleased at the arrival of the new-comer. The governor pronounced that he was a man thoroughly to be depended upon; the public prosecutor said that he was a practical man; the colonel of the gendarmes said that he was a well-educated man; the president of the court said that he was a well-informed and estimable man; the police-master that he was an estimable and agreeable man; the police-master's wife that he was a most agreeable and most amiable man. Though Sobakevitch rarely said anything good of any one, yet even he, after returning rather late from town, undressing and getting into bed beside his scraggy wife, said to her: "I spent the evening at the governor's, my love, and dined at the police-master's and made the acquaintance of a collegiate councillor called Pavel Ivanovitch Tchitchikov, a very agreeable man!" To which his spouse responded with: "H'm," and kicked him.

Such was the very flattering opinion that was formed of the visitor in the town, and it was maintained until a strange peculiarity and enterprise of his, or, as they say in the provinces, a 'passage,' of which the reader will soon hear more, reduced almost the whole town to utter perplexity.

CHAPTER 2

Our new-comer had stayed for over a week in the town, driving about to evening-parties and dinners and so passing his time, as it is called, very agreeably. At last he made up his mind to carry his visits beyond the town and to go and see Manilov and Sobakevitch as he had promised. Perhaps he was impelled to this by another more essential reason, by something more serious and nearer to his heart. . . . But of all this the reader will learn by degrees in due season, if only he has the patience to read through the following narrative, a very long one, since it was later on to cover a wider and wider ground as it approaches its conclusion.

Selifan the coachman was given orders to put the horses into the familiar chaise early in the morning; Petrushka was instructed to remain at home to look after the room and portmanteau. It will not be amiss for the reader to be made acquainted with these two serfs of our hero's. Although of course they are not very prominent characters but are rather what are called secondary or even tertiary, though the principal events and the mainsprings of the poem do not rest upon them, and only here and there touch and lightly catch upon them, yet the author likes to be extremely circumstantial in everything and in that respect, though a Russian, prefers to be as precise as a German. This however will not take up much time and space, since we need not add much to what the reader knows already, that is, that Petrushka wore a rather roomy brown coat that had been his master's, and had, as usual with persons of his calling, a thick nose and lips. He was rather of a taciturn than of a talkative disposition; he even had a generous yearning for enlightenment, that is, for reading books, over the subject of which he did not trouble himself: it was precisely the same to him whether it was the story of a love-sick hero's adventures, or simply a dictionary or a prayer-book—he read everything with equal attention. If he had been offered a manual of chemistry he would not have refused it. He liked not so much what he read as the reading itself, or rather the process of reading, the fact that the letters continually made up a word and the devil knows what it might sometimes mean. His reading was for the most part done in a recumbent position on the bedstead in the passage and on a mattress which had through this habit been flattened out as thin as a wafer. Apart from his passion for reading he had two other characteristics; he slept without undressing, just as he was, in the same coat, and he always brought with him his own peculiar atmosphere, his individual odour which was suggestive of a room which has been lived in a long time, so that it was enough for him to put up his bedstead somewhere even in a room hitherto uninhabited, and to instal there his greatcoat and belongings for it to seem at once as though people had been living in the room for the last ten years. Tchitchikov, who was a very fastidious and in some cases an over-particular man, would pucker up his face when he sniffed the air in the morning and, shaking his head, would say: "Goodness knows what it is, my boy, you are in a sweat or something, you should go to the bath." To which Petrushka made no reply but tried to be very busy about something at once: either he went with a brush to his master's dress coat hanging on a peg, or simply put something in its place. What was he thinking while he was silent? Perhaps he was saying to himself: "You are a nice one too, you are never tired of saying the same thing forty times over. . . ." God knows, it is hard to tell what a serf is thinking when his master is giving him a lecture. So much then may be said of Petrushka to start with. Selifan, the coachman, was quite a different man. . . . But the author is really ashamed of occupying his readers' attention so long with persons of a low class, knowing from experience how reluctant they are to make acquaintance with the lower orders. It is characteristic of the Russian that he has a great passion for making the acquaintance of any one who is ever so little higher in rank, and a nodding acquaintance with a count or a prince is more precious to him than the closest friendship of ordinary human beings. The author, indeed, is a little anxious over his hero who is only a collegiate councillor. Court councillors perhaps will consent to make his acquaintance, but those who have attained the rank of general may perhaps—God knows—cast upon him one of those contemptuous glances which a man proudly casts at everything which grovels at his feet, or, worse still perhaps, pass by with an indifference that will stab the author to the heart. But however mortifying either of these alternatives would be, we must in any case return now to our hero.

And so, having given his orders overnight, he woke up very early in the morning, washed, rubbing himself from head to foot with a wet sponge, an operation only performed on Sundays—and it happened to be a Sunday—he shaved so thoroughly that his cheeks were like satin for smoothness and glossiness, he put on his shot cranberry-coloured swallow-tail coat, then his overcoat lined with thick bearskin; then, supported first on one side and then on the other by the waiter, he went downstairs and got into his chaise. The chaise drove rumbling out of the gates of the hotel into the street. A passing priest took off his hat, some street urchins in dirty shirts held out their hands, saying, "Something for a poor orphan, sir!" The coachman, noticing that one of them was very zealous to stand on the footboard, gave him a lash with the whip, and the chaise went jolting over the cobble stones. It was not without relief that our hero saw in the distance the striped barrier post that indicated that to the cobbled road as to every form of torture there would soon be an end, and after striking his head rather violently against the sides of the chaise two or three times more, Tchitchikov glided at last over the soft earth. As soon as the town was left behind, all sorts of wild rubbish and litter made its appearance on both sides of the road, as is usually the case in Russia: mounds of earth, firwoods, low scanty thickets of young pines, the charred stumps of old ones, wild heather and such stuff. They came upon villages consisting of a string of huts, looking like old timber shacks, covered with grey roofs with carvings under them, that resembled embroidered towels. As usual a few peasants sat gaping on benches in front of their gates, dressed in their sheepskins; peasant women, tightly girt above the bosom, showed their fat faces at the upper windows; from the lower ones a calf stared or a pig poked out its small-eyed snout. In short, there were the familiar sights.

After driving about ten miles our hero remembered that from Manilov's account his village ought to be here, but the eleventh mile was passed and still the village was not to be seen, and if they had not happened to meet two peasants they could hardly have reached their destination. To the question, "Is the village of Zamanilovka far from here?" the peasants took off their hats and one of them with a wedge-shaped beard, somewhat more intelligent than the rest, answered: "Manilovka perhaps, not Zamanilovka?"

"Yes, I suppose, Manilovka."

"Manilovka! Well, if you go on another half mile then you turn straight off to the right."

"To the right," repeated the coachman.

"To the right," said the peasant. "That will be your road to Manilovka; but there is no such place as Zamanilovka. That is what it is called, its name is Manilovka, but as for Zamanilovka there is no such place here about. There straight before you on the hill you will see the house, built of brick, two storeys high—the manor house, that is, where the gentleman himself lives. There you have Manilovka, but there is no Zamanilovka here and never has been."

They drove on to look for Manilovka. After going on another mile and a half they came to a by-road to the right; but they drove on another mile, and two miles, and three miles and still no brick house of two storeys was to be seen. At that point Tchitchikov recalled the fact that if a friend invites one into the country a distance of ten miles it always turns out to be twenty. Few people would have been attracted by the situation of the village of Manilovka. The manor house stood on a bluff, that is, on a height exposed to every wind that might chance to blow; the slope of the hill on which it stood was covered with closely-shaven turf. Two or three flower-beds with bushes of lilac and yellow acacia were scattered about it in the English fashion; birch-trees in small groups of five or six together lifted here and there their skimpy tiny-leaved crests. Under two such birch-trees could be seen an arbour with a flattish green cupola, blue wood pillars, and an inscription: "The Temple of solitary meditation"; lower down there was a pond covered with green scum, which is however nothing uncommon in the English gardens of Russian landowners. Grey log huts, which our hero for some unknown reason instantly proceeded to count, and of which he made out over two hundred, lay here and there at the foot of the hill and for some distance up the slope of it. Nowhere was there a growing tree or any kind of greenery among them to relieve the monotony of the grey logs. The scene was enlivened by two peasant women who, with their skirts picturesquely tucked up on all sides, were wading over their knees in the pond, dragging by two wooden poles a torn net in which two crayfish were entangled and a gleaming roach* could be seen; the women seemed to be quarrelling and were scolding each other about something. A pine forest of a dreary bluish colour made a dark blur in the distance. Even the very weather was in keeping. The day was neither bright nor gloomy but of a light-grey tint,—such as is only seen in the uniforms of garrison soldiers, those peaceful—though on Sundays apt to be intemperate—forces. To complete the picture, a cock, herald of changing weather, crowed very loudly, though his head had been pecked to the brain by other cocks during his flirtations, and even flapped his wings plucked bare as old bast mats.

As he drove up to the courtyard, Tchitchikov noticed on the doorstep the master of the house himself, who attired in a green coat of shalloon† was standing, holding his hand to his forehead to screen his eyes from the sun and get a better view of the approaching carriage. The nearer it came, the more delighted he looked and the broader was his smile.

"Pavel Ivanovitch!" he cried, as Tchitchikov alighted from the chaise. "So you have remembered us at last!"

The friends kissed each other very warmly and Manilov led his visitor indoors. Though the time spent by them in passing through the vestibule, the hall, and the dining-room will be somewhat brief, yet we must snatch the opportunity to say a few words about the master of the house. But at this point the author must confess that the task is a very difficult one. It is much easier to describe characters on a grander scale: then you simply have to throw the colour by handfuls on the canvas—black, glowing eyes, overhanging brows, a forehead lined by care, a black or fiery crimson cloak flung over the shoulder, and the portrait is complete. But all the gentlemen (of whom there are so many in the world) who look so very much alike and yet, when you inspect them more closely, have many extremely elusive peculiarities, are fearfully difficult to describe. One has to strain one's attention to the utmost to make all the delicate almost indiscernible traits stand out, and altogether one needs to look deeply with an eye sharpened by long practice in the art.

God alone could say what Manilov's character was like. There are

---

*European freshwater, carp-like fish.
†Light, twilled woolen fabric.

people who are always spoken of as being "so-so," neither one thing nor the other, neither flesh, fowl, nor good red herring, as the saying is. Possibly Manilov must be included in their number. In appearance, he was good-looking; the features of his countenance were rather agreeable, but in that agreeableness there was an overdose of sugar; in his deportment and manners there was something that betrayed an anxiety to win goodwill and friendship. He smiled ingratiatingly, he had fair hair and blue eyes. At the first moment of conversation with him one could not but say, "What a kind and agreeable man!" The next minute one would say nothing, and the third minute one would say, "What the devil is one to make of it?" and would walk away; if one did not walk away one would be aware of a deadly boredom. You would never hear from him a hasty or even over-eager word, such as you may hear from almost any one if you touch on a subject that upsets him. Every one has his weak spot: in one man it takes the form of hounds, another imagines that he is a great amateur of music and has a wonderful feeling for its inmost depths; a third is proud of his feats at the dining-table. A fourth is for playing a part if only one inch higher than that allotted him by fate; a fifth with more limited aspirations, dreams waking and sleeping of being seen on the promenade with a court adjutant to the admiration of his friends and acquaintances, and of strangers, too, indeed; a sixth is endowed with a hand which feels a supernatural prompting to turn down the corner of an ace of diamonds or of a two, while a seventh positively itches to maintain discipline everywhere and to enforce his views on stationmasters and cabmen. In short every one has some peculiarity, but Manilov had nothing. At home he spoke very little, and for the most part confined himself to meditation and thought, but what he thought about, that too, God only knows. It could not be said that he busied himself in looking after his land, he never even drove out into the fields; the estate looked after itself somehow. When the steward said, "It would be a good thing to do this or that, sir," "Yes, it would not be amiss," he would usually reply, smoking his pipe, a habit he had taken to while he was in the army, in which he was considered a most modest, refined, and highly-cultured officer. "Yes, it certainly would not be amiss," he would repeat. When a peasant came to him and, scratching the back of his head, said, "Master, give me leave of absence to earn money for my taxes," "You can go," he would say, smoking his pipe, and it would never enter his head that the peasant was going for a drinking-bout. Sometimes, looking from the steps into the yard or at the pond, he would say how nice it would be to make an underground passage from the house, or build a bridge over the pond with stalls on each side of it and shopmen sitting in them, selling all sorts of small articles of use to the peasants. And as he did so, his eyes would become extraordinarily sugary, and an expression of the greatest satisfaction would come into his face. All these projects ended in nothing but words, however. In his study there always lay a book with a marker at the fourteenth page, which he had been reading for the last two years. In his home something was always lacking: in the drawing-room there was excellent furniture upholstered in smart silken material which had certainly cost a good price, but there had not been enough of it to cover everything and two of the easy-chairs had remained simply swathed in sacking. The master of the house had been for some years past in the habit of warning his guests, "Don't sit on those armchairs, they are not finished yet." In some of the rooms there was no furniture at all, although in the early days after their marriage he had said to his wife: "To-morrow, my love, we must see about putting some furniture into those rooms if only for a time." In the evening a very handsome candlestick of dark bronze with antique figures of the three Graces* and an elegant mother-of-pearl shield was put on the table, and beside it was set a humble copper relic, unsteady on its legs and always covered with tallow, though this never attracted the notice of the master of the house, the mistress, or the servants. His wife was . . . however they were thoroughly satisfied with each other. Although they had been married over eight years they would still each offer the other a piece of apple or a sweet or a nut, and say in a touchingly tender voice expressive of the most perfect devotion: "Open your little mouth, my love, and I will pop it in." It need hardly be said that on such occasions the little mouth was gracefully opened. For birthdays they prepared surprises for each other—such as a beaded case for a toothbrush. And very often as they sat on the sofa, all at once, entirely without any apparent cause, he would lay down his pipe and she her

---

*In classical mythology, daughters of Zeus, goddesses who embodied and bestowed beauty, charm, and grace.

needle-work, if she happened to have it in her hands at the time, and they would imprint on each other's lips a kiss so prolonged and languishing, that a small cigar might easily have been smoked while it lasted. In short, they were what is called happy. Of course, it might be observed that there are many other things to be done in a house besides exchanging prolonged kisses and preparing surprises, and many different questions might be asked. Why was it, for instance, that the cooking was foolishly and badly done? Why was it that the storeroom was rather empty? Why was it the housekeeper was a thief? Why was it that the servants were drunken and immoral? Why was it all the house-serfs slept in a conscienceless way and spent the rest of their time in loose behaviour? But all these subjects were low, and Madame Manilov had had a good education. And a good education, as we all know, is received in a boarding-school; and in boarding-schools, as we all know, three principal subjects lay the foundation of all human virtues: the French language, indispensable for the happiness of family life; the pianoforte, to furnish moments of agreeable relaxation to husbands; and finally domestic training in particular, *i.e.* the knitting of purses and other surprises. It is true that there are all sorts of improvements and changes of method, especially in these latter days: everything depends on the good sense and capacity of the lady-principals of these establishments. In some boarding-schools, for instance, it is usual to put the pianoforte first, then French, and then domestic training. While in others domestic training, that is, the knitting of "surprises," takes the foremost place, then comes French, and only then the pianoforte. There are all sorts of variations. It may not be out of place to observe also that Madame Manilov . . . but, I must own, I feel frightened of talking about ladies, besides it is time for me to get back to my heroes, whom we have left standing for some minutes before the drawing-room door, each begging the other to pass in first.

"Pray don't put yourself out on my account, I will follow you," said Tchitchikov.

"No, Pavel Ivanovitch, no, you are the visitor," said Manilov, motioning him to the door with his hand.

"Don't stand on ceremony, please; please go first," said Tchitchikov.

"No, you must excuse me, I cannot allow such an agreeable, highly-cultured guest to walk behind me."

"Why highly-cultured? . . . Please pass in."

"No, you, pray walk in."

"But why?"

"Why, because!" Manilov said with an agreeable smile.

Finally the two friends walked in at the door sideways, somewhat squeezing each other.

"Allow me to introduce my wife," said Manilov. "My love, this is Pavel Ivanovitch!"

Tchitchikov did indeed observe a lady whom he had not noticed while bowing and scraping with Manilov in the doorway. She was not bad-looking and was becomingly dressed. Her loose brocaded silk gown of a pale colour hung well upon her: her delicate little hand flung something hurriedly on the table and crushed a cambric handkerchief with embroidered corners. She got up from the sofa on which she was sitting. Tchitchikov not without satisfaction bent to kiss her hand. Madame Manilov said, even speaking with a slight lisp, that they were greatly delighted at his visit and that not a day passed without her husband's mentioning him.

"Yes," observed Manilov, "she has been continually asking me, 'Why doesn't your friend come?' 'Wait a little, my love,' I told her, 'he will come.' And here at last you have honoured us with a visit. It really is a pleasure you have given us . . . a May day . . . a festival of the heart."

Tchitchikov was actually a little embarrassed on hearing that it had already come to festivals of the heart, and answered that he had no great name nor distinguished rank.

"You have everything," Manilov pronounced with the same agreeable smile, "you have everything: more, indeed."

"What do you think of our town?" inquired Madame Manilov. "Have you passed your time there pleasantly?"

"A very nice town, a fine town," replied Tchitchikov, "and have I spent a most agreeable time: the society is most amiable."

"And what did you think of our governor?" said Madame Manilov.

"He really is a most estimable and genial man, isn't he?" added Manilov.

"Perfectly true," assented Tchitchikov, "a most estimable man.

And how thoroughly he throws himself into his duties, how thoroughly he understands them! If only there were more men like him!"

"How well he understands, you know, entertaining all sorts; what delicacy he displays in his manners!" Manilov chimed in with a smile, and he almost closed his eyes with gratification like a tom-cat who is being scratched behind his ears.

"A most affable and agreeable man," continued Tchitchikov, "and what a clever man he is! I could never have imagined it: how well he embroiders all sorts of patterns. He showed me some of his handiwork, a purse: not many ladies could have embroidered it so well."

"And the deputy-governor, isn't he a charming man?" said Manilov, again screwing up his eyes.

"A most worthy man, most worthy," answered Tchitchikov.

"And let me ask you, what was your impression of the police-master? He is a very agreeable man, is he not?"

"Extremely agreeable, and what an intelligent, well-read man! We were playing whist at his house with the public prosecutor and the president of the court till cock-crow. A most worthy man, most worthy!"

"And what did you think of the police-master's wife?" added Madame Manilov. "A most amiable woman, isn't she?"

"Oh, she is one of the most estimable ladies I have ever known," answered Tchitchikov.

Then they did not omit to mention the president of the court and the postmaster, and in this way ran through the names of almost all the officials in the town, who were, as it appeared, all excellent persons.

"Do you spend all your time in the country?" inquired Tchitchikov, venturing upon a question in his turn.

"Most of the time we do," answered Manilov. "Sometimes, however, we do visit the town simply in order to see something of cultured people. One grows too rustic if one stays shut up for ever."

"That is true, that is true," said Tchitchikov.

"Of course," Manilov went on, "it would be a different matter if we had nice neighbours, if for instance there were some one with whom one could to some extent converse on polished and refined subjects, pursue some sort of study that would stir the soul, it would give one inspiration, so to say . . ." He would have expressed something more, but, perceiving that he was wandering a little from the point, he merely twiddled his fingers in the air, and went on: "In that case, of course, the country and solitude would have many charms. But there is absolutely no one. . . . Sometimes one is reduced to reading the *Son of the Fatherland*. . . ."*

Tchitchikov agreed with this view entirely, adding that nothing could be more agreeable than to live in solitude, to enjoy the spectacle of nature and from time to time to read. . . .

"But you know," added Manilov, "if one has no friends with whom one can share . . ."

"Oh, that is true, that is perfectly true," Tchitchikov interrupted him. "What are all the treasures in the world then! Not money, but good company, a wise man has said."

"And do you know, Pavel Ivanovitch," said Manilov, while his face wore an expression not merely sweet but sickly cloying sweet, like a dose some tactful society doctor has mercilessly over-sweetened, thinking to gratify his patient, "then one feels to some extent a spiritual enjoyment. . . . Here now, for instance, when chance has given me the rare, one may say unique, happiness of conversing with you and enjoying your agreeable conversation . . ."

"Upon my word, how can my conversation be agreeable? I am an insignificant person and nothing more," answered Tchitchikov.

"Oh, Pavel Ivanovitch, allow me to be open with you! I would gladly give half my fortune to possess some of the qualities with which you are endowed!"

"On the contrary, I for my part should esteem it the greatest . . ."

There is no saying what pitch the mutual outpouring of sentiment between these two friends might have reached, had not a servant entered to announce a meal.

"Pray come to dinner," said Manilov. "You must excuse it if we have not a dinner such as you get in parqueted halls and great cities; we have simply cabbage soup in Russian style, but we offer it from our hearts. Pray go in."

At this point they spent some time in disputing which should

---

*Nineteenth-century Russian political, historical, and literary journal.

pass in first, and finally Tchitchikov walked sideways into the dining-room.

In the dining-room there were already two boys, Manilov's sons, children of an age to sit at the dinner table but still on high chairs. With them was their tutor, who bowed politely with a smile. The lady of the house sat behind the soup tureen; the visitor was placed between his host and hostess. A servant tied dinner napkins round the children's necks.

"What charming children!" said Tchitchikov, looking at them. "How old are they?"

"The elder is eight and the younger was six yesterday," said Madame Manilov.

"Themistoclus,"* said Manilov, addressing the elder boy who was trying to free his chin which had been tied up in the dinner napkin by the footman. Tchitchikov raised his eyebrows a little when he heard this somewhat Greek name, which for some unknown reason Manilov ended with the syllable us; but he tried at once to bring his countenance back to its usual expression.

"Themistoclus! tell me which is the finest town in France?"

At this point the tutor concentrated his whole attention on Themistoclus and looked as though he were going to spring into his face, but was completely reassured at last and nodded his head when Themistoclus said: "Paris."

"And which is our finest town?" Manilov asked again.

The tutor pricked up his ears again.

"Petersburg," answered Themistoclus.

"And any other?"

"Moscow," answered Themistoclus.

"The clever boy, the darling!" Tchitchikov said upon this. "Upon my soul," he went on, addressing the Manilovs with an air of some astonishment, "at his age, and already so much knowledge. I can assure you that that child will show marked abilities!"

"Oh, you don't know him yet," answered Manilov, "he has a very keen wit. The younger now, Alkides,† is not so quick, but this fellow

---

*Pretentiously named (or misnamed) after Themistocles (c.524–c.460 B.C.), Athenian statesman and commander.

†After Alcides, a name for Hercules, the mythical Greek hero known for his strength.

if he comes upon anything such as a beetle or a lady-bird, his eyes are racing after it at once; he runs after it and notices it directly. I intend him for the diplomatic service. Themistoclus," he went on, addressing the boy again, "would you like to be an ambassador?"

"Yes, I should," answered Themistoclus, munching bread, and wagging his head from right to left.

At that moment the footman standing behind his chair wiped the ambassador's nose, and he did well as something very unpleasant might else have dropped into the soup. The conversation at the dinner table began upon the charms of a tranquil life, interspersed with observations from the hostess about the town theatre and the actors in it. The tutor kept an attentive watch upon the speakers, and whenever he saw they were on the point of laughing, he instantly opened his mouth and laughed vigorously. Probably he was a man of grateful disposition and wished to repay the master of the house for his kindly treatment of him. On one occasion, however, his face assumed a severe expression and he sternly tapped on the table, fastening his eyes on the children sitting opposite him. This was in the nick of time, for Themistoclus had just bitten Alkides' ear, and Alkides, screwing up his eyes and opening his mouth, was on the point of breaking into piteous sobs, but, reflecting that he might easily lose the rest of his dinner, he brought his mouth back to its normal position and, with tears in his eyes, began gnawing a mutton bone till both his cheeks were greasy and shining.

The lady of the house often addressed Tchitchikov with the words: "You are eating nothing, you have taken such a little." To which Tchitchikov invariably answered: "Thank you very much, I have done very well. Agreeable conversation is better than the best of good fare."

They got up from the table. Manilov was extremely delighted and, supporting his visitor's backbone with his arm, was preparing to conduct him to the drawing-room, when all at once the visitor announced with a very significant air that he was proposing to speak to him about a very important matter.

"In that case allow me to invite you into my study," said Manilov, and he led him into a small room, the window of which looked out towards the forest, bluish in the distance.

"This is my den," said Manilov.

"A pleasant little room," said Tchitchikov, scanning it. The room certainly was not without charm: the walls were painted a greyish-blue colour; there were four chairs, one easy-chair, a table on which lay the book and in it the book-marker which we have already had occasion to mention; but what was most in evidence was tobacco. It was conspicuous in various receptacles: in packets, in a jar, and also scattered in a heap on the table. In both the windows also there were little heaps of ashes, carefully arranged in very elegant lines. It might be gathered that their arrangement at moments afforded the master of the house a pastime.

"Allow me to beg you to take this easy-chair," said Manilov. "You will be more comfortable."

"Excuse me, I will sit on this chair."

"Allow me not to excuse you," said Manilov with a smile. "This easy-chair is always assigned to my guests; whether you like it or not you must sit in it."

Tchitchikov sat down.

"Allow me to offer you a pipe."

"No, thank you, I do not smoke," said Tchitchikov affably and with an air of regret.

"Why not?" asked Manilov also affably and with an air of regret.

"I am not used to it, I am afraid of it; they say smoking a pipe dries up the system."

"Allow me to observe that that is a prejudice. I imagine, indeed, that it is far better for the health to smoke a pipe than to take snuff. There was a lieutenant in our regiment, a very excellent and highly-cultured man, who never had a pipe out of his mouth, not only at the table, but, if I must say so, in every other place. By now he is over forty but, thank God, he is as strong and well as any one could wish to be."

Tchitchikov observed that it did happen like that and that there were many things in nature that could not be explained even by the profoundest intellect.

"But allow me first to ask one question . . . ," he added in a voice in which there rang a strange, or almost strange, intonation, and thereupon for some unknown reason he looked round behind him. And Manilov too for some unknown reason looked behind him. "How long is it since you made out a census return?"

"Oh, not for a long time; in fact, I don't remember when."

"So that since then a good many of your peasants have died?"

"About that I can't say; I think we must ask my steward. Hey, boy! Call the steward; he was to be here to-day."

The steward appeared. He was a man about forty who shaved his beard, wore a frock-coat and apparently led a very easy life, for his face looked plump and puffy, and the yellow complexion and little eyes betrayed that he was not a stranger to feather beds and pillows. It could be seen at once that he had made his way in life as all gentlemen's stewards do: he had once been simply a boy in the household who could read and write, then had married some Agashka, a housekeeper and favourite of the mistress, had himself become keeper of the stores and then steward. And, having become a steward, he behaved, of course, like all stewards; he hob-nobbed with those who were richer in the village and added to the burdens of the poorer; when he woke after eight o'clock in the morning he waited for the samovar and drank his tea before he went out.

"I say, my good man, how many of our peasants have died since the census was taken?"

"How many? A good many have died since then," said the steward, and he hiccoughed, putting his hand before his mouth like a shield.

"Yes, I confess I thought so myself," Manilov assented. "A great many have died."

Then he turned to Tchitchikov and added: "Certainly, a very great many."

"And what number, for instance?" Tchitchikov inquired.

"Yes, how many precisely?" Manilov chimed in.

"Why, how can I say what number? There is no telling, you know, how many have died, no one has counted them."

"Yes, precisely," said Manilov, addressing Tchitchikov. "I, too, supposed there had been a considerable mortality; it is quite uncertain how many have died."

"Please count them," said Tchitchikov to the steward, "and make an exact list of all of them by name."

"Yes, of all of them by name," said Manilov.

The steward said, "Yes, sir," and went out.

"And for what reason do you want to know?" Manilov inquired when the steward had gone.

This question seemed to put the visitor in some difficulty: his face betrayed a strained effort which even made him flush crimson, an effort to express something not easily put into words. And indeed Manilov did at last hear things more strange and extraordinary than human ears had ever heard before.

"You ask for what reason. The reason is this, I should like to buy the peasants . . ." said Tchitchikov, hesitating and not finishing his sentence.

"But allow me to ask," said Manilov, "how do you wish to buy peasants, with land or simply to take away, that is, without land?"

"No, it's not exactly the peasants," said Tchitchikov. "I want to have dead ones . . ."

"What? Excuse me, I am a little deaf, I fancied I heard something very odd . . ."

"I propose to purchase dead ones who would yet appear on the census list as alive," said Tchitchikov.

Manilov at that point dropped his pipe on the floor and stood with his mouth open for several minutes. The two friends, who had so lately been discussing the charms of friendship, remained motionless, staring at each other like those portraits which used in old days to be hung facing each other on each side of a looking-glass. At last Manilov picked up his pipe and looked up into his guest's face, trying to discern whether there were not a smile on his lips, whether he were not joking; but there was no sign of anything of the sort, indeed his countenance looked more sedate than usual. Then he wondered whether his guest could by some chance have gone out of his mind and in alarm looked at him intently; but his visitor's eyes were perfectly clear; there was no wild uneasy gleam in them, such as is common in the eyes of a madman; all was decorum and propriety. However profoundly Manilov pondered how to take it and what to do, he could think of nothing but to blow out in a thin coil the smoke left in his mouth.

"And so I should like to know whether you could transfer such peasants, not living in reality but living from the point of view of the law, or bestow them, or convey them as you may think best?"

But Manilov was so embarrassed and confused that he could only gaze at him.

"I believe you see objections?" observed Tchitchikov.

"I? . . . no, it's not that," said Manilov, "but pardon me . . . I cannot quite grasp it . . . I, of course, have not been so fortunate as to receive the brilliant education which is perceptible, one may say, in your every movement; I have no great art in expressing myself. Perhaps in this, in what you have just expressed, there is some hidden significance. Perhaps you have expressed yourself in this way as a figure of speech?"

"No," Tchitchikov interposed. "No, I mean just what I say, that is, the souls which are really dead."

Manilov was completely bewildered. He felt he ought to do something, to put some question, but what the devil to ask, he could not tell. He ended at last by blowing out smoke again, not from his mouth but through his nostrils.

"And so if there are no obstacles we might, with God's blessing, proceed to draw up a deed of sale," said Tchitchikov.

"What . . . a sale of dead souls?"

"Oh no," said Tchitchikov, "we shall write them as living, just as it actually stands in the census list. It is my habit never to depart one jot from the law; though I have had to suffer for that in the service, but pardon me: duty is for me a sacred thing, the law—before the law I am dumb."

Manilov liked these last words but he had not the faintest inkling of what was meant, and, instead of answering, fell to sucking at his pipe so vigorously that it began to wheeze like a bassoon. It seemed as though he were trying to draw out of it some opinion in regard to this incredible incident; but the pipe wheezed—and nothing more.

"Perhaps you have some hesitation?"

"Oh, indeed, not the slightest! I don't say this as passing any criticism on you at all, but allow me to suggest, will not this undertaking or, to express it more precisely, negotiation—will not this negotiation be inconsistent with the civic code and ultimate welfare of Russia?"

At this point Manilov making a movement with his hand looked very significantly into Tchitchikov's face, displaying in his tightly-compressed lips and in all the features of his face an expression more

profound than has perhaps ever been seen on the human countenance, unless indeed on that of some extremely wise minister at a
critical moment in a most perplexing situation.

But Tchitchikov said that such an undertaking or negotiation
would be in no way inconsistent with the civic code and the ultimate
welfare of Russia, and a minute later he added that the government
would indeed gain by it as it would receive legal fees.

"That is your opinion?"

"It is my opinion that it will be quite right."

"Oh, if it is quite right that is another thing; I have nothing
against it," said Manilov, and he was completely reassured.

"Now we have only to agree upon the price . . ."

"The price?" inquired Manilov again and he stopped. "Surely
you don't imagine I am going to take money for souls which in a certain sense have ended their existence? Since you have conceived this,
so to speak, fantastic desire, I am ready for my part to give them to
you gratis, and will undertake the legal expenses myself."

The historian of the foregoing events would be greatly to blame
if he omitted to state that the visitor was overcome with delight at the
words uttered by Manilov. Sober and dignified as he was, yet he could
hardly refrain from executing a caper like a goat's, which, as we all
know, is a demonstration confined to moments of acute delight. He
wriggled about so violently in his chair that he slit the woollen material that covered the cushion; Manilov himself looked at him in
some perplexity. Stirred by gratitude he poured out such a flood of
thanks that Manilov was embarrassed, flushed crimson, made a dep-
recating movement with his head, and at last declared that it was
really nothing, that he certainly would be glad to show in some way
the heartfelt attraction, the magnetism of soul of which he was sensible; but that dead souls were in a sense utterly worthless.

"Not worthless at all," said Tchitchikov, pressing his hand.

At this point a very deep sigh escaped him. It seemed that he was
inclined to pour out his heart; not without feeling and expression, he
uttered at last the following words:

"If only you knew the service that with those apparently worthless souls you are doing to a man of no rank or family! What have I
not suffered indeed! Like some ship on the stormy waves . . . what
ill-usage, what persecution have I not endured, what grief have I not

known! And for what? For having followed the path of justice, for being true to my conscience, for giving a helping hand to the forlorn widow and orphan in distress! . . ."

At this point he actually wiped away a tear with his handkerchief.

Manilov was deeply touched. The two friends spent a long time pressing each other's hands and gazing in silence into each other's eyes in which the tears were starting. Manilov would not let go of our hero's hand, but went on pressing it so warmly that the latter did not know how to release it. At last, stealthily withdrawing it, he said that it would not be amiss to draw up the deed of sale as soon as possible, and that it would be as well for him to pay a visit to the town himself; then he picked up his hat and began taking leave.

"What? You want to go already?" said Manilov, suddenly coming to himself and almost frightened.

At that moment Madame Manilov walked into the study.

"Lizanka," said Manilov with a rather plaintive air, "Pavel Ivanovitch is leaving us!"

"Because we have worried Pavel Ivanovitch," said Madame Manilov.

"Madame! Here," said Tchitchikov, "here is where . . ."—he laid his hand on his heart—"Yes, here the delightful time I have spent with you will be treasured! And, believe me, there could be no greater bliss than to live for ever, if not in the same house, at least in the near neighbourhood."

"And you know, Pavel Ivanovitch," said Manilov, who was highly delighted by this idea, "how nice it would be really, if we could live like this together, under one roof, or in the shade of some elm-tree, discuss philosophy, go deeply into things! . . ."

"Oh, that would be paradise!" said Tchitchikov with a sigh. "Farewell, madame," he went on, kissing Madame Manilov's hand. "Farewell, my honoured friend. Do not forget my request."

"Oh, trust me!" answered Manilov, "I am parting with you for no more than two days!"

They all went into the dining-room.

"Good-bye, sweet children!" said Tchitchikov, seeing Alkides and Themistoclus, who were busy over a wooden soldier which had neither arms nor nose. "Good-bye, my darlings, you must forgive me for not having brought you any presents, for I must own that I did not even know of your existence; but now I will certainly bring you some when I come again. I will bring you a sword; would you like a sword?"

"Yes," answered Themistoclus.

"And you a drum. You would like a drum, wouldn't you?" Tchitchikov went on, bending down to Alkides.

"Yes," Alkides answered in a whisper, hanging his head.

"Very well, I'll bring you a drum, such a lovely drum; it will go: Toorrrr . . . roo . . . tra-ta-ta, ta-ta-ta. Good-bye, my dear! Good-bye!" Then he kissed the child on the head and turned to Manilov and his wife with the little laugh with which people commonly insinuate to parents the innocence of their children's desires.

"You really must stay, Pavel Ivanovitch!" said Manilov when they had gone out on the steps. "Look what storm-clouds."

"They are only little ones," answered Tchitchikov.

"And do you know the way to Sobakevitch's?"

"I wanted to ask you about it."

"If you will allow me, I will tell your coachman at once."

And Manilov proceeded with the same politeness to explain the way to the coachman.

The coachman, hearing that he had to pass two turnings and take the third, said: "We shall find it, your honour."

And Tchitchikov drove away while the gentleman and lady left behind stood for a long time on tiptoe on the steps, sending greetings after him and waving their handkerchiefs.

Manilov watched the chaise disappearing into the distance, and even after it was completely out of sight, still went on standing on the steps, smoking his pipe. At last he went into the house, sat down to the table and gave himself up to meditation, genuinely delighted at having given his visitor pleasure. Then his thoughts passed imperceptibly to other subjects, and goodness knows where they landed at last. He mused on the bliss of life spent in friendship, thought how nice it would be to live with a friend on some bank of a river, then a bridge began to rise across the river, then an immense house with such a high belvedere* that one could see even Moscow from it, and then he dreamed of drinking tea there in the evenings in the open air

---

*Building designed and sited to look on an impressive view.

and discussing agreeable subjects. Then he dreamed that he and Tchitchikov drove in fine carriages to some party, where they charmed every one by the agreeableness of their behaviour, and that the Tsar, hearing of their great friendship, made them both generals, and so passed into goodness knows what visions, such as he could not clearly make out himself. Tchitchikov's strange request suddenly cut across all his dreams. It seemed as though his brain could not assimilate the idea, and however much he turned it about he could not explain it to himself, and so he sat on, smoking his pipe till suppertime.

CHAPTER 3

Meanwhile Tchitchikov in a contented frame of mind was sitting in his chaise which had for some time been rolling along the high-road. From the foregoing chapter it can now be seen what was the chief subject of his interests and inclinations, and so it is not surprising that he was soon completely absorbed in it. The suppositions, calculations, and reflections of which signs passed over his face were evidently very agreeable, for at every moment traces of a gratified smile were left by them. Engrossed in them, he paid no attention to the fact that his coachman, well-satisfied with the reception given him by Manilov's servants, was making very sagacious observations to the dappled trace-horse* harnessed on the right side. This dappled grey horse was extremely sly and only made a show of pulling, while the bay in the shafts and the other trace-horse, of a chestnut colour and called the Assessor because it had been purchased from some tax assessor, worked with all their hearts, so that the satisfaction they derived from it was actually perceptible in their eyes.

"Be as sly as you like! I'll be even with you!" said Selifan, rising in his seat and lashing the laggard with his whip. "You mind your job, you German pantaloon! The bay is a gentlemanly horse, he does his duty; I'll be glad to give him an extra handful, for he is a gentlemanly horse, and the Assessor, he is a good horse too. . . . Now then, why are you shaking your ears? You should listen when you are spoken to, you fool! I am not going to teach you any harm, you dunce. There, where is he off to?" Here he lashed him, observing: "Ugh, you savage! you damned Bonaparte! . . ."

Then he shouted at all of them:

"Hey, you darlings!" And he gave a flick to all three, not by way of punishment but to show that he was pleased with them. After having gratified himself in this way he again addressed the dappled

---

*Harnessed horse, one of two on either side of the middle shaft-horse, that helps to pull a carriage.

trace-horse: "You think you will hide your conduct. No, you must act straightforwardly, if you want to be treated with respect. At that landowner's now where we have been there are good folks. I am always glad to talk to a good man; a good man and I can always get on together, we are always close friends. Whether it's drinking a cup of tea with anybody or taking a snack of something, I do it with a relish if he's a good man. Every one pays respect to a good man. Here's our master now, every one respects him because he has served his Tsar, do you hear, he is a collegiate councillor . . ."

Reasoning in this way Selifan rose at last to the most abstract generalisations. If Tchitchikov had been listening, he would have learned many details relating to himself. But his thoughts were so engrossed with his pet idea that nothing but a loud clap of thunder made him rouse himself and look about him. The whole sky was completely covered with clouds and the dusty high-road was being sprinkled with drops of rain. Then there came a second clap of thunder louder and nearer and the rain spurted down in bucketfuls. At first falling in a slanting direction, it lashed on one side of the chaise, then on the other; then, changing its direction and coming down quite straight, it pattered on the roof of the carriage; and finally drops spurted straight into our hero's face. This made him draw the leather curtains, with two little round windows in them to give a view of the road, and tell Selifan to drive faster. Selifan, interrupted in the middle of his talk, realised that it certainly would not do to dawdle, pulled out from under the box seat some ragged garment of grey cloth, put it on, snatched up the reins, and shouted at his horses, who were scarcely moving their legs, for they felt agreeably relaxed by his edifying admonitions. But Selifan could not remember whether he had passed two, or three, turnings. On reflecting and recalling the road, he surmised that he had passed many. As in critical moments a Russian always decides what to do without further reflection, he turned to the right at the next crossroad and, shouting, "Hey, honoured friends!" put his horses into a gallop without considering long where the road he had taken might lead them.

The rain however seemed as though it would go on for hours. The dust lying on the high-road was soon churned into mud and it seemed harder every minute for the horses to draw the chaise. Tchitchikov was beginning to feel very uneasy at still seeing no sign of Sobakevitch's village. According to his calculations they ought to have arrived long before. He kept looking out on either side, but it was so dark that you could not see your hand before your face.

"Selifan," he said at last, poking his head out of the chaise.

"What is it, master?" answered Selifan.

"Look out, isn't there a village in sight?"

"No, master, there is nothing in sight anywhere!" After which Selifan, brandishing his whip, struck up—not precisely a song but a sort of long rigmarole without an ending. Everything went into it; all the calls of encouragement and incitement with which horses are regaled all over Russia from one end to the other, adjectives of all kinds without discrimination just as they came first to his tongue. It came at last to his beginning to call them secretaries.

Meanwhile Tchitchikov began to notice that the chaise was swaying in all directions and jolting him violently: this made him aware that they had turned off the road and were probably jolting over a freshly harrowed field. Selifan seemed to perceive this himself but did not say a word.

"Why, you scoundrel, what road are you taking me?" said Tchitchikov.

"I can't help it, sir, it is such weather; there is no seeing the whip, it is so dark!"

As he said this, he gave the chaise such a lurch that Tchitchikov had to hold on with both hands. It was only then that he noticed that Selifan had been making merry.

"Take care, take care, you'll upset us!" he shouted to him.

"No, master, how can I upset you?" said Selifan. "It wouldn't be right to upset you, I know that myself; I won't upset you for anything!"

Then he began slightly turning the chaise: he turned it and turned it till at last he tipped it on its side. Tchitchikov went splash on his hands and knees into the mud. Selifan stopped the horses, however; though they would have stopped of themselves for they were exhausted. This unforeseen mishap completely bewildered him. Clambering off the box he stood facing the chaise with his arms akimbo, while his master was floundering in the mud, trying to scramble out of it, and said after some pondering: "Well, I never did! It has upset, too!"

"You are as drunk as a cobbler!" said Tchitchikov.

"No, master, how could I be drunk! I know that it is not the right thing to be drunk. I had a chat with a friend, because one may have a chat with a good man, there is no harm in that,—and we had a snack together. There is nothing to hurt in a snack: one can take a snack of something with a good man."

"And what did I tell you the last time when you got drunk, eh? Have you forgotten?" said Tchitchikov.

"No, your honour, as though I could forget! I know my duty. I know it is not right to get drunk. I had a chat with a good man because . . ."

"I will give you a thrashing that will teach you to have a chat with a good man."

"That is as your honour thinks best," answered Selifan, ready to agree to anything, "if it's to be a thrashing, a thrashing let it be; I have nothing against it. Why not a thrashing, if it's deserved? That's what you are master for. There must be thrashing, for the peasants are too fond of their ease; order must be kept up. If it's deserved, then thrash, why not thrash?"

His master found absolutely no reply to make to this line of argument. But at that instant it seemed as though fate itself had determined to take pity on them. They heard a dog barking in the distance. Tchitchikov, overjoyed, told Selifan to whip up the horses. The Russian driver has a keen scent that takes the place of his eyes; that is how it is he jolts along at full speed with his eyes shut and always arrives somewhere in the end. Though Selifan could not see his hand before his face, he drove the horses so straight to the village that he didn't stop till the shafts of the chaise struck against a fence and he could absolutely drive no further. All Tchitchikov could discern through the thick curtain of streaming rain was something that looked like a roof. He sent Selifan to seek for the gate, an operation which would undoubtedly have taken a long time if it were not that in Russia ferocious dogs do duty for house-porters, and these proclaimed its whereabouts so loudly that he put his fingers into his ears. There was a gleam of light in one little window which sent a misty glimmer as far as the fence and showed our travellers the gate. Selifan fell to knocking and soon a figure clad in a smock was thrust out at the gate, and the master and his servant heard a husky female voice ask: "Who is knocking? Why do you make such a row?"

"We are travellers, my good woman, put us up for the night," answered Tchitchikov.

"Well, you are a sharp one," said the old woman, "what a time to come! This isn't an inn: this is a lady's place."

"What can we do, my good woman? You see we have lost our way. We can't spend the night on the steppe in such weather."

"Yes, it is dark weather, it is not good weather," added Selifan.

"Hold your tongue, you fool," said Tchitchikov.

"Why, who are you?" said the old woman.

"A nobleman, my good woman."

The word nobleman seemed to make the old woman consider a little. "Wait a minute, I will tell the mistress," she said, and two minutes later she came back with a lantern in her hand. The gates were opened. There was a gleam of light in another window. Driving into the yard the chaise stopped before a little house which it was difficult to make out in the darkness. Only one half of it was lighted up by the light from the window; a pool in front of the house on which the light fell directly was also visible. The rain was pattering noisily on the wooden roof and running in gurgling streams into the water-butt. Meanwhile the dogs were barking on every possible note: one throwing up its head executed a howl as prolonged and brought it out with as much effort as though it were getting a handsome salary for it; another snapped it out quickly like a sacristan, and between them there rang out like the bell of a post-cart an indefatigable falsetto, most likely of a young puppy, and it was completed by a bass, possibly an old fellow endowed with a sturdy doggy nature, for he was as husky as the bass in a choir when the concert is in full swing: when the tenors rise on tiptoe in their intense desire to bring out a high note, and all heads are flung back and straining upwards, while he alone, with his unshaven chin thrust into his cravat, squatting and almost sinking to the floor, lets out a note that sets the window-panes shaking and tinkling. From the mere barking of the dogs that made up such an orchestra it might be surmised that the village was a decent one; but our drenched and chilled hero thought of nothing but his bed. The chaise had not quite stopped when he leapt out on to the steps, gave a lurch, and almost fell down. Another woman, somewhat younger than the first, but very much like her, came out on to the steps. She led him into the house. Tchitchikov took two cursory glances at the room: it was hung with old striped paper; there were pictures of birds; between the windows there were little old-fashioned looking-glasses with dark frames in the shape of turned-back leaves; behind each looking-glass was stuffed either a letter or an old pack of cards or a stocking; there was a clock on the wall with flowers painted on the face, but he could distinguish nothing more. He felt that his eyelids were sticking together as though some one had smeared them with honey. A minute later the mistress of the house walked in, an elderly woman in some sort of nightcap hurriedly put on and with a piece of flannel round her neck, one of those good dames owning a small estate, who lament over the failure of their crops and their losses and hold their heads a little on one side, and yet little by little put away a tidy sum of money in different drawers of their chests. In one little bag they save up all the roubles, in another the half roubles, in a third the quarter roubles, though it looks as though there were nothing in the chest but underlinen and night-jackets and reels of cotton and an unpicked pelisse,* intended to be turned into a dress later on, if the old one should be scorched in frying the holiday cakes, doughnuts, and fritters of all sorts, or should be worn out of itself. But the dress does not get scorched and is not worn out, the old lady is careful, and the pelisse is destined to lie unpicked for years and then to come later on to a niece, together with all sorts of other rubbish.

Tchitchikov apologised for disturbing her with his unexpected visit.

"It's all right, it's all right!" said the old lady. "In what weather God has brought you! Such a storm of wind and rain. . . . You ought to have something to eat after your journey, but it is night-time, we can't cook anything."

Her words were interrupted by a strange hissing sound so that Tchitchikov was somewhat alarmed: the sound suggested that the whole room was full of snakes, but glancing upwards he was reassured, for he noticed that the clock on the wall was disposed to strike. The hissing was followed at once by a wheezing, and at last with a desperate effort it struck two o'clock with a sound as though some one were hitting a broken pot with a stick, after which the pendulum returned to its tranquil ticking, to right and to left.

---

*Woman's long, fur-trimmed cloak with slits for the arms.

Tchitchikov thanked the old lady, saying that he wanted nothing, that she was not to put herself out, that he asked for nothing but a bed and was only curious to know to what place he had come, and whether it was far from here to the estate of Sobakevitch. To which the old lady replied that she had never heard the name and that there was no such landowner.

"You know Manilov anyway?" said Tchitchikov.

"Why, who is Manilov?"

"A landowner, ma'am."

"No, I have never heard of him, there is no such landowner here."

"Who are the landowners here?"

"Bobrov, Svinyin, Kanapatyev, Harpakin, Trepakin, Plyeshakov."

"Are they well-to-do people?"

"No, my good sir, not very well-to-do. One has twenty souls, another thirty; but there are none about here with as many as a hundred."

Tchitchikov perceived that he had come quite into the wilds.

"Is it far to the town, anyway?"

"It will be some forty miles. What a pity I have nothing to give you! Won't you have a cup of tea, my good sir?"

"No thank you, ma'am, I want nothing but a bed."

"After such a journey you must need a rest indeed. You can lie down here, my good sir, on this sofa. Hey, Fetinya, bring a feather bed, pillows, and a sheet. What weather God has sent us: such thunder—I have had a light burning before the holy image all night. Oh, my good sir, why, all your back and side is muddy as a hog's; where have you got so dirty?"

"It's a mercy that I am only muddy. I must be thankful that I did not break my ribs."

"Holy Saints, how dreadful! But shouldn't your back be rubbed with something?"

"Thank you, thank you. Don't trouble, but only bid your maid dry my clothes and brush them."

"Do you hear, Fetinya?" said the old lady, addressing the woman who had come out on to the steps with a light and who had now dragged in a feather bed and, beating it up on both sides, was scattering a perfect shower of feathers all over the room. "You take the gentleman's coat together with his underthings, and first dry them before the fire as you used to do for the master, and afterwards give them a good brushing and beating."

"Yes, ma'am," said Fetinya, spreading a sheet over the feather bed and laying the pillows on it.

"Well, here's your bed ready," said the old lady. "Good-bye, sir, I wish you good-night, but is there nothing you would like? Perhaps you are accustomed, my good sir, to have some one tickle your heels at night? My poor dear husband could never get to sleep without it."

But the visitor refused the heel-tickling also. The lady of the house retired and he made haste at once to undress, giving Fetinya all his garments, upper and lower, and Fetinya, wishing him a good-night too, carried off his wet array. Left alone he glanced with satisfaction at his bed which almost reached the ceiling. Fetinya was evidently a mistress of the art of beating up feathers. When, putting a chair beside it, he climbed on to the bed, it sank almost to the floor under his weight, and the feathers squeezed out of the cover flew into every corner of the room. Putting out the candle he drew the cotton quilt over him and, curling up under it, fell asleep that very minute. He woke rather late next morning. The sun was shining straight into his face, and the flies which had the night before been quietly asleep on the walls and the ceiling were all paying attention to him: one was sitting on his lip, another on his ear, a third was trying to settle on his eye; one who had had the indiscretion to settle close to his nostril he had in his sleep drawn up into his nose, which set him sneezing violently—the circumstance which caused him to wake up. Looking about the room he noticed now that the pictures were not all of birds: among them hung a portrait of Kutuzov,* and an old gentleman painted in oils with red revers on his uniform as worn in the reign of Paul I.† The clock again emitted a hissing sound and struck ten: a woman's face peeped in at the door, and instantly withdrew seeing that Tchitchikov had flung off absolutely everything to sleep more at his ease. The face that peeped in seemed to him somehow familiar. He began trying to recall who it was and at last re-

---

*Mikhail Kutuzov (1745–1813), Russian commander who fought and pursued the retreating army of French emperor Napoléon I in 1812.
†Emperor of Russia; born in 1754, he ruled from 1796 to 1801.

membered that it was the mistress of the house. He put on his shirt; his clothes, dried and brushed, were lying beside him. After dressing he went up to the looking-glass and sneezed again so loudly that a turkey-cock who had come up to the window at that moment—the window was very near the ground—gabbled something very quickly to him in his queer language, probably "God bless you," on which Tchitchikov called him a fool. Going to the window he scrutinised the view before him; the window might be said to look into the poultry yard. At least the narrow little yard that lay before him was filled with fowls and domestic animals of all sorts. There were turkeys and hens beyond all reckoning; among them a cock was strutting about with measured steps, shaking his comb and turning his head on one side as though listening to something; a sow too was there with her family; poking about in a heap of litter, she ate a chicken in passing and, without noticing it, went on gobbling melon rinds as before. This little yard was shut in by a paling fence beyond which stretched a spacious kitchen garden with cabbages, onions, potatoes, beetroot, and other vegetables. Apple trees and other fruit trees were dotted here and there about the kitchen garden and were covered with nets to protect them from the magpies and sparrows, the latter of which were flitting from place to place in perfect clouds. With the same end in view, several scarecrows had been rigged up on long posts with outstretched arms; one of them was adorned with a cap belonging to the mistress of the house herself. Beyond the kitchen garden there were peasants' huts which, though placed at random and not arranged in straight rows, yet from what Tchitchikov could observe showed the prosperity of their inhabitants, for they were well-kept: where the wood on the roof had rotted it had everywhere been replaced by new; the gates were nowhere on the slant, and, in the peasants' covered sheds turned towards him, he noticed in one almost a new cart and in another even two.

"Why, she hasn't such a very little village," he said, and at once resolved to have a good talk with the lady of the house and to make her closer acquaintance. He glanced through the crack of the door from which her head had appeared and, seeing her sitting at the tea-table in the next room, went in to her with a good-humoured and friendly air.

"Good-morning, my good sir. How have you slept?" said the old lady, getting up from her seat. She was better dressed than she had been the night before, in a dark gown, and wore no nightcap, but she still had something wrapped round her neck.

"Very well, very well indeed," said Tchitchikov, seating himself in an easy-chair. "And what sort of a night had you, ma'am?"

"Very bad, sir."

"How's that?"

"It's sleeplessness. My back keeps aching and my leg above the knee is painful too."

"That will pass, that will pass, ma'am. You mustn't take any notice of that."

"God grant it may; I've rubbed it with lard and bathed it with turpentine. And what do you take with your tea? There's home-made wine in that bottle."

"That's not amiss, ma'am. We will have a drop of home-made wine too."

The reader has, I imagine, already observed that in spite of his friendly air Tchitchikov spoke with more freedom and easiness than with Manilov and did not stand on ceremony at all. It must be said that if we in Russia have not caught up with foreigners in other things, we have far outstripped them in the knowledge of how to behave. All the shades and subtleties of our manners cannot be counted. A Frenchman or a German would never catch and understand all its peculiarities and distinctions; he will speak in almost the same tone of voice and almost the same language to a millionaire and to a little tobacconist, though of course in his soul he will grovel quite sufficiently before the former. It is not so with us: there are among us persons so clever that they can talk to a landowner with two hundred souls quite differently from the way in which they speak to one with three hundred, and to the one with three hundred they will speak differently again from the manner in which they will address one with five hundred; and to one with five hundred they do not talk as they do to one with eight hundred; in short there are shades all up to a million. Let us suppose, for instance, that there is a government office—not here but in some fairy kingdom—and let us suppose that in the office there is a head of the office. I beg you to look at him when he is sitting among his subordinates—one is simply too awestricken to utter a word. Pride and dignity . . . and what else is not expressed upon his face? You should take a brush and paint him: a Prometheus,* a perfect Prometheus! He looks like an eagle, he moves with a measured step. That very eagle, when he has left his own room and is approaching the sanctum of his chief, flutters along like a partridge with papers under his arm as best he may. In company and at an evening-party if all present are of a low rank, Prometheus remains Prometheus, but if they are ever so little above him, Prometheus undergoes a metamorphosis such as Ovid† never imagined: he is a fly, less than a fly indeed, he humbles himself into the dust! "But this isn't Ivan Petrovitch," you say, looking at him. "Ivan Petrovitch is taller, and this fellow is both short and thin; Ivan Petrovitch talks in a loud bass voice and never laughs, while there is no making this fellow out, he pipes like a bird and keeps laughing." You go near, you look, it really is Ivan Petrovitch! "Aha!" you think to yourself. . . . However, we will return to the characters of our story.

Tchitchikov, as we have seen already, had made up his mind not to stand on ceremony at all, and so, taking the cup of tea in his hand and pouring some home-made wine into it, he spoke as follows:

"You have a nice little village, ma'am. How many souls in it?"

"Close upon eighty, my good sir," said his hostess. "But the times are bad, I am sorry to say. Last year, too, we had such a bad harvest, as I never wish to see again."

"The peasants look sturdy enough, though, and their huts are solid. Allow me to ask your surname. I was so distracted . . . arriving in the night . . ."

"Korobotchka."

"Thank you very much, and your Christian name and father's name?"

"Nastasya Petrovna."

"Nastasya Petrovna? A good name, Nastasya Petrovna; I have an aunt, my mother's sister, called Nastasya Petrovna."

"And what is your name?" asked the lady. "You are a tax assessor, for sure?"

---

*In classical mythology, a Titan who stole fire from the gods and was punished by being chained to a rock where eagles tore his liver.

†Roman poet (43 B.C.–A.D. 18), author of *Metamorphoses*, a collection of legends recounting miraculous transformations.

"No, ma'am," answered Tchitchikov, grinning, "not a tax assessor for sure, but just travelling on a little business of my own."

"Oh, then you are a dealer! What a pity, really, that I sold my
honey to the merchants so cheap; very likely you would have bought
it from me, sir."

"Your honey I shouldn't have bought."

"What else then? Hemp perhaps? But there, I have very little
hemp now, not more than half a pood."*

"No, ma'am, I buy a different sort of ware. Tell me, have any of
your peasants died?"

"Oh, sir, eighteen of them," said the old lady, sighing, "and such
a good lot died, all workmen. It's true that some have been born
since, but what use are they? They are all such small fry. And the assessor came—you must pay the tax by the soul, said he. The peasants
are dead, but I must pay as though they were alive. Last week my
blacksmith was burnt, such a clever blacksmith and he could do lock-
smith's work too."

"Did you have a fire, ma'am?"

"God preserve us from such a misfortune; a fire would be worse
still: he caught fire of himself, my good sir. His inside somehow
began burning, he had had a terrible lot to drink: all I can say is that
a blue flame came out of him and he smouldered and smouldered
away and turned black as a coal; and he was such a very clever blacksmith! And now I can't drive about, I have no one to shoe my horses."

"It is all God's will, ma'am," said Tchitchikov with a sigh, "it is
no use murmuring against the wisdom of God. . . . Let me have
them, Nastasya Petrovna."

"Have whom, sir?"

"Why, all those who are dead."

"Why, how let you have them?"

"Oh, quite simply. Or if you like, sell them, I'll pay you for
them."

"Why, how's that, I really don't take your meaning. Surely you
don't want to dig them out of the ground, do you?"

Tchitchikov saw that the old lady was quite at sea, and that he absolutely must explain what he wanted. In a few words he explained

---

*Russian unit of weight equal to about 36 pounds.

to her that the transfer or purchase would take place only on paper and that the souls would be described as though alive.

"But what use will they be to you?" said the old lady, looking at him with round eyes.

"That's my business."

"But you know they are dead."

"Well, who says they are alive? That's just why they are a loss to you, that they are dead: you have to pay the tax on them, but now I will save you from all that trouble and expense. Do you understand? And I will not only do that, but give you fifteen roubles besides. Well, is it clear now?"

"I really don't know," the old lady brought out hesitatingly, "you see I've never sold the dead before."

"I should think not! It would be a wonder indeed if you could sell them to any one. Or do you suppose that there is some profit to be made out of them, really?"

"No, I don't suppose that! What profit could there be in them? They are no use at all. The only thing that troubles me is that they are dead."

"Well, the woman's thick-headed, it seems," Tchitchikov thought to himself. "Listen, ma'am, just look at it fairly yourself: you are being ruined, paying for them as though they were living. . . ."

"Oh, my good sir, don't speak about it," the old lady caught him up. "Only the week before last I paid more than a hundred and fifty roubles, beside presents to the assessor."

"There you see, ma'am! And now take into consideration the mere fact that you won't have to make presents to the assessor again, because now I shall have to pay for them,—I and not you; I take all the taxes on myself, I will even pay all the legal expenses, do you understand?"

The old lady pondered. She saw that the transaction certainly seemed a profitable one, only it was too novel and unusual, and so she began to be extremely uneasy that the purchaser might be trying to cheat her. God knows where he had come from, and he arrived in the middle of the night, too.

"Well, ma'am, how is it to be then, is it a bargain?" said Tchitchikov.

"Upon my word, sir, it has never yet happened to me to sell the

dead. The year before last I did sell some living ones, two girls to Pro-
topopov, two girls for a hundred roubles each, and very grateful he
was for them too: they turned out capital girls to work; they even
weave table napkins."

"Well, it is not a question of the living; God bless them! I am asking for the dead."

"Really, at first sight, I am afraid that it may be a loss to me. Perhaps you are deceiving me, sir, and they, er . . . are worth more, perhaps."

"Listen, my good woman . . . ech, what nonsense you talk! What
can they be worth? Just consider: why, they are dust, you know. Do
you understand, they are nothing but dust. Take the most worthless,
humblest article, a simple rag for instance—and even the rag has a
value: rags are bought for making into paper, anyway, but what I am
speaking of is no use for anything. Come, tell me yourself, what is it
of use for?"

"That is true, certainly. They are of no use for anything at all. The
only thing that makes me hesitate is that, you see, they are dead."

"Ugh, she is as stupid as a post," said Tchitchikov to himself, beginning to lose patience. "However is one to come to terms with her!
She makes me feel hot all over, the confounded old woman!" And,
taking a handkerchief out of his pocket, he began mopping his perspiring brow. Tchitchikov need not have been moved to anger, however: many a highly respected man, many a statesman indeed is a
regular Korobotchka in business. Once he has taken a notion into his
head there is no getting over it, anyhow: however many arguments as
clear as daylight you put before him, they all rebound from him as
an india-rubber ball bounces from a wall.

After mopping his brow Tchitchikov made up his mind to try
whether he could not get round her from some other side.

"Either you don't want to understand what I say, ma'am, or you
talk like that, simply for the sake of saying something. I'll give you fifteen paper roubles—do you understand? That's money, you know.
You won't pick it up in the road. Come, let me know what you sold
your honey for?"

"Twelve roubles a pood."

"You are taking a little sin upon your soul, ma'am, you didn't sell
it for twelve roubles."

"Upon my word, I did."

"Well, do you see? That was for something—it was honey. You had been collecting it perhaps for about a year with work and trouble and anxiety, you went and killed the bees, and fed the bees in the cellar all winter. But dead souls are not a thing of this world at all. In this case, you have taken no trouble whatever about them, it was God's will that they should leave this world to the loss of your estate. In the case of the honey, for your work, for your exertions you have received twelve roubles, but in this case you will get gratis, for nothing, not twelve but fifteen roubles, and not in silver but all in blue notes."

After these powerful arguments Tchitchikov had no doubt that the old lady would give way.

"Really," answered the old lady, "I am an inexperienced widow; I had better wait a little, maybe the dealers will be coming and I shall find out about prices."

"For shame, my good woman, it is simply shameful. Come, just think over what you are saying. Who is going to buy them? Why, what use could any one put them to?"

"Well, perhaps they may be put to some use somehow . . . ," replied the old lady, but she broke off and gazed open-mouthed at him, almost with horror, waiting to see what he would say to it.

"Dead men be put to some use! Ugh, what next! To scare the sparrows at night in your kitchen garden or what?"

"God have mercy on us! What dreadful things you do say!" said the old lady, crossing herself.

"What else do you want to do with them? Besides, the bones and the graves, all that will be left to you; the transfer is only on paper. Well, what do you say? How is it to be? Give me an answer, anyway."

The old lady pondered again.

"What are you thinking about, Nastasya Petrovna?"

"I really can't make up my mind what to do; I had really better sell you my hemp."

"Hemp! Upon my soul, I asked you about something quite different and you foist hemp upon me. Hemp is hemp, another time I'll come and take your hemp, too. So how is it to be, Nastasya Petrovna?"

"Oh dear, it is such a strange, quite unheard-of thing to sell."

At this point Tchitchikov was completely driven out of all patience; he banged his chair upon the floor in his anger and consigned her to the devil.

The old lady was extremely frightened of the devil.

"Oh, don't speak of him, God bless him!" she cried, turning quite pale. "Only the night before last I was dreaming all night of the evil spirit. I took a fancy to try my fortune on the cards after saying my prayers that night and it seems the Lord sent him to punish me. He looked so horrid and his horns were longer than our bull's."

"I wonder you don't dream of them by dozens. From simple Christian humanity I wanted to help you: I saw a poor woman struggling and in poverty. . . . But the plague take you and all your village!"

"Oh, what shocking words you are using!" said the old lady, looking at him with horror.

"Well, there is no knowing how to talk to you! Why, you are like some—not to use a bad word—dog in the manger that won't eat the hay itself and won't let others. I was meaning to buy all sorts of produce from you, for I take government contracts too . . ."

This was a lie, though quite a casual one, uttered with no ulterior design, but it was unexpectedly successful. The government contract produced a strong effect on Nastasya Petrovna. Anyway she brought out, in a voice of supplication almost:

"But why are you in such a terrible rage? If I had known before that you were so hot-tempered I wouldn't have contradicted you."

"There's nothing to be angry about! The business is not worth a rotten egg, as though I should get in a rage about it!"

"Oh, very well then, I am ready to let you have them for fifteen paper roubles! Only, my good sir, about these contracts, mind, if you should be taking my rye or buckwheat flour or my grain or my carcasses, please don't cheat me."

"No, my good woman, I won't cheat you," he said, while he wiped away the perspiration that was streaming down his face. He began inquiring whether she had any lawyer in the town or friend whom she could authorise to complete the purchase and do everything necessary.

"To be sure! The son of the chief priest, Father Kirill, is a clerk in the law-court," said the old lady. Tchitchikov asked her to write a letter of authorisation to him, and, to save unnecessary trouble, undertook to compose it himself.

"It would be a good thing," the old lady was thinking to herself meanwhile, "if he would take my flour and cattle for the government. I must soften his heart: there is some dough left from yesterday evening, so I'll go and tell Fetinya to make some pancakes; it would be a good thing to make an egg turnover too. They make turnovers capitally and it doesn't take long to do."

The old woman departed to carry out her idea about the turnovers, and probably to complete it with other masterpieces of domestic baking and cookery; while Tchitchikov went into the drawing-room in which he had spent the night, in order to get the necessary papers out of his case. The drawing-room had been swept and dusted long before, the luxurious feather beds had been carried away, before the sofa stood a table laid for a meal. Putting his case upon it he paused for a little while, for he felt that he was wet with perspiration as though he were in a river: everything he had on from his shirt to his stockings was soaked.

"Ugh! how she has wearied me, the confounded old woman!" he said, resting for a little before he opened the case. The author is persuaded that there are readers so inquisitive as to be desirous of knowing the plan and internal arrangement of the case. By all means, why not satisfy them? This was the internal arrangement: in the very middle was a box for soap; above the soap-box six or seven narrow divisions for razors; then square places for a sand box and an inkpot, with a little boat hollowed out between them for pens, sealing-wax, and things that were rather longer; then various divisions with covers and without covers for things that were shorter, full of visiting cards, funeral cards, theatre tickets, and other things kept as souvenirs. All the upper tray with its little divisions lifted out, and under it there was a space filled with packets of sheets of paper; then followed a little secret drawer for money, which came out from the side of the case. It always came out so quickly and was moved back at the same minute by Tchitchikov, so that one could not tell for certain how much money there was in it. He set to work at once, and mending a pen began to write. At that moment the old lady came in.

"You have a nice box there," said she, sitting down beside him, "I'll be bound you bought it in Moscow?"

"Yes, in Moscow," said Tchitchikov, going on writing.

"I knew it; the work there is always good. The year before last my sister brought me little warm boots for the children from there: such good material, it has lasted till now. Oh la! what a lot of stamped paper you have in it!" she went on, peeping into the case. And there certainly was a good deal of stamped paper in it. "You might make me a present of a sheet or two! I am so badly off for it; if I want to send in a petition to the court I have nothing to write it on."

Tchitchikov explained to her that the paper was not the right sort for that, that it was meant for drawing up deeds of purchase and not for petitions. To satisfy her, however, he gave her a sheet worth a rouble. After writing the letter he gave it to her to sign and asked her for a little list of the peasants. It appeared that the old lady kept no lists or records, but knew them all by heart. He made her dictate their names to him. He was astonished at some of the peasants' surnames and still more at their nicknames, so much so that he paused on hearing them before beginning to write. He was particularly struck by one Pyotr Savelyev Ne-uvazhay-Koryto (Never mind the Trough), so that he could not help saying: "What a long name." Another had attached to his name Korovy-Kirpitch (Cow's Brick), another simply appeared as Ivan Koleso (Wheel). When he had finished writing he drew in the air through his nose and sniffed a seductive fragrance of something fried in butter.

"Pray come and have lunch," said the old lady. Tchitchikov looked round and saw that the table was already spread with mushrooms, pies, fritters, cheesecakes, doughnuts, pancakes, open tarts with all sorts of different fillings, some with onions, some with poppy seeds, some with curds, and some with fish, and there is no knowing what else.

"Some egg pie," said his hostess.

Tchitchikov drew up to the pie and, after consuming a little more than half of it on the spot, praised it. And the pie was indeed savoury, and after all his worry with the old lady seemed still more so.

"Some pancakes?" said his hostess.

In reply to this Tchitchikov folded three pancakes together and, moistening them in melted butter, directed them towards his mouth and then wiped his lips and hands with a table napkin. After repeating this operation three times, he asked his hostess to order the chaise to be brought round. Nastasya Petrovna at once despatched Fetinya, bidding her at the same time to bring in some more pancakes.

"Your pancakes are very nice, ma'am," said Tchitchikov, attacking the hot ones as they were brought in.

"Yes, they fry them very nicely," said the old lady, "but the worst of it is that the harvest is poor and the flour is so unprofitable. . . . But why are you in such a hurry?" she said, seeing that Tchitchikov was taking up his cap. "Why, the horses are not in yet."

"They soon will be, ma'am, my servants don't take long to get ready."

"Well, then, please don't forget about the government contracts."

"I won't forget, I won't forget," said Tchitchikov, going out into the passage.

"And won't you buy salt pork?" said the old lady, following him.

"Why not? I'll certainly buy it, only later."

"I shall have salt pork by Easter."

"We'll buy it, we'll buy everything, we'll buy salt pork too."

"Perhaps you'll be wanting feathers. I shall have feathers too, by St. Philip's fast."*

"Very good, very good," said Tchitchikov.

"There, you see, my good sir, your chaise isn't ready yet," said his hostess when they had gone out on to the steps.

"It will be, it will be directly. Only tell me how to reach the highroad."

"How am I to do that?" said the old lady. "It is hard to explain, there are so many turnings; perhaps I had better let you have a girl to show you the way. You have room, I daresay, on the box."

"To be sure we have."

"Very well, I'll let you have a little girl, she knows the way; only mind you don't carry her off, some merchants have carried off one of mine already."

Tchitchikov assured her that he would not carry off the girl, and Madame Korobotchka, reassured, began scanning everything that was going on in her yard. She stared at the housekeeper who was bringing a wooden tub of honey out of the storeroom, at a peasant who appeared at the gate, and, little by little, was completely re-absorbed

---

*Fast beginning on November 14.

in the life of her farm. But why spend so long over Madame Korobotchka? Enough of Madame Korobotchka and Madame Manilov, of their well-ordered or ill-ordered lives! Or—as it is so strangely ordained in this world—what is amusing will turn into being gloomy, if you stand too long before it, and then God knows what ideas may not stray into the mind. Perhaps one may even begin thinking: "But, after all, is Madame Korobotchka so low down on the endless ladder of human perfectibility?" Is there really such a vast chasm separating her from her sister, who, inaccessibly immured within the walls of her aristocratic house with its perfumed cast-iron staircases, its shining copper fittings, its mahogany and carpets, yawns over her unfinished book while she waits to pay her visits in witty fashionable society? There she has a field in which to display her intelligence and express the views she has learnt by heart—not ideas of her own, about her household and her estate, both neglected and in disorder, thanks to her ignorance of housekeeping and farming—but those opinions that by fashion's decree interest the town for a whole week, ideas about the political revolution brewing in France and the tendencies of fashionable Catholicism. But enough, enough! Why talk of this? Why is it that even in moments of unthinking careless gaiety a different and strange mood suddenly comes upon one? The smile has scarcely faded from the lips when, even among the same people, one is suddenly another man and already the face shines with a different light.

"Here is the chaise! Here is the chaise!" cried Tchitchikov, seeing his chaise drive up at last. "Why have you been dawdling about so long, stupid? I suppose the drink you had yesterday has not quite gone off?"

Selifan made no answer to this.

"Good-bye, ma'am! But, I say, where is your little girl?"

"Hey, Pelageya!" said the old lady to a girl of eleven who stood near the steps in a frock of home-dyed linen, with bare legs so coated with fresh mud that at a little distance they might have been taken for boots. "Show the gentleman the way!"

Selifan gave a hand to the girl who, putting her foot on to the carriage step and covering it with mud, clambered up and sat down on the box beside him. Tchitchikov put his foot on the step after her and tilting the chaise down on the right side, for he was no light weight, settled himself in at last, saying, "We are all right now! Good-bye, ma'am!"

The horses set off.

Selifan was sullen all the way and at the same time very attentive to his driving, as he always was whenever he had been drunk or to blame in any way. The horses had been marvellously groomed. The collar on one of them, which had almost always hitherto been put on with a rent in it, so that the stuffing peeped out under the leather, had been skilfully repaired. All the way he was silent; he merely lashed the horses and did not address any words of admonition to them, though the dappled grey was doubtless longing for a sermon, for the reins were always slack and the whip was merely passed over their backs as a matter of form when the garrulous driver was holding forth. On this occasion, however, no sound came from his sullen lips but monotonous and unpleasant exclamations: "Now then! now! raven! crawling along!" Even the bay and the Assessor were dissatisfied at not once hearing the usual terms of endearment. The dappled grey felt the lashes on his broad, plump sides extremely disagreeable. "I say, how he is going it," he thought to himself, twitching his ears a little. "He knows right enough where to hit! He doesn't simply switch one on the back, but just picks out the spot that is tenderest; he flicks one on the ear or lashes one under the belly."

"To the right?" was the curt question Selifan addressed to the girl sitting beside him, as he pointed with his whip towards the rain-darkened road between the fresh bright green fields.

"No, no, I'll show you," answered the girl.

"Which way?" asked Selifan, when they were getting nearer.

"That way," answered the girl, pointing with her hand.

"Well, you are one," said Selifan. "Why, that is to the right: she doesn't know her right hand from her left!"

Though it was a very fine day, the ground was so thick with mud that the chaise wheels, flinging it up, were soon thickly coated, and that made the carriage considerably heavier. Moreover, the soil was of exceptionally sticky clay. Owing to these difficulties it was midday before they got on to the high-road. They would have hardly done that without the girl, for the by-roads ran zig-zagging to and fro like crabs when they are shaken out of a sack, and Selifan might well have gone astray through no fault of his own. Soon the girl pointed to a dingy-looking building in the distance, saying: "Yonder is the high-road!"

"And the house?" asked Selifan.

"It's the tavern," said the girl.

"Well, now we can get along by ourselves," said Selifan, "you can run home."

He stopped and helped her to get down, muttering through his teeth: "Oh, you grubby legs!"

Tchitchikov gave her a copper and she sauntered home highly delighted at having had a ride on the box.

CHAPTER 4

As they approached the tavern, Tchitchikov told Selifan to stop for two reasons, that the horses might rest and also that he might himself have a little refreshment. The author must admit that he greatly envies the appetite and digestion of such people. He has no great opinion of all the grand gentlemen living in Petersburg and Moscow who spend their time in deliberating what to eat tomorrow and what to have for dinner the day after, and who invariably put pills into their mouths before beginning on the dinner, then swallow oysters, lobsters, and other strange things and afterwards go for a cure to Carlsbad* or the Caucasus.† No, those gentlemen have never excited his envy. But the gentlemen of the middling sort who ask for ham at one station and sucking-pig at the next, a slice of sturgeon or some fried sausage and onion at the third, and then, as though nothing had happened, sit down to table at any time you please, and with a hissing, gurgling sound gulp down a sturgeon-soup full of eel-pouts‡ and soft roes to the accompaniment of a turnover or a fish patty, so that it makes other people hungry to look at them—yes, these gentlemen certainly do enjoy a blessing that may well be envied! More than one grand gentleman would any minute sacrifice half his peasants and half his estates, mortgaged and unmortgaged, with all the improvements in foreign and Russian style, only to possess a digestion such as that of a middle-class gentleman. But the worst of it is that no money, nor even estates with or without improvements can procure a digestion like that of a middle-class gentleman.

The wooden tavern, blackened by age, received Tchitchikov under its narrow hospitable porch which stood on carved wooden

---

*Now Karlovy Vary; town in the Czech Republic known for its spa with mineral waters.
†Mountainous region in southwestern Russia, between the Black Sea and the Caspian Sea.
‡Burbots; elongated freshwater fish.

posts like old-fashioned church candlesticks. The tavern was something in the style of a Russian peasant's hut but on a rather larger scale. The cornices of new wood carved in patterns round the windows and under the roof stood out vividly against the dark walls; pots of flowers were painted on the shutters.

Going up the narrow wooden steps into the wide outer room, Tchitchikov met a door, that opened with a creak, and a fat woman in a bright chintz gown, who said: "Please come this way!" In the inner room he found the usual old friends that are always to be seen in all the little wooden taverns of which not a few are built by the roadside; that is, a begrimed samovar, smoothly-planed deal walls, a three-cornered cupboard containing cups and teapots in the corner, gilt china eggs hanging on red and blue ribbons in front of the ikons, a cat who had recently had kittens, a looking-glass that reflected four eyes instead of two, and transformed the human countenance into a sort of bun, bunches of scented herbs and pinks* stuck before the ikons, so dry that any one who tried to sniff them would be sure to sneeze.

"Have you any sucking-pig?" was the question Tchitchikov addressed to the woman.

"Yes, we have."

"With horse-radish and sour cream?"

"Yes, with horse-radish and sour cream."

"Let me have some!"

The old woman went off to rummage and brought a plate and a table napkin, starched till it was as stiff as a dried crust and would not lie flat, then a knife with a bone handle yellow with age, and a blade as thin as a penknife, a two-pronged fork and a salt-cellar, which would not stand straight on the table.

Our hero, as his habit was, instantly entered into conversation with her, and inquired whether she kept the tavern herself or whether there was a master, and what income the tavern yielded and whether their sons were living at home with them and whether the eldest son was a married man or a bachelor and whether he had married a wife with a big dowry or not, and whether the bride's father was satisfied or had been vexed at not getting presents enough at the

---

*Carnations.

wedding; in fact, he went into everything. I need hardly say that he was anxious to find out what landowners there were in the neighbourhood and learned that there were landowners of all sorts: Blohin, Potchitaev, Mylnoy, Tcheprakov, the Colonel, and Sobakevitch.

"Ah! you know Sobakevitch!" he said, and at once heard that the old woman knew not only Sobakevitch, but also Manilov, and that Manilov was more refined than Sobakevitch: he would order a fowl to be boiled at once, and would ask for veal too; if they had sheep's liver he would ask for that too, and would take no more than a taste of everything, while Sobakevitch would only ask for one dish, but then he would eat up every morsel and would even expect a second helping for the same price.

While he was talking in this way and eating the sucking-pig, of which only the last slice by now remained, he heard the rumbling wheels of an approaching carriage. Looking out of window he saw a light chaise drawn by three good horses pull up at the tavern. Two men got out of the chaise: one tall and fair-haired, the other somewhat shorter and dark. The fair-haired man was wearing a dark-blue braided jacket, the black-haired man simply a striped jerkin. Another wretched-looking carriage was crawling up in the distance, empty and drawn by four shaggy horses with torn collars and harness made of cord. The fair man at once went upstairs while the dark fellow stayed behind, fumbling for something in the chaise while he talked to his servant and at the same time waved to the carriage that was following. His voice struck Tchitchikov as somehow familiar. While he was looking more closely at him, the fair man felt his way to the door and opened it. He was a tall man, with a thin or what is called worn face and red moustache. From his tanned face it might be gathered that he was familiar with tobacco smoke anyway, if not with that of gunpowder. He gave Tchitchikov a polite bow, to which the latter responded with equal politeness. Within a few minutes they would have probably been talking freely and making acquaintance, for the ice had already been broken and they were both almost at the same moment expressing their satisfaction that the dust on the road had been completely laid by the rain of the previous day, and that now it was cool and pleasant for driving, when his dark-haired companion walked in, flinging his cap down on the table, and jauntily ruffling up his thick black hair with his fingers. He was a fine, very well-made young fellow of medium height, with full ruddy cheeks, snow-white teeth, and pitch-black whiskers. He was as fresh as milk and roses, his face looked simply bursting with health.

"Bah, bah, bah!" he exclaimed, flinging wide his hands at the sight of Tchitchikov. "How did you come here?"

Tchitchikov recognised Nozdryov, the young man with whom he had dined at the public prosecutor's and who had within a few minutes become very intimate in his manner and taken up a familiar tone, though our hero had given him no encouragement.

"Where are you going to?" said Nozdryov, and without waiting for an answer he went on: "I have just come from the fair, old man. Congratulate me, I've been cleaned out! Would you believe it, I have never been so thoroughly cleaned out in my life. Why, I have driven here with hired horses! Do just take a look at them!"

Hereupon he bent Tchitchikov's head down so that the latter almost knocked it against the window frame.

"Do you see what wretched hacks they are? They could scarcely crawl here, the damned brutes; I had to get into his chaise."

Saying this Nozdryov pointed to his companion.

"You are acquainted, are you? My brother-in-law, Mizhuev! We have been talking about you all the morning. 'You see now,' I said, 'if we don't meet Tchitchikov.' Well, old man, if only you knew how I have been fleeced! Would you believe it, I have not only dropped my four fast trotters, I have got rid of every mortal thing. Why, I have no watch or chain left."

Tchitchikov glanced at him, and saw that he was in fact wearing neither watch nor chain. He even fancied that one of his whiskers was shorter and not so thick as the other.

"But if I had only twenty roubles in my pocket," Nozdryov went on, "no more than twenty roubles, I would win it all back, and I'd not only win it all back, on my honour, I'd put thirty thousand in my pocketbook at once."

"You said the same thing then, though," retorted the fair man, "but when I gave you fifty roubles, you lost them on the spot."

"I should not have lost them, upon my soul, I shouldn't! If I hadn't done such a silly thing, I shouldn't! If I hadn't laid two to one on that damned seven after the stakes had been doubled, I might have broken the whole bank."

"You didn't break it, though," observed the fair man.

"I didn't break it because I laid two to one on the seven at the wrong minute. But do you suppose your major is a good player?"

"Whether he is good or bad, he beat you."

"As though that mattered," said Nozdryov; "I shall beat him all the same. Just let him try playing doubles, then I shall see; I shall see then how much of a player he is. But what a roaring time we had the first days, friend Tchitchikov. The fair really was a first-rate one. The very dealers said there had never been such a crowd. Everything I had brought from the village sold at tip-top prices. Ah, my boy, didn't we have a time! Even now when one thinks of it . . . dash it all! What a pity you weren't there! Only fancy, there was a regiment of dragoons stationed only two miles from the town. Would you believe it, all the officers, forty of them, were in the town, every man-jack of them. . . . When we began to drink, my boy . . . the staff-captain Potsyeluev . . . such a jolly fellow . . . such fine moustaches, my boy! He calls Bordeaux simply 'bordashka.' 'Bring us some bordashka, waiter!' he would say. Lieutenant Kuvshinnikov . . . ah, my boy, what a charming man! One might say he is a regular dog! He and I were together all the time. What wine Ponomarey brought out for us! You must know he is a regular cheat; you shouldn't buy anything in his shop; he puts all sorts of rubbish into his wine, sandalwood, burnt cork, and even colours it with elderberries, the rogue: but if he brings out from some remote place they call the special room, some choice little bottle, well then, old boy, you will find yourself in the empyrean.* We had champagne . . . what was the governor's compared with it?—no better than cider. Just fancy, not Cliquot but a special Cliquot-Matradura which means double Cliquot. And he got us a bottle of French wine too, called Bon-bon, with a fragrance!—of roses and anything you like! Didn't we have a roaring time! A prince who came after us sent to the shop for champagne, there wasn't a bottle to be had in the town: the officers had drunk it all. Would you believe it, I drank seventeen bottles of champagne myself at dinner!"

"Come, you can't drink seventeen bottles," observed the fair man.

"As a man of honor I tell you I did," answered Nozdryov.

"You can tell yourself what you like, but I tell you that you can't drink ten."

---

*the highest reaches of heaven; paradise.

"Well, would you like to bet I can't?"

"Bet for what?"

"Well, bet me the gun that you bought in the town."

"I won't."

"Oh, do bet it, try!"

"I don't want to try."

"Yes, you would lose your gun if you did, as you lost your cap. Oh, friend Tchitchikov, how sorry I was you weren't there! I know that you would never have parted from Lieutenant Kuvshinnikov, how he and you would have got on together! He is very different from the public prosecutor and all the old niggards in our town who tremble over every farthing. He's ready to play any game you like. Oh, Tchitchikov, you might just as well have come! You really were a pig not to, you cattle-breeder! Kiss me, my dear soul, I like you awfully! Just fancy, Mizhuev, here fate has brought us together! Why, what was he to me or I to him? He has come here God knows where from and I, too, am living here. . . . And what lots of carriages there were, old boy, and it was all *en gros*.* I tried my luck and won two pots of pomatum, a china cup and a guitar; and then I staked once more and lost more than six roubles, damn it all. And what a flirt that Kuvshinnikov is if you only knew! We went with him to almost all the balls. There was one girl dressed up to the nines, all frills and flounces, and the deuce knows what. I thought to myself: 'Dash it all!' But Kuvshinnikov, he is a devil of a fellow, sat down beside her and let off such compliments in French. . . . Would you believe it, he wouldn't let the peasant women alone either. That's what he calls 'gathering roses while we may.'† There were wonderful fish and dried sturgeon for sale; I did bring one away with me, it's a good thing I thought to buy it while I had the money left. Where are you off to now?"

"I am going to see somebody," said Tchitchikov.

"Come, what does somebody matter? Chuck him, come home with me!"

"I can't, I can't, I have business."

---

*At wholesale; a great many (French).

†Allusion to the first line of "To the Virgins, to Make Much of Time," by English poet Robert Herrick (1591–1674): "Gather ye rosebuds while ye may"—that is, take pleasures while you can.

"There now, it's business! What next. Oh you, Opodeldoc Ivanovitch!"

"I really have business and very urgent business too."

"I bet you are lying. Come tell me, who is it you are going to see?"

"Why, Sobakevitch."

At this point Nozdryov burst into a loud resounding guffaw, laughing as only a man in the best of health laughs when every one of his teeth white as sugar are displayed and his cheeks tremble and quiver, and his fellow-lodger three rooms away leaps up from his sleep and, with his eyes starting from his head, cries: "Well, he is going it!"

"What is there funny about it?" asked Tchitchikov, somewhat disconcerted by this laughter.

But Nozdryov went on roaring with laughter as he ejaculated: "Oh spare me, I shall split with laughing!"

"There is nothing funny in it; I promised him to go," said Tchitchikov.

"But you know you won't enjoy yourself staying with him: he's a regular skinflint! I know your character: you are cruelly mistaken if you think you will find a game of cards and a good bottle of Bonbon there. I say, old boy: hang Sobakevitch! Come home with me! What a sturgeon I'll set before you! Ponomarev kept bowing away, the beast, and saying: 'I got it expressly for you, you might look all through the fair,' he said, 'and you wouldn't find one like it.' He is an awful rogue, though. I told him so to his face. 'Our government contractor and you are the two greatest cheats going!' I said. He laughed and stroked his beard, the brute. Kuvshinnikov and I had lunch every day in his shop. Oh, there's something I forgot to tell you about; I know you'll never leave off about it, but for ten thousand roubles I won't let you have it, so I give you fair warning. Hey, Porfiry!" going to the window, he shouted to his servant, who in one hand was holding a knife and in the other a crust of bread and a slice of sturgeon, which he had succeeded in cutting for himself while getting something out of the chaise. "Hey, Porfiry, bring the pup up here! Such a pup," he went on, addressing Tchitchikov.

"Stolen, it must be, the owner would never have parted with it of his own accord. I offered my chestnut mare for it, the one you remember Hvostyrev swopped me."

Tchitchikov however had never in his life seen the chestnut mare or Hvostyrev.

"Won't you have something to eat, sir?" said the old woman, going up to him at that moment.

"No, nothing. Ah, my boy, what a roaring time we had! Give me a glass of vodka, though. What sort have you got?"

"Flavoured with aniseed," answered the old woman.

"Give me a glass, too," said the fair man.

"At the theatre there was an actress who sang like a canary, the hussy! Kuvshinnikov who was sitting by me, 'I say, my boy,' says he, 'there's a rose that wants gathering.' There must have been quite fifty booths, I believe. Fenardi turned somersaults for four hours." At this point he took the glass out of the hands of the old woman who made him a low bow for doing so.

"Ah, give him here," he shouted, seeing Porfiry come in with the puppy. Porfiry was dressed like his master in a sort of a jerkin, wadded and somewhat greasy, however.

"Bring him here, put him down on the floor!"

Porfiry set down the puppy which, stretching out all its four legs, sniffed at the floor.

"Here's the pup!" said Nozdryov, picking it up by its back and holding it up in the air. The puppy gave a rather plaintive howl.

"But you haven't done what I told you," said Nozdryov, addressing Porfiry and carefully scrutinising the puppy's belly; "and didn't you think to comb him?"

"Yes, I did comb him."

"Well, why has he got fleas then?"

"I can't tell. They may have got on to him from the chaise."

"You are lying, you are lying, you never thought of combing him; and I expect, you fool, you let him catch yours too. Just look here, Tchitchikov, look what ears; here, feel them."

"But why? I can see without that: it's a good breed," answered Tchitchikov.

"No, take him, feel his ears."

To gratify him Tchitchikov felt the dog's ears, saying as he did so: "Yes, he will make a good dog."

"And feel how cold his nose is. Take hold of it."

Not wishing to offend him Tchitchikov touched the dog's nose too, and said: "He'll have a good scent."

"He's a real bull-dog," Nozdryov went on. "I must own I've been keen to get a bull-dog for ever so long. Here, Porfiry, take him away."

Porfiry, putting his arm around the puppy, carried him off to the chaise.

"I say, Tchitchikov, you absolutely must come back with me now; it's only three miles, we shall whisk there like the wind, and then, if you like, you can go on to Sobakevitch."

"Well," thought Tchitchikov to himself, "why shouldn't I really go to Nozdryov's. Isn't he as good as any one else and he has just lost money too. He is ready for anything as one can see. So one might get him to give one something for nothing. Very well, let us go," he said, "but on condition you don't keep me; my time's precious."

"Well, you darling, that's right! That's capital! Stay! I must give you a kiss for that."

Hereupon Nozdryov and Tchitchikov kissed each other.

"First-rate; we will set off, the three of us!"

"No, let me off, please," said the fair man, "I must get home."

"Nonsense, nonsense, old man: I won't let you go."

"My wife will be cross, really; now you can get into the gentleman's chaise."

"No, no, no! Don't you think it."

The fair man was one of those people in whose character a certain obstinacy is at first sight apparent. Before you have time to open your lips, they are ready to begin arguing and it seems as though they will never agree to what is openly opposed to their way of thinking, that they will never call what is foolish sensible, and above all will never dance to another man's piping. But it always ends in their displaying a weakness of will, in their agreeing to what they have denied, calling what is foolish sensible and dancing in fine style to another man's piping—in fact they begin well and end badly.

"Nonsense," said Nozdryov in reply to some protest on the part of the fair man; then he put the latter's cap on his head and—the fair man followed them.

"For the drop of vodka, sir, you have not paid," said the old woman.

"Oh, all right, all right, my good woman. I say, dear boy! pay it for me please, I haven't a farthing in my pocket."

"How much do you want?" asked his brother-in-law.

"Why, twenty kopecks, sir," said the old woman.

"Nonsense, nonsense, give her half. It's quite enough for her."

"That's very little, sir," said the old woman. She took the money with gratitude, however, and ran with alacrity to open the door. She was not a loser by the transaction, for she had asked four times the cost of the vodka.

The travellers took their seats. Tchitchikov's chaise drove by the side of the one in which Nozdryov and his brother-in-law were seated, and so they could all talk freely together on the way. Nozdryov's wretched little carriage drawn by the lean hired horses followed behind, continually halting. Porfiry was in it with the puppy.

As the conversation which the travellers kept up was of no great interest to the reader, we shall do better if we say something about Nozdryov himself, since he is perhaps destined to play not the least important part in our poem.

The personality of Nozdryov is certainly to some extent familiar to the reader already. Every one must have met more than a few like him. They are called dashing fellows and are known even in childhood and at school as good companions, though they are apt to get a good many hard knocks for all that. There is always something open, direct, and reckless in their faces. They are quick to make friends, and you can hardly look round before they have begun addressing you as though they had known you all their lives. One would think they were friends for life; but it almost always happens that their new friend quarrels with them the very evening when they are celebrating their friendship. They are always great talkers, rakes, and dare-devils, and are always to the fore in everything. At thirty-five, Nozdryov was exactly the same as he had been at eighteen and twenty: given up to the pursuit of pleasure. His marriage did not change him in the least, especially as his wife departed to a better world soon after it, leaving him two small children who were not at all what he wanted. The children, however, were looked after by an engaging little nurse. He could never stay at home for more than a day at a time. He never failed to get wind of any fairs, assemblies, or balls for miles around; in a twinkling of an eye he was there, squabbling and getting up a row at the green table, for like all men of his kind, he had a great passion for cards.

As we have seen in the first chapter, his play was not quite above suspicion, he was up to all sorts of tricks and dodges, and so the game often ended in sport of a different kind: either he got a good drubbing or had his fine thick whiskers pulled out, so that he often returned home with only one whisker and that somewhat attenuated. But his fully healthy cheeks were so happily constituted and capable of such luxuriant growth, that his whiskers soon sprouted and were finer than ever. And what is strangest of all and only possible in Russia, within a short time he would meet again the very friends who had given him such a dressing, and meet them as though nothing had happened: he, as the saying is, did not turn a hair and they did not turn a hair.

Nozdryov was in a certain sense an *historical* character. No gathering at which he was present went off without some "history." Some sort of scandal invariably occurred: either he was conducted out of the ballroom by the police, or his friends were forced to eject him themselves. If that did not occur, something would be sure to happen that never would happen to any one else: either he would get so drunk at the refreshment bar that he did nothing but laugh, or he would tell such fantastic lies that at last he felt ashamed of himself. And he would lie without any provocation: he would suddenly assert that he had a horse whose coat was a light blue or pink colour, and nonsense of that sort, so that at last his listeners would walk away from him, saying: "Well, my lad, it seems you are drawing the long-bow." There are people who have a passion for playing nasty tricks on their neighbours, sometimes without the slightest provocation. Even a man of good position and gentlemanly appearance, with a decoration on his breast will, for instance, shake hands, and converse with you on intellectual subjects that call for deep reflection, and in another minute before your very eyes he is playing you a nasty trick like the humblest little copying clerk and not at all like a man with a decoration on his breast conversing on subjects that call for deep reflection, so that you simply stand amazed and can do nothing but shrug your shoulders. Nozdryov had this strange passion too. The more intimate any one was with him, the readier he was to do him a bad turn; he would spread the most incredible tales which would have been hard to beat for silliness, upset a wedding or a business transaction, and all the while would be far from regarding himself as your enemy; on the contrary, if chance threw you with him again, he would behave in the most friendly way again and would even say: "You are a wretch, you never come to see me." In a certain sense Nozdryov was a many-sided man, that is, a man who could turn his hand to anything. In the same breath he would offer to go with you to the furthest ends of the earth, to undertake any enterprise you might choose, to swop anything in the world for anything you like. Guns, dogs, horses, anything would do for a swop, not with the slightest idea of gain; it all sprang from an irresistible impetuosity and recklessness of character. If he had the luck to hit upon a simpleton at a fair and rook him, he bought masses of things because they caught his eye in the shops: horse collars, fumigating candles, kerchiefs for the nurse, a stallion, raisins, a silver washing-basin, holland linen, fine wheaten flour, tobacco, pistols, herrings, pictures, a lathe, pots, boots, china—as long as his money lasted. However, it rarely happened that all this wealth was carried home; almost the same day it would pass into the hands of some luckier gambler, sometimes even with the addition of a peculiar pipe with a tobacco pouch and a mouth-piece, and another time with all his four horses, carriage, and coachman, so that their former owner had to set to work in a short jacket or a jerkin to look out for a friend to give him a lift in his carriage. Such was Nozdryov! Perhaps he will be called a hackneyed character, and it will be said that there are no Nozdryovs now. Alas! those who say so are wrong. It will be many long years before the Nozdryovs are extinct. They are everywhere among us, and the only difference perhaps is that they are wearing a different cut of coat; but people are carelessly unobservant and a man in a different coat seems to them a different man.

Meanwhile the three carriages rolled up to the steps of Nozdryov's house. There was no sort of preparation for their reception within. There were wooden trestles in the middle of the dining-room, and two peasants standing on them were whitewashing the walls, carolling some endless song; the floor was all splashed with whitewash. Nozdryov ordered the peasants and the trestles out of the room on the spot and ran out into the next room to give instructions. The guests heard him giving the cook directions about dinner; Tchitchikov, who was already beginning to be aware of an appetite, saw clearly that they would not sit down to table within five hours. On his return Nozdryov conducted his visitors to see everything he had in the village, and in the course of a little more than two hours showed them absolutely everything, so that there was nothing else to be shown. First of all, they went to inspect the stable where they saw two more mares, one a dappled grey, the other a chestnut, then a bay stallion, not very handsome to look at, though Nozdryov swore that he had paid ten thousand for it.

"You didn't give ten thousand for him," said his brother-in-law. "He's not worth one."

"Upon my soul, I did give ten thousand for him," said Nozdryov.

"You can swear as much as you like," answered his brother-in-law.

"Well, will you take a bet on it?" said Nozdryov.

His brother-in-law did not care to bet on it.

Then Nozdryov showed them the empty stalls in which there had once been other good horses. In the same stables they saw a goat, which in accordance with the old superstition they considered it essential to keep with the horses, and which seemed to be on the best of terms with them and walked about under their bellies as though it were at home there. Then Nozdryov led them to view a wolf-cub which was kept tied up. "Here's the wolf-cub!" he said. "I feed him on raw meat on purpose. I want him to be quite fierce." They went to look at the pond, in which according to Nozdryov there were fish of such size that two men could with difficulty pull one out. His brother-in-law did not fail to express his doubts of the fact.

"I am going to show you, Tchitchikov, a couple of first-rate dogs: the strength of their black flesh is simply amazing, their hair is like needles"; and he led them into a very picturesquely built little house, surrounded by a large yard, fenced in on all sides. When they went into the yard they saw dogs of all kinds, borzoys of several breeds of all shades and colours, dark brown, black and tan, black and white, brown and white, red and white, with black ears and with grey ears. . . . They had all sorts of names, often in the imperative mood: Shoot-away, Growl-away, Dash-away, Fire, Cross-eye, Pointer, Bakewell, Scorcher, Swallow, Hasty, Treasure, Caretaker. With them Nozdryov was just like a father among his children: they all flew to meet and welcome the visitors with their tails in the air in accordance with the rules of canine etiquette. A dozen of them put their paws on

Nozdryov's shoulders, Growl-away displayed great affection for Tchitchikov and, getting on his hindlegs, licked him right on the lips, so that our friend turned aside and spat at once. They inspected the dogs the strength of whose "black flesh" was so amazing—they were fine dogs. Then they went to look at a Crimean* bitch who was blind and in Nozdryov's words would soon be dead, but had two years ago been a very good bitch. They looked at the bitch, she certainly was blind. Then they went to look at a water-mill, it had lost the iron ring on which the upper stone rests as it turns rapidly on the axle— whisks round, to use the delightful expression of the Russian peasant. "And the smithy is close by," said Nozdryov; and going on a little further they saw the smithy, and that too they inspected.

"Look, in that field," said Nozdryov, pointing to it, "there are such masses of hares that you can't see the ground; I caught one by the hind-legs with my own hands."

"Come, you can't catch a hare with your hands," observed his brother-in-law.

"But I say I did catch one, I caught one on purpose!" answered Nozdryov. "Now," he said, addressing Tchitchikov, "I am going to take you to see the boundaries of my property."

Nozdryov led his visitors across fields which in many places were covered with hillocks. The guests had to make their way between rough fallow land and ploughed fields. Tchitchikov began to feel tired. In many places the water squelched up under their feet, it was such low-lying ground. At first they were careful and picked their way, but afterwards, seeing that it was of no use, walked straight on without looking out for the mud. After walking a considerable distance they did indeed see the boundary which consisted of a wooden post and a narrow ditch.

"This is the boundary," said Nozdryov, "all that you see on this side is mine and even on the other side of it, all that forest which you see in the blue distance over there and all that beyond the forest is mine too."

"But when did that forest become your property?" asked the brother-in-law. "Surely you haven't bought it lately? It used not to be yours, you know."

---

*Referring to the Crimea, a peninsula in southwestern Russia, between the Black Sea and the Sea of Azov.

"Yes, I bought it lately," answered Nozdryov.

"When did you manage to buy it so quickly?"

"Oh, I bought it the day before yesterday and paid a lot for it too, dash it all!"

"Why, but you were at the fair then."

"Ough, you duffer! Can't one be at a fair and yet buy land? I was at the fair and while I was away my steward bought it for me."

"But how could the steward?" said his brother-in-law; but at that moment he looked dubious and shook his head.

The visitors returned to the house by the same disgusting road. Nozdryov led them to his study, in which however there was nothing commonly seen in studies, such as books or papers; on the walls there hung swords and two guns, one that had cost three hundred and the other eight hundred roubles. The brother-in-law after examining them merely shook his head. Then they were shown some Turkish daggers, on one of which there had been engraved by mistake: Made by Savely Sibiryakov. Then the friends were shown a barrel-organ. Nozdryov immediately turned the handle. The barrel-organ played not unpleasantly, but something seemed to go wrong with it in the middle, for the mazurka ended up with the song, "Marlbrook s'en va-t-en guerre,"* and Marlbrook wound up unexpectedly with an old familiar waltz. Nozdryov had left off turning, but there was one pipe in the organ that was very irrepressible and, unwilling to be silenced, went on for a long time fluting by itself.

Then they were shown pipes made of wood, of clay, or of meerschaum, smoked and unsmoked, wrapped up in chamois leather and not wrapped up, a chibouk† with an amber mouthpiece lately won at cards, a tobacco pouch embroidered by a countess who had fallen head over ears in love with him somewhere at a posting station, and whose hands were, in his words, *subtilement superflues*,‡ words that apparently to him suggested the acme of perfection. After a preliminary snack of salt sturgeon they sat down to dinner about five o'clock.

---

*"Marlborough goes to war" (French); popular song about the battles of the English general the Duke of Marlborough in the War of Spanish Succession (1701–1714), when King Louis XIV sought to extend France's powers.

†Long pipe smoked by Turks.

‡Subtly superfluous (French).

Dinner evidently was not the chief interest in Nozdryov's life; the dishes did not make a very fine show, some were burnt, others quite uncooked. It was evident the cook was guided by inspiration and put in the first ingredient he laid his hand on, if the pepper happened to stand by him he put in pepper, if cabbage turned up, in it went, he flung in milk, ham, peas—in short he pitched in everything pell-mell so long as it was hot, thinking it would be sure to have some sort of taste. On the other hand Nozdryov was strong on wines; even before the soup was handed round he had already poured out for each of his guests a big glass of port and another of Haut Sauterne,* for in provincial towns there is no such thing as simple Sauterne. Then Nozdryov sent for a bottle of Madeira, "no field-marshal ever drank better," he said. The Madeira† certainly did burn their mouths, for the wine merchants know the tastes of country gentlemen who are fond of good Madeira, and doctor it mercilessly with rum and sometimes put plain vodka in it, confidently relying on the fortitude of the Russian stomach. Then Nozdryov ordered a special bottle to be fetched of a wine which, according to him, was a mixture of Burgundy and champagne. He poured it very freely into the glasses of both—to right and to left, to his brother-in-law and Tchitchikov. Tchitchikov noticed, however, out of the corner of his eye that his host took very little for himself. This put him on his guard, and as soon as Nozdryov's attention was distracted by talking or pouring out wine for his brother-in-law he upset his wine-glass into his plate. After a brief interval a liqueur made from rowan berries was put on the table and described by Nozdryov as tasting exactly like cream, though to their surprise it tasted strongly of corn-brandy. Then they drank some sort of balsam which had a name difficult to remember, and, indeed, the master of the house called it by a different name later on. The dinner had long ago been finished and all the wines tasted, but the guests still sat at the table. Tchitchikov was not at all anxious to broach the great subject to Nozdryov before the brother-in-law: the latter was in any case a third person and the subject called for privacy and friendly talk. At the same time the brother-in-law could hardly be a man to be afraid of, for he was apparently quite tipsy and was nod-

---

*Sweet white French wine.
†Strong Portuguese wine, similar to sherry.

ding in his chair. Perceiving himself that he was in a somewhat unstable condition, he began to talk of going home, but in a voice as languid and listless as though, to use the Russian expression, he were putting on a horse's collar with a pair of pincers.

"No, no, I won't let you go," said Nozdryov.

"No, don't worry me, my dear boy, I am going really," said the brother-in-law, "you treat me very badly."

"Nonsense, nonsense! We will have a game of bank in a minute."

"No, you play yourself, my boy, but I can't: my wife will be dreadfully upset, I must tell her all about the fair. I must, my boy, I really must do that to please her. No, don't keep me!"

"Oh, your wife can go to . . . ! Very important business that is! . . ."

"No, my boy! She is such a good wife. She is really exemplary, so faithful and estimable. She does so much for me . . . you wouldn't believe it, it brings tears into my eyes. No, don't keep me, as I am an honest man, I am going. On my word of honour, I assure you."

"Let him go; what's the use of keeping him?" said Tchitchikov to Nozdryov.

"Ah, you are right there," said Nozdryov. "I simply hate such wet blankets"; and he added aloud: "Well, confound you, you can go and spoon with your wife, you muff."

"No, my boy, don't call me names," answered his brother-in-law, "I am indebted to her, to my wife. She is so kind and good really, she is so sweet to me, she touches me to tears. She will ask me what I saw at the fair, I must tell her all about it . . . she is so sweet really."

"Well, be off then. . . . Tell her a lot of tosh! Here is your cap."

"No, you oughtn't to talk like that about her, my boy; you are insulting me, I may say, when you do it, she is so sweet."

"Well, then, make haste and take yourself off to her."

"Yes, my boy, I'm going, you must excuse me but I really can't stay. I should love to, but I can't." The brother-in-law went on a long while repeating his apologies without observing that he had for some time past been sitting in his chaise, had driven out beyond the gates and was facing nothing but the empty fields. It may be assumed that his wife heard but little of the incidents of the fair.

"What a paltry fellow!" said Nozdryov, standing before the window and looking at the carriage as it drove away. "Look how it rolls along. The trace-horse isn't bad, I have long wanted to hook it. But there is no getting round him. He is a muff, a regular muff!"

Thereupon they went into another room. Porfiry brought candles, and Tchitchikov noticed in his host's hands a pack of cards that seemed to have appeared from nowhere.

"Well, my boy," said Nozdryov, pressing the side of the pack with his fingers and slightly bending it so that the paper round it split and flew off, "to pass the time I'll put three hundred roubles in the bank."

But Tchitchikov made as though he had not heard what was said, and observed as though suddenly recollecting: "Oh, while I think of it: I have something I want to ask you."

"What is it?"

"Promise first that you will do it."

"But what is it?"

"Come, promise first."

"Very well."

"On your honour?"

"On my honour."

"This is what it is; I expect you have a great many dead serfs whose names have not been struck off the census list?"

"Yes I have, what of it?"

"Transfer them to me, to my name."

"What do you want them for?"

"Oh well, I want them."

"What for?"

"Oh well, I want them . . . that's my business, in fact I need them."

"Well, I suppose you have some scheme in your head. Own up now, what is it?"

"Why, what scheme? There is nothing one could plan over such rubbish."

"But what do you want them for?"

"Oh, how inquisitive he is! He wants to have his finger in every petty business and to poke his nose into it too!"

"And why won't you tell me?"

"What good will it do you to know? Oh well, it is just a fancy of mine."

"Oh, all right then: unless you tell me I won't do it."

"Come, now, you see that's not honourable on your part: you have given your word—and now you are going back on it."

"Well, that is just as you please, but I won't do it till you tell me."

"What am I to say to him," thought Tchitchikov, and after a minute's reflection he informed him he needed the dead souls to obtain a position in society, that at present he had not big estates, so that until he had, he would be glad of souls of any sort.

"That's a lie, that's a lie!" said Nozdryov, not allowing him to finish. "That's a lie, old man!"

Tchitchikov himself realised that his fiction was not very plausible and that the pretext was rather a feeble one.

"Oh, very well, then I will tell you straight out," he said, to set himself right, "only please don't speak of it to any one. I am going to be married, but I must tell you that the father and mother of my betrothed are very ambitious people. It's a regular nuisance. I regret the engagement: they are set on their daughter's husband having at least three hundred souls, and as I am quite a hundred and fifty souls short of that . . ."

"Come, that's a lie, that's a lie," cried Nozdryov again.

"I assure you," said Tchitchikov, "I haven't lied this little bit," and he pointed with his thumb to the top of his little finger.

"I bet my head you are lying!"

"This is really insulting. What do you take me for? Why are you so sure that I am lying?"

"Why, I know you, you see; you are a great rascal—let me tell you in a friendly way! If I were your chief, I'd hang you on the nearest tree."

Tchitchikov was offended by this observation. Any expression in the least coarse or derogatory to his dignity was distasteful to him. He even disliked any sort of familiarity, except on the part of some personage of very high rank. And so on this occasion he was greatly offended.

"Upon my soul, I would hang you," repeated Nozdryov. "I tell you so openly not to insult you, I only speak as a friend."

"There is a limit to everything," said Tchitchikov with an air of dignity. "If you want to display your wit in this way, you had better go to the barracks"; and then he added, "If you don't care to give them to me, you might sell them."

"Sell them! But you see I know you, you are a rascal, I know you won't give much for them."

"Ugh! you are a nice one, really! Think, what use are they to you, are they diamonds or what?"

"Well, there you are! I knew you'd say that."

"Upon my word, my dear fellow, what Jewish propensities you have! You ought simply to give them to me."

"Well, listen then; to show you that I am not a shark, I won't take anything for them. Buy my stallion and I will throw them in as a makeweight."

"Upon my soul, what do I want with a stallion?" said Tchitchikov, genuinely astounded at such a proposition.

"What do you want with one? But you know I gave ten thousand for him, and I will sell him to you for four."

"But what do I want with a stallion? I don't keep a stud farm."

"But listen, you don't understand; why, I will let you have him for three thousand and the other thousand you can pay me later."

"But I don't want the stallion, God bless him!"

"Well, buy the chestnut mare then."

"I don't want the mare either."

"I will let you have the mare and the grey horse you saw in the stable for two thousand."

"But I don't want the horses."

"You can sell them, they will give you three times as much for them at the first fair."

"Well, you had better sell them yourself then, if you are sure you will get three times as much."

"I know it would pay me better, but I want you to make something out of it."

Tchitchikov thanked him for his kind intention, and refused point-blank both the grey horse and the chestnut mare.

"All right, then, buy some dogs. I'll sell you a couple—that will simply make your hair stand on end! Such whiskers; their coat stands up like a brush; and the barrel-shape of their ribs is beyond all conception, and their paws are so soft and supple—they don't leave a mark on the ground."

"But what do I want with dogs? I am not a sportsman."

"But I should like you to have dogs. Well, I say, if you don't want dogs, buy my barrel-organ. It's a wonderful organ. As I am an honest man, it cost me fifteen hundred roubles. I'll let you have it for nine hundred."

"But what do I want with a hurdy-gurdy, I am not a German to go trudging about the roads with it, begging."

"But this isn't the sort of barrel-organ Germans go about with, you know. It's an organ; take a good look at it; it's all mahogany. I'll show it to you again!" At this point Nozdryov seizing Tchitchikov by the arm dragged him into the adjoining room and, though he held his ground firmly and declared that he knew what the barrel-organ was like, he had to hear how Marlborough went to war once more.

"If you don't want to buy it, I tell you, I'll give you the barrel-organ and all the dead souls I have got, and you give me your chaise and three hundred roubles thrown in."

"What next! What should I do for a carriage?"

"I'd give you another chaise. Come along to the coach-house, I'll show it you! You have only to give it a coat of paint and it will be a capital chaise."

"Ough, the devil is egging him on!" Tchitchikov thought to himself, and he made up his mind that, come what might, he would refuse all chaises, barrel-organs, and any conceivable dog in spite of ribs, barrel-shaped beyond all conception, and paws so soft and supple.

"But, you see, you'll have the chaise, the barrel-organ, and the dead souls all together."

"I don't want them!" Tchitchikov said once more.

"Why don't you want them?"

"Because I simply don't want them, and that's all about it."

"Well, you are a fellow! I see there is no doing business with you as between good friends and comrades. . . . You really are . . . one can see at once that you are a double-faced man!"

"Why, do you take me for a fool or what? Judge for yourself: why should I take a thing absolutely of no use to me?"

"Oh, it is no use your talking. I understand you very well now. You are really such a cad. But I tell you what. If you like we'll have out the cards, I'll stake all my dead souls on a card, the barrel-organ too."

"Well, staking it on a card means leaving it in uncertainty," said Tchitchikov, while he glanced askance at the cards that were in

Nozdryov's hands. Both the packs looked to him as though they had been tampered with and the very spots on the back looked suspicious.

"Why uncertainty?" said Nozdryov. "There is no uncertainty. If only the luck's on your side, you'll win a devilish lot. There it is! What luck!" he said, beginning to lay out the cards to tempt him to play. "What luck, what luck; take everything."

"There's that damned nine that I lost everything on! I felt that it would sell me and, half shutting my eyes, I thought to myself: damnation take you, you may sell me, you brute!"

While Nozdryov was saying this, Porfiry brought in a bottle. But Tchitchikov absolutely refused either to drink or to play.

"Why won't you play?" said Nozdryov.

"Oh, because I don't feel inclined. And, indeed, I must own that I am not particularly fond of cards at any time."

"Why aren't you?"

Tchitchikov shrugged his shoulders and added: "Because I am not."

"You are a paltry fellow!"

"What's to be done? I am as God made me."

"You are a regular muff! I did think at first that you were more or less of a gentleman, but you don't know how to behave at all. One can't speak to you as one would to a friend. . . . There is no straightforwardness, no sincerity. You are a regular Sobakevitch, just such a scoundrel!"

"What are you swearing at me for? Am I to blame for not playing? Sell me the souls alone, since you are so made that you worry about such trifles."

"Devil a one of them you shall have! I was meaning to let you have them for nothing, but now you shan't have them! I wouldn't give them for the riches of the world. You are a pickpocket, a nasty sweep. I won't have anything to do with you from this time forth. Porfiry, go and tell the stable-boy not to give his horses any oats, don't let them have anything but hay."

Tchitchikov had not in the least expected this conclusion.

"I wish I had never set eyes on you," said Nozdryov.

In spite of this little misunderstanding, however, the two gentlemen had supper together, though on this occasion there were no wines with fanciful names on the table. There was only one bottle containing Cypress wine,* which was as sour as sour can be. After supper Nozdryov said to Tchitchikov, taking him into a room where a bed had been made up for him: "Here's your bed. I don't want to say good-night to you."

On Nozdryov's departure Tchitchikov was left in a most unpleasant frame of mind. He was inwardly annoyed with himself and swore at himself for coming here and wasting his time. But he blamed himself still more for having spoken to Nozdryov of business; he had behaved as recklessly as a child, as a fool, for his business was not of the sort that could safely be confided to Nozdryov . . . Nozdryov was a worthless fellow. Nozdryov might tell lies, exaggerate, spread abroad God knows what stories, and it might lead to all sorts of scandal . . . it was bad, it was bad. "I am simply a fool," he said to himself. He slept very badly. Some small and very lively insects bit him mercilessly, so much so that he scratched with all his fingers on the smarting place, saying as he did so: "The devil take you and Nozdryov too." He woke up early in the morning. His first action, after putting on his dressing-gown and boots, was to cross the yard to the stable to tell Selifan to put the horses in the chaise at once. As he crossed the yard on his way back, he met Nozdryov, who was also in his dressing-gown and had a pipe between his teeth.

Nozdryov gave him a friendly greeting and asked him what sort of a night he had had.

"So-so," answered Tchitchikov very drily.

"As for me, my boy," said Nozdryov, "such nasty things haunted me all night that it is loathsome to tell of them; and it seemed as though there were a regiment of soldiers encamped in my mouth after yesterday. Only fancy, I dreamed that I was being thrashed, upon my soul! And would you believe it? You will never guess by whom: Captain Potsyeluev and Kuvshinnikov."

"Yes," thought Tchitchikov to himself, "it would be a good thing if you really were thrashed."

"Upon my soul! And it hurt too! I woke up, dash it all, something really was stinging me, I suppose it was those hags of fleas. Well, you go and get dressed; I will come to you directly. I have only got to pitch into that rogue of a steward."

---

*From the Mediterranean island of Cyprus.

Tchitchikov went back to his room, to wash and dress. When, after that, he went into the dining-room, the table was already laid for morning tea together with a bottle of rum. There were still traces about the room of the dinner and supper of the previous day and it seemed that no broom had been used. There were bread-crumbs on the floor and tobacco-ash even on the tablecloth. The master of the house himself who came in soon after had nothing on under his dressing-gown, and displayed a bare chest with something like a beard growing on it. Holding a chibouk in his hands and sipping from a cup, he would have been a very good subject for one of those painters who detest sleek gentlemen with hair properly cut or curled like a barber's block.

"Well, so how is it to be?" said Nozdryov after a brief pause, "won't you play for the souls?"

"I have told you, my boy, that I don't play. I will buy them if you like."

"I don't want to sell them: that wouldn't be acting like a friend. I am not going to make filthy lucre from the devil knows what. Playing for it is a different matter. Let us have one game anyway."

"I have told you already I won't."

"And you won't change?"

"I won't."

"Well, I tell you what, let us have a game at draughts;* if you win they are all yours. I have got lots, you know, that ought to be struck off the census list. Hey, Porfiry, bring the draughtboard here!"

"No need to trouble; I am not going to play."

"But this isn't cards; there is no question of chance or deception about it: it all depends on skill, you know. I must warn you beforehand that I can't play a bit, in fact you ought to give me something."

"Well, suppose I do," Tchitchikov thought to himself. "I will play draughts with him. I don't play badly, and it will be difficult for him to be up to any tricks at draughts."

"Very well, I will play at draughts."

"The souls against a hundred roubles!"

"Why? Fifty would be quite enough."

"No, fifty is not much of a stake. I had better make it up with a puppy of some sort or a gold seal for your watch-chain."

---

*Checkers.

"Very well!" said Tchitchikov.

"What piece will you give me?" said Nozdryov.

"Whatever for? Certainly not."

"You might at least give me the first two moves."

"I won't, I am a poor player myself."

"I know what sort of a poor player you are!" said Nozdryov, moving forward a draught.

"It's a long time since I touched a draughtsman," said Tchitchikov, and he too advanced a piece.

"We know what sort of a poor player you are," said Nozdryov, moving a draughtsman and at the same time pushing forward another with the cuff of his sleeve.

"I haven't touched one for ever so long! . . . Aie, aie! What's this, put it back," said Tchitchikov.

"Which?"

"That draught there," said Tchitchikov, and at the same moment saw almost under his nose another which had, it seemed, reached the point of becoming a king. Where it had come from, goodness only knows. "No," said Tchitchikov, getting up from the table. "It is quite impossible to play with you. You can't play three moves at once!"

"Why three? It is a mistake. One was moved by accident; I'll put it back if you like."

"And where did that other one come from?"

"What other one?"

"Why, that other one which is just going to be a king."

"Well, I say! don't you remember?"

"No, my friend, I have counted every move and I remember them all, you have only just put it there. Its proper place is here!"

"What, which place?" said Nozdryov, turning crimson. "I see you are a story-teller, old fellow."

"No, old fellow, it is you who tell stories, I fancy, but you don't tell them successfully."

"For what do you take me?" said Nozdryov. "Do you suppose I cheat?"

"I don't take you for anything, but I'll never play with you again."

"No, you can't refuse," said Nozdryov, getting hot, "the game has begun."

"I have a right to refuse, for you don't play as an honourable man should."

"No, that's a lie, you mustn't say that!"

"No, you are lying yourself."

"I didn't cheat and you can't refuse to go on, you ought to finish the game!"

"You won't make me do that," said Tchitchikov, coolly, and going up to the draughtboard he mixed the draughts together.

Nozdryov flushed crimson and advanced so close to Tchitchikov that the latter stepped back a couple of paces.

"I'll make you play. It does not matter that you have moved the pieces. I remember all the moves. We'll put them back as they were."

"No, my dear fellow, that's the end: I am not going to play with you again."

"So you won't play?"

"You can see yourself that it is impossible to play with you."

"No, say straight out, won't you play?" said Nozdryov, advancing closer.

"No," said Tchitchikov, and at the same time he brought both his hands nearer to his face in case of need, for things were really getting rather too hot for him. This precaution was very well-timed for Nozdryov swung his arm . . . and it might easily have happened that one of our hero's plump and prepossessing cheeks would have received an insult that nothing could have wiped out, but, fortunately warding off the blow, he seized Nozdryov by his two menacing arms and held him firmly.

"Porfiry, Pavlushka!" shouted Nozdryov in a fury, struggling to free himself.

Hearing this shout, Tchitchikov, not wishing the serfs to witness this seductive scene, and at the same time feeling it was useless to hold Nozdryov, let go of his arms. At that instant Porfiry entered followed by Pavlushka, a stalwart fellow with whom it would be distinctly unprofitable to come to blows.

"So you won't finish the game?" said Nozdryov. "Give me a straightforward answer!"

"It's impossible to finish the game," said Tchitchikov and glanced out the window. He saw his chaise standing quite ready and Selifan waiting apparently for a signal to drive up to the steps; but there was no possibility of getting out of the room, two sturdy fools of serfs were standing in the doorway.

"So you won't finish the game," said Nozdryov with a face as hot as fire.

"If you played as an honourable man should . . . but as it is, I can't."

"So you can't, you scoundrel! As soon as you see you are losing, you can't! Beat him!" he shouted frantically, turning to Porfiry and Pavlushka, while he caught hold of his cherrywood chibouk. Tchitchikov turned as pale as a sheet. He tried to say something, but felt his lips move without uttering a sound.

"Beat him!" cried Nozdryov, dashing forward with the cherry-wood chibouk, as hot and perspiring as though he were attacking an impregnable citadel. "Beat him!" he shouted in the voice with which some desperate lieutenant shouts "Forward, lads!" to his men, though his hot-headed valour has attained such notoriety that special instructions have been given him to curb it when advancing to the attack. But the lieutenant is stirred by martial ardour, everything whirls round in his head, he has visions of Suvorov* and yearns for deeds of heroism. "Forward, lads!" he shouts, regardless of the fact that he is ruining the plan laid down for the general attack, that innumerable guns are ranged in the embrasure of the impregnable fortress walls that vanish into the skies, that his helpless company will be blown to atoms, and that already the fatal bullet that will still his shouts and close his mouth for ever is whistling through the air. But if Nozdryov did suggest a desperate and frantic lieutenant attacking a fortress, it must be admitted that the fortress that he was attacking was by no means an impregnable one. On the contrary, the object of his attack was so overwhelmed with terror that his heart sank into his heels. Already the chair with which he had thought to protect himself had been wrenched from his hands by the servants, already closing his eyes, more dead than alive, he was expecting to feel his host's Circassian† chibouk, and God only knows what might not have happened to him in another moment; but the fates were pleased to spare

---

*Alexander Suvorov (1729–1800), heroic Russian commander in wars against the Poles, Turks, and French.
†From a region in the northern Caucasus, bordering the Black Sea.

the sides, the shoulders, and all the well-bred person of our hero.
Suddenly and unexpectedly, as though from the clouds, came the tinkle of jangling bells, there was a distinct sound of the rattling wheels
of a trap flying up to the steps, and the heavy snorts and laboured
breathing of the over-heated horses resounded even in the room.
Every one involuntarily glanced out of window: a man with a moustache, in a semi-military uniform, got out of the trap. After inquiries
in the hall, he walked in before Tchitchikov could recover from his
terror and while he was in the most pitiful position in which mortal
could be placed.

"Allow me to inquire which of the present company is Mr.
Nozdryov?" said the stranger, looking with some perplexity at
Nozdryov who was standing with his chibouk in his hand, and at
Tchitchikov who had scarcely begun to recover from his ignomin-
ious position.

"Allow me to ask first, to whom I have the honour of speaking?"
said Nozdryov, going up to him.

"I am the police-captain."

"And what do you want?"

"I have come to inform you that you are placed under arrest until
your case has been settled."

"What nonsense, what case?" said Nozdryov.

"You are implicated in the assault by thrashing on a gentleman
by name of Maximov whilst in the state of intoxication."

"That's a lie! I have never set eyes on a gentleman called Maximov."

"Sir! Allow me to remind you that I am an officer. You may say
that to your servant, but not to me."

At this point Tchitchikov, without waiting for Nozdryov's answer, made haste to pick up his hat, slipped behind the police-
captain's back, and out to the steps, got into his chaise and told
Selifan to drive at his topmost speed.

CHAPTER 5

Our hero was thoroughly scared, however. Though the chaise flew along at full speed and Nozdryov's estate was soon left behind, out of sight, hidden behind fields and the rise and fall of the ground, he still looked behind him in terror as though expecting every moment to be pursued and overtaken. His breathing was laboured, and when he tried laying his hands on his heart he found that it was fluttering like a quail in a cage. "Well, he has given me a treat! Just think what a fellow!" At this point there followed a number of angry and violent imprecations referring to Nozdryov, and indeed some bad language was uttered. How could it be otherwise? He was a Russian, and in a rage too! Besides, it was no joking matter. "Say what you like," he said, "if the police-captain had not turned up in the nick of time I might well have looked my last on the light of day. I should have disappeared like a bubble on the water without leaving a trace, leaving no descendants and bequeathing to my future children neither fortune nor honour!" Our hero was always very much troubled about his descendants.

"What a nasty gentleman!" Selifan was thinking to himself. "I have never seen such a gentleman before. He deserves to be spat upon! Better give a man nothing to eat than not feed the horses properly, for a horse likes oats. They are a treat to him; oats for him are what a feast is for us: it's his pleasure."

The horses too seemed to have an unflattering opinion of Nozdryov: not only the bay and Assessor but even the dappled-grey seemed dissatisfied. Though the worst of the oats always fell to his share and Selifan never poured them into his manger without first saying, "Ah, you rascal," still they were oats and not simply hay: he munched them with satisfaction and often thrust his long nose into his companions' mangers to try their portion, especially when Selifan was not in the stable; but on this occasion there was nothing but hay—it was too bad! Every one was displeased.

But they were all interrupted in their expressions of displeasure in a sudden and quite unexpected manner. All of them, not excluding the coachman, only came to themselves and realised what had happened when a carriage with six horses dashed into collision with them and they heard almost over their heads the screams of ladies in the carriage, the threats and swearing of the coachman: "You scoundrel, I shouted to you at the top of my voice: 'Turn to the right, you crow.' Are you drunk?" Selifan was very conscious of his negligence, but as a Russian is not fond of admitting before others that he is to blame, he drew himself up with dignity and promptly retorted: "And you, why were you galloping in such style? Have you left your eyes in pawn at the pot-house or what?" Then he proceeded to back the horses so as to extricate them, but there was no managing it—everything was in a tangle. The dappled-grey sniffed with curiosity at the new friends whom he found on each side of him. Meanwhile the ladies in the carriage looked at it all with an expression of alarm on their faces. One was an old lady, the other a young girl of sixteen, with golden hair very charmingly and skilfully coiled about her little head. The pretty oval of her face was rounded like an egg, and had the transparent whiteness of one when, fresh and new-laid, it is held up to the light by the housekeeper's dark-skinned hand and the rays of the flashing sun filter through it: her delicate ears were also transparent and flushed crimson by the light that penetrated through them. The terror on her parted lips, the tears in her eyes were all so charming that our hero stared at her for some minutes without noticing the uproar that was going on among the horses and the coachmen, "Back, do, you Nizhni-Novgorod* crow!" yelled the other coachman. Selifan tugged at the reins as hard as he could, the other coachman did the same, the horses shuffled back a little and then stepping over the traces† were entangled again. While this was going on, the dappled-grey was so attracted by his new companions that he felt no inclination to get out of the predicament in which an unforeseen destiny had placed him and, laying his nose upon the neck of his new friend, whispered in his ear probably something dreadfully foolish, for the stranger constantly twitched his ears.

Peasants from the village which was fortunately close at hand ran

---

*City located about 250 miles east of Moscow; between 1932 and 1991 known as Gorki.
†Straps for harnessed horses.

up to give assistance. Since such a spectacle is a real godsend to a peasant, just as a newspaper or a club is to a German, numbers of them were soon swarming round the carriages and there was no one left in the village but the old women and little children. The traces were taken off, a few prods on the nose of the dappled-grey forced him to back; in short they were separated and led apart, but either owing to the annoyance felt by the horses at being parted from their friends or through foolishness, they would not move however much the coachman thrashed them but stood as though turned to stone. The sympathetic interest of the peasants reached an incredible pitch. Each one of them was continually volunteering advice: "You go, Andryushka, you look after the trace-horse, the one on the right side, and let Uncle Mitya get on the shaft-horse! Get on, Uncle Mitya!" Uncle Mitya, a long lean peasant with a red beard, mounted the shaft-horse and looked like the village belfry or like the crane with which they draw water from the well. The coachman lashed the horses but it was no use, Uncle Mitya was no help at all. "Stay, stay," shouted the peasants. "You get on the trace-horse, Uncle Mitya, and let Uncle Minyay get on the shaft-horse." Uncle Minyay, a broad-shouldered peasant with a coal-black beard and a paunch that looked like the gigantic samovar in which honey posset* is brewed for the chilly crowds in a market, jumped with gusto on to the shaft-horse who was almost bowed to the ground under his weight. "Now it will be all right," bawled the peasants. "Make him smart, make him smart! Touch him up with the whip, that one yonder, the bay. Make him wriggle, like a daddy-long-legs." But seeing that no progress was made and that no whipping was any use, Uncle Mitya and Uncle Minyay both mounted the shaft-horse while Andryushka got on to the trace-horse. At last the coachman, losing patience, drove both uncles away; and it was as well that he did for the horses were in a steam as though they had raced from one posting station to another without taking breath. He gave them a minute to rest and then they set off of themselves. While all this was going on, Tchitchikov looked very attentively at the young lady in the carriage. Several times he made an effort to speak to her, but he somehow could not bring himself to do so. And meanwhile the ladies drove off, the pretty little head together

*Sweet spiced drink made of honey and hot milk curdled with ale or wine.

with the delicate features and the slender waist vanished almost like
a vision—and there remained only the road, the chaise, the three
horses with whom the reader is familiar, Selifan, Tchitchikov, the desolate flatness of the surrounding fields. Everywhere in life, wherever
it may be, among the coarse, cruelly poor, and dirtily squalid lower
ranks, or among the monotonously frigid and tediously decorous
higher orders—in every class a man is met at least once in his life by
an apparition unlike anything that it has been his lot to see before,
which for once awakens in him a feeling unlike what he is destined
to feel all his life. In every life, joy flashes gay and radiant across the
sorrows of all sorts of which the web of our life is woven, just as
sometimes a splendid carriage with glittering harness, picturesque
horses, and windows flashing in the light suddenly darts by some
poor squalid little village which has till then seen nought but rustic
carts: and long afterwards the peasants stand, hat in hand, gaping
with open mouths, though the wonderful carriage has long since
whirled by and vanished out of sight. Just in the same way this fair
young lady has appeared utterly unexpectedly in our story and vanished again. Had some boy of twenty been in Tchitchikov's place—
an hussar,* a student, or simply a young man beginning his career in
life—my God, what would not have awakened, what would not have
stirred, what would not have spoken in his heart! For long minutes
he would have stood bewildered on the spot, gazing vacantly into the
distance, forgetting the road and the reproofs and chidings that await
him for his delay, forgetting himself, his duty, the world and everything in it.

But our hero was a man of mature years and of a cool and calculating temper. He too grew pensive and reflected but more practi-
cally, his reflections were not so irresponsible but were, one may say,
very much to the point. "A fine wench," he said, opening his snuff-
box and taking a pinch of snuff. "But what is it that is especially fine
in her? What is best in her is that she is evidently fresh from some
school or college, that there is so far nothing of what is called feminine about her, which is precisely what is most distasteful in them.
Now she is like a child; everything about her is simple; she says what
comes into her head, laughs when she is inclined to laugh. Anything

---

*Light cavalry officer in flamboyant uniform.

could be made of her. She might become something wonderful and she might turn out worthless—and she will turn out worthless, too! Wait till the mammas and the aunties set to work on her. In one year they will fill her head with such feminine flummery that her own father will hardly know her. Conceit and affectation will make their appearance; she will begin to move and hold herself according to the instructions she has learned; she will puzzle her brains and consider with whom and how much to talk, how and at whom she must look; every minute she will be afraid of saying more than she ought; she will get caught in the snares herself at last and will end by lying all her life, and the devil knows what she will turn into!" At this point he paused for a minute and then added: "But it would be interesting to know who she is, and what her father is, whether he is a wealthy landowner of respectable character or simply a well-meaning man with a fortune made in the service. Why, supposing there is a nice little dowry of two hundred thousand with that girl, it would make her a very tempting little morsel. She might, so to speak, make the happiness of the right sort of man." The thought of two hundred thousand took such an attractive shape in his mind that he began to be inwardly annoyed with himself for not having ascertained from the postillion or the coachman who the ladies were. Soon however the sight of Sobakevitch's house in the distance distracted his thoughts and made them turn to their invariable subject.

The village struck him as being a fairly large one. Two copses, one of pines, the other of birches, lay like two wings to right and left of it, one darker, one lighter in colour; in the middle was a wooden house with a mezzanine, a red roof, and dark-grey or, to be more accurate, natural-coloured walls; the house was after the style of those that are built amongst us in Russia for military settlements or German colonists. It was noticeable that the architect had been in a continual conflict with the owner's tastes in the building of it. The architect was a pedant and aimed at symmetry, while the owner aimed at comfort and had consequently boarded up all the windows at one side and in place of them had cut one tiny one probably required for a dark loft. The front façade too had not succeeded in getting into the centre in spite of the architect's struggles, for the owner had insisted on rejecting a column on one side, so that instead of four columns as in the original design, there were only three. The yard was enclosed by

a strong and immensely thick wooden fence. It was evident that
Sobakevitch thought a great deal of solidity. Beams heavy and thick
enough to last for centuries had been used for the stables, the barns,
and the kitchens. The peasants' huts in the village were also wonderfully solid: there were no brick walls, carved patterns, or anything
fanciful, but everything was firmly and properly built. Even the well
was made of that strong oak which is usually reserved for mills and
ships. In short, wherever he looked everything was solid and substantial in a strong and clumsy style. As he drove up to the steps he
observed two faces peeping out of the window almost at the same
moment: a woman's face in a cap as long and narrow as a cucumber,
and a man's as full and round as the Moldavian* pumpkins called
gorlyankas out of which the Russians make balalaikas,† light two-
stringed balalaikas, the adornment and delight of the jaunty twenty-
year-old peasant lad, the saucy dandy winking and whistling to the
white-bosomed, white-throated maidens who gather round to listen
to the tinkle of his thrumming. The two faces at the window vanished
simultaneously. A flunkey in a grey livery with a light-blue stand-up
collar came out on to the steps and led Tchitchikov into the hall,
where the master of the house was already awaiting him. Seeing his
visitor, he said abruptly, "Please," and conducted him into the inner
apartments.

When Tchitchikov stole a sidelong glance at Sobakevitch, he
struck him on this occasion as being extremely like a middle-sized
bear. To complete the resemblance his dress coat was precisely the
colour of a bear's skin, his sleeves were long, his trousers were long,
he ambled from side to side as he walked and was continually treading on other people's feet. His face was burnt as dark red as a copper
penny. We all know that there are a great many faces in the world,
over the carving of which nature has spent no great pains, has used
no delicate tools such as files or gimlets, but has simply rough-hewn
them with a swing of the arm: one stroke of the axe and there's a
nose, another and there are the lips, the eyes are bored with a great
drill, and without polishing it off, nature thrusts it into the world,

---

*From Moldavia, historic region in southwestern Russia (now the Republic of
Moldova).
†Russian stringed musical instruments with a triangular body and a guitarlike neck.

saying, "This will do." Just such an uncouth and strangely-hewn countenance was that of Sobakevitch: he held it rather drooping than erect, he did not turn his neck at all, and in consequence of this immobility he rarely looked at the person to whom he was speaking but always stared away at the corner of the stove or at the door. Tchitchikov stole another glance at him as they reached the dining-room; he was a bear, a regular bear! To complete the strange resemblance, his name was actually Mihail Semyonovitch. . . . Knowing his habit of treading on people's feet, Tchitchikov moved his own feet very cautiously and made way for him to go first. Apparently Sobakevitch was aware of this failing and at once asked whether he had caused him any inconvenience, but Tchitchikov thanked him and said that he had so far suffered no discomfort.

When they entered the drawing-room Sobakevitch pointed to an empty chair and again said, "Please." Sitting down, Tchitchikov glanced at the walls and the pictures hanging on them. They were all portraits of gallant heroes, Greek generals painted at full length, Mavrocordato in red trousers and uniform, with spectacles on his nose, Miaoulis, Kanaris.* All these heroes had such thick calves and incredible moustaches that they sent a shiver down one's spine. Among these Greek heroes, goodness knows why, was a portrait of Bagration,† a lean gaunt figure with little flags and cannons below in a very narrow frame. Then followed the portrait of the Greek heroine Bobelina‡ whose leg seemed stouter than the whole body of a dandy such as those that fill our drawing-rooms nowadays. It seemed as though the master of the house, being himself strong and sturdy, desired to have his room decorated with people strong and sturdy also. Near Bobelina, right in the window, hung a cage out of which peeped a thrush of a dark colour speckled with white who was also much like Sobakevitch. The master of the house and his guest had not sat in silence for more than two minutes, when the drawing-room door opened and the lady of the house, a very tall figure in a cap,

---

*Aléxandros Mavrocordáto, Andreas Miaoulis, and Konstantínos Kanáris, heroes in the Greek War of Independence fought against the Ottoman Empire (1821–1829).
†Prince Peter Bagration (1765–1812), Georgian hero in the Napoleonic Wars, killed in the battle of Borodino (the Russian defense of Moscow).
‡Also Bobolina; the embodiment of female strength, derived from Bouboulina Laskarina (1771–1825), Albanian-Greek heroine in the Greek War of Independence.

adorned with home-dyed ribbons, walked in. She entered with dignity, holding her head as erect as a palm-tree.

"This is my Feoduliya Ivanovna," said Sobakevitch.

Tchitchikov stopped to kiss the hand of Feoduliya Ivanovna while she almost thrust it at his lips. As he kissed it he had the opportunity of observing that it had been washed in cucumber water.

"My love," Sobakevitch went on, "let me introduce Pavel Ivanovitch Tchitchikov; I had the honour of making his acquaintance at the governor's and at the police-captain's."

Feoduliya Ivanovna asked him to sit down, like her husband saying no more than "Please," with a motion of her head like an actress in the part of a queen. Then she seated herself upon the sofa, wrapping her merino shawl about her, and sat without moving an eye or an eyebrow.

Tchitchikov again raised his eyes and again saw Kanaris with his thick calves and endless moustaches, Bobelina and the thrush in the cage.

For the space of fully five minutes they all remained silent; the only sound was the tap of the thrush's beak on the cage as he picked up grains from the floor of it. Tchitchikov looked round at the room again and everything in it, everything was solid and clumsy to the last degree and had a strange resemblance to the master of the house. In a corner of the room stood a paunchy walnut bureau on four very absurd legs looking exactly like a bear. The table, the armchairs, the chairs were all of the heaviest and most uncomfortable shape; in short, every chair, every object seemed to be saying, "I am a Sobakevitch too!" or "I too am very like Sobakevitch!"

"We were speaking of you last Thursday at Ivan Grigoryevitch's, I mean the president of the court of justice," said Tchitchikov at last, seeing that no one was disposed to begin the conversation. "We had a very pleasant evening."

"Yes, I wasn't at the president's that day," answered Sobakevitch.

"He is a splendid man!"

"Who's that?" asked Sobakevitch, staring at the corner of the stove.

"The president."

"Well, perhaps he seems so to you. Although he is a freemason, he is the greatest fool on earth."

Tchitchikov was a little disconcerted by this rather harsh description, but recovering himself he went on: "Of course every man has his weaknesses, but the governor now, what a delightful man!"

"The governor a delightful man?"

"Yes, isn't he?"

"He is the greatest ruffian on earth!"

"What, the governor a ruffian!" said Tchitchikov, and was utterly at a loss to understand how the governor could be a ruffian. "I must own I should never have thought so," he continued. "Allow me to observe, however, that his behaviour is not at all suggestive of it: on the contrary, in fact, there is a great deal of softness in him." At this juncture he referred in support of his words to the purses embroidered by the governor's own hands; and alluded appreciatively to the amiable expression of his face.

"He has the face of a ruffian!" said Sobakevitch. "If you put a knife in his hand and let him loose on the public highway he would cut your throat for a farthing, that he would! He and the vice-governor are a pair of them—a regular Gog and Magog."*

"He is on bad terms with them," Tchitchikov thought to himself. "But I'll begin talking about the police-master, I fancy they are friends." "Though as far as I am concerned," he said, "I must own the one I like best is the police-master. Such a straightforward, open character; there is a look of such simple warm-heartedness in his face."

"A scoundrel!" said Sobakevitch with perfect coolness; "he'll betray you and cheat you and then he'll dine with you. I know them all: they are all rascals: the whole town is the same. Scoundrels sit upon scoundrels and prosecute scoundrels. They are all Judases. There is only one decent man among them, the prosecutor, and even he is a pig, to tell the truth."

After such eulogistic though somewhat brief biographies, Tchitchikov saw it would be useless to mention any other officials, and remembered that Sobakevitch did not like to hear any one spoken well of.

"Well, my love, shall we go in to dinner?" said Madame Sobakevitch to her husband.

---

*In the Bible, Ezekiel (chapters 38–39) foresees that Gog, king of Magog, will lead his armies against Israel and be defeated by God.

"Please!" said Sobakevitch. Whereupon the two gentlemen, going up to the table which was laid with savouries, duly drank a glass of vodka each; they took a preliminary snack as is done all over the vast expanse of Russia, throughout the towns and villages, that is, tasted various salt dishes and other stimulating dainties; then all proceeded to the dining-room; the hostess sailed in at their head like a goose swimming. The small table was laid for four. In the fourth place there very shortly appeared—it is hard to say definitely who—whether a married lady, or a girl, a relation, a housekeeper or simply some one living in the house—a thing without a cap, about thirty years of age, in a bright-coloured handkerchief. There are persons who exist in the world not as primary objects but as incidental spots or specks on objects. They sit in the same place and hold their head immovably; one is almost tempted to take them for furniture and imagine that no word has ever issued from those lips; but in some remote region, in the maids' quarters or the storeroom, it is quite another story!

"The cabbage soup is particularly good to-day," said Sobakevitch, taking spoonfuls of the soup and helping himself to an immense portion of a well-known delicacy which is served with cabbage soup and consists of sheep's stomach, stuffed with buckwheat, brains and sheep's trotters. "You won't find a dish like this in town," he went on, addressing Tchitchikov, "the devil only knows what they give you there!"

"The governor keeps a good table, however," said Tchitchikov.

"But do you know what it is all made of? You won't eat it when you do know."

"I don't know how the dishes were cooked, I can't judge of that; but the pork chops and the stewed fish were excellent."

"You fancy so. You see I know what they buy at the market. That scoundrelly cook who has been trained in France buys a cat and skins it and sends it up to the table for a hare."

"Faugh, what unpleasant things you say!" said his wife.

"Well, my love! That's how they do things; it's not my fault, that's how they do things, all of them. All the refuse that our Alkulka throws, if I may be permitted to say so, into the rubbish pail, they put into the soup, yes, into the soup! In it goes!"

"You always talk about such things at table," his wife protested again.

"Well, my love," said Sobakevitch, "if I did the same myself, you might complain, but I tell you straight that I am not going to eat filth. If you sprinkle frogs with sugar I wouldn't put them into my mouth, and I wouldn't taste oysters, either: I know what oysters are like. Take some mutton," he went on, addressing Tchitchikov. "This is saddle of mutton with grain, not the fricassees that they make in gentlemen's kitchens out of mutton which has been lying about in the market-place for days. The French and German doctors have invented all that; I'd have them all hanged for it. They have invented a treatment too, the hunger cure! Because they have a thin-blooded German constitution, they fancy they can treat the Russian stomach too. No, it's all wrong, it's all their fancies, it's all . . . ." Here Sobakevitch shook his head wrathfully. "They talk of enlightenment, enlightenment, and this enlightenment is . . . faugh! I might use another word for it but it would be improper at the dinner table. It is not like that in my house. If we have pork we put the whole pig on the table, if it's mutton, we bring in the whole sheep, if it's a goose, the whole goose! I had rather eat only two dishes, and eat my fill of them." Sobakevitch confirmed this in practice; he put half a saddle of mutton on his plate and ate it all, gnawing and sucking every little bone.

"Yes," thought Tchitchikov, "the man knows what's what."

"It's not like that in my house," said Sobakevitch, wiping his fingers on a dinner napkin, "I don't do things like a Plyushkin: he has eight hundred souls and he dines and sups worse than any shepherd."

"Who is this Plyushkin?" inquired Tchitchikov.

"A scoundrel," answered Sobakevitch. "You can't fancy what a miser he is. The convicts in prison are better fed than he is: he has starved all his servants to death . . ."

"Really," Tchitchikov put in with interest. "And do you actually mean that his serfs have died in considerable numbers?"

"They die off like flies."

"Really, like flies? Allow me to ask how far away does he live?"

"Four miles."

"Four miles!" exclaimed Tchitchikov and was even aware of a

slight palpitation of the heart. "But when one drives out of your gate, is it to the right or to the left?"

"I don't advise you even to learn the road to that cur's," said Sobakevitch. "There is more excuse for visiting the lowest haunt than visiting him."

"Oh, I did not ask for any special . . . but simply because I am interested in knowing all about the locality," Tchitchikov replied.

The saddle of mutton was followed by curd cheese-cakes, each one of which was much larger than a plate, then a turkey as big as a calf, stuffed with all sorts of good things: eggs, rice, kidneys, and goodness knows what. With this the dinner ended, but when they had risen from the table Tchitchikov felt as though he were two or three stones* heavier. They went into the drawing-room where they found a saucer of jam already awaiting them—not a pear, nor a plum, nor any kind of berry—and neither of the gentlemen touched it. The lady of the house went out of the room to put out some more on other saucers.

Taking advantage of her absence, Tchitchikov turned to Sobakevitch, who lying in an easy-chair, was merely gasping after his ample repast and emitting from his throat undefinable sounds while he crossed himself and continually put his hand before his mouth.

Tchitchikov addressed him as follows: "I should like to have a few words with you about a little matter of business."

"Here is some more jam," said the lady of the house, returning with a saucer, "it's very choice, made with honey!"

"We will have some of it later on," said Sobakevitch. "You go to your own room now. Pavel Ivanovitch and I will take off our coats and have a little nap."

The lady began suggesting that she should send for feather beds and pillows, but her husband said, "There's no need, we can doze in our easy-chairs," and she withdrew.

Sobakevitch bent his head slightly, and prepared to hear what the business might be.

Tchitchikov approached the subject indirectly, touched on the Russian empire in general, and spoke with great appreciation of its vast extent, said that even the ancient Roman empire was not so large,

---

*Equal to 42 pounds.

and that foreigners might well marvel at it . . . (Sobakevitch still listened with his head bowed), and that in accordance with the existing ordinances of the government, whose fame had no equal, souls on the census list who had ended their earthly career were, until the next census was taken, reckoned as though they were alive, in order to avoid burdening the government departments with a multitude of petty and unimportant details and increasing the complexity of the administrative machinery so complicated as it is . . . (Sobakevitch still listened with his head bowed), and that, justifiable as this arrangement was, it put however a somewhat heavy burden on many landowners, compelling them to pay a tax as though for living serfs, and that, through a sentiment of personal respect for him, he was prepared to some extent to relieve him of this burdensome obligation. In regard to the real subject of his remarks, Tchitchikov expressed himself very cautiously and never spoke of the souls as dead, but invariably as non-existent.

Sobakevitch still listened as before with his head bent, and not a trace of anything approaching expression showed on his face. It seemed as though in that body there was no soul at all, or if there were, that it was not in its proper place, but, as with the immortal Boney* somewhere far away and covered with so thick a shell that whatever was stirring at the bottom of it produced not the faintest ripple on the surface.

"And so . . . ?" said Tchitchikov, waiting not without some perturbation for an answer.

"You want the dead souls?" inquired Sobakevitch very simply, with no sign of surprise as though they had been talking of corn.

"Yes," said Tchitchikov, and again he softened the expression, adding, "non-existent ones."

"There are some; to be sure there are," said Sobakevitch.

"Well, if you have any, you will doubtless be glad to get rid of them?"

"Certainly, I am willing to sell them," said Sobakevitch, slightly raising his head, and reflecting that doubtless the purchaser would make some profit out of them.

---

*Ogrish character based on Napoléon Bonaparte (Napoléon I, 1769–1821), emperor of the French and enemy of Russia.

"Deuce take it!" thought Tchitchikov to himself. "He is ready to sell them before I drop a hint of it!" And aloud he said, "And at what price, for instance? Though, indeed, it is a queer sort of goods . . . it seems odd to speak of price."

"Well, not to ask you too much, a hundred roubles a-piece," said Sobakevitch.

"A hundred!" cried Tchitchikov, staring into his face, with his mouth open, not knowing whether his ears had deceived him or whether Sobakevitch's tongue in its heavy clumsiness had brought out the wrong word.

"Oh, is that too dear for you?" said Sobakevitch, and then added, "Why, what may your price be then?"

"My price! We must be making some mistake or misunderstanding each other, and have forgotten what it is we are talking about. I protest, laying my hand on my heart, I can offer no more than eighty kopecks a soul,—that's the very highest price!"

"Ech, what an idea, eighty kopecks! . . ."

"Well, in my judgment, I can offer no more."

"Why, I am not selling bark shoes."

"You must admit, however, that they are not men either."

"Do you suppose you would find anybody fool enough to sell you a soul on the census for a few paltry kopecks."

"But excuse me, why do you speak of them like that? Why, the souls have been dead a long while, nothing is left but an insubstantial name. However, to avoid further discussion, I'll give you a rouble and a half if you like, but beyond that I cannot go."

"You ought to be ashamed to mention such a sum. You are haggling, tell me your real price."

"I cannot give more, Mihail Semyonovitch; you may believe my word, I cannot; what cannot be done, cannot be done," said Tchitchikov; he added half a rouble, however.

"But why are you so stingy?" said Sobakevitch; "it really is not dear! Another man would cheat you and sell you some rubbish instead of souls; but mine are as sound as a nut, all first-class: if not craftsmen, they are sturdy peasants of one sort or another. Look here, Mihyeev the wheelwright, for instance, he never made a carriage that wasn't on springs. And they were not like some of the Moscow workmanship, made to last an hour . . . all so solid . . . he lines them himself and varnishes them!"

Tchitchikov was opening his lips to say that Mihyeev had however left this world; but Sobakevitch was carried away, as the saying is, by his own eloquence, and the vehemence and flow of his language was surprising.

"And Probka Stepan the carpenter! I'll stake my head you would never find another peasant like him. What a giant of strength he was! If he had served in the Guards, God knows what they would have given him, over seven foot high!"

Tchitchikov tried again to say that Probka too had departed this life; but such streams of words followed that he had no choice but to listen.

"Milushkin the bricklayer could build a stove in any house you like. Maxin Telyatnikov the bootmaker: no sooner does he put the awl through the leather than it's a boot; and you must be thankful that it is a boot; and he never touched a drop. And Yeremy Sorokoplyohin! That peasant alone is worth all the rest. He traded in Moscow and sent me as much as five hundred roubles at a time in lieu of labour. That's the sort of fellows they are! They are not what a Plyushkin would sell you."

"But excuse me," said Tchitchikov at last, amazed at this flood of eloquence which seemed as though it would be endless. "Why are you enumerating all their qualifications? They are no good now, you know, they are all dead. A dead man is no use even to prop up a fence, as the proverb says."

"Yes, of course they are dead," said Sobakevitch, as though reflecting and recalling the fact that they really were dead; and then he added: "though it must be said, that these fellows who are reckoned alive are not worth calling men, they are no better than flies."

"Still they do exist, while the others are a dream."

"But no, they are not a dream! I tell you, Mihyeev was a man you won't find the like of again! He was such a giant, he couldn't have walked into this room: no, he's not a dream! He had more strength in his huge great shoulders than a horse. I should like to know where else you would find a dream like that!" These last words he uttered, addressing the portraits of Bagration and Kolokotrones,* as commonly happens with people who are talking, when one of them for

---

*Theódoros Kolokotrónis (1770–1843), hero of the Greek War of Independence.

some unexplained reason addresses himself not to the person whom
his words concern but to some third person who happens to be present, even a total stranger from whom he knows that he will receive
no answer, no opinion, no support, though he stares at him as intently as if appealing to him as an arbitrator; and, somewhat embarrassed, the stranger does not for the first minute know whether to
answer him about the business of which he has heard nothing, or to
stay as he is, maintaining perfect propriety of demeanour and afterwards to get up and walk away.

"No, I can't give more than two roubles," said Tchitchikov.

"If you like, that you may not complain that I have asked you too
much and will not show you any consideration, if you like—seventy-
five roubles per soul—it's only because you are a friend really!"

"Does he take me for a fool or what?" Tchitchikov thought to
himself, and then he added aloud: "I am really puzzled: it seems to
me as though we are taking part in some theatrical performance or
farce: that's the only way I can explain it to myself . . . I believe you
are a fairly intelligent man, you have all the advantages of education.
Why, the goods you are selling are simply . . . ough! What are they
worth? What use are they to any one?"

"But you see you are buying them, so they are of use."

At this point Tchitchikov bit his lip and could not think of a suitable answer. He was beginning to say something about private family circumstances but Sobakevitch answered simply:

"I don't want to know your circumstances, I don't meddle in
other people's private affairs, that's your business. You have need of
the souls, I am selling them, and you will regret it if you don't buy
them."

"Two roubles," said Tchitchikov.

"Ugh, really, the magpie knows one name and calls all men the
same, as the proverb has it: since you have pitched on two, you won't
budge. Do give your real price!"

"Oh, deuce take him!" thought Tchitchikov, "I'll give him another half rouble, the cur." "Well, if you like I'll say another half rouble."

"Oh, very well, and I'll give you my final word too: fifty roubles!
It's really selling at a loss, you would never buy such fellows anywhere else!"

"What a close-fisted brute!" Tchitchikov said to himself; and then continued aloud with some vexation: "Why really, upon my soul . . . as though it were something real! Why, I could get them for nothing elsewhere. What's more, any one else would be glad to let me have them simply to get rid of them. Only a fool would want to keep them and go on paying the tax on them!"

"But, you know, a transaction of this kind—I say this between ourselves as a friend—is not permissible everywhere, and if I or some one else were to mention it, such a man would have no security for the purchase or profitable fulfillment of the contract."

"What the devil is he hinting at, the scoundrel!" thought Tchitchikov, and at once brought out with a most unconcerned air: "It is just as you like, I am not buying them from any special necessity as you imagine, but just . . . simply from an inner prompting. If you won't take two and a half roubles, good-bye!"

"There's no wringing it out of him, he's stubborn!" thought Sobakevitch. "Well, God bless you, give me thirty and you shall have them!"

"No, I see you don't want to sell them, good-bye!"

"Excuse me, excuse me," said Sobakevitch, retaining his hold of Tchitchikov's hand and stepping on his foot, for our hero forgot to be on his guard and the punishment for the carelessness made him flinch and stand on one leg. "I beg your pardon! I'm afraid I have caused you discomfort. Please sit down here! Please!"

Whereupon he sat Tchitchikov down in an easy-chair with a certain dexterity, like a bear who has been trained and knows how to turn somersaults and to perform various tricks when he is asked such questions as: "Come show us, Misha, how do peasant women have a steam bath?" or "How do little children steal peas, Misha?"

"I am wasting time really, I must make haste."

"Stay just a minute longer, and I'll say something you would like to hear." At this point Sobakevitch moved to a seat near him, and said softly in his ear as though it were a secret, "Will a quarter suit you?"

"You mean twenty-five roubles? No, no, no! I wouldn't give a quarter of a quarter, I won't add a single farthing."

Sobakevitch did not speak; Tchitchikov too was silent. The silence lasted for two minutes. Bagration with his eagle nose looked down attentively at the transaction.

"What is your final price?" Sobakevitch asked at last.

"Two and a half."

"You have a soul like a boiled turnip. You might at least give me three roubles!"

"I can't."

"Oh, there's no doing anything with you, very well! It's a loss. But there, I'm like a dog, I can't help doing anything I can to please a fellow creature. I suppose I must make out a deed of purchase, so that it may all be done properly."

"Of course."

"And what's more, I shall have to go to the town."

So the business was settled, they both decided to visit the town next day and to arrange the deed of purchase. Tchitchikov asked for a list of the peasants. Sobakevitch readily agreed, went to his bureau at once, and began writing with his own hand not merely a list of all the names but also an enumeration of their valuable qualities.

And Tchitchikov, having nothing better to do, and being seated behind him, scrutinised his ample frame. As he looked at his back, broad as a thickset Vyatka* horse, and at his legs which looked like the iron posts stuck in pavements, he could not help inwardly exclaiming: "Ough, God has been bountiful to you! It is a case of what they call, badly cut but strongly sewn! . . . I wonder whether you were born a bear or have you been turned into a bear by living in the wilds, tilling the cornfields, dealing with peasants, and through all that have you become what they call a 'fist'? But no; I believe you would have been just the same if you had had a fashionable education, had gone into society and lived in Petersburg instead of in the wilds. The only difference is, that now you will gorge upon half a saddle of mutton and grain, and eat cheese-cakes as big as a plate, while in Petersburg you would have eaten cutlets with truffles. As it is you have peasants in your power, you get on well with them and don't ill-treat them because they are yours, and it would be to your disadvantage; but up in town you would have clerks under you whom you would have bullied horribly, reflecting that they were not your serfs, or you would have stolen government money! No, if a man has a close fist there is no making him open it! Or if he does

_____

*Or Kirov, a city about 500 miles northeast of Moscow.

open one or two fingers, it makes it all the worse. If he skims the surface of some branch of knowledge, afterwards when he is in a prominent position, he'll make those who really know something of the subject feel it! And maybe he will say afterwards too: 'Let me show what I can do!' And then he'll invent such a sage regulation that many people will have to smart for it. . . . Ough, if all men were as close-fisted . . ."

"The list is ready!" said Sobakevitch turning round.

"Is it ready? Please hand it over!" He ran his eyes over it and was surprised at its neatness and precision; not only the trade, the calling, the age, and family circumstances were minutely entered, but there were even marginal notes regarding behaviour and sobriety—in fact it was a pleasure to look at it.

"Now for the deposit, if you please," said Sobakevitch.

"What do you want a deposit for? You shall have all the money at once in the town."

"It's always done," protested Sobakevitch.

"I don't know how I am to give it you, I have not brought any money with me. But here, I have ten roubles."

"What's the good of ten? Give me fifty at least."

Tchitchikov was about to protest that he had not got it; but Sobakevitch declared with such conviction that he had, that he brought out another note, saying: "Here is another fifteen roubles for you, making twenty-five altogether. But please give me a receipt."

"Yes, but why do you want a receipt?"

"It's always better to have a receipt, you know. In case of accidents . . . anything may happen."

"Very good, give the money here."

"What do you want the money for? Here it is in my hand. As soon as you have written the receipt, you shall have it the same minute."

"But excuse me, how can I write the receipt, I must see the money first."

Tchitchikov let Sobakevitch take the notes from his hand and the latter, going up to the table and covering the notes with his left hand, with the other wrote on a scrap of paper that a deposit of twenty-five roubles on a purchase of souls had been paid in full. After signing the receipt he looked through the notes once more.

"This note's an old one," he commented, holding one of them up to the light, "rather frayed; but there, one can't look at that between friends."

"The fist, the fist!" Tchitchikov thought to himself, "and he's a brute into the bargain."

"And don't you want any of the female sex?"

"No, thank you."

"I wouldn't charge you much for them. For the sake of our good acquaintance, I will only ask a rouble a-piece."

"No, I have no need of females."

"Well, since you don't want any, it is useless to discuss it. Every one to his taste, one man loves the priest and another the priest's wife, as the proverb says."

"Another thing I want to ask you is that this transaction should be strictly between ourselves," said Tchitchikov as he said good-bye.

"Oh, that is a matter of course. There is no reason to mix a third person up in it; what is done in all straightforwardness between two friends should be left to their mutual friendship. Good-bye. Thank you for your visit; I beg you to think of us again; when you have a free hour, come to dinner and spend a little time with us. Possibly we may be able to be of service to each other again."

"Not if I know it," Tchitchikov thought to himself as he got into his chaise. "He has squeezed two and a half roubles a soul out of me, the damned skinflint!"

He was displeased with Sobakevitch's behaviour. After all, look at it how you would, he was an acquaintance, and they had both met at the governor's and at the police-master's, but he had treated him exactly as though he were a stranger and squeezed money out of him! When the chaise had driven out of the yard he looked back and saw that Sobakevitch was still standing on the steps and seemed to be watching to see which way his guest was going.

"The rascal, he is still standing there!" he muttered through his teeth, and he bade Selifan turn towards the peasants' huts and drive away so that the carriage could not be seen from the house. He wanted to drive to Plyushkin, whose serfs, according to Sobakevitch, were dying off like flies; but he did not want Sobakevitch to know it. When the chaise had reached the end of the village; he called to the first peasant he met, a man who had picked up a very thick log, and

like an indefatigable ant was dragging it on his shoulders along the
road towards his hut.

"Hey, bushy beard! How's one to get from here to Plyushkin's
without passing your master's house?"

The peasant seemed to be perplexed by the question.

"Why, don't you know?"

"No, sir, I don't know."

"Tut, tut! Why, you have grey hairs coming! Don't you know the
miser Plyushkin who doesn't feed his serfs properly?"

"Oh, the . . . in rags and patches!" cried the peasant. He put in a
substantive which was very apt but impossible in polite conversation,
and so we omit it. It may however be surmised that the expression
was very appropriate, for long after the peasant was out of sight,
when they had driven a good way further, Tchitchikov was still
laughing as he sat in his chaise. The Russian people express themselves vividly. And if a nickname is bestowed on any one, it becomes
part and parcel of him, he carries it along with him into the service
and into retirement and to Petersburg and to the ends of the earth.
And whatever dodge he tries to ennoble his nickname, even though
he may get the scribbling gentry for a consideration to trace his pedi-
gree from an ancient aristocratic family, it is all of no use: the very
sound of the nickname, like the caw of a crow, betrays where the bird
has come from. A word aptly uttered or written cannot be cut away
by an axe. And how good the sayings are that come out of the depths
of Russia, where there are neither Germans nor Finns nor any foreigners, but only the native, living, nimble Russian intelligence,
which never fumbles for a word nor broods over a phrase like a sitting hen, but sticks it on like a passport to be carried all one's life,
and there is no need to add a description of your nose or your lips:
with one stroke you are drawn from head to foot!

Like the innumerable multitude of churches and monasteries
with their cupolas, domes and crosses scattered over holy, pious Russia, swarms the innumerable multitude of races, generations and peoples, a many-coloured crowd shifting hither and thither over the face
of the earth. And each people, bearing within itself the pledge of
powers, full of creative, spiritual faculties, of its own conspicuous in-
dividuality, and of other gifts of God, is individually distinguished
each by its own peculiar sayings, in which, whatever subject it de-

scribes, part of its own character is reflected. The sayings of the Briton resound with the wisdom of the heart and sage comprehension of life; the Frenchman's short-lived phrase is brilliant as a sprightly dandy and soon fades away; the German fancifully contrives his intellectually thin sayings, not within the grasp of all; but there are no sayings of so wide a sweep and so bold an aim, none that burst from the very heart, bubble up and vibrate with life like an aptly uttered Russian saying.

CHAPTER 6

Long ago in the days of my youth, in the days of my childhood, now vanished for ever, I used to enjoy going for the first time to an unknown place; it made no difference to me whether it were a little village, a poor, wretched district town, a hamlet, or a suburb, my inquisitive childish eyes discovered much that was of interest in it. Every building, everything that was marked by some noticeable peculiarity arrested my attention and impressed me. Whether it were a brick government building of the usual architecture with half its windows mere blank spaces, sticking up, lonely and forlorn, in the midst of a group of one-storied workmen's cottages with walls of logs and shingled roofs; or a round cupola all covered with sheets of white metal, rising above the snowy, white-washed new church, or a market, or a beau of the district who was in the town—nothing escaped my fresh, alert attention, and poking my nose out of my cart, I stared at the novel cut of some coat, and at the wooden chests of nails, of sulphur, yellow in the distance, of raisins and of soap, of which I caught glimpses through the door of a grocer's shop, together with jars of stale Moscow sweets. I stared too, at the infantry officer who had been cast by fate from God knows what province into the boredom of this remote district, and at the dealer in his long overcoat, flying by in his racing droshky,* and in my thoughts I was carried along with them into their poor lives. If a local official walked by, at once I fell to speculating where he was going, whether it was to spend the evening with some fellow-clerk, or straight home to lounge for half an hour on the steps till the twilight had turned to darkness, and then to sit down to an early supper with his mother, his wife, his wife's sister and all his family, and what their talk would be about, while a serf-girl in necklaces, or a boy in a thick, short jacket, brought in, but only after the soup, a tallow candle in a candlestick that had seen long years of service in the household. As I drove up to some landowner's village, I looked with curiosity at the

---

*Light, two- or four-wheeled open carriage.

tall, narrow, wooden belfry, or at the spacious old church of dark
wood. Through the green of the trees the red roofs and white chimneys of the owner's house gleamed alluringly in the distance, and I
waited with impatience for a gap through the gardens that screened
it on both sides, that I might get a full view of its, in those days
(alas!), not at all vulgar exterior, and from it I tried to guess what the
owner himself was like, whether he was a fat man, and whether he
had sons or a full set of six daughters with ringing girlish laughter
and games, and the youngest sister, of course, a beauty, and whether
they had black eyes, and whether he was a merry fellow himself, or,
gloomy as the last days of September, looked at the calendar and
talked about the rye and wheat, while the young people sat bored.

Now I drive into any strange village with indifference, and with
indifference look at its vulgar exterior; to my cooler gaze it is un-
inviting and does not amuse me, and what in former years would
have set my face working with excitement and roused me to laughter and unceasing chatter now slips by me, and my lips remain sealed
in unconcerned silence. Oh, my youth! Oh, my fresh eagerness!

While Tchitchikov was meditating and inwardly laughing at the
nickname the peasant had given to Plyushkin, he did not notice that
he had driven into the middle of a large village, with a number of
peasant's huts and streets. He was soon, however, roused to notice it
by a rather violent jolting, as they passed over the bridge of logs,
compared with which our town bridge of cobble-stones is nothing.
The logs hop up and down like the keys of a piano, and the incautious traveller gets a bump on the back of his head, or a bruise on his
forehead, or may chance to bite the tip of his tongue very painfully.
He noticed signs of age and decay in all the village buildings; the logs
of which the huts were built were old and dark. Many of the roofs
were as full of holes as a sieve; on some nothing was left but the
ridge-pole and the transverse pieces like ribs. It seemed as though the
owners themselves had removed the laths and shingles, arguing, and
no doubt quite correctly, that as huts cannot be roofed in the rain,
while in fine weather the rain keeps off of itself, there is no need to
mess about indoors, while there is plenty of room in the tavern and
on the high-road—wherever one chooses, in fact. The windows in
the huts had no panes, some were stuffed up with a rag or a coat. The
little balconies with railings which for some inexplicable reason are

put just below the roof in some Russian huts were all aslant and too black to be picturesque, even. In several places immense stacks of corn stretched in rows behind the huts, and evidently they had been standing there for years; in colour they were like an old, badly baked brick, all sorts of weeds were sprouting on the top of them, and bushes growing at the side were tangled in them. The corn was evidently the master's. Behind the stacks of corn and dilapidated roofs two village churches, standing side by side, one wooden and disused, the other built of brick with yellow walls covered with stains and cracks, stood up in the pure air and showed in glimpses, first on the right and then on the left, as the chaise turned in one direction or another. Parts of the owner's house came into sight, and at last the whole of it could be seen where there was a gap in the chain of huts, and there was the open space made by a kitchen garden or a cabbage patch, enclosed by a low, and in places broken, fence. This strange castle, which was of quite disproportionate length, had the air of a decrepit invalid. In parts it was of one storey, in parts of two; on its dark roof, which did not everywhere furnish it with secure protection, there stood two belvederes facing each other, both were infirm, and here and there bare of the paint that had once covered them. The walls of the house showed here and there the bare laths under the plaster and had evidently suffered a great deal from all sorts of weather, rain and hurricane, and the changes of autumn. Of the windows only two were uncovered, the others were closed with shutters or even boarded up. Even the two windows were half blind. On one of them was a triangular dark patch where a piece of the blue paper in which sugar is wrapped had been pasted.

The big overgrown and neglected old garden which stretched at the back of the house, and coming out behind the village, disappeared into the open country, seemed the one refreshing feature in the great rambling village, and in its picturesque wildness was the only beautiful thing in the place. The interlacing tops of the unpruned trees lay in clouds of greenery and irregular canopies of trembling foliage against the horizon. The colossal white trunk of a birch-tree, of which the crest had been snapped off by a gale or a tempest, rose out of this green maze and stood up like a round shining marble column; the sharp slanting angle, in which it ended instead of in a capital, looked dark against the snowy whiteness of the trunk, like a cap or a blackbird. A hop, after smothering bushes of elder, mountain-ash and hazel, and then running along the top of the whole palisade, finally darted upwards and twined round half of the broken birch-tree. After reaching the middle of it, it drooped down from it, caught on to the tops of other trees, or hung in the air, its festoons of delicate clinging tendrils faintly stirring in the breeze. Here and there, the green thicket, lighted up by the sun, parted and exposed the unlighted depths between them, yawning like a dark gulf. It was all plunged in shadow, and in its black depths there were faint glimpses of a narrow path, broken-down railings, a rickety arbour, a decaying willow stump full of holes, a grey-foliaged caragana* thrusting forward like a thick brush from behind the willow, leaves and twigs interlaced and crossing one another, withered from growing so terribly close, and a young branch of maple stretching sideways its claw-like leaves, under one of which the sun, somehow piercing its way, suddenly transformed it into a transparent, fiery hand, gleaming marvellously in that dense darkness. On one side, at the very edge of the garden, a few high-growing aspens above the level of the other trees lifted high into the air immense ravens' nests upon their tremulous tops. From some of them, branches, twisted back but not yet broken off, hung downwards with their withered leaves. In short, it was all beautiful, as neither the work of nature nor that of art is alone, but as only happens when they work together, when nature's chisel gives the final touches to the often unintelligent clumsy work of man, relieves the heavy masses, obliterates the crudely conceived symmetry, the bare gaps through which the plan is too nakedly apparent, and gives a marvellous warmth to all that has been created in the frigid stiffness of calculated neatness and accuracy.

After turning round two or three corners, our hero found himself at last in front of the house, which looked even gloomier at close quarters. The old wood of the gates and fence was covered with green lichen. The yard was crowded with buildings, servants' quarters, barns and storehouses, evidently falling into decay; on the right and the left were gates leading to other yards. There was every indication that things had once been done on a grand scale here, and now every-

---

*Siberian pea tree.

thing looked dejected. There was nothing in sight to enliven the scene, no opening doors, no servants coming out, none of the hurry and bustle of a household. Only the principal gates stood open, and they had evidently been opened merely because a peasant had driven in with a loaded cart covered with sacking; he seemed to have made his appearance expressly to bring life into the dead place; at other times it was evidently kept locked, for a huge padlock hung in the iron staple. At one of the buildings, Tchitchikov soon perceived a human figure wrangling with the peasant. For a long time he could not make out the sex of the figure, whether it was a man or a woman. Its clothes were quite indefinite and very much like a woman's dressing-gown; on the head was a cap such as women wear in the country; only the voice struck him as rather husky for a woman's; "Oh, a female!" he thought, and at once added, "Oh no!" "Of course it's a woman," he said at last after looking more closely. The figure on its side stared intently at him too. It seemed as though a visitor were a strange marvel, for she scrutinised not only him, but Selifan and the horses from their tails to their heads. From the fact that there were keys hanging from her belt, and that she scolded the peasant in rather abusive language, Tchitchikov concluded that this was probably the housekeeper.

"I say, my good woman," he said, getting out of the chaise, "is the master . . . ?"

"Not at home," answered the housekeeper, without waiting for him to finish his question, and then a moment later, added: "What do you want?"

"I have business."

"Go indoors," said the housekeeper, turning round and showing him her back, dusty with flour, and a big slit in her skirt.

He stepped into a wide, dark hall, which struck as chill as a cellar. From the hall he went into a room, which was also dark, with a faint light coming from a big crack at the bottom of the door. Opening this door he found himself in the light, and was startled at the scene of disorder that met his eyes. It looked as though they were having a house-cleaning, and all the furniture were piled up in this room. There was even a broken chair standing on a table, and near it a clock with a stationary pendulum on which a spider had already spun a web. Close by stood a cupboard leaning sideways against the

wall, with old-fashioned silver decanters and china in it. On the bureau, inlaid with a mosaic in mother-of-pearl, bits of which had
fallen out, leaving yellow gaps filled with glue, lay a vast number of
all sorts of things; a pile of closely written papers, covered with a
marble egg-shaped paper-weight, green with age, and an old-
fashioned book, bound in leather with a red pattern on it, a lemon
shrivelled up to the size of a hazelnut, the arm of a broken easy-chair,
a wineglass containing some liquid and three flies, covered with an
envelope, a bit of sealing-wax, a rag that had been picked up somewhere, two pens crusted with ink, dried up as though in consump-
tion, a toothpick yellow with age which the master might have used
to pick his teeth with before the invasion of Russia by the French.*

On the walls there were pictures, hung very close together and
all anyhow. A long engraving, yellow with time and without a glass,
depicting some sort of battle, with huge drums, shouting soldiers in
three-cornered hats and drowning horses, was in a mahogany frame
with thin strips of bronze and bronze discs at the corners. Next it,
filling half the wall, was a huge blackened picture in oils, depicting
flowers, fruit, a cut melon, a boar's head and a duck with its head
hanging down. From the middle of the ceiling, hung a chandelier in
a linen cover, so thick with dust that it looked like a cocoon of a silk-
worm. On the floor lay a heap of coarser articles unworthy of a place
on the table. It was difficult to make out precisely what was in the
heap, for the dust lay on it so thick that the hands of any one who
touched it at once looked like gloves; the most conspicuous objects
in the heap were a piece of a broken wooden spade and the old sole
of a boot. It would have been impossible to say that a living being
was inhabiting this room, if a shabby old skull-cap lying on the table
had not testified to his existence. While Tchitchikov was examining
his strange surroundings, a sidedoor opened, and the same housekeeper that he had met in the yard walked in. But now he saw that it
was more like a steward than a housekeeper; a housekeeper does not
anyway shave a beard, while this person on the other hand did, and
apparently not too often, for his chin and the lower parts of his
cheeks were like those curry-combs made of wire, with which horses

---

*Reference to the disastrous campaign of Napoléon I in 1812, which resulted in his
retreat and the decimation of his huge army.

are combed down in the stable. Tchitchikov, assuming an inquiring expression, waited with patience to hear what the steward would say to him. The steward for his part, too, waited to see what Tchitchikov had to say to him. At last the latter, wondering at this strange hesitation, made up his mind to ask:

"Where is your master? Is he at home?"

"The master is here," said the steward.

"Where is he?" Tchitchikov repeated.

"Why, are you blind, my good sir?" said the steward. "Upon my soul! I am the master!"

At this our hero involuntarily stepped back and stared at him. He had met a good many sorts of people, among them some such as neither the reader nor I are ever likely to see; but he had never seen any one like this before. There was nothing out of the way about his face, it was not unlike that of many lean old men, the only peculiarity was that his chin was very prominent, so that he always had to put his handkerchief on it to avoid spitting on it. His little eyes were not dim with age, but darted about under their overhanging brows like mice when, poking their sharp noses out of their dark holes, pricking up their ears and twitching their whiskers, they peep out to see whether the cat or a mischievous boy is lying in ambush, and sniff the very air with suspicion. His costume was a great deal more remarkable. No effort or investigation could have discovered of what his dressing-gown was composed: the sleeves and the upper part of the skirts were so greasy and shiny that they looked like the polished leather of which high boots are made; at the back instead of two there were four tails out of which cotton wool hung in tufts! Then there was something round his neck, too, which it was impossible to identify: it might have been a stocking, or a bandage or a stomach-belt, but it certainly could not be a cravat. In fact if Tchitchikov had met him thus arrayed outside a church he would probably have given him a copper, for to our hero's credit it must be said, that he had a compassionate heart, and could never refrain from giving a poor man a copper. But before him stood not a beggar but a landowner. This landowner had more than a thousand souls, and one might try in vain to find another with so much corn, grain, flour, simply in stacks, with storehouses and granaries and drying sheds, piled up with such masses of linen, cloth, sheepskins, dressed and undressed, dried fish, all sorts of garden produce and fruits and mushrooms from the woods. If any one had caught sight of him in his work yard where he had stores of wood of all sorts and vessels never used, he might have fancied that he somehow had been transported to the "chip fair" in Moscow, where brisk mothers-in-law repair daily with their cooks behind them to replenish their household stocks, and where wooden articles of all sorts, nailed together, turned, dove-tailed and woven, lie in white heaps—tubs, mincers, buckets, casks, wooden jugs with spouts and without spouts, loving cups, bark baskets, baskets in which the women keep their spinning materials and all sorts of odds and ends, baskets of thin bent aspen wood, baskets of plaited birch-bark and many other articles in use by rich and poor in Russia. One might wonder what Plyushkin wanted with such a mass of things. He could not have used them all in his lifetime, even if his estate had been twice the size it was, but all this was not enough for him. Not satisfied with it, he used to go every day about the streets of his village, peeping under bridges and planks, and everything he came across, an old sole, a peasant woman's rag, an iron nail, a bit of broken earthenware, he dragged home with him, and added to the heap that Tchitchikov had noticed in the corner. "Yonder is the old angler at his sport again!" the peasants used to say when they saw him in search of booty. And indeed there was no need to sweep the street after he had been over it. If an officer riding along the road dropped a spur, the spur immediately found its way to the same heap. If a peasant woman loitering at the well forgot her pail, he carried off the pail too. When, however, a peasant caught him in the act, he gave up his plunder without dispute; but, once it had got into the heap, then it was all over with it: he would swear that the thing had been bought by him at some time from somebody, or that it had come down to him from his grandfather. In his room he picked up everything he saw on the floor, sealing-wax, scraps of paper, feathers, and laid them all on the bureau or on the windowsill.

And yet there had been a time when he was only a careful manager! He was married and the father of a family, and the neighbours would drive over to dine with him and learn from him how to manage an estate with wise economy. The work was done briskly and everything followed its regular course; the mills and the fullers'*

---

*Cloth-fullers, who shrink and thicken woolen cloth.

works were running, the cloth factories, the carpenters' lathes, and the spinning wheels were all busily at work; the master's sharp eye was everywhere looking into everything, and like an industrious spider, he ran anxiously but efficiently from one end to another of his industrial web. His features did not express over-intense feelings, and his eyes were full of intelligence. His words were weighty with experience and knowledge of the world, and his guests were glad to listen to him. The lady of the house, gracious and ready of speech, was famed for her hospitality; two little daughters, both fair and fresh as roses, came out to greet visitors, the son, a free and easy lad, would run in and kiss every one, without considering whether his attentions were welcome. All the windows in the house were open to the light. In the entre-sol* were the apartments of the French tutor, who shaved to perfection and was devoted to shooting: he brought home a woodcock or a wild duck nearly every day for dinner, though sometimes nothing but sparrows' eggs, which he would have made into an omelette for himself, as no one else in the house would touch them. His compatriot, the daughters' governess, lived in the entre-sol also. The master of the house came to dinner in a somewhat shabby but tidy frock-coat: there were no holes in the elbows and no sign of a patch anywhere. But the kind mistress of the house died; the keys and with them the petty cares of housekeeping passed into his hands. Plyushkin became more anxious and, like all widowers, more suspicious and niggardly. He could not altogether depend on his elder daughter, Alexandra Stepanovna, and indeed he was right not to do so, for Alexandra Stepanovna soon afterwards eloped with a lieutenant of a cavalry regiment, goodness knows which, and hastily married him in some village church, knowing that her father disliked officers, and had a strange conviction that they were all gamblers and spendthrifts. Her father sent his curse after her and did not trouble to pursue her. The house became still emptier. Miserliness began to be a more conspicuous characteristic of the master, and developed more rapidly as his rough hair was silvered, for white hair is always the trusty ally of avarice. The French tutor was dismissed, as the time came for the son to enter the service. The governess was turned away, as it appeared she had not been quite exemplary in regard to Alexan-

---

*Mezzanine floor (French), just above the ground floor.

dra Stepanovna's elopement. The son, who had been sent to the chief town of the province to go into the department of justice, which in his father's opinion, was a sound branch of the service, obtained a commission in a regiment instead, and, only after receiving it, wrote to his father for money for his equipment; but naturally all he got was a rebuff. At last, the second daughter, who had remained with him at home, died, and the old man found himself the sole keeper, guardian and master of his riches. His solitary life furnished ample food for his avarice to batten upon, for that vice, as we all know, has the appetite of a wolf and grows more insatiable the more it devours. The human feelings, which had never been very deep in him, grew shallower every hour, and every day something more dropped away from the decrepit wreck. As though expressly to confirm his prejudices against the military, it happened at this time that his son lost money at cards; he sent him a paternal curse that came from the heart, and never troubled himself afterwards to ascertain whether he was alive or dead. Every year more windows were boarded up in the house, at last only two were left, and one of these, as the reader has seen already, was pasted up with paper; every year the important part of the management passed more out of his sight; his petty anxieties were more and more concentrated on the scraps of paper and feathers he picked up in his room. He became more and more uncompromising with the dealers who used to come to purchase his produce, they haggled and haggled and at last threw him up altogether, saying that he was a devil, not a man. The hay and the corn rotted, the stores and stacks decayed into manure only of use for growing cabbages: the flour in the cellars got hard as a stone, and had to be chopped with an axe. It was risky to handle the cloth, linen and home-made materials, for they turned to dust at the touch. By now he had himself forgotten how much he had of anything and only remembered the place in the cupboard where he had put a decanter with a little of some liqueur in it, and the mark he had made on it, that no one might thievishly help himself, and the spot where a bit of sealing-wax or a feather had been laid. And meanwhile the revenue from the estate came in as before: the peasants had to pay the same rent in lieu of labour, every peasant woman had to bring the same contribution of nuts, and to furnish so many pieces of the linen she weaved. All this was heaped together in the storehouses, and all was falling into decay and tatters, and he himself was at last turning into a mere tatter of humanity. Alexandra Stepanovna came on one or two occasions to visit him with her little son, in hope of getting a little help from him; evidently a life on active service with the lieutenant was not as attractive as she had fancied before her marriage. Plyushkin forgave her, however, and even gave his little grandson a button that was lying on the table to play with, but he gave her no money. Another time Alexandra Stepanovna came with two little ones and brought him a cake for tea and a new dressing-gown, for her father was wearing a dressing-gown which was not merely a shocking but positively a shameful sight. Plyushkin fondled both his grandsons and, putting one on his right knee and one on his left, jogged them up and down precisely as though they were on horseback. He accepted the cake and the dressing-gown, but gave his daughter absolutely nothing; and with that Alexandra Stepanovna departed.

And so this was the landowner that stood facing Tchitchikov! It must be said that such a phenomenon is rare in Russia, where every one prefers rather to expand than to contract, and it was the more striking because close by, in the same neighbourhood, there was a landowner who was spending his money right and left with all the devil-may-care recklessness of the old Russian serf-owner, burning his way through life, as the saying is. The passing stranger stopped in amazement at the sight of his dwelling, wondering what sovereign prince had suddenly appeared in the midst of the petty, obscure landowners: the white house with its innumerable chimneys, belvederes and turrets, surrounded by a crowd of lodges and all sorts of buildings for visitors, looked like a palace. Nothing was lacking. There were theatres, balls; every night the garden was brilliantly decorated with lights and lamps, and resounded to the strains of music. Half the province gaily promenaded under the trees, dressed up in their best, and no one felt it strange and sinister when out of the dark shade of the trees a branch stood out theatrically in the artificial light, robbed of its bright green, and the night sky looked darker and more gloomy and twenty times more terrible through it, and the austere tree-tops with their leaves quivering in the heights as they vanished into the impenetrable darkness seemed to resent the tawdry brilliance that lighted up their roots below.

Plyushkin had been standing for some minutes without uttering a word, and still Tchitchikov, distracted both by the appearance of the landowner himself and by all that was in his room, could not think how to begin the conversation. For a long while he could not imagine in what words to explain the object of his visit. He had intended to use some such expression as "that having heard of his virtues and the rare qualities of his soul, he had thought it his duty to pay him his respects in person"; but he hesitated and felt that this was too much. Casting another sidelong look at all the things in the room, he felt that the words "virtues" or "rare qualities of soul," might be suitably replaced by the words "economy" and "good management," and so, adapting his speech accordingly, he said, that, having heard of his economy and rare skill in the management of his estates, he had thought it his duty to make his acquaintance and pay his respects in person. No doubt a better reason might have been found, but nothing else occurred to him at the moment.

To this Plyushkin muttered something between his lips,—he had no teeth,—what it was exactly is not certain, but probably the gist of it was: "The deuce take you and your respects"; but, as hospitality is so traditional a duty among us that even a miser cannot bring himself to transgress its laws, he added a little more distinctly: "Pray sit down!"

"It's a long time since I have seen visitors," he said, "and I must own I don't see much use in them. A most unseemly habit of visiting one another has come into fashion, and it means neglecting one's work . . . and one has to give hay to their horses too! I had my dinner hours ago, my kitchen is humble and in very bad state, and the chimney is completely in ruins: if one were to begin to heat the stove, one would set fire to the place."

"So that's how the land lies!" thought Tchitchikov to himself. "It's a good thing I did eat a cheese-cake and a good slice of saddle of mutton at Sobakevitch's."

"And what is so tiresome is that there is not a bundle of hay on the whole estate!" Plyushkin went on. "And indeed how is one to have any? I have a wretched little bit of land and the peasants are lazy, they are not fond of work, they are always trying to get off to the tavern. . . . If I don't look out, I shall be begging my bread in my old age!"

"I have been told, however," said Tchitchikov modestly, "that you have more than a thousand serfs."

"And who told you that? You ought to have spat in his face when he said that, my good sir. It seems he was jeering, he wanted to have a joke with you. Here they chatter about a thousand serfs, but you should just go and count them, and you'll find nothing of the sort! During the last three years the cursed fever has carried off a terrible number of my peasants."

"You don't say so! And have many died?" exclaimed Tchitchikov with sympathy.

"Yes, many are in their graves."

"And allow me to ask you, how many?"

"Eighty souls."

"No?"

"I shouldn't tell you a lie, my good sir."

"Allow me to inquire too: I suppose that you reckon that number from the time the last census was taken?"

"I should be thankful if it were so," said Plyushkin, "the number dead since then runs up to a hundred and twenty."

"Really! a hundred and twenty?" exclaimed Tchitchikov, and he positively gaped with astonishment.

"I am an old man, sir, and not likely to tell you a lie: I am over seventy!" said Plyushkin. He seemed rather offended by Tchitchikov's almost joyful exclamation. Tchitchikov realised that such lack of sympathy with another man's trouble really was shocking, and so he immediately sighed and said that he deeply sympathised.

"But sympathy is nothing you can put in your pocket," said Plyushkin. "Here there is a captain living near, the devil knows where he has come from; he says he is a relation. It's 'uncle,' all the time, and he kisses my hand; and when he begins sympathising he sets up such a howl that one wants to stuff one's fingers in one's ears. He is all red in the face; he's too fond of good brandy, I'll be bound. No doubt he wasted his money, being an officer, or some stage actress turned his head, so now he has to sympathise!"

Tchitchikov tried to explain that his sympathy was not of the same sort as the captain's, and that he was ready to prove it, not in hollow words, but in action, and, coming straight to business, he announced his readiness to take upon himself the duty of paying the tax for all the peasants who had died in this unfortunate way. The offer seemed to astound Plyushkin. He stared at him with wide-open eyes and finally asked: "Why, have you been in military service, sir?"

"No," said Tchitchikov rather slyly, "I was in the civil service."

"In the civil service," said Plyushkin, and he began munching his lips, as though he were eating something. "But how do you mean? Why, it will be a loss to you?"

"To please you, I am ready to face the loss."

"Ah, my good sir! ah, my benefactor!" cried Plyushkin, not observing in his delight that a piece of snuff of the colour of coffee grounds was peeping out of his nose in a most unpicturesque way, and that the skirts of his dressing-gown had grown apart and were displaying undergarments not at all suitable for exhibition. "You are bringing comfort to an old man! Oh Lord! Oh holy saints! . . ." Plyushkin could say no more. But before a minute had passed, the joy that had appeared so instantaneously on his wooden face just as instantaneously passed away, as though it had never been there, and the anxious expression came into his face again. He even wiped his face with his handkerchief and, rolling it up into a ball, began to pass it over his upper lip.

"How do you mean, if I may make bold to inquire without offending you; do you undertake to pay the tax for them every year, and will send the money to me or to the tax collector?"

"Oh, this is what we will do: we will draw up a deed of purchase of them, as though they were alive, and as though you were selling them to me."

"Yes, a deed of purchase," said Plyushkin; he sank into thought and began again munching his lips. "But you see a deed of purchase is an expense. The clerks have no conscience. In old days one could get off with half a rouble in copper and a sack of flour, but now you have to send them a whole cartload of grain, and add a red note too, they are such money-grubbers. I don't know how it is no one notices it. They might at least say a word of admonition to them, you know you can touch any one with a word, say what you like, but there is no resisting a word of admonition."

"Come, I fancy you would resist it!" Tchitchikov thought to himself, and he at once declared that out of respect for him he was even ready to take the expenses of the purchase upon himself.

Hearing that he was prepared to do this, Plyushkin concluded that his visitor must be a perfect fool, was only pretending to have been in the civil service, and had probably been an officer and dangled after actresses. For all that he could not conceal his delight and called down all sorts of blessings, not only upon him but upon his children, without inquiring whether he had any or not. Going to the window he tapped on the pane and shouted: "Hey, Proshka!" A minute later there was the sound of some one running in hot haste into the hall, moving about there for a long time and tramping with his boots. At last the door opened and Proshka, a boy of thirteen, walked in, wearing boots so huge that they almost flew off his feet at every step. Why Proshka had such big boots the reader may be told at once. Plyushkin kept for the use of all his house serfs, however many they might be, only one pair of boots, which had always to be kept in the hall. Every one summoned to the master's apartments used as a rule to prance barefoot across the yard, to put on the boots on entering the hall and so to appear at the master's door. When he went out, he left his boots in the hall and set off again on his own soles. If any one had glanced out of window in the autumn, especially when the frosts were beginning, he would have seen all the house serfs cutting such capers as the most agile dancer scarcely succeeds in executing at the theatre.

"Just look, my good sir, what a loutish face," Plyushkin said to Tchitchikov, pointing to Proshka's. "He is as stupid as a block of wood, but try putting anything down, he'll steal it in a minute! Well, what have you come for, fool, tell me what?" Here he paused for a space, and Proshka responded with equal silence.

"Set the samovar, do you hear—and here, take the key and give it to Mavra for her to go to the store-room: on the shelf there is a piece of the cake Alexandra Stepanovna brought, it can be served for tea . . . Stay, where are you off to, stupid fool, tut, tut, stupid fool. . . . Is the devil tickling your feet or what? . . . You should listen first. The cake may be a little mouldy on the top, so let her scrape it with a knife, but don't throw away the crumbs; take them to the hens, and mind now, you are not to go into the store-room, my boy, if you do—I'll give it you with a birch, you know, to give you an appetite! You've a fine appetite as it is, so that would improve it! You just try to go into the store-room! I shall be looking out of window all the time . . . You can't trust them with anything," he went on, addressing Tchitchikov, after Proshka had taken himself off with his boots. Then he began looking suspiciously at Tchitchikov, too. Such extraordinary generosity struck him as incredible, and he thought to himself:

"The devil only knows what he is up to; maybe he is only boasting, like all these spendthrifts. He goes on lying and lying, just to talk, and get a drink of tea, and then he will go off!"

And therefore as a precaution and at the same time wishing to test him a little, he said that it would not be amiss to complete the purchase as quickly as possible, since there was no reckoning on anything in human affairs: one is alive to-day but to-morrow is in God's hands.

Tchitchikov expressed his readiness to complete the purchase that very minute, and asked for nothing but a list of all the peasants.

This reassured Plyushkin. It could be seen that he was considering doing something, and taking his keys he did in fact approach the cupboard and opening the door, rummaged for a long time among the glasses and cups, and at last articulated: "Why, there is no finding it, but I did have a drop of splendid liqueur, if only they have not drunk it up, they are such a set of thieves! Oh, isn't this it, perhaps!"

Tchitchikov saw in his hands a little decanter which was enveloped in dust as though in a vest.

"My wife made it herself." Plyushkin went on. "The slut of a housekeeper was for flinging it away altogether and did not even keep it corked, the wretch! Ladybirds and all sorts of rubbish had got into it, but I took all that out and now it's quite clean, and I will give you a glass."

But Tchitchikov tried to refuse the liqueur, saying that he had already eaten and drunk.

"Eaten and drunk already!" said Plyushkin. "To be sure, one can recognise a man of good society anywhere; he does not eat but has had all he wants; but when one of these impostors come, you have to feed him endlessly. . . . That captain turns up: 'Uncle,' he says, 'give me something to eat,' and I am no more his uncle than he is my grandfather; he has nothing to eat at home I expect, so he comes dangling round here! So you want a list of all these wastrels? To be sure, I know I made a list of them on a special bit of paper, so that they might be all struck off at the next revision of the census."

Plyushkin put on his spectacles and began fumbling among his papers. Untying all sorts of papers he regaled his visitor with so much dust that the latter sneezed. At last he pulled out a bit of paper covered closely with writing. It was covered as thickly with peasants' names as a leaf with green fly. There were some of all sorts: Paramons and Pimens and Panteleymons, and there was even one Grigory Never-get-there. There were over a hundred and twenty in all. Tchitchikov smiled at the sight of so many. Putting it into his pocket he observed to Plyushkin that he would have to go to the town to complete the purchase.

"To the town? But how can I? . . . And how can I leave the house? Why, my serfs are all thieves or scoundrels: in one day they would strip me, so I'd have nothing left to hang my coat on."

"Haven't you some one of your acquaintance?"

"Some one of my acquaintance? All my acquaintances are dead or have dropped my acquaintance. . . . Ah, my good sir, to be sure I have!" he cried. "Why, the president himself is a friend of mine, he used to come and see me in old days. I should think I do know him! We were boys together, we used to climb the fences together. Not know him? I should think I do! . . . Shouldn't I write to him?"

"Why, of course, write to him!"

"To be sure, he is a friend! We used to be friends at school."

And, all at once, something like a ray of warmth glided over that wooden face, there was an expression not of feeling, but of a sort of pale reflection of feeling.

It was an apparition, like the sudden appearance of a drowned man at the surface of the water, that calls forth a shout of joy in the crowd upon the bank; but in vain the rejoicing brothers and sisters let down a cord from the bank and wait for another glimpse of the back or the arms exhausted with struggling—that appearance was the last. All is still and the unrippled surface of the implacable element is still more terrible and desolate than before. So the face of Plyushkin, after the feeling that glided for an instant over it, looked harder and meaner than ever.

"There was a sheet of clean paper lying here on the table," he said, "but I don't know what could have become of it, my servants are so untrustworthy!" Thereupon he began looking on the table and under the table and fumbled everywhere, and at last shouted: "Mavra, Mavra!" His summons was answered by a woman with a plate in her hand on which lay the piece of dry cake of which the reader has heard already. And the following conversation took place between them.

"Where did you put that paper, you wretch of a woman?"

"Upon my word, your honour, I have not seen any except the little bit you were pleased to give me to cover the wine-glass."

"But I see from your face that you filched it."

"What should I filch it for? I should have no use for it: I can't read or write."

"That's a lie, you took it to the sacristan! he knows his A B C, so you took it to him."

"Why, the sacristan can get paper for himself if he wants it. He's not seen your bit of paper!"

"You wait a bit. At the dread Day of Judgment, the devils will toast you on their iron forks for this. You will see how they will toast you!"

"Why should they toast me, when I have never touched the paper? Other womanish weaknesses maybe, but thieving nobody has ever charged me with before."

"But the devils will toast you! They will say: 'Here, this is for deceiving your master, you wicked woman,' and they'll toast you on hot coals!"

"And I shall say: 'There's no reason to! upon my word, there's no reason! I didn't take it. . . .' But there it lies yonder on the table; you are always scolding me for nothing!"

Plyushkin did, indeed, see the paper; he stood still for a minute chewing his lips, and then brought out: "Well, why are you running on like that? You are such a stuck-up thing! If one says a word to her, she answers back a dozen. Go and bring a light for me to seal a letter. Stay! You will snatch up a tallow candle; a tallow is so soft; it burns away to nothing, it's a waste; you bring me a burning stick!"

Mavra went out and Plyushkin, sitting down in an armchair and taking up a pen, turned the paper over and over in his hand, wondering whether he could not tear a scrap off it, but, coming to the conclusion at last that he could not, he dipped the pen into an inkstand containing some sort of mildewy liquid with a number of flies at the bottom, and began writing, forming the letters like musical notes, and continually checking the impetuosity of his hand, and preventing it from galloping too freely over the paper, fitting each line close up to the next and thinking, not without regret, that in spite of his efforts a lot of blank space would be wasted.

And could a man sink to such triviality, such meanness, such nastiness? Could he change so much? And is it true to life? Yes, it is all true to life. All this can happen to a man. The ardent youth of to-day would start back in horror if you could show him his portrait in old age. As you pass from the soft years of youth into harsh, hardening manhood, be sure you take with you on the way all the humane emotions, do not leave them on the road: you will not pick them up again afterwards! Old age is before you, threatening and terrible, and it will give you nothing back again! The grave is more merciful; on the tomb is written: "Here lies a man," but you can read nothing on the frigid, callous features of old age.

"And do you know any one among your friends," said Plyushkin as he folded up the letter, "who is in want of runaway souls?"

"Why, have you runaway ones too?" asked Tchitchikov, quickly pricking up his ears.

"That's just it, I have. My brother-in-law did make inquiries: but he says there is no trace to be found of them; of course, he is a military man, he can clank his spurs well enough, but as for legal business . . ."

"And what number may there be of them?"

"Why, there are seventy of those too."

"No, really?"

"Yes, indeed! Not a year passes without some running away. They are a shockingly greedy lot, from idleness they have taken to drinking, while I have nothing to eat myself. . . . Really I would take anything I could get for them. So you might advise your friend: if he can only find one in ten, it will be all profit. You know a serf is worth fifty roubles."

"No, I am not going to let any friend have an inkling of it," thought Tchitchikov to himself: and then he explained that such a friend could not be found, since the expenses of the business would cost more than that, seeing that one had better cut off the skirts of one's coat than not get away from the courts, but if he really was so pressed for money, then he was ready out of sympathy to give . . . but really it was a trifle scarcely worth discussing.

"Why, how much would you give?" asked Plyushkin, and he "went Jewish"; his hands quivered like quicksilver.

"I'd give you twenty-five kopecks the soul."

"And how would you buy them—for ready money?"

"Yes, money down."

"Only, my good sir, considering my great need, you might give me forty kopecks apiece."

"My honoured friend," said Tchitchikov, "I should be glad to pay you not forty kopecks, but five hundred roubles each! I would pay it with pleasure, for I see a good, worthy old man suffering through his own kindness of heart."

"Yes indeed, that's true! It's really the truth!" said Plyushkin, hanging his head and shaking it regretfully. "It's all through kindness of heart."

"There, you see I grasped your character at once. And so I should be glad to give five hundred roubles, but . . . I have not the means. I am ready to add five kopecks so that the souls would be thirty apiece."

"Well, my good sir, as you will, but you might raise it two kopecks."

"I will raise it another two kopecks, certainly. How many of them have you? I believe you said seventy."

"No, altogether there are seventy-eight."

"Seventy-eight, seventy-eight at thirty-two kopecks each, that makes. . . ." At this point our hero thought for one second, not more. "That makes twenty-four roubles, ninety-six kopecks! . . ." He was good at arithmetic. He immediately made Plyushkin write out a list of the serfs and paid him the money, which the latter took in both hands and carried to his bureau with as much care as though he were carrying some liquid and was in fear every minute of spilling it. On reaching the bureau he looked over the money once more and, with the same care, put it in a drawer where it no doubt was destined to be buried, till such time as Father Karp and Father Polikarp, the two priests of his village, came to bury him himself, to the indescribable joy of his son-in-law and his daughter, and possibly of the captain who claimed relationship with him. After putting away the money, Plyushkin sat down in his armchair, and seemed unable to find a subject for further conversation.

"Why, are you going already," he said, noticing a slight movement on the part of Tchitchikov, who was however only intending to get out his handkerchief.

This question reminded him that he really had no reason for lingering. "Yes, I must be off," he said, taking his hat.

"And what about tea?"

"No, I must have a cup of tea with you next time I come."

"Why, I ordered the samovar; I must own I am not very fond of tea myself: it is an expensive drink and the price of sugar has gone up cruelly. Proshka, we don't need the samovar! Take the cake back to Mavra, do you hear? Let her put it back in the same place; no, I will put it back myself. Good-bye, my good sir, and God bless you. And you will give my letter to the president. Yes! Let him read it, he is an old friend of mine. Why, we were boys together!"

Whereupon this strange apparition, this miserable, shrunken old man accompanied him to the gate, after which he ordered the gate to be locked up at once; then he made the round of his storehouses to see whether all the watchmen who were stationed at every corner and had to tap with wooden spades on empty barrels, instead of on a sheet of iron, were in their proper places; after that, he peeped into the kitchen where, on the pretext of ascertaining whether the servants were being properly fed, he had a good feed of cabbage soup and boiled grain, and after abusing every one of them for stealing and bad behaviour, he returned to his room. When he was again alone, he began actually thinking how he could show his gratitude to his guest for his unexampled generosity. "I will give him a watch," he thought to himself, "it's a good silver watch, and not one of your pinchbeck or bronze ones, something has gone wrong with it, but he can have it done up; he is still a young man, so he wants a watch to please his young lady. No," he added, after some reflection, "I had better leave it him in my will that he may remember me."

But, even without the watch, our hero was in the best of spirits. Such an expected haul was a real godsend. And actually, after all, not only dead souls, but runaway ones too, altogether more than two hundred! To be sure, even on his way to Plyushkin's he had had a presentiment that he would get something good, but such a profitable bargain he had never expected. He was exceptionally cheerful all the way, he whistled, played a tune with his fingers, put his fists to his mouth like a trumpet, and at last broke into a song so extraordinary that Selifan listened and listened, and then shaking his head a little, said: "I say, if the master isn't singing." It was quite dusk as they drove into the town. Light was merging into darkness and the very objects merged into indistinct blurs, too. The parti-coloured flagstaff was of an indefinite tint; the moustache of the soldier, standing on sentry duty, seemed to be on his forehead and a long way above his eyes, while his nose had disappeared entirely. The rattle and jolting made it evident that the chaise was rumbling over the cobble-stones. The street lamps were not yet lighted, but, here and there, the windows of the houses began lighting up, and, in the alleys and at the street corners, snatches of talk were audible such as are inseparable from that hour of the day in all towns where there are many soldiers, cab-men, workmen and peculiar creatures in the shape of ladies in red shawls and in slippers with no stockings, who flit about like bats at the street corners. Tchitchikov did not notice them and did not even observe many genteel government clerks with little canes, who were probably returning home from a walk. From time to time exclama-tions, sounds of feminine voices, reached his ears: "That's a lie, you drunken sot, I never let him take such a liberty!" or, "Don't fight, you low fellow, but go along to the police-station; I'll show you!" words, in fact, such as fall like scalding water on the ears of a dreamy youth of twenty, when returning from the theatre with his head full of a street of Spain, a summer night and an exquisite feminine figure with curls and a guitar. What fancies are now floating in his brain? He is in the clouds, or off on a visit to Schiller,* when suddenly the fatal words burst upon him like thunder: and he sees that he is back on earth, and even in the hay market and near a pothouse, and life in its workaday garb flaunts itself before him again.

At last the chaise with a violent jolt seemed to drop into a hole, as it passed in at the gates of the hotel, and Tchitchikov was met by Petrushka, who with one hand held the skirts of his coat, for he could not bear them to fly apart, and with the other began helping his mas-ter out of the chaise. The waiter ran out with a candle in his hand and a napkin over his shoulder. Whether Petrushka was pleased at his

---

*Friedrich Schiller (1759–1805), a great German poet and dramatist, author of *The Robbers* and *Don Carlos*.

master's arrival no one can tell; anyway, Selifan and he winked at each other, and his usually sullen countenance seemed for a moment to brighten.

"Your honour has been away a long time," said the waiter, as he held the candle to light up the stairs.

"Yes," said Tchitchikov, as he mounted the stairs. "And how have you been getting on?"

"Very well, thank God," answered the waiter, bowing. "A lieutenant, a military gentleman of some sort, arrived yesterday and has number sixteen."

"A lieutenant?"

"I don't know who he is, from Ryazan,* bay horses."

"Very well, very well, behave well for the future too," said Tchitchikov, and he went into his room. As he went through the outer room he puckered up his nose and said to Petrushka, "You might at least have opened the windows!"

"I did open them," said Petrushka, but he was lying. And his master knew he was lying, but he did not care to contest it.

He felt greatly fatigued after his expedition. Ordering the very lightest of suppers, consisting of sucking-pig, he undressed immediately after it, and getting under the bedclothes, fell into a sound sleep, fell into that sweet sleep which is the privilege of those happy mortals who know nothing of piles or fleas, or of over-developed intellectual faculties.

---

*City about 120 miles southeast of Moscow.

CHAPTER 7

Happy is the traveller who, after a long and wearisome journey with its cold and sleet, mud, posting-station superintendents waked out of their sleep, jingling bells, repairs, disputes, drivers, blacksmiths and all sorts of rascals of the road, sees at last the familiar roof with its lights flying to meet him. And there rise before his mind the familiar rooms, the delighted outcry of the servants running out to meet him, the noise and racing footsteps of his children, and the soothing gentle words interspersed with passionate kisses that are able to efface everything gloomy from the memory. Happy the man with a family and nook of his own, but woe to the bachelor!

Happy the writer who, passing by tedious and repulsive characters that impress us by their painful reality, attaches himself to characters that display the loftiest virtues of humanity, who, from the great whirlpool of human figures flitting by him daily, has selected only the few exceptions, who has never tuned his lyre to a less exalted key, has never stooped from his pinnacle to his poor, insignificant fellow-creatures, but without touching the earth has devoted himself entirely to his elevated images that are utterly remote from it. His fair portion is doubly worthy of envy; he lives in the midst of them as in the midst of his own family; and, at the same time, his fame resounds far and wide. He clouds men's vision with enchanting incense; he flatters them marvellously, covering up the gloomy side of life, and exhibiting to them the noble man. All run after him, clapping their hands and eagerly following his triumphal chariot. They call him a great world-famed poet, soaring high above every other genius as the eagle soars above the other birds of the air. Young ardent hearts are thrilled at his very name; responsive tears gleam in every eye. . . . No one is his equal in power—he is a god! But quite other is the portion, and very different is the destiny of the writer who has the temerity to bring to the surface what is ever before men's sight and is unseen by their indifferent eyes—all the terrible overwhelming mire of trivialities in which our life is entangled, all that is hidden in the often cold, petty every day characters with which our bitter and dreary path through life swarms, and with the strong hand of a relentless sculptor dares to present them bold and distinct to the gaze of all! It is not for him to receive the applause of the people, it is not his lot to behold the grateful tears and single-hearted rapture of souls stirred by his words; no girl of sixteen, with her head turned, flies to meet him with heroic enthusiasm. It is not his lot to lose himself in the sweet enchantment of sounds he has himself evoked. And lastly, it is not his lot to escape the contemporary critic, the hypocritical callous contemporary critic, who will call his cherished creations mean and insignificant, will assign him an ignoble place in the ranks of writers who have insulted humanity, will attribute to him the qualities of her heroes, will strip him of heart and soul and the divine fire of talent. For the contemporary critic does not recognise that the telescope through which we behold the sun and the microscope which unfolds to us the movements of unnoticed insects are equally marvellous. For the contemporary critic does not recognise that great spiritual depth is needed to light up a picture of ignoble life and transform it into a gem of creative art. For the contemporary critic does not admit that the laughter of lofty delight is worthy to stand beside exalted lyrical emotion, and that there is all the world of difference between it and the antics of clowns at a fair! All this the critic of to-day does not admit, and he will turn it all into the censure and dishonour of the unrecognised writer. Without sympathy, without response, without compassion, he is left by the roadside like the traveller without a family. Hard is his lot and bitterly he feels his loneliness.

And for long years to come I am destined by some strange fate to walk hand in hand with my odd heroes, to gaze at life in its vast movement, to gaze upon it through laughter seen by the world and tears unseen and unknown by it! And far away still is the time when the terrible storm of inspiration will burst into another stream, and my head be wreathed with holy terror and brilliance, and men will hear with a confused tremour the majestic thunder of other words. . . .

But forward! forward! Away with the wrinkles that furrow the brow, away with stern and gloomy looks! Let us plunge at once into life with all its silent clamour and jingling bells, and let us see what Tchitchikov is doing.

Tchitchikov woke up, stretched his arms and legs and felt that he had had a good sleep. After lying for two minutes on his back, he snapped his fingers, and with a beaming face remembered that he had now almost four hundred souls. He jumped out of bed on the spot and did not even look at his face, of which he was very fond, finding, so it appears, the chin extremely attractive, for he very often praised it to some one of his friends, especially if one happened to be present while he was shaving. "Just look," he would say, stroking it with his hand, "what a chin I have: perfectly round." On this occasion, however, he looked neither at his chin nor at his face, but, just as he was, put on his dressing-gown and his morocco boots with decorated tops of many colours (the sort of boots in which the town of Torzhok* does a brisk trade, thanks to the Russians' love of comfort), and forgetting his dignity and his decorous middle age, he pranced like a Scotchman, in nothing but his shirt, across the room in two skips, very neatly striking himself on the back with his heels. Then he instantly set to work. Rubbing his hands before his box with as much pleasure as an incorruptible district judge displays on going into lunch, he at once drew out some papers from it. He wanted to conclude the whole business as quickly as possible without putting it off. He made up his mind to draw up the deed of purchase himself, to write it out and copy it, to avoid the expense of lawyers' clerks. He was quite familiar with legal formalities: he put at the top, in bold figures, the date, then after it in small letters, So-and-so, landowner, and everything as it should be. In a couple of hours it was all done. When afterwards he glanced at the lists, at the peasants who really had once been peasants, had worked, ploughed, got drunk, been drivers, cheated their masters, or perhaps were simply good peasants, a strange feeling which he could not himself comprehend, took possession of him. Each list had as it were an individual character, and through it the peasants themselves seemed to have an individual character, too. The peasants belonging to Madam Korobotchka almost all had nicknames and descriptions. Plyushkin's list was distinguished by the brevity of its style: often only the initial letters of the name

---

*Town about 150 miles northwest of Moscow.

were given. Sobakevitch's catalogue was distinguished by its extraordinary fullness and circumstantial detail; not one characteristic of the peasants was omitted: of one it was stated that he was "a good cabinetmaker," of another it was noted that "he understands his work and does not touch liquor." As circumstantially were entered the names of their fathers and mothers, and how they had behaved: of one only, a certain Fedotov, it was stated: "father unknown; he was the son of the peasant girl Kapitolina, but he was of good character and not a thief." All these details gave a peculiar air of freshness: it seemed as though the peasants had been alive only yesterday. After gazing a long time at their names, his heart was stirred and with a sigh he brought out, "Goodness, what a lot there are of you crowded in here! What did you do in your day, my dear souls? How did you all get along?" And his eyes unconsciously rested on one name. It was Pyotr Savelyev (Never mind the Trough), of whom the reader has heard already, and who once belonged to Madame Korobotchka. Again he could not refrain from saying: "What a long name, it has spread all over the line. Were you a craftsman or simply a peasant, and what death carried you off? Was it at the pothouse or did a clumsy wagon run over you when you were asleep in the middle of the road? 'Probka Stepan, carpenter, of exemplary sobriety.' Ah, here he is, here is Probka Stepan, the giant who ought to have been in the Guards! He went about all the provinces with an axe in his belt and his boots slung over his shoulder, eating a hap'orth of bread and a couple of dried fish, though I bet he carried home a hundred silver roubles in his purse every time, or perhaps sewed up a note in his hempen breeches, or thrust it in his boot. Where did you meet your death? Did you clamber up the church cupola to earn a big fee, or perhaps you even dragged yourself up to the cross, and slipping down from a crossbeam, fell with a thud on the ground and some Uncle Milhey, standing by, simply scratched his head and said: 'Ech, Vanya, you have done the trick this time!' and tying himself to the cord climbed up to take your place. 'Maxim Telyatnikov, bootmaker.' Hey, a bootmaker! As drunk as a cobbler, says the proverb. I know you, I know you, my dear fellow; I can tell you your whole story if you like. You were apprenticed to a German who used to feed all of you together, beat you on the back with a strap for carelessness, and wouldn't let you out into the streets to lark about, and you were a marvel, not an ordinary bootmaker; and the German couldn't say enough in your praise when he talked with his wife or his comrade. And when your apprenticeship was over: 'I'll set up on my own account now!' you said, 'and I won't make a farthing profit at a time like the German, I'll get rich at once.' And so, sending your master a good sum in lieu of labour, you set up a little shop, took a number of orders and went to work. You got hold of cheap bits of rotten leather and made twice their value on every pair of boots, and within a week or two your boots split and you were abused in the coarsest way. And your shop began to be deserted and you took to drinking and loafing about the streets, saying: 'This life's a poor look-out. There is no living for a Russian, the Germans always stand in your way!' What peasant is this? Elizaveta Vorobey? Ough, you plague, you are a woman! How did she get in here? That scoundrel Sobakevitch has done me again!"

Tchitchikov was right, it really was a woman. How she got there there was no knowing, but she had been so skilfully introduced, that at a distance she might have been taken for a man, and the name in fact ended in t instead of a, not Elizaveta but Elizavet. However, he paid no attention to that but crossed it out at once. "Grigory-never-get-there! What sort of a fellow were you? Were you a carrier by trade, did you get a team of three horses and a cart with a cover of sacking, and renounce your home for ever, your native lair, and go trailing off with merchants to the fairs? And did you give up your soul to God on the road, or did your companions do for you on account of some fat red-cheeked soldier's wife, or did some tramp in the forest cast a covetous eye on your leather gloves and your three short-legged but sturdy horses or, perhaps, lying on the rafter bed, you brooded and brooded, and for no rhyme or reason turned into the pothouse, and then straight to a hole in the ice, and vanished for ever! Ah, the Russian people! They don't care to die a natural death! And what about you, my darlings!" he went on, casting his eyes on the page on which Plyushkin's runaway serfs were inscribed: "though you are alive, what is the good of you? You might as well be dead. And where are your nimble legs carrying you now? Did you have a bad time with Plyushkin, or is it simply to please yourselves that you are wandering in the forest and robbing travellers? Are you in prison or have you found other masters and are tilling the land? Yeremy Karyakin, Nikita Flitter and his son, Anton Flitter. One can see by their

very names that they were nimble-footed gentry. Popov, a house-
serf. . . . He must have been able to read and write: I bet he never
took a knife in his hand, but did his thieving in a gentlemanly way.
But then a police-captain caught you without a passport. You stood
your ground boldly when you were examined. 'Whose man are you?'
says the police-captain, flinging some strong language at you on this
appropriate occasion. 'Mr. So-an-so's,' you answer smartly. 'Why are
you here?' says the police-captain. 'Away on leave for a fixed payment,' you answer without hesitation. 'Where is your passport?' 'My
employer, Pimenov, has it.' 'Call Pimenov.' 'Are you Pimenov?' 'I am
Pimenov.' 'Did he give you his passport?' 'No, he never gave me a
passport.' 'Why are you lying?' says the police-captain, with the addition of some strong language. 'Just so,' you answer boldly, 'I did not
give it to him because I got home late, but gave it to Antip Prohorov,
the bell-ringer, to take care of.' 'Call the bell-ringer. Did he give you
his passport?' 'No, I took no passport from him.'

" 'Why are you lying again?' says the police-captain, fortifying
his words with more strong language. 'Where is your passport?' 'I did
have it,' you answer promptly, 'but, maybe I dropped it on the road.'
'And why,' asks the police-captain, again throwing in a little strong
language, 'have you carried off a soldier's overcoat and the priest's
box with coppers in it?' 'Never yet,' you say, without turning a hair,
'have I been mixed up in any sort of dishonesty.' 'Then how is it they
found the overcoat in your possession?' 'I can't say: somebody else
must have brought it.' 'Ah, you brute, you brute,' says the police-
captain shaking his head, with his arms akimbo. 'Rivet fetters on his
legs and take him to prison.' 'By all means, I'll go with pleasure,' you
answer. And then, taking a snuff-box out of your pocket, you genially
offer it to the two veterans who are putting on your fetters, and ask
them how long they have left the army and what wars they were in.
And then you settle down in prison till your case comes on for trial.
And the judge orders that you are to be taken from Tsarevo-
Kokshaisk* prison to the prison of some other town, and from there
the court sends you on to Vesyegonsk,† and you move about from

---

*Town (now called Yoshkar-Ola) in eastern Russia, between Nizhniy Novgorod and
Kirov.
†Town about 200 miles north of Moscow.

prison to prison, and say when you have inspected your new abode: 'Well, the Vesyegonsk prison is smarter; there is room even for a game of skittles* there, and there's more company."

"Abukum Fryrov! What about you, my boy? Where are you wandering now? Have you drifted to the Volga, fallen in love with the free life and joined the hauliers?" . . . At this point Tchitchikov stopped and sank into the daydream. What was he dreaming about? Was he dreaming of the lot of Abakum Fyrov, or was he simply dreaming on his own account as every Russian dreams, whatever may be his years, his rank, and condition, when he thinks of the reckless gaiety of a free life. And indeed, where is Fyrov now? He leads a gay and jolly life on the corn wharf, bargaining with the merchants. Flowers and ribbons on their hats, the whole gang of hauliers are merry, taking leave of their wives and mistresses, tall, well-made women in beads and ribbons; there are dances and songs; the whole place is surging with life, while to the sound of shouts and oaths and words of encouragement, the porters hooking some nine poods on their backs, pour peas and wheat rattling into the deep holds, pile up bags of oats and corn, and the heaps of sacks, piled up in a pyramid like cannon balls, are seen all over the quay, and the huge arsenal of grain towers up immense till it is all loaded into the deep holds, and, with the melting of the ice in spring, the endless fleet files away. Then you get to work, you hauliers! and all together, just as before you made merry, you set to, toiling and sweating, pulling at the strap, to the sound of a song as unending as Russia!

"Aha! Twelve o'clock!" said Tchitchikov, at last, looking at his watch. "Why have I been dawdling like this? It wouldn't have been so bad, if I had been doing something, but, for no rhyme or reason, at first I set to spinning yarns and then fell to dreaming. What a fool I am, really!" Saying this he changed his Scotch costume for a European one, drew tightly the buckle over his somewhat round stomach, sprinkled himself with eau-de-Cologne, picked up his warm cap, and with his papers under his arm, went off to the government offices to complete the deed of purchase. He made haste, not because he was afraid of being late—he was not afraid of being late, for he knew the president, and the latter could prolong or curtail the sitting to please

---

*Bowling game in which a wooden ball is used to knock down pins.

himself, like Homer's Zeus, who lengthened the days or brought on night prematurely when he wanted to cut short the battle of his favourite heroes, or to give them an opportunity to fight to a finish— but he felt a desire to get the business over as quickly as possible; he felt uneasy and uncomfortable until it was done, he was haunted by the thought that the souls were not quite real, and that it was always as well to get a load of that sort off his back as quickly as possible. Reflecting on these things and at the same time pulling on his shoulders his bearskin overcoat, covered with brown cloth, he reached the street, and, instantly on turning into a side street, met another gentleman in a bearskin coat, covered with brown cloth and a warm cap with earflaps. The gentleman cried out—it was Manilov. They immediately folded each other in a mutual embrace, and remained clasped in each other's arms for five minutes in the street. Their kisses were so ardent on both sides that their front teeth ached all the rest of the day. Manilov's delight was so great that only his nose and his lips remained in his face, his eyes completely disappeared. For a quarter of an hour he held Tchitchikov's hand clasped in both of his and made it terribly hot. In the most refined and agreeable phrases, he described how he had flown to embrace Pavel Ivanovitch; his speech wound up with a compliment only suitable for a young lady at a dance. Tchitchikov opened his mouth without knowing how to thank him, when Manilov took from under his fur coat a roll of paper tied up with pink ribbon.

"What is that?"

"The peasants."

"Ah!" he immediately unfolded it, ran his eyes over it, and admired the neatness and beauty of the handwriting. "It's well written," he said, "there's no need to copy it. And a margin ruled all round it! Who made that margin so artistically?"

"You mustn't ask," said Manilov.

"You?"

"My wife."

"Oh, dear, I am really ashamed to have given so much trouble."

"Nothing is a trouble for Pavel Ivanovitch!"

Tchitchikov bowed his acknowledgment. Learning that he was going to the government offices to complete the purchase, Manilov expressed his readiness to accompany him. The friends took each the other's arm and walked on together. At the slightest rise in the ground, whether it was a hillock or a step, Manilov supported Tchitchikov and almost lifted him up, saying with an agreeable smile, as he did so, that he could not let Pavel Ivanovitch hurt his precious foot. Tchitchikov was abashed, not knowing how to thank him and conscious that he was no light weight. Paying each other these attentions they reached at last the square in which the government offices were to be found in a big three-storied brick house, painted white as chalk all over, probably as a symbol of the purity of heart of the various departments located in it. The other buildings in the square were out of keeping with the huge brick house. They were a sentry-box at which a soldier was standing with a gun, a cabstand, and lastly a long fence adorned with the inscriptions and sketches in charcoal and chalk usual on fences. There was nothing else in this desolate or, as the expression is among us, picturesque place. From the windows of the second and third storeys, the incorruptible heads of the votaries of Themis* were thrust out and instantly disappeared again: probably their chief entered the room at the moment. The friends rather ran than walked up the stairs, for Tchitchikov, trying to avoid being supported by Manilov, quickened his pace, while Manilov dashed forward, trying to assist Tchitchikov, that he might not be tired, so both the friends were breathless when they reached the dark corridor at the top. The eye was not impressed with the high degree of cleanliness either of the corridor or of the rooms. At that time, they did not trouble about it and what was dirty remained dirty, and no attempt was made at external charm. Themis received her visitors, just as she was, in negligée and dressing-gown. The offices through which our heroes passed ought to be described, but our author cherishes the deepest awe for all such places. If he has chanced to pass through them even when they were in their most brilliant and dignified aspect with polished floors and tables, he has tried to hasten through them as quickly as he could, with bowed head and eyes meekly cast down, and so he has not the slightest idea how flourishing and prosperous it all looked.

Our hero saw a vast amount of paper, rough drafts and fair

---

*Titaness of classical mythology; the personification of justice, who summons assemblies of men.

copies, bent heads, thick necks, dress coats, frock coats of provincial cut, even a light grey jacket which stood out conspicuously among the others, and the wearer of which, with his head on one side and almost touching the paper, was writing in a bold and flourishing hand a report on a successful lawsuit concerning misappropriation of land or the inventory of an estate, of which a peaceable country gentleman had taken possession, and on which he had spent his life, maintained himself, his children and his grandchildren while the lawsuit went on over his head: and brief phrases uttered in a husky voice were audible by snatches: "Oblige me with case No. 368, Fedosey Fedoseyitch!" "You always carry off the cork of the office inkpot!" From time to time a more majestic voice, doubtless that of one of the chiefs, rang out peremptorily: "Copy it out again, or they shall take your boots away, and you shall stay here for six days and nights with nothing to eat." There was a great scratching of pens, which sounded like a cartful of brushwood driving through a copse a quarter of a yard deep in dead leaves.

Tchitchikov and Manilov went up to the first table, where two clerks of tender years were sitting, and inquired: "Allow me to ask where is the business of deeds of sale transacted here?"

"Why, what do you want?" asked both the clerks, turning round.

"I want to make an application."

"Why, what have you bought?"

"I want first to know where is the table for matters relating to sales—here or in some other office?"

"Why, tell me first what you are buying, and at what price, and then we can tell you where; but we can't tell without."

Tchitchikov saw at once that the clerks were inquisitive, like all young clerks, and trying to give more importance and consequence to their duties.

"Look here, gentlemen," he said, "I know perfectly well that all business relating to the purchase of serfs, irrespective of the price paid, is transacted in the same office, and so I beg you to point out which is the table, and, if you don't know what is done in your office, we will ask some one else." The clerks made no reply, one of them merely jerked his finger towards a corner of the room, where an old man was sitting at a table making notes on some official paper.

Tchitchikov and Manilov passed between the tables and went straight up to him. The old man became deeply absorbed in his work.

"Allow me to ask," said Tchitchikov with a bow, "is this where I have to apply concerning deeds of sale?"

The old man raised his eyes and brought out deliberately: "This is not the place to apply concerning deeds of sale."

"Where then?"

"In the sales section."

"And where is that section?"

"At Ivan Antonovitch's table."

"And where is Ivan Antonovitch?"

The old man jerked his finger towards another corner of the room. Tchitchikov and Manilov made their way to Ivan Antonovitch. Ivan Antonovitch had already cast a glance behind him and stolen a sidelong look at them, but became instantly more deeply engrossed than ever in his writing.

"Allow me to ask," said Tchitchikov with a bow, "is this the right table to apply to concerning the sale of serfs?"

Ivan Antonovitch appeared not to hear the question and became absolutely buried in his papers, making no response whatever. It could be seen at once that he was a man of reasonable years, very different from a young chatterbox and featherhead. Ivan Antonovitch seemed to be a man of over forty; his hair was thick and black; all the outline of his face stood out prominently, and ran out to meet his nose, in short it was the sort of face that is popularly called a "jug snout."

"Allow me to ask, is this the section for business relating to the purchase of serfs?" said Tchitchikov.

"Yes," said Ivan Antonovitch, turning his jug snout, but going on with his writing.

"Well, this is the business I have come about; I have bought peasants from different landowners of this district; the deed of purchase is here, I have only to complete the formalities."

"And are the sellers here in person?"

"Some are here, and from others I have an authorisation."

"And have you brought an application?"

"I have the application too. I should be glad. . . . I am obliged to be in haste . . . so would it be possible, for instance, to complete the business to-day?"

"Oh, to-day! . . . It can't be done to-day," said Ivan Antonovitch, "inquiries must be made, we must know whether there are any impediments."

"It may hasten matters, however, if I mention that Ivan Grigoryevitch, the president, is a great friend of mine. . . ."

"But Ivan Grigoryevitch is not the only one, you know; there are other people too," Ivan Antonovitch said surlily.

Tchitchikov understood the hint Ivan Antonovitch had given him, and said: "Other people will not be the worse for it either; I've been in the service, I understand business. . . ."

"Go to Ivan Grigoryevitch," said Ivan Antonovitch in a somewhat more friendly voice. "Let him give the order to the proper quarter, it is not in our hands."

Tchitchikov took a note out of his pocket and put it before Ivan Antonovitch, who completely failed to notice it, and instantly put a book over it. Tchitchikov was about to point it out to him, but with a motion of his head Ivan Antonovitch gave him to understand that there was no need for him to point it out.

"Here, he'll show you to the office," said Ivan Antonovitch, with a nod of his head, and one of the votaries standing near—he had sacrificed so zealously to Themis that his sleeves were in holes at the elbows and the lining was sticking out, for which sacrifices he had been rewarded with the grade of collegiate registrar—performed for our friends the office that Virgil once performed for Dante,* and brought them to an apartment in which there was one roomy armchair, and, in it, solitary as the sun, the president sat at a table behind a Double Eagle and two thick books. In this place the new Virgil was so overcome by awe that he did not venture to set foot within its portals, but turned round, displaying his back worn as threadbare as a bit of matting, and with a hen's feather sticking on it. On entering the office, they saw that the president was not alone. With him was sitting Sobakevitch, completely screened by the Double Eagle. The entrance of the guests was greeted with an exclamation, the presidential

---

*In the Italian poet Dante's *The Divine Comedy* (c.1310–1314), the Roman poet Virgil guides Dante through hell.

chair was noisily pushed back. Sobakevitch, too, got up from his chair, and became visible from all sides, with his long sleeves. The president clasped Tchitchikov in his arms, and the room resounded with kisses; they inquired after each other's health; it appeared that both were suffering from pains in the back, which were at once set down to a sedentary life. The president seemed to have been already informed of the purchase by Sobakevitch, for he began congratulating our hero, which at first rather embarrassed the latter, especially when he saw Sobakevitch and Manilov, two vendors, with each of whom the business had been transacted in private, now standing face to face. He thanked the president, however, and addressing Sobakevitch, asked: "And how are you?"

"Thank God, I have nothing to complain of," said Sobakevitch. And certainly he had nothing to complain of. Iron might as soon catch cold and cough, as that marvellously constituted gentleman.

"Yes, you have always been famous for your health," said the president. "And your good father was just as strong."

"Yes, he used to tackle a bear alone," answered Sobakevitch.

"I believe you could knock a bear down alone, too," said the president, "if you cared to tackle him."

"No, I couldn't," said Sobakevitch, "my father was stronger than I am." And with a sigh, he went on: "No, people aren't the same as they used to be; take my life, for instance, what can one say for it? It's not up to much. . . ."

"What's wrong with your life?" said the president.

"It's all wrong, it's all wrong," said Sobakevitch, shaking his head. "Only think, Ivan Grigoryevitch: I am fifty and I have never been ill in my life; I might at least have had a sore throat or a boil or a carbuncle. . . . No, it will bring me no good. Some day I shall have to pay for it." Here Sobakevitch sank into melancholy.

"What a fellow!" Tchitchikov and the president thought simultaneously, "what will he grumble at next?"

"I have a letter for you," said Tchitchikov, taking Plyushkin's letter out of his pocket.

"From whom?" said the president, and breaking the seal he exclaimed, "Oh, from Plyushkin! So he is still freezing on in life. What a fate! A most intelligent man he used to be and very wealthy! And now . . ."

"He is a cur," said Sobakevitch, "a scoundrel. He has starved his peasants to death."

"Certainly, certainly," said the president, reading the letter. "I am ready to act for him. When do you want to complete the purchase, now or later?"

"Now," said Tchitchikov. "I will even ask you if possible to have it done to-day, as I should like to leave the town to-morrow. I have brought the deeds of purchase and my application."

"That's all right, only, say what you like, we are not going to let you go so soon. The purchase shall be completed to-day, but you must stay with us a little all the same. I'll give the order at once," he said, and opened the door of an office filled with clerks who might be compared to industrious bees busy upon their combs, if indeed honeycomb can be compared with legal duties. "Is Ivan Antonovitch there?"

"Yes, here," answered a voice from within.

"Kindly send him here."

Ivan Antonovitch, the "jug snout" with whom the reader is already familiar, entered the presidential chamber, making a respectful bow.

"Here, Ivan Antonovitch, take all these deeds of purchase. . . ."

"And don't forget, Ivan Grigoryevitch," put in Sobakevitch, "we must have witnesses, two at least for each party. Send now to the prosecutor: he is a man of leisure and no doubt he is at home now. Zolotuha the attorney, the most grasping scoundrel on earth, does all his work for him. The inspector of the medical board is another gentleman of leisure and sure to be at home, unless he has gone off somewhere for a game of cards; and there are lots of others, too, somewhat nearer, Truhatchevsky, Byegushkin—they all cumber the earth and do nothing."

"Just so, just so," said the president, and at once sent a messenger to fetch them all.

"Another request I have to make of you," said Tchitchikov: "send for the authorised representative of a lady from whom I have also made purchases, the son of Father Kirill, the head priest, he is employed here."

"To be sure, we will send for him too," said the president, "everything shall be done, and do not give anything to the clerks; that

I beg of you. My friends are not to pay." Saying this he at once gave some order to Ivan Antonovitch, which evidently did not please him. The purchase of serfs evidently made a good impression on the president, especially when he saw that the purchases mounted up to a hundred thousand roubles. For some minutes he looked into Tchitchikov's face with an expression of great satisfaction, and at last said:

"Well, I must say! That's the way to do things, Pavel Ivanovitch! Well, you have got something worth having."

"Yes, I have," answered Tchitchikov.

"It's a good deed, it's a good deed really."

"Yes, I see myself that I could not do anything that would be better. In any case a man's goal remains undefined, if he does not firmly take his stand at last on a solid foundation and not on some free-thinking chimera of youth."

Hereupon he very appropriately fell to abusing the liberalism of all young people—not without reason, indeed. But it is a remarkable fact that there was all the while a lack of assurance in his words, as though he were saying to himself: "Ah, my lad, you are lying and lying hard too!"

He did not even glance at Sobakevitch or Manilov for fear of detecting something in their faces. But he had no need to be afraid. Sobakevitch's face did not stir a muscle, while Manilov, enchanted by his phrases, merely nodded his head approvingly in the attitude of a musical amateur when a prima donna outdoes the violin and shrills out a note higher than any bird's throat could produce.

"But why don't you tell Ivan Grigoryevitch," Sobakevitch put in, "what sort of stuff you have got? And you, Ivan Grigoryevitch, why don't you ask what his new acquisitions are like? They are something like peasants! Real gems! Do you know I have sold him Miheyev, my coachbuilder?"

"You don't mean to say you have sold your Miheyev?" said the president. "I know Miheyev the coachbuilder, a splendid craftsman; he did up my light cart. But, excuse me, how's that . . . Why, you told me that he was dead. . . ."

"Who? Miheyev dead?" said Sobakevitch, without a trace of embarrassment. "It's his brother that's dead, but he is full of life and better than he has ever been. The other day he made me a chaise better than anything they make in Moscow. He really ought to be working for the Tsar."

"Yes, Miheyev is a fine craftsman," said the president, "and indeed I wonder you could bring yourself to part with him."

"If it were only Miheyev! but Stepan Probka, my carpenter, Milushkin, my brickmaker, Maxim Telyatnikov, my bootmaker. They are all gone, I have sold them all!" And when the president asked him why he had got rid of them, considering that they were craftsmen whose work was essential for the house and estate, Sobakevitch answered with a wave of his hand: "Well, it was simply my foolishness; 'Come, I'll sell them,' I thought, and I sold them in my foolishness." Thereupon he hung his head as though he were regretting what he had done and added: "Here my hair is turning grey, but I have got no sense yet."

"But excuse me, Pavel Ivanovitch," said the president, "how is it you are buying peasants without land? Are you going to settle them elsewhere?"

"Yes."

"Well, that's a different matter; in what part of the country?"

"In the Kherson province."*

"Oh, there is excellent land there!" said the president, and referred with great appreciation to the luxuriant growth of the grass in that district. "And have you sufficient land?"

"Yes, as much as I shall need for the peasants I have bought."

"Is there a river or a pond?"

"There is a river. There is a pond too, though," Tchitchikov chanced to look at Sobakevitch, and, although Sobakevitch was as immovable as ever, he could read in his face: "Oh, you are lying! I doubt whether there is a river or a pond, or any land at all."

While the conversation continued, the witnesses began to turn up, one by one, the winking prosecutor, already known to the reader, the inspector of the medical board, Truhatchevsky, Byegushkin and the others whom Sobakevitch had described as cumberers of the earth. With some of them Tchitchikov was quite unacquainted. The number was made up by taking some clerks from the office. Not only the son of Father Kirill but Father Kirill himself was brought. Each of

---

*Rich agricultural province in southern Ukraine.

the witnesses put down his name with all his grades and qualifications, some in an upright hand, others in a slanting handwriting, others forming letters almost upside down, such as had never been seen in the Russian alphabet. Ivan Antonovitch, known already to the reader, got through the business very rapidly, the purchase deeds were drawn up, revised, entered in a book and wherever else was necessary, and the half per cent, and charge for publication in the *Gazetteer* were made out, and Tchitchikov had to pay the merest trifle. The president even gave orders that only half the usual dues should be charged to him, and the other half was in some mysterious way transferred to the account of some other applicant.

"And now," said the president when all the formalities were over, "all that is left to do is to 'sprinkle' the purchase."

"I am quite ready," said Tchitchikov. "You have only to name a time. It would be remiss if for such excellent company I did not uncork two or three bottles of fizz."

"No, you have got it wrong," said the president, "we'll stand the fizz: that is what we ought to do, it is our duty. You are our guest, it is for us to entertain you. Do you know what, gentlemen? For the time being, this is what we will do, we'll go, all of us as we are, to the police-master; he's our wonder-worker; he has only to wink as he walks through the fish market or by the wine merchants; and we shall have a grand lunch, don't you know! And a little game of whist for the occasion."

No one could refuse such a proposition. The mere mention of the fish market gave the witnesses an appetite; they all picked up their hats and caps, and the presidential office was closed. As they walked through the clerks' rooms, Ivan Antonovitch, the jug scout, bowing politely, said on the quiet to Tchitchikov: "You have bought peasants for a hundred thousand and only twenty-five roubles for my trouble."

"But what sort of peasants are they?" Tchitchikov answered, also in a whisper, "a wretched, good-for-nothing lot, not worth half that." Ivan Antonovitch saw that he was a man of strong character and would not give more.

"And what made you buy souls from Plyushkin?" Sobakevitch whispered in his other ear.

"And why did you stick in Vorobey?" Tchitchikov retorted.

"What Vorobey?" said Sobakevitch.

"Why a woman, Elizaveta Vorobey, and you left out the *a* at the end of her name, too."

"No, I did not stick in any Vorobey," said Sobakevitch, and he walked off to rejoin the others.

The visitors arrived all together at the police-master's door. The police-master certainly was a wonder-worker: as soon as he heard what was wanted he called a policeman, a smart fellow in polished high boots, and seemed to whisper only a couple of words in his ear, merely adding: "understand?" and at once, while the guests were playing whist, on the table in the next room there appeared a great sturgeon, dried salmon, pressed caviare and fresh caviare, herrings, star sturgeon, cheese, smoked tongue and dried sturgeon, all this came from the direction of the fish market. Then came various supplementary dishes created in the kitchen; a pie, made of the head and trimmings of a giant sturgeon, another pie made of mushrooms, tarts, buttercakes, fritters. The police-master was in a sense the father and benefactor of the town. Among the people of the town, he was as though in the bosom of his family, and looked after the shops and bazaar as though they were his own storeroom. Altogether, he was, as the saying is, the right man in the right place, and understood his duties to perfection. It was hard, indeed, to say whether it was he who was created for his job or his job for him. His duties were so ably performed, that his income was double that of any of his predecessors, and at the same time he had won the love of the whole town. The merchants particularly loved him, just because he was not proud, and indeed he stood godfather to their children, and was friendly and convivial with them, though he did at times fleece them dreadfully, but he did it extremely cleverly. He would slap a man on the shoulder and laugh, treat him to tea, promise to come and play draughts, inquire about everything, how business was doing, and why and wherefore; if he heard that a child was ailing, he would advise a medicine. In short, he was a jolly fellow! He drove in his racing sledge and gave orders, and at the same time would drop a word here and there: "I say, Mihyevitch, you and I ought to finish our rubber one of these days." "Yes, Alexey Ivanovitch," the man would answer, taking off his hat, "we ought to." "Hey, Ilya Paramonitch, old man, come round and have a look at my trotting horse, he'll beat yours in a race, and you must put yours in a racing droshky: we'll try him." The merchant, who was mad on trotting horses, would smile at this with peculiar relish and, stroking his beard, say: "We'll try him, Alexey Ivanovitch." Even the shopmen, who usually stood hat in hand at such times, looked at one another delighted, and seemed as though they would say: "Alexey Ivanovitch is a splendid man!" In short he had succeeded in gaining great popularity and it was the opinion of the merchants, that though Alexey Ivanovitch "does take his share he never gives you away."

Observing that the savouries were ready, the police-master suggested that they should finish their game after lunch, and they all trooped into the room, the smell issuing from which had begun some time previously to tickle their noses agreeably, and in at the door of which Sobakevitch had for some time been peeping, having noted from a distance the sturgeon lying on a big dish. After drinking a glass of a dark vodka, of that olive colour which is only seen in the transparent Siberian stones of which seals are carved in Russia, the guests approached the table from all sides, with forks in their hands and began to display, as the saying is, each his character and propensities, one falling on the caviare, another on the dried salmon, another on the cheese. Sobakevitch, paying no attention to all these trifles, established himself by the sturgeon, and while the others were drinking, talking and eating, he in a little over a quarter of an hour had made his way through it, so that when the police-master recollected it, and saying: "And what do you think, gentlemen, of this product of nature?" went up, fork in hand, with others of the company towards it, he saw that nothing was left of the product of nature but its tail, while Sobakevitch effaced himself, and as though it were not his doing, went up to a dish at a little distance from the rest, and stuck his fork into some little dried fish. Having had enough with the sturgeon, Sobakevitch sat down in an easy-chair, ate and drank nothing more; he simply frowned and blinked. The police-master was apparently not given to sparing the wine; the toasts were innumerable. The first toast was, as the reader can probably guess for himself, drunk to the health of the new Kherson landowner, then to the prosperity of his peasants and their successful settlement in their new home, then to the health of that fair lady, his future bride, which elicited an agreeable smile from our hero. The company surrounded him on all sides and began earnestly pleading with him to remain with them, if only for another fortnight: "Come, Pavel Ivanovitch! say what you will, to go off like this, it's just cooling the hut for nothing as the saying is: coming to the door and going back again! Come, you must stay a little time with us! We'll make a match for you. We will, Ivan Grigoryevitch, won't we, we'll make a match for him?"

"We will, we will," the president agreed. "You may struggle hand and foot, but we will marry you all the same! No, my good sir, once you are here, it is no good your complaining. We are not to be trifled with."

"Why struggle hand and foot?" said Tchitchikov, simpering, "matrimony is not such a . . . er . . . if there were but a bride."

"There shall be, there shall be! No fear about that. You shall have everything you want! . . ."

"Oh, well, if so. . . ."

"Bravo, he will stay," they all cried: "hurrah, hurrah, Pavel Ivanovitch! Hurrah!"

And they all pressed round him with their glasses in their hands to clink with his. Tchitchikov clinked glasses with everyone. "Again, again," cried some of the more persistent and clinked glasses again, some pushed forward a third time and they clinked glasses once more. In a little while they were all extraordinarily lively. The president who was a most charming person when he was a little elevated, embraced Tchitchikov several times, exclaiming in the fullness of his heart: "My dear soul, my precious!" and even, snapping his fingers, fell to pirouetting round him, humming the well-known song, "You are this and you are that, you Kamarinsky peasant!"* After the champagne, they opened some bottles of Hungarian wine, which put still more spirit into the party and made them merrier than ever. The whist was completely forgotten. They disputed, shouted, talked about everything, about politics, even about military matters, giving expression to advanced ideas for which at any other time they would have thrashed their own children. They settled on the spot a number of the most difficult questions. Tchitchikov had never felt so merry, he imagined himself already a genuine Kherson landowner, talked of various improvements he meant to make, of the three-field system of

---

*Subject of a still-popular humorous Russian song and dance.

cropping, of the bliss and happiness of two kindred souls, and began repeating to Sobakevitch Werther's letter in verse to Charlotte,* on which the latter merely blinked as he sat in an armchair, for after the sturgeon he felt a great inclination for sleep. Tchitchikov perceived himself that he had begun to be a little too expansive, he asked for his carriage, and accepted the offer of the prosecutor's racing droshky. The prosecutor's coachman was, as it turned out on the way, an efficient and experienced fellow, for he drove with one hand only, while he held the gentleman on with the other hand thrust out behind him. It was in this fashion that our hero arrived at his hotel, where his tongue still went on babbling all sorts of nonsense about a fair-haired bride with a rosy complexion and a dimple in her right cheek, estates in Kherson, and investments. Selifan even received some orders in regard to the management of the estate, he was told to collect together all the newly settled peasants that they might all answer to a roll-call. Selifan listened for a long time in silence and then went out of the room, saying to Petrushka: "Go and undress the master!" Petrushka set to work to pull off his boots and nearly pulled his master on to the floor with them. At last the boots were off, the master was properly undressed, and after turning over several times on the bed, which creaked mercilessly, he fell asleep like a genuine Kherson landowner. Meanwhile Petrushka carried out into the passage his master's breeches and his shot cranberry-coloured coat, and spreading them out on a wooden hatstand, began beating and brushing them, filling the whole corridor with dust. As he was about to take the clothes down, he glanced over the bannisters, and saw Selifan coming in from the stable. Their eyes met, they understood each other: the master had gone to sleep and they could go and look in somewhere. Instantly taking the coat and trousers into the room, Petrushka went downstairs and they set off together, without one word to each other as to the object of their journey, chattering on the way upon quite extraneous matters. They did not walk far: in fact they only went to the other side of the street to a house that was opposite the hotel, and in at a low grimy glass door, which led down almost to the cellar, where many people of different sorts, shaven and un-

---

*The doomed hero and his married loved one in the German author Johann Wolfgang von Goethe's novel *The Sorrows of Young Werther* (1774).

shaven, in plain sheepskins or simply in their shirt sleeves, and here and there a frieze overcoat, were sitting at the wooden tables. What Petrushka and Selifan did there, God only knows; but they came out an hour later, arm in arm, maintaining complete silence, showing great solicitude for each other, and steering each other clear of all corners. Still arm in arm they spent a quarter of an hour getting up the stairs, at last got the better of them and reached the top. Petrushka stood for a minute facing his low bed, considering which way it would be more suitable to lie on it, and finally lay across it at right angles, so that his legs were on the floor. Selifan lay down on the same bed with his head on Petrushka's stomach, oblivious of the fact that he ought not to have been sleeping there, but perhaps in the servants' room, or even in the stable, with the horses. They both fell asleep at the same instant and raised a snore of an incredibly deep note, to which their master responded from the next room with a refined nasal whistle. Soon afterwards everything was still and all the hotel was wrapped in profound slumber; only in one window a light was still to be seen, from the room occupied by the lieutenant from Kazan,* apparently a great connoisseur in boots, for he had already bought himself four pairs and was continually trying on a fifth. Several times he went up to his bed to take them off and go to bed, but could not bring himself to do so; the boots were certainly well made, and he still sat a long while lifting up his foot and scrutinising the smartly and beautifully shaped heel.

*City about 200 miles east of Nizhniy Novgorod.

CHAPTER 8

Tchitchikov's purchases became the subject of conversation. Discussions took place in the town, views and opinions were expressed as to whether purchasing serfs for removal to another district were a profitable undertaking. From the controversy it appeared that many possessed a thorough understanding of the subject. "Of course it's all right," said some people, "there is no disputing it: the land in the southern provinces is undoubtedly good and fertile, but how are Tchitchikov's peasants going to get on without water? You know there is no river."

"That wouldn't matter, there being no water; that wouldn't matter, Stepan Dmitryevitch; but transporting peasants is a risky business. We all know what the peasant is; put down on fresh land and set to till it, and with nothing for him, no hut, no firewood—why he'd run away as sure as twice two makes four, he'd take to his heels and leave no trace behind him."

"No, Alexey Ivanovitch, excuse me, I don't agree with what you say that Tchitchikov's peasants will run away. The Russian is capable of tackling anything, and can stand any climate. Send him to Kamchatka* and just give him warm gloves, he'll clap his hands together, pick up his axe and go off to hew logs for his new hut."

"But, Ivan Grigoryevitch, you have lost sight of one important point; you haven't asked yourself what sort of peasants Tchitchikov's are, you have forgotten that a good man is never sold by his master. I'll stake my head that Tchitchikov's peasants are thieves, hopeless drunkards, sluggards and of unruly behaviour."

"To be sure, to be sure, I quite agree, that's true, no one will sell good serfs, and Tchitchikov's peasants are drunkards, but you must take into consideration that there is a moral point involved, that it is a moral question; they are good-for-nothing fellows now but, settled

---

*Remote peninsula on the Bering Sea in the Russian Far East; notorious as a place of banishment.

on new land, they may become excellent serfs. There are many such instances in both daily life and history."

"Never, never," said the superintendent of the government factories, "believe me, that can never be, for Tchitchikov's peasants will have two terrible foes to face. The first is the proximity of the provinces of Little Russia,* where as you all know there is no control of the Liquor Trade. I assure you within a fortnight they will all be as drunk as cobblers. The other danger arises from their inevitably growing used to a wandering life during their migration. They will have to be constantly before Tchitchikov's eyes, and he will have to keep a very tight hold over them, punish them for every trifle, and it will be no good for him to rely on any one else, he must give them a punch in the face or a bang on the head when necessary with his own hands."

"Why should Tchitchikov have to bother and to knock them about himself? He may get a steward."

"Well, you get him a steward: they are all rogues!"

"They are rogues because the masters don't go into things themselves."

"That's true," several persons assented. "If the master has some notion of management himself and is a judge of character, he always gets a good steward."

But the superintendent of the factories said that you couldn't get a good steward for less than five thousand roubles. Then the president maintained that you could find one for three thousand. But the superintendent protested: "Where are you going to find him, he is not just under your nose?"

And the president said: "No, not under my nose, but in this district; I mean Pyotr Petrovitch Samoylov; he is the steward Tchitchikov's peasants need!"

Many threw themselves warmly into Tchitchikov's position, and the difficulty of transporting so vast a number of peasants alarmed them extremely; they began to be greatly apprehensive of an actual mutiny arising among peasants so unruly as Tchitchikov's. To this the police-master observed that there was no need to be afraid of a mutiny, that the authority of the police-captain himself need not go, that if he merely sent his cap, the sight of the cap would be enough

---

*Former name of the Ukraine.

to take the peasants all the way to their new home. Many persons offered suggestions for eradicating the mutinous spirit agitating Tchitchikov's peasants. The suggestions were of various kinds. There were some which had a strong flavour of military harshness and even severity, though there were others distinguished by their mildness. The post-master observed that Tchitchikov had a sacred duty before him, that he might become, as he expressed it, something like a father to his peasants, that he might carry out the philanthropic work of enlightenment, and incidentally, he referred with approval to the Lancastrian system of education.*

So they argued and discussed it in the town, and many persons, moved by their sympathy, communicated some of this advice to Tchitchikov, and even offered him an escort to ensure the arrival of the peasants in safety at their new homes. Tchitchikov thanked them for their advice, saying that he would not fail to follow it should occasion arise, but he resolutely declined to escort, maintaining that it was quite unnecessary, that the peasants he had bought were of an exemplarily docile character, and were themselves favourably disposed to migration, and that there could not possibly be a mutiny among them.

All these arguments and discussions, however, led to a more agreeable result than Tchitchikov could possibly have expected, that is, to the rumour that he was neither more nor less than a millionaire. The people of the town had already, as we have seen in the first chapter, taken a great liking to Tchitchikov, and after this rumour spread among them, their liking for him was even greater. Though, to tell the truth, they were all good-natured people, got on well together, and behaved in a friendly way to each other, and indeed, there was a peculiar note of kindliness and good humour in their conversation: "My dear friend, Ilya Ilyitch!" . . . I say, Antipator Zaharyevitch, old man!" . . . "You are drawing the long bow, Ivan Grigoryevitch, my precious." . . . When addressing Ivan Andreyevitch, people always added: "Sprechen Sie Deutsch,† Ivan Andreyevitch." . . . In short they were all like one family. Many of them had

---

*English Quaker and educator Joseph Lancaster (1778–1838) used bright older children to teach younger ones.
†"Speak German" (German).

some degree of culture; the president of the court of justice knew by heart Zhukovsky's "Ludmila,"* which was then a great novelty, and recited many passages in masterly fashion, especially, "The forest sleeps, the valley slumbers," and the word "Tchoo!" so that they really seemed to see the valley slumbering; for greater effect he actually closed his eyes at the passage. The postmaster was more devoted to philosophy and read diligently even at night, Young's *Night Thoughts*† and *The Key to the Mysteries of Nature*,‡ by Eckartshausen, from which he copied out very long extracts; but no one knew what they were about. He was however a wit, flowery in his language, and fond as he expressed it of flavouring his words. And he did flavour his words with a number of all sorts of little phrases such as: "My dear sir, you know, you understand, you can fancy, as regards, so to say, in a certain sense," and so on, which he scattered freely about him; he flavoured his language also rather successfully by winking and screwing up one eye, which gave a very biting expression to many of his satirical allusions. The others were all more or less cultured people, one read Karamzin,§ another read the *Moscow News*, while there were others who actually read nothing at all. Some were the sort of men who need a kick to make them rise to anything; others were simply sluggards lying all their lives on one side, as the saying is, and it would have been a waste of time to lift them up, they wouldn't have stood up under any circumstances. As far as health and appearance goes, they were all, as we have said already, sound people, there wasn't one consumptive among them. They were all of the kind to whom wives in moments of tender tête-à-tête‖ use such endearing epithets as "tubby," "fatty," "chubby," "dumpling," "zou-zou," and so on. But, take them all in all, they were a good-natured set, full of hospitality, and a man who had eaten their salt or spent the evening playing whist with them was at once near and dear to them, and Tchitchikov, with his fascinating qualities and manners, and his real

---

*Ballad (1808) by Russian Romantic poet Vasily Zhukovsky.

†English poet Edward Young's long narrative poem (1742–1745) on death and immortality.

‡Religious-mystical work (1791) by German author Karl von Eckartshausen.

§Nikolai Karamzin (1766–1826), novelist and historian, leader of Russia's Sentimental school.

‖Private conversation between two people; literally, "head to head" (French).

understanding of the great secret of pleasing was, of course, especially so. They had grown so fond of him that he did not know how to tear himself from the town; he heard nothing but: "Come, a week, just one short week more, you must stay with us, Pavel Ivanovitch!" In fact he was, as the saying is, carried along in triumph. But incomparably more remarkable (truly a marvel!) was the impression which Tchitchikov made upon the ladies. To make even a partial explanation of it, one would have to say a great deal of the ladies themselves, of their society and their surroundings, to describe in living colours, as it is called, their spiritual qualities; but that is very difficult for the author. On the one hand he is restrained by his unbounded respect for the spouses of the higher officials, and on the other hand . . . on the other hand, it is simply too difficult. The ladies of the town of N. were . . . no, I really can't: I really feel shy. What was most remarkable in the ladies of the town of N. was . . . It is positively strange my pen refuses to move, as though it were weighted with lead. So be it: it seems I must leave the painting of their characters to some one whose colours are more vivid, and who has a greater variety on his palette; while I confine myself to a few words about their exterior and their superficial characteristics. The ladies of the town of N. were what is called *presentable*, and in that respect one may boldly hold them up as an example to all others. As regards deportment, elevation of tone, observance of etiquette and of a multitude of the most refined rules of propriety, and, above all, as regards following the fashion to its minutest details, they actually surpassed the ladies of Petersburg and Moscow. They dressed with great taste, and drove about the town in carriages, with a footman perched up behind, in a livery with gold lace on it, as prescribed by the latest fashion. A visiting card, even if it were written on a two of clubs or an ace of diamonds, was a very sacred thing. Two ladies, great friends and even relations, were completely estranged on account of a card, just because one of them had somehow failed to return a call. And in spite of all the efforts of their husbands and relations to reconcile them afterwards, it appeared that one may do anything else in the world, but that one thing is impossible—to reconcile two ladies who have quarrelled over failure to leave a card. And so the two ladies were left, "mutually indisposed" as the society of the town expressed it. The question of precedence also gave rise to many violent scenes, inspiring sometimes in their husbands a chivalrous and noble-minded conception of the duty of championing them. Duels of course did not occur because the gentlemen were all in the civil service, but on the other hand they tried to play each other nasty tricks wherever possible, and that as every one knows, is sometimes worse than any duel. In moral principles the ladies of N. were severe, full of noble indignation at everything vicious, and every form of depravity, and they punished every weakness without mercy. If what is known as a "thing or two" did occur, it was kept dark so that there was no outward sign of its having occurred; every dignity was preserved and the husband himself was so well primed, that if he did see a "thing or two," or heard of it, he responded mildly and reasonably with the popular saying: What does it matter to any one else, if the godfather sits with the godmother?

Another thing I must mention about the ladies of N. is that, like many Petersburg ladies, they were distinguished by great niceness and propriety in their choice of words and expressions. They never said: "I blew my nose, I got into a sweat, I spat," but used instead some such expression as: "I made use of my handkerchief." It was out of the question to say under any circumstances "that glass or that plate stinks," or even to say anything that would suggest it; they said instead "that glass is not quite agreeable," or something of the sort. To refine and elevate the Russian language, fully half the words in it were rejected from their vocabulary, and so it was very often necessary to have recourse to French; but in French it was quite a different matter; in that language they permitted themselves expressions far coarser than those mentioned above. So much for what may be said of the ladies of N., speaking superficially. Though, of course, if one were to look more deeply, many other things would be discovered, but it is very dangerous to look too deeply into the feminine heart.

And so, confining ourselves to the superficial, we will continue. Hitherto the ladies had said very little of Tchitchikov, although they gave him full credit for his agreeable demeanour in company, but from the time that there were rumours of his being a millionaire, other qualities were discerned in him. Though, indeed, the ladies were not at all mercenary-minded: the word millionaire was to blame—not the millionaire himself but just the word; for in the mere sound of that word, altogether apart from the moneybags, there is something which produces an effect upon people who are scoundrels, upon people who are neither one thing nor the other, and upon good people too, that is, it produces an effect upon all. The millionaire has the advantage of meeting with servility that is quite disinterested, pure servility resting on no secondary motives: many people know perfectly well that they will never get a farthing from him and have no right to expect it, but yet will not fail to run to anticipate his wishes, to laugh at his jokes, to take off their hats, to wring an invitation for themselves to a dinner where they know he will be. It cannot be said that this tender inclination to servility was felt by the ladies; in many drawing-rooms, however, it began to be said that Tchitchikov was, of course, not strikingly handsome, but he was quite what a man ought to be, that if he were stouter or fatter, it would be a pity. And incidentally the observation was made—somewhat slighting to thin men in general—that they were more like toothpicks than men. All sorts of additional touches appeared in the attire of the ladies. There was quite a crowd, almost a crush in the arcade; there were so many carriages driving up to it that they were a regular procession. The shopkeepers were astonished at seeing that some pieces of material, which they had brought from the fair and could not get rid of on account of the price, had suddenly become the rage, and were snapped up regardless of expense. At mass in church one lady had a stiff flounce at the bottom of her skirt, which stuck it out so far all round her, that the police inspector of the quarter, who happened to be present, ordered the people to move further back, that they might not crush her honour's costume. Tchitchikov himself could not help noticing the extraordinary attention paid him. One day on returning home he found a letter lying on his table. He could not find out from whom it came or who had brought it: the waiter informed him that it had been brought with orders not to say from whom it came. The letter began with great determination, in these words in fact: "Yes, I must write to you!" then something was said about a mysterious affinity of souls; this truth was confirmed by a number of dots which filled up half a line. Then followed several reflections so remarkable for their justice, that we feel it almost essential to quote them: "What is our life? A vale in which grief has taken up its abode. What is the world? The crowd of the unfeeling." Then the writer mentioned that she was bedewing the lines with tears for a tender mother, who twenty-five years before had left this earthly sphere; Tchitchikov was invited to flee to the desert, to abandon for ever the town where, shut in by spiritual barriers, people did not breathe the air of freedom; the latter part of the letter had a note of positive despair, and ended with the following verses:

> "Two turtle doves will show thee
> Where my cold ashes lie
> And sadly murmuring tell thee
> How in tears I did die."*

The last line did not scan, that did not matter, though: the letter was written in the spirit of the day. There was no signature: neither Christian name nor surname nor even the date. But a postscript was added to the effect that his own heart should divine who was the writer, and that the author would be at the governor's ball that was to take place on the following day.

This greatly interested him. There was so much that was alluring and that excited the curiosity in the anonymity of it, that he read the letter through a second and a third time, and said at last: "It would be interesting, though, to know who the writer is!" In fact, things were becoming serious, as may be seen. He spent more than an hour brooding over it. At last, flinging wide his hands and nodding his head, he said: "The letter is very, very fancifully written!" Then, I need hardly say, the letter was folded up and put in his case beside an advertisement and an invitation to a wedding, which had been preserved for seven years in the same place and position. Shortly afterwards an invitation actually was brought him for the governor's ball, a very common event in provincial towns: where there is a governor, there is a ball, or the nobility would not pay him due respect and love.

Every other consideration was instantly dismissed and thrust aside, and every thought was concentrated on preparations for the ball, for indeed there were many exciting and stimulating circumstances connected with it. Probably so much time and effort had never since the creation of the world been devoted to the toilet. A whole hour was spent merely in scrutinising his countenance in the

---

*Loose quotation from Karamzin's poem "Content with My Fate."

looking-glass. Attempts were made to assume a great variety of expressions: at one moment important and dignified, at the next, respectful with a smile, then, simply respectful without a smile; several bows were made to the looking-glass, accompanied by vague sounds, somewhat resembling French, though Tchitchikov did not know French at all. He even attempted several new and surprising tricks, twisted his eyebrows and his lips and even tried to do something with his tongue; as a matter of fact, there is no limit to what one may do when left alone and feeling that one is a handsome fellow and convinced, moreover, that no one will be looking through a crack. At last he gave his chin a slap, saying, "Bless me, what a mug!" and began dressing. The whole process of dressing was accompanied by an agreeable and contented feeling: as he put on his braces or tied his cravat, he bowed and scraped with peculiar sprightliness, and though he had never danced in his life, he cut a caper. This caper had a small and harmless consequence: the chest of drawers shook and the brush fell on the floor.

His arrival at the ball made an extraordinary impression. Every one turned to greet him, one with cards in his hand, another at the most interesting point in the conversation as he uttered the words: "And the lower district court maintains in answer to that . . ." but what the district court did maintain he abandoned altogether and hastened to welcome our hero. "Pavel Ivanovitch! Ah, goodness me, Pavel Ivanovitch! Dear Pavel Ivanovitch! Honoured Pavel Ivanovitch! My dear soul, Pavel Ivanovitch! Ah, here you are, Pavel Ivanovitch! Here he is, our Pavel Ivanovitch! Allow me to embrace you, Pavel Ivanovitch! Hand him over, let me give him a good kiss, my precious Pavel Ivanovitch!" Tchitchikov instantly felt himself clasped in the embrace of several friends. He had hardly succeeded in completely extricating himself from the embrace of the president, when he found himself in the arms of the police-master; the police-master passed him on to the inspector of the medical board; the inspector of the medical board handed him over to the government contractor, and the latter passed him on to the architect. . . . The governor, who was at the moment standing by some ladies, with a motto from a bon-bon* in one hand and a lap-dog in the other, dropped both

---

*Sweet or candy (French).

motto and lap-dog on the floor on seeing him—the dog raised a
shrill yelp—in short, Tchitchikov was the centre of extraordinary joy
and delight. There was not a face that did not express pleasure or at
least a reflection of the general pleasure. So it is with the faces of government clerks when the offices in their charge are being inspected
by a newly arrived chief: when their first panic has passed off, and
they see that he is pleased with a great deal and when he has graciously condescended to jest, that is to pronounce a few words with
an agreeable simper, and the clerks standing near him laugh twice as
much in response, those who have scarcely caught his words laugh
with all their hearts too, and last of all a policeman, standing far away
at the door at the very entrance, who has never laughed in his life,
and has just before been shaking his fist at the people, is moved by
the unalterable laws of reflection to show upon his face a smile,
though it looks more as though he were sneezing after a strong pinch
of snuff.

Our hero responded to all and each, and was aware of a peculiar
ease: he bowed to right and to left, a little to one side as he always
did, but with perfect grace, so that he charmed every one. The ladies
surrounded him with a galaxy of beauty, and wafted with them perfect clouds of sweet scents, one smelt of roses, another was breathing
of spring and violets, another was saturated through and through
with mignonette.* Tchitchikov could only throw up his nose and
sniff. A vast deal of taste was displayed in their attire; muslins, satins,
chiffons were of those pale, fashionable shades, for which it is impossible to find a name, so refined is modern taste! Bows of ribbon
and bunches of flowers were dotted here and there about their
dresses in most picturesque disorder, though this disorder had cost
an orderly brain a great deal of trouble. The light ornaments that
adorned their heads held on only by the ears, and seemed to be saying: "Aie! I am taking flight, and the only pity is that I can't carry the
beauty away with me!" The waists were tightly laced and had the
most firm and agreeable contour (it must be noted that generally
speaking the ladies of the town of N. were rather plump, but they
laced so skillfully and held themselves so gracefully, that their stoutness was not noticeable). Everything had been thought out and

*Plant with fragrant, greenish-white flowers.

looked after with special care: necks and shoulders were bared just as far as was right and not a bit further; each one displayed her possessions so far as she felt from her inner conviction that they were calculated to slay her man. The rest was all covered up with extraordinary taste; either some light ribbon neck-band, dainty as the sweets known as "kisses," ethereally encircled the neck, or little scalloped edgings of fine batiste known as "modesties," emerged under the dress behind the shoulders. These "modesties" concealed in front and at the back what was not calculated to play havoc with the heart of man, and at the same time they aroused the suspicion that the very centre of danger was there. The long gloves were drawn up not quite to meet the sleeves, but the most alluring part of the arm above the elbow, in many cases of an enviable plumpness, was intentionally left bare; some ladies had even split their kid gloves in the effort to push them up higher—in short everything seemed to be imprinted with the words: "No, this is not a provincial town, this is Petersburg, this is Paris!" Only here and there a cap of a species never seen on earth before, or some feather, perhaps from a peacock, stood up in accordance with individual taste and in defiance of the dictates of fashion. But there is no escaping that; such originality is characteristic of a provincial town, it is bound to break out somewhere. Tchitchikov stood before them, wondering who could be the authoress of the letter, and he was about to crane his head forward for a better look round when a whole procession of elbows, cuffs, sleeves, ends of ribbons, perfumed chemisettes* and dresses flashed by under his very nose. The gallop was at its height: the postmaster's wife, the police-captain, a lady with a pale blue feather, a lady with a white feather, the Georgian prince, Tchiphaihilidzev, an official from Petersburg,† an official from Moscow, a French gentleman called Coucou, Perhunovsky, Berebendovsky, all pranced up and down and flew by. . . .

"Well, they are all at it!" Tchitchikov said to himself as he stepped back, and, as soon as the ladies had sat down in their places, he began scanning them again to see whether from the expression on some face or the look in some eyes he could recognise the authoress of the letter; but it was utterly impossible to recognise either from the ex-

---

*Lace or muslin used to decorate the open front of a woman's dress.
†From Georgia, the Caucasus region on the Black Sea.

pression of the face or the look in the eyes which was she. Everywhere there could be discerned something faintly betrayed, something elusively subtle—oh, how subtle! . . .

"No," Tchitchikov said to himself, "women really are . . . a subject. . . ." Here he waved his hand hopelessly. "It's simply no use talking! Go and try to describe all that is flitting over their faces, all the roundabout devices, the hints. . . . But you simply couldn't describe it. Their eyes alone are a boundless realm which a man explores—and is lost for ever! You can never get him back by hook or by crook. Just try describing, for instance, the mere light in them: melting, velvety, full of sweetness and goodness knows what besides; cruel and soft and quite languishing too, or as some say, voluptuous, or not voluptuous, but especially when voluptuous—and it catches the heart and plays upon the soul like a violin bow. No, there is simply no finding the words: the *fine fleur** half of the human species and that's all about it."

I beg your pardon! I believe an expression overheard in the street has just escaped from the lips of my hero. I could not help it! Such is the sad plight of an author in Russia! Though, indeed, if a word overheard in the streets does creep into a book, it is not the author who is to blame, but the readers, and especially the readers of the best society; it is from them, above all others, that you never hear a decent Russian word, but they must reel off French, German and English phrases beyond anything you could wish for, and they even keep to every possible pronunciation—French they speak through their nose with a lisp, English they twitter like a bird in the correct way; and even look like birds as they speak it, and positively laugh at those who cannot make their faces look like birds. They never contribute anything Russian, at most their patriotism leads them to build a peasant's hut in the Russian style for a summer bungalow. So that's what readers of the best society are like, and all who rank themselves as such follow their example. And at the same time how exacting they are! They insist that everything must be written in the most rigidly correct language, purified and refined—in fact they want the Russian language to descend of itself from the clouds, all finished and polished, and settle on their tongue, leaving them nothing to do but open their mouth and stick it out. Of course, the feminine half of the

---

*Finest flower (French).

human species is not easy to understand; but our worthy readers are sometimes even more difficult to make out.

And meanwhile Tchitchikov was completely puzzled to decide which of the ladies was the authoress of the letter. Trying to look more intently, he perceived on the ladies' side, too, an expression calculated to inspire at once such hope and such sweet torture in the heart of a poor mortal that he said at last: "No, there is no guessing!" This, however, did not detract from his cheerful frame of mind. In the most unconstrained way he exchanged a few agreeable phrases with some of the ladies, went up first to one and then to another with little mincing steps, with the tripping gait affected by little foppish old gentlemen with high heels, midget bucks, as they are called, who skip very nimbly to and fro among the ladies. Turning rather adroitly to right and to left, as he tripped along, he scraped with one foot as though drawing a short tail or a comma on the floor. The ladies were very well pleased with him and not only discovered in him a wealth of agreeable and amiable qualities, but even discerned a majestic expression in his countenance, even something martial and military which, as we all know, greatly attracts the fair sex. They even began quarrelling a little over him. Noticing that he generally stood near the door, some hastened abruptly to take seats nearer the door, and, when one succeeded in doing so first, there was very nearly an unpleasant scene, and such forwardness seemed positively revolting to many who had been desirous of doing the same.

Tchitchikov was so absorbed in his conversation with the ladies, or to be more accurate, the ladies so engrossed and overwhelmed him with their conversation, interspersing a number of ingenious and subtly allegorical remarks—his brow was perspiring with the effort to interpret their meaning—that he forgot the rules of good manners and did not go up first to his hostess. He thought of this only when he heard the voice of the governor's wife who had been standing before him for some minutes. The lady, shaking her head archly, said in a rather caressing and insinuating voice: "Ah, so this is where you are, Pavel Ivanovitch!" I cannot accurately reproduce the lady's words, but something was said, full of the greatest politeness, in the style in which ladies and gentlemen express themselves in the works of the society novelists who devote themselves to describing drawing-rooms and pride themselves on their knowledge of aristocratic manners, something in the style of—"Have they taken such possession of your heart that you have no room left in it, not even the tiniest corner for those you have so mercilessly forgotten?" Our hero instantly faced about to the governor's wife, and was on the point of making a reply, probably in no way inferior to those uttered by the Zvonskys, the Linskys, the Lindins, the Gremins and all the other accomplished officers in fashionable novels, when, chancing to raise his eyes, he stood rooted to the spot.

It was not the governor's wife alone who stood before him; on her arm was a fresh-looking fair-haired girl of sixteen, with delicate and graceful features, a pointed chin, and a face of an enchantingly rounded oval, such as an artist might have taken as a model for his Madonna, and such as is rarely seen in Russia, where everything, whatever it may be, is apt to be on a broad scale: mountains, forests, steppes, faces, lips, and feet. It was the same fair-haired girl whom he had met on his way back from Nozdryov's when through the stupidity of the coachman or the horses, their carriages had come so strangely into collision, when their harness was entangled and Uncle Mitya and Uncle Minyay undertook to extricate them.

Tchitchikov was so overcome that he could utter nothing coherent, and goodness knows what he mumbled, something that certainly no Gremin, Zvonsky or Lidin would have said.

"You don't know my daughter?" said the governor's wife, "she has only just left school."

He said that he had already by chance had the happiness of making her acquaintance; he tried to say something more, but the something more did not come off. The governor's wife said two or three words, and then went off with her daughter to the other end of the drawing-room to talk to other guests; while Tchitchikov still remained motionless at the same spot, like a man who having gaily sallied out into the street for a walk, with eyes disposed to observe everything, suddenly stands stock-still thinking he has forgotten something; and nothing can look stupider than such a man: instantly, the careless expression vanishes from his face; he struggles to recall what he has forgotten: was it his handkerchief?—but his handkerchief is still in his pocket; was it his money?—but his money too is in his pocket, he seems to have everything, but yet some unseen spirit keeps whispering in his ear that he has forgotten something. And

now he looks blankly and absent-mindedly at the moving crowd before him, at the carriages dashing by, at the shakos* and guns of the
regiment marching by, at the signboard on the shop, and sees nothing clearly. So Tchitchikov suddenly became aloof from all that was
passing around him. Meanwhile a number of hints and questions
saturated with refinement and politeness were aimed at him from the
fragrant lips of the ladies, such as: "Is it permissible for us, poor
dwellers in this earthly sphere, to be so audacious as to ask the subject of your dreams?" "Where may those happy regions be to which
your thoughts have taken flight?" "May we know the name of her
who has plunged you into this sweet vale of reverie." But he paid absolutely no attention, and the agreeable phrases were completely
thrown away. He was even so uncivil as to walk away from them hurriedly to the other end of the room, anxious to find out where the
governor's wife had gone with her daughter. But the ladies were not,
it seemed, disposed to let him escape so easily, every one of them inwardly determined to use all those weapons so menacing to the
peace of our hearts, and to turn her best points to the best possible
advantage. I must observe that some ladies—I say some, that is, not
all ladies—have a little weakness: if a lady notices anything particularly attractive in herself—whether lips or brow or hand—she is apt
to imagine that her best point is conspicuous and is attracting the notice of every one, and that all are saying with one voice: "Look, look,
hasn't she a lovely Grecian nose!" or, "What a smooth and fascinating brow!" One who has good shoulders is confident that all the
young men will be completely captivated, and will be continually repeating when she passes: "What marvellous shoulders she has!" and
that they will not glance at her face, her hair, her nose, her brow, or
if they do, it will be as at something quite apart. That is what some
ladies imagine. Every lady took an inward vow to be as fascinating as
possible in the dances, and to display in all the brilliance of its perfection whatever was most perfect in her. The postmaster's wife put
her head on one side so languishingly as she waltzed that it really
gave one a feeling of something unearthly. One very amiable lady
who had come with no idea of dancing at all on account of, as she
herself expressed it, a slight incommodity in the shape of a small callos-

---

*Military caps with visor and plume.

ity on her right foot, in consequence of which she had actually been obliged to put on plush boots, could not resist joining the dance and taking a few turns in her plush boots, solely to prevent the postmaster's wife from really thinking too much of herself.

But all this did not produce the effect anticipated on Tchitchikov. He did not even look at the circles described by the ladies, but was continually rising on tiptoe to peep over people's heads, and see where the interesting fair one had gone; he stooped down too, to look between backs and shoulders; at last his search was successful, and he saw her sitting with her mother, on whose head a sort of oriental turban with a feather was nodding majestically. He seemed to mean to take them by storm. Whether the influence of spring affected him or some one was pushing from behind, he pressed resolutely forward, regardless of everything: the spirit tax contractor was so violently pushed aside by him, that he staggered and only just succeeded in balancing himself on one leg, or he would have brought a whole row of others down with him; the postmaster too stepped back and looked at him in amazement mixed with rather subtle irony, but he did not look at them: he saw nothing but the fair girl in the distance, pulling on a long glove, and no doubt burning with impatience to be flying over the parquet floor.

And already four couples were dancing the mazurka,* heels were tapping on the floor, and an army captain was working hard with body and soul, and arms and legs, executing such steps as no one had ever executed before in his wildest dreams. Tchitchikov dashed by the mazurka almost on the dancers' heels, and straight to the place where the governor's wife was sitting with her daughter. He approached them, however, very timidly, he did not trip up to them with jaunty and foppish little steps, he even shifted from one foot to the other uneasily, and there was an awkwardness in all his movements.

It cannot be said for certain that the passion of love was stirring in our hero's heart: it is doubtful, indeed, if gentlemen of his sort, that is, not precisely fat and yet not what you would call thin, are capable of falling in love; but for all that there was something strange about it, something which he could not have explained to himself; it seemed to him, as he admitted to himself afterwards, as though the

---

*Lively Polish folk dance.

whole ball with all its noise and conversation became for a few minutes, as it were, far away; the fiddles and trumpets droned somewhere
in the distance, and all were lost in fog like some carelessly painted
background in a picture. And from this foggy, roughly sketched background nothing stood out clearly but the delicate features of the fair
charmer: the oval little face, the slender, slender figure such as one
sees only in girls who have just left school, the white, almost plain
dress lightly and elegantly draping her graceful young limbs, and following their pure lines. It seemed as though she were like some toy,
delicately carved out of ivory; she alone stood out white, transparent,
and full of light against the dingy and opaque crowd.

It seems that it does sometimes happen; it seems that even the
Tchitchikovs are for a few moments in their lives transformed into
poets; though the word "poet" is too much. Anyway he felt quite like
a young man, almost an Hussar. Seeing an empty chair beside them,
he instantly took it. Conversation flagged at first, but afterwards
things went better, he even began to gain confidence. . . . At this
point to my great regret I must observe that dignified persons occupying important posts are somewhat ponderous in conversation with
ladies; at this lieutenants are first-rate, no officers of a rank higher
than a captain's are any good at it. Goodness only knows how they
manage it: it seems as though they are not saying anything very subtle, but the young lady is continually rocking with laughter. Goodness
knows what a civil councillor will talk to her about, either he will
begin informing her that Russia is a vast empire, or will launch out
into a compliment which, though doubtless wittily conceived, has a
terribly bookish flavour; if he says something funny, he will laugh at
it himself ever so much more than the fair one who is listening to
him. This fact is here noted that the reader may see why it was that
the governor's daughter yawned while our hero was talking to her.
The latter completely failed, however, to observe this, as he repeated
to her a number of agreeable things, which he had already said on
various occasions before in various places, to wit: in the Simbirsk*
province at Sofron Ivanovitch Bezpetchny's, where there were three
young ladies, Adelaida Sofronovna and her three sisters-in-law—

*Also Ulyanovsk; city about 120 miles south of Kazan.

Marie Gavrilovna, Alexandra Gavrilovna and Adelheida Gavrilovna; at Fyodor Fyodorovitch Perekroev's in the province of Ryazan;* at Frol Vassilyevitch Pobyedonosny's in the province of Penza,† and at the house of his brother, Pyotr Vassilyevitch, where were his sister-in-law, Katerina Mihailovna and her second cousins Rosa Fyodorovna and Amilia Fyodorovna: in the province of Vyatka, at the house of Pyotr Varsonofyevitch in the presence of his betrothed's sister, Pelageya Yegorovna and his niece, Sofya Rostislavna and her two half-sisters Sofya Alexandrovna and Maklatura Alexandrovna.

All the ladies were greatly displeased with Tchitchikov's behaviour. One of them purposely walked by him in order to let him see this, and even rather carelessly brushed against the fair charmer with the thick flounce of her dress, and managed so that the end of the scarf that fluttered round her shoulders flapped right into the young lady's face; at the same time a rather biting and malignant observation floated together with the scent of violets from the lips of a lady behind him. But either he really did not hear, or he pretended not to hear, and in either case he did wrong, for one must attach importance to the opinions of the ladies: he regretted it, but only afterwards, and consequently, too late.

An expression of perfectly justifiable indignation was apparent on many faces. Whatever weight Tchitchikov might have in society, though he might be a millionaire, though there might be an expression of majesty and even something martial and military in his face, yet there are things that ladies can forgive in no one, whoever he may be, and then one must simply write him down—lost! There are cases in which a woman, however weak and helpless compared with a man, becomes all at once harder, not merely than a man, but than anything on earth. Tchitchikov's almost unconscious neglect restored among the ladies the concord and harmony which had been on the brink of ruin through the competition for a seat next him. Sarcastic allusions were discovered in brief and ordinary phrases he had uttered at random. To make things worse, one of the young men present composed on the spot some satirical verses on the dancers; as we all know, no provincial ball is complete without some such display of

---

*City southeast of Moscow.
†City about 360 miles southeast of Moscow.

wit. These verses were immediately ascribed to Tchitchikov. The indignation grew, and in different corners, ladies began to speak of him in the most unflattering terms; while the poor schoolgirl was completely doomed, and sentence had already been passed on her.

Meanwhile a most unpleasant surprise was in store for our hero. While the young lady was yawning and he was telling her various incidents that had occurred to him at various times, and even referred to the Greek philosopher Diogenes, Nozdryov appeared from the furthest room. Either he had torn himself from the refreshment room, or had come, possibly of his own free will, or more probably from being ejected, from the little green drawing-room where the play was more fast and furious than ordinary whist. Anyway, he appeared in the liveliest spirits, hanging on to the arm of the prosecutor, whom he had probably been dragging along with him for some time, for the prosecutor was twitching his thick eyebrows in all directions, as though trying to find a way of escape from this over-affectionate arm-in-arm promenade. It certainly was insufferable. Nozdryov, who had sipped inspiration with two cups of tea, not of course unaccompanied by rum, was pouring out the most fabulous tales. Seeing him in the distance, Tchitchikov at once resolved to make a sacrifice, that is, to leave his enviable position and to beat a retreat as quickly as possible: he foresaw nothing good from this meeting. But, as ill-luck would have it, that moment the governor turned up, and expressing the utmost pleasure at having found Pavel Ivanovitch, detained him by asking him to arbitrate between him and two ladies with whom he had been arguing whether women's love were lasting or not; and meanwhile Nozdryov had seen him and came straight towards him.

"Ah, the Kherson landowner, the Kherson landowner!" he shouted, as he came up, and he went off into a guffaw so that his cheeks, fresh and red as a spring rose, shook with laughter. "Well, have you bought a lot of dead souls? I expect you don't know, your Excellency," he bawled, addressing the governor, "he deals in dead souls! Upon my word! I say, Tchitchikov! Let me tell you, I say it as a friend, we are all your friends here, and here is his Excellency too—I'd hang you, upon my soul, I would!"

Tchitchikov did not know whether he was standing on his head or his feet.

"Would you believe it, your Excellency," Nozdryov went on, "when he said to me, 'Sell me your dead souls,' I fairly split with laughing. As I came along, I was told he had bought three millions worth of serfs to take to a settlement. Fine settlers! But he was bargaining with me for dead ones. I say, Tchitchikov: you are a beast, upon my soul, you are a beast! Here's his Excellency here too . . . isn't he, prosecutor?"

But the prosecutor and Tchitchikov and the governor himself were thrown into such confusion, that they could not think of anything to say; and meanwhile Nozdryov made a half tipsy speech without taking the slightest notice of them.

"I say, old boy, you, you . . . I won't let you alone till I find out what you are buying dead souls for. I say, Tchitchikov, you really ought to be ashamed, you know yourself you have no better friend than me. . . . And here's his Excellency here too . . . isn't he, prosecutor? You wouldn't believe, your Excellency, what friends we are. It's the simple fact, if you were to say—with me standing here, if you were to say: 'Nozdryov, tell me on your honour, which is dearer to you, your own father or Tchitchikov?' I should say 'Tchitchikov.' Upon my soul. . . . Let me imprint a *baiser** on your cheek, love. You will allow me to kiss him, your Excellency. Yes, Tchitchikov, it's no use your resisting, let me imprint one little *baiser* on your snow-white cheek!"

Nozdryov was so violently repulsed with his *baisers* that he was almost thrown to the floor. Every one drew away from him and would hear no more. But still what he had said about the purchase of dead souls had been uttered at the top of his voice and accompanied by such loud laughter that it had attracted the attention even of persons sitting at the furthest ends of the room. This piece of news was so astounding that it left every one with a sort of wooden, stupidly interrogative expression. Tchitchikov noticed that many of the ladies glanced at each other with a spiteful, sarcastic smile, and in the expression of several countenances there was something ambiguous which further increased his confusion. That Nozdryov was a desperate liar was a fact known to all, and there was nothing to be surprised at in hearing the wildest fabrication from him, but mortal man—it

---

*Kiss (French).

really is difficult to understand what mortal man is made of; however silly a piece of news may be, so long as it is news, every mortal immediately passes it on to another, if only to say: "Just think what lies people are putting about!" And the other mortal listens eagerly, though he too will say afterwards: "Yes, that's a perfectly silly lie, not worth noticing!" And thereupon he sets off to look for a third mortal, in order that after telling the story he may exclaim with righteous indignation: "What a silly lie!" And it will certainly go the round of the whole town and all the inhabitants, every one of them, will discuss it till they are sick of it, and will then admit that it's not worth noticing and too silly to think of.

This apparently nonsensical incident unmistakably upset our hero. However stupid a fool's words may be, they are sometimes enough to upset a sensible man. He began to feel uncomfortable and ill at ease, exactly as though with highly polished boots he had stepped into a filthy, stinking puddle—in short, it was nasty, very nasty. He tried not to think of it, he tried to turn the current of his thoughts, to distract his mind, and sat down to whist, but everything went awry like a crooked wheel: twice he revoked and forgetting that one should not rump in the third place, threw away his whole hand and spoilt his game by his foolishness. The president simply could not understand how Pavel Ivanovitch, who had such a good and, one might say, subtle understanding of the game, could make such blunders and had even trumped his king of spades in whom, to use his own expression, he had trusted as in God. Of course the postmaster and the president and even the police-master bantered our hero, asking whether he was in love, and declaring that Pavel Ivanovitch's heart had been smitten, and that they knew from whom the dart had come; but all that was no comfort to him, though he did his best to laugh and turn it off with a joke. At supper, too, he was not able to recover himself, although the company at the table was agreeable and Nozdryov had been ejected some time before, for even the ladies had observed that his conduct was becoming extremely scandalous. In the middle of the cotillion, he had sat down on the floor and clutched at the skirts of the dancers, which was really beyond anything, to use the ladies' expression.

The supper was very lively; all the faces, flitting to and fro before the three-stemmed candlesticks, the flowers, the sweets and the bottles, were beaming with the most spontaneous satisfaction. Officers, ladies, gentlemen in dress coats—everything was polite to mawkishness. The gentlemen jumped up from their chairs and ran to take the dishes from the servants to offer them with rare adroitness to the ladies. One colonel handed a lady a plate of sauce on the tip of his drawn sword. The gentlemen of respectable age, among whom Tchitchikov was sitting, argued loudly, absorbing a few words about business with the fish or the beef, which was ruthlessly smothered in mustard. They discussed the very subjects in which he was always interested; but he was like a man wearied or knocked up by a long journey who has not an idea in his head and who is not capable of entering into anything. He did not even stay to the end of the supper, but went home much earlier than he generally did.

There in the little room so familiar to the reader, with the chest of drawers blocking up one door, and the cockroaches peering out of the corners, his mind and his soul were as comfortable as the easy-chair on which he was sitting. There was an unpleasant confused feeling in his heart; there was an oppressive emptiness in it. "Damnation take all those who arranged that ball!" he said to himself in anger. "What are they so pleased about in their foolishness? The crops have failed and there is dearth in the province, and they are all for balls! A fine business! they dress themselves up in their feminine rags! It's a monstrous thing for a woman to waste a thousand roubles on her trappings! And of course it's at the expense of the peasants' earnings or what's worse still, of the consciences of our dear friends. We all know why a man takes a bribe and overcomes his scruples: it's to get his wife a shawl or robes of some sort, plague take them, whatever they are called! And what for? That some low woman shouldn't say that the postmaster's wife was better dressed, and bang goes a thousand roubles because of her. They cry out, 'A ball, a ball! delightful!' A ball's a silly rubbishy thing, it's not in the Russian spirit, nor true to the Russian nature; what the devil is one to make of it? A grown-up man, getting on in years, suddenly skips in, all in black, as trim and tight as a devil, and sets to working away with his legs. Even while they are standing in couples, a man will begin talking to another about something of importance, and all the while his legs will be capering to right and to left like a goat. . . . It is all apishness, apishness! Because a Frenchman is as childish at forty as he was fifteen, we must be the same! Yes, really, after every ball one feels as though one had committed a sin and does not like to think of it. One's head is as empty as it is after talking to one of these society gentlemen. He talks about everything, touches lightly on everything, he says everything he has filched out of books brightly and picturesquely, but he hasn't got anything of it in his head; and you see afterwards that a talk with a humble merchant who knows nothing but his own business but does know that thoroughly and by experience, is better than all these chatterboxes. Why, what do you get out of this ball? Come, suppose some writer were to take it into his head to describe all that scene just as it was. Why, it would be just as senseless in a book as it is in nature. What was it, moral or immoral? God knows what to make of it! You would simply spit and shut the book."

Such were Tchitchikov's unfavourable criticisms of balls in general; but I fancy that there was partly another reason for his indignation. His chief vexation was not with the ball, but with the fact that he had happened to come off rather badly at it, that he had been made to look like goodness knows what, that he had played a strange and ambiguous part of it. Of course, looking at it as a sensible man, he could see that it was all nonsense, that a foolish word is of no consequence, especially now when his chief business was successfully concluded. But—strange is man: he was deeply mortified at being in disfavour with the very people whom he did not respect, and whose vanity and love of dress he derided. This annoyed him all the more because when he analysed the matter clearly, he saw that he was to some extent himself to blame. He was not, however, angry with himself, and there, of course, he was quite right. We all have a little weakness for sparing ourselves, and we try to find some neighbour on whom to pour out our vexation, for instance, our servant, our subordinate at the office who turns up at the moment, our wife, or even a chair which is sent flying, goodness knows where, right against the door, so that its arms and back are broken—let it have a taste of one's wrath, one feels. So Tchitchikov soon found some one on whose shoulders to throw everything his vexation suggested to him. This was Nozdyrov, and it is needless to say that he came in for a storm of abuse, for a storm of abuse such as is only poured on some rogue of a village elder or driver by some experienced captain on his travels, or even by a general who, to the many expressions that have become classical, adds others unfamiliar, for the invention of which he can claim the credit. All Nozdryov's kith and kin came in for abuse, and many members of his family were severely dealt with.

But while our hero was sitting in his hard armchair, troubled by sleeplessness and his thoughts, and vigorously cursing Nozdryov and all his relations, while before him glowed a tallow candle with a black cowl of soot on the wick, which threatened every minute to go out, while the blind, dark night, on the point of turning blue with the approaching dawn, looked in at the window, and in the distance cocks were crowing to one another, and in the slumbering town perhaps some poor fellow of unknown class and rank in a fustian* overcoat trudged along knowing nothing of aught but the highway, too well worn (alas!) by the vagabonds of Russia—at that very moment an event was taking place at the other end of the town that was destined to increase the unpleasantness of our hero's position. To be precise, a strange equipage, for which it is puzzling to find a name, was creaking through the further streets and alleys of the town; it was not like a coach, nor a carriage, nor a chaise, but it was more like a full-cheeked rounded melon on wheels. The cheeks of this melon, that is the doors, which bore tracks of yellow paint, shut very badly owing to the rickety condition of the handles and locks, which were tied up with string. The melon was full of cotton cushions in the shape of pouches, rolling-pins and simple pillows, stuffed up with sacks of bread, fancy loaves, doughnuts and pasties, and bread rings made of boiled dough. Chicken pies and saltfish pies peeped out at the top. The footboard was occupied by an individual of the flunkey order, with an unshaven chin, slightly touched with grey, in a short jacket of bright-coloured homespun—the sort of individual known as a "fellow." The clank and squeaking of the iron clamps and rusty screws woke a sentry at the other end of the town, who picking up his halberd shouted half awake at the top of his voice: "Who goes there?" but seeing that no one was passing, and only hearing a creaking in the distance, caught a beast of some sort on his collar, and, going up to a lamp-post, executed it on the spot with his nail, then laying aside his halberd, fell asleep again in accordance with the rules of his chivalry. The horses kept falling on their knees, for they had not been

*Stout fabric of cotton and flax.

shod, and evidently the quiet cobbled streets of the town were unfamiliar to them. This grotesque equipage, after turning several times from one street into another, at last turned into a dark side-street next the little parish church of St. Nikolay, and stopped before the head priest's gate. A girl clambered out of the vehicle, wearing a short warm jacket, with a kerchief on her head, and beat on the gate with both fists as though she were beating a man (the "fellow" in the bright-coloured homespun jacket was afterwards dragged down by his legs, for he was sleeping like the dead). Dogs began barking, the gates yawned, and at last, though with difficulty, swallowed up this uncouth monster of the road.

The carriage drove into the narrow yard which was filled up with stacks of wood, poultry-houses and sheds; a lady alighted: this lady was no other than Madame Korobotchka. Soon after our hero's departure, the old lady had been overcome by such anxiety as to the possibility of his deceiving her, that after lying awake for three nights in succession she made up her mind to drive into the town, regardless of the fact that the horses were not shod, hoping there to find out for certain what price dead souls were going for, and whether she had not—God forbid—made a terrible blunder by selling them at a third of their proper price. The effect produced by this incident may be understood by the reader from a conversation which took place between two ladies. This conversation—but this conversation had better be kept for the following chapter.

CHAPTER 9

In the morning, earlier than the hour usually fixed for calls in the town of N., a lady in a smart checked cloak darted out of the door of an orange-coloured wooden house with a mezzanine and blue columns. She was escorted by a footman in a livery coat, with many collars and gold braid on his round, shining hat. With unusual haste the lady at once skipped up the lowered steps of a carriage that stood at the door. The footman instantly slammed the carriage door, pulled up the steps and catching hold of a strap at the back of the carriage, shouted to the coachman: "Off!" The lady was taking with her a piece of news she had only just heard, and was conscious of an irresistible longing to communicate it as soon as possible. She was every minute looking out of the window and seeing to her unspeakable vexation that they had only gone half-way. Every house seemed longer than usual; the white almshouse with its narrow windows seemed interminable, so that at last she could not resist saying: "The confounded building, there is no end to it." Already twice the coachman had received the order: "Make haste, make haste, Andryushka! You are insufferably slow to-day." At last the goal was reached. The carriage stopped before a dark grey wooden house of one storey, with little white bas-reliefs above the windows, and high trellis fences just in front of the windows, and a narrow little front garden, in which the slender trees were always white with the dust of the town that covered their leaves.

In the windows could be seen pots of flowers, a parrot swinging in a cage and holding the ring in its beak, and two lap-dogs asleep in the sun. In this house lived the lady's bosom friend. The author is extremely perplexed how to name these ladies in such a way as to avoid exciting an outburst of anger, as he has done in the past. To call them by a fictitious surname is dangerous. Whatever name one thinks of, in some corner of our empire—well-called great— some one is sure to be found bearing it, and he is bound to be not slightly but mortally offended, and will declare that the author has secretly paid a visit to the neighbourhood on purpose to find out what he is like, and what sort of a sheepskin he wears, and what Agrafena Ivanovna he visits, and what he likes best to eat. As for speaking of them by their rank in the service, God forbid, that is more dangerous still. All grades and classes now are so mortally sensitive, that everything they find in a book seems to them a personality: apparently this sensitiveness is in the air. It is enough to say that in a certain town there is a stupid man—even that is a personality: a gentleman of respectable appearance will pop up at once and cry out, "Why, I am a man too, so it seems I am stupid"; in fact he perceives at once what is meant. And so in order to avoid all this I will call the lady to whom the visit was made, as she was almost unanimously called in the town of N., that is, a lady agreeable in every respect. She had gained this appellation quite legitimately, for she certainly spared no effort to be obliging in the extreme, although of course through that amiability there stole a glimpse of—oh! what a swift rush of femininity!—and even in her most agreeable phrase would be thrust—oh! what a sharp pin! And God forbid that she should be moved to fury against some one who had somehow poked herself in some way in front of her. But all this would be wrapped up in the most refined politeness such as is only found in provincial towns. Every movement she made was with good taste, she was even fond of poetry; and could hold her head pensively, and every one agreed that she really was a lady agreeable in every respect.

The other lady, that is, the visitor, had not a character so many-sided, and so we will call her the simply agreeable lady. The arrival of the visitor woke the dogs that were sleeping in the sun: shaggy Adèle, always entangled in her own coat, and thin-legged Potpourri.* Both began describing circles with their tails in the hall where the visitor, divested of her cloak, appeared in a dress of fashionable design and colour with long streamers from her neck; a scent of jasmine was wafted all over the hall. As soon as the lady agreeable in all respects heard of the arrival of the simply agreeable lady, she ran out into the hall. The ladies grasped each other's hands, kissed each other and screamed as schoolgirls scream on meeting again after a holiday, before their mothers have managed to explain to them that one is

---

*Motley collection; comic name for a mongrel.

poorer and of a lower rank than another. The kiss was a noisy one, for the dogs began barking again, and were flicked with a handkerchief for doing so, and both of the ladies went off into the drawing-room, which was, of course, pale blue, with a sofa, an oval table and even a little screen with ivy climbing up it; shaggy Adèle and tall Potpourri on his slender legs ran in after them growling. "This way, this way, sit in this corner!" said the lady of the house, installing her friend in the corner of the sofa. "That's right, that's right, and here is a cushion for you." Saying this, she stuffed a cushion in behind her, on which there was a knight worked in wool, as such figures always are worked on canvas, with a nose looking like a ladder and lips forming a square. "How glad I am that it's you. . . . I heard some one drive up and I wondered who it could be so early. Parasha said, 'It's the vice-president's lady,' and I said, 'There, here's that silly creature come to bore me again,' and I was on the point of telling them to say I was not at home."

The visitor was meaning to communicate her piece of news without delay, but an exclamation uttered at that instant by the lady agreeable in all respects gave another turn to the conversation.

"What a sweet bright little print!" exclaimed the lady agreeable in all respects, looking at the dress of the simply agreeable lady.

"Yes, it is very sweet, but Praskovya Fyodorovna thinks it would have been nicer if the checks had been smaller, and if the spots had been pale blue instead of brown. I sent my sister a piece of material: it was so absolutely fascinating, it's simply beyond all words. Just fancy, narrow, narrow little stripes, beyond anything the human fancy can imagine, and a pale blue ground, and all over the stripes, spots and sprigs, spots and sprigs, spots and sprigs . . . in fact quite unique! One may really say there has never been anything like it in the world."

"My dear, that's too gaudy!"

"Oh no, it's not gaudy!"

"Oh, it must be gaudy."

It must be noted that the lady who was agreeable in all respects was something of a materialist, disposed to doubts and scepticism, and there were a great many things she refused to believe in.

Here the simply agreeable lady protested that it was not at all gaudy, and exclaimed: "Oh, I congratulate you, flounces are not to be worn."

"Not worn?"

"Little festoons are coming instead."

"Oh, that's not nice—little festoons!"

"Little festoons, it's all festoons: a pelerine* made of festoons, festoons on the sleeves, epaulettes of little festoons, festoons below and festoons everywhere."

"It's not nice, Sofya Ivanovna, if it's all festoons."

"It's sweet, Anna Grigoryevna, you would never believe how sweet. It's made with two seams, there are wide armholes, and above . . . but now, now you will be astonished, now you will say . . . well, you may wonder: only fancy, the waists are longer than ever, coming down to a point in front, and the front busk is more extreme than ever; the skirt is gathered all round just as in the old-fashioned farthingale, they even stick on a little padding at the back to make you quite a belle-femme."†

"Well, that really is . . . I must say!" said the lady who was agreeable in all respects, tossing her head with a sense of her own dignity.

"Yes, precisely so; I must say!" answered the simply agreeable lady.

"Do what you like, I shall never follow that fashion."

"I feel just the same. . . . Really, when you come to think what extremes fashion will sometimes go to . . . it's beyond anything! I asked my sister to send me the pattern just for fun; my Melanya undertook to make it."

"Why, have you actually got the pattern!" cried the lady agreeable in all respects, with a perceptible throbbing of her heart.

"Yes, my sister brought it."

"My darling, do let me have it, for the sake of all that's holy."

"Oh, I have already promised it to Praskovya Fyodorovna. When she has done with it, perhaps."

"Who is going to wear it after Praskovya Fyodorovna? It is very odd on your part to put strangers before your friends."

"But you know she is my own cousin."

---

*Woman's short cape.
†Beautiful woman (French).

"Queer sort of cousin, only on your husband's side. . . . No, Sofya Ivanovna, you needn't talk to me; it seems you want to put a slight upon me. . . . It's clear that you are tired of me; I see you want to give up being friends with me."

Poor Sofya Ivanovna did not know what to do. She felt she had put herself between the devil and the deep sea. That is what comes of bragging! She felt ready to bite off her silly tongue.

"Well, what news of our charming gentleman?" the lady agreeable in all respects asked.

"Ah, my goodness! Why am I sitting here like this! What an idea! Do you know what I have come to you about, Anna Grigoryevna?" Here the visitor took a deep breath, the words were ready to fly like hawks one after another out of her mouth, and no one less inhuman than her bosom friend could have been so ruthless as to stop her.

"You may praise him up and say all sorts of nice things of him," she said with more vivacity than usual, "but I tell you straight out and I will tell him to his face, that he is a good-for-nothing fellow, good-for-nothing, good-for-nothing."

"But only listen to what I have to tell you. . . ."

"They spread rumours that he was a nice man, but he is not a nice man at all, not at all, and his nose is . . . a most unattractive nose."

"Do let me, do let me only tell you . . . my love, Anna Grigoryevna, let me tell you! Why it's a scandal, do you understand: it's a story, *skonapel eestwah*,"* said the visitor in a voice of entreaty, with an expression almost of despair. I may as well mention that the ladies introduced many foreign words into their conversation, and sometimes whole French sentences. But great as is the author's reverence for the inestimable benefits conferred by the French language on Russia, and great as is his respect for the praiseworthy custom in our aristocratic society of expressing themselves at all hours in that language, entirely, of course, through their love for their fatherland, yet he cannot bring himself to introduce sentences in any foreign language into this Russian poem. And so we will continue in Russian.

"What story?"

---

*Clumsy attempt to pronounce the French phrase *ce qu'on appelle* "*histoire*," meaning "what they call a 'story.' "

"O my precious Anna Grigoryevna! If you could only imagine the state I am in! Only fancy, Father Kirill's wife came to see me this morning, and what do you think? Our visitor who seems so meek, he is a fine one, isn't he?"

"What, do you mean to say he has been making advances to the priest's wife?"

"Ah, Anna Grigoryevna, if it were no worse than that, that would be nothing. Just listen to what she told me. She says that Madame Korobotchka, a lady from the country, came to her, panic-stricken and pale as death, and told her a tale, such a tale! Only listen, it's a regular novel: all at once at dead of night when every one was asleep there came a knock at the gate more awful than anything you could imagine; there was a shout of 'Open, open, or we'll smash open the gate!' . . . What do you think of that? He's a charming fellow after that, isn't he?"

"And what's this Korobotchka like? Is she young and good-looking?"

"Not at all, she's an old lady."

"Oh, how charming! So he's after an old lady? It speaks well for the taste of our ladies; they have pitched on a nice person to fall in love with."

"Well no, Anna Grigoryevna, it's not at all as you suppose. Only imagine, he makes his appearance armed to the teeth like some Rinaldo Rinaldini,* and demands: 'Sell me all your souls that are dead.' Korobotchka answers him very reasonably, saying: 'I can't sell them because they are dead.' 'No,' he said, 'they are not dead, they are mine, it's my business to know whether they are dead or not,' says he. 'They are not dead, not dead,' he shouts, 'not dead!' In fact he makes a fearful scene; all the village rushes up, the children cry, everybody is shouting, no one can make out what's the matter, it was simply an *horreur, horreur, horreur!* . . . You simply can't imagine, Anna Grigoryevna, how upset I was when I heard all this. 'Mistress darling,' my Mashka said to me, 'look in the looking-glass and see how pale you are.' 'Don't talk to me of looking-glasses,' said I, 'I must go and tell Anna Grigoryevna.' I instantly ordered the carriage to be brought round; my coachman Andryushka asked me where to drive and I couldn't speak a word, I simply stared in his face like a fool; I do believe he

---

*Outlaw robber and hero of eponymous German novel (1800) by Christian Vulpius.

thought I had gone mad. Oh, Anna Grigoryevna, if you could only fancy how upset I was!"

"It certainly is odd," said the lady agreeable in all respects. "What can be the meaning of these dead souls? I can't make it out, I must own. This is the second time I have heard of these dead souls; though my husband still declares that Nozdryov's lying, there must be something in it."

"But just fancy, Anna Grigoryevna, what a state I was in when I heard of it. 'And now,' Korobotchka says, 'I don't know,' she says, 'what I'm to do. He made me sign some forged document, threw down fifteen roubles in notes; I am a helpless and inexperienced widow,' she says, 'I know nothing about it. . . .' You see what things are happening! If you could only imagine how upset I am!"

"But, say what you like, it's not a question of dead souls, there's something behind all this."

"I confess I think so too," the simply agreeable lady pronounced, not without surprise, and was instantly aware of an intense desire to find out what it could be that was behind it. She even articulated hesitatingly: "Why, what do you suppose is behind it?"

"Well, what do you think?"

"What do I think? I must own I am completely at a loss."

"All the same, I should like to know what you think about it."

But the agreeable lady could think of nothing to say. She was only capable of being upset, but was quite incapable of forming a coherent hypothesis and that is why she, more than most, stood in need of tender affection and advice.

"Well, let me tell you what's the meaning of these dead souls," said the lady agreeable in all respects, and at these words her visitor was all attention; her ears seemed to prick up of themselves, she rose up in her seat, scarcely touching the sofa, and though she was a somewhat solid lady, seemed to grow slimmer, and as light as a feather which might fly off into the air at a puff of wind.

So when a hare, startled by the beaters, darts out of the forest, the sportsman with his horse and his riding whip is suddenly like powder waiting for the match to be applied. He gazes into the murky air and is already with faultless aim striking at the beast, has already slain it, however the whirling snowy steppe may rise up against him, scattering silvery stars on his lips, his moustache, his eyes, his brows, and on his beaver cap.

"The dead souls . . ." pronounced the lady agreeable in all respects.

"Well, well!" cried her visitor, all excitement.

"The dead souls! . . ."

"Oh, speak, for God's sake!"

"They are simply a cover, but this is what he is really after: he is trying to elope with the governor's daughter."

This conclusion was indeed utterly unexpected and in every way extraordinary. The agreeable lady, on hearing it, was simply petrified, she turned pale, she turned pale as death, and certainly was upset in earnest. "Oh dear!" she cried, clasping her hands, "that I never should have supposed!"

"But as soon as you opened your mouth, I saw what was in the wind," answered the lady who was agreeable in all respects.

"Well, what is one to think of boarding-school education after this, Anna Grigoryevna! So this is their innocence!"

"Innocence, indeed! I have heard her say such things as I could not bring myself to repeat!"

"It's heartrending, you know, Anna Grigoryevna, to see what lengths depravity can go to."

"And the men are all wild over her, though for my part I must own I can see nothing in her. . . . She is insufferably affected."

"Ah, my precious, Anna Grigoryevna! she's a statue, if only she had a little expression in her face."

"Ah, how affected she is! Ah, how affected! My goodness, how affected! Who taught her to behave like that I don't know; but I have never seen a girl give herself such airs."

"My darling, she is like a statue and deathly pale."

"Oh, don't talk to me, Sofya Ivanovna, she rouges shamelessly."

"What do you mean, Anna Grigoryevna? she is like chalk, chalk, simply chalk."

"My dear, I was sitting beside her, the rouge was as thick as my finger and kept peeling off like plaster. The mother has set her an example; she is a coquette and the daughter is worse than the mother!"

"Oh, excuse me, come, I'll swear by anything you like, I'll wager my children, my husband, all my property this minute, if there is a single drop, a grain, a shadow of rouge upon her!"

"Oh, what are you saying, Sofya Ivanovna!" said the lady agreeable in all respects, and she clasped her hands.

"Oh, what a woman you are, Anna Grigoryevna, really! I wonder at you!" said the agreeable lady, and she too clasped her hands.

The reader must not be surprised that the ladies were not agreed about what they had both seen almost at the same moment. There are indeed many things in the world, which have the peculiar property of appearing absolutely white when one lady looks at them, and as red as a cranberry in the eyes of another.

"Well, here's another proof for you that she is pale," the agreeable lady went on, "I remember as though it were now, how I was sitting beside Manilov and said to him: 'Just look how pale she is.' Any one must be as senseless as our gentlemen here to be so fascinated by her. And our charming gentleman . . . How hateful I thought him! You can't imagine, Anna Grigoryevna, how hateful I thought him."

"Yet there were ladies who were quite taken with him."

"I, Anna Grigoryevna? No, you can never say that, never, never!"

"But I am not talking about you, as though there were nobody but you."

"Never, never, Anna Grigoryevna! Allow me to tell you what I know myself very well indeed! Perhaps there may have been something on the part of some ladies who give themselves out as so unapproachable."

"I beg your pardon, Sofya Ivanovna! Allow me to tell you that there has never been any scandalous gossip about me. About any one else, perhaps, but not about me, allow me to tell you."

"What are you taking offence for? There were other ladies there, you know, such as those who made a rush for the chairs by the door so as to sit near him."

It might have seemed inevitable that a storm should follow these observations of the agreeable lady, but, marvellous to relate, both ladies suddenly subsided and nothing whatever followed. The lady agreeable in all respects remembered that the pattern of the new fashion was not yet in her possession, and the simply agreeable lady reflected that she had not yet succeeded in extracting any details of the affair that her bosom friend had just revealed to her, and so peace was very quickly restored. It could not be said, however, of either of the ladies that the desire to make herself disagreeable was characteristic; indeed there was nothing spiteful in their disposition, it was simply that in conversation a slight inclination to stick pins in one another sprang up of itself unconsciously. It was simply that each derived some slight gratification from slipping in a sharp word at the expense of the other, as much as to say: "That's one for you!" "Take that to yourself!" There are all sorts of impulses in the hearts of the feminine as well as of the masculine sex.

"The only thing I can't understand, though," said the simply agreeable lady, "is how Tchitchikov, a stranger in these parts, could venture to attempt such an audacious proceeding. There surely must be others implicated in the affair."

"Why, did you suppose there were not?"

"Why, who do you think can be assisting him?"

"Well, Nozdryov anyway."

"Nozdryov! really?"

"Why, it is just in his line. You know that he tried to sell his own father, or worse still, staked him at cards."

"Oh dear, what interesting things you tell me! I never could have imagined that Nozdryov was mixed up in this affair."

"I always took it for granted."

"Really, the things that do happen in the world, when you come to think of it; who could have supposed when Tchitchikov first came among us, do you remember, that he would make such a strange upset in the world. O Anna Grigoryevna, if only you knew how upset I feel! If it were not for your friendship and affection . . . I should really be on the brink of despair. What are we coming to! My Mashka saw I was as pale as death; 'Mistress, darling!' said she, 'you are as pale as death.' 'Mashka,' I cried, 'I can't think of that now.' What a thing to happen! So Nozdryov's in it! Well I declare!"

The agreeable lady was very eager to hear further details concerning the elopement, that is, at what o'clock it would take place and so on, but she wanted too much. The lady agreeable in all respects professed her entire ignorance of all this. She was incapable of lying: to assume the truth of a supposition was a different matter, but even then the supposition must be founded on her inner conviction; if she were conscious of an inner conviction she was quite capable of defending her position, and any lawyer renowned for his power of turning other people's opinions might have tried his powers on her and he would have seen what an inner conviction means.

That both ladies were in the end fully convinced of what they had at first assumed as a mere supposition is nothing out of the way. We learned people, as we call ourselves, behave in almost the same way, and our learned theories are a proof of it. At first our savants approach them in almost a cringing spirit, they begin timidly, discreetly, they begin with the humblest suggestion: "Is not this the origin? Does not such a country derive its name from such and such a spot?" or, "Is not this document connected with another of a later period?" or, "Should we not take such and such a people to mean this or that other people?" He immediately quotes such and such ancient writers, and if he can only detect a hint or what he takes for a hint, he grows audacious and confident, talks to the writers of antiquity without ceremony, asks them questions and himself supplies the answers, quite forgetting that he had begun with a timid hypothesis; he soon fancies that he sees it, that it is clear, and his argument is concluded with the words, "This is how it was: so this is the people that is meant by this name! This is how we must look at the subject!" Then it is proclaimed to all from the platform—and the newly discovered truth is sent on its travels round the world, gathering to itself followers and disciples.

While the two ladies were so cleverly and successfully interpreting this intricate affair, the public prosecutor with his invariably immobile face, his thick eyebrows and winking eyelid, walked into the room. The ladies vied with each other in explaining the whole episode, they told him of the purchase of the dead souls, and of the plot to carry off the governor's daughter, and completely bewildered him, so that in spite of his standing on the same spot winking with his left eye, and flicking his beard with his handkerchief to brush off some snuff from it, he was utterly unable to make head or tail of it. And so the two ladies left him standing and went each on her way to rouse the town. They succeeded in carrying out this enterprise in a little over half an hour. The town certainly was roused; everything was in a ferment and no one knew what to think. The ladies succeeded in throwing such a mist over the eyes of every one, that all, and especially the officials, were for a time completely overwhelmed.

They found themselves for the first moment in the position of a schoolboy whose schoolfellows have thrust a twist of paper full of snuff up his nose while he is asleep. Breathing up all the snuff with the energy of sleep, he wakes and jumps up, looks about him like an idiot with his eyes starting out of his head and cannot grasp where he is, what has happened to him, and then recognises the walls lighted up by the slanting rays of the sun, the laughter of his companions hiding in the corners, and glancing out of window, sees the early morning with the awakening forest resounding with the notes of a thousand birds, and the shining river, lost here and there in gleaming zigzags among the slender reeds, and dotted with naked boys calling each other to bathe—and last of all perceives what has been put in his nose.

Such was exactly the position of the inhabitants and officials of the town for the first moment. Each one of them stood like a sheep with his eyes starting out of his head. Dead souls, the governor's daughter and Tchitchikov were mixed together in the strangest confusion in their brains; and only later on, after the first stupefaction had passed, they began as it were to disentangle and separate them, they began to demand explanations and to be vexed, seeing that the affair refused to become intelligible. "What is the meaning of it really, what is the meaning of these dead souls? There is no sense in dead souls, how can one buy dead souls? Who would be such a fool as to accept them? And queer sort of money one would pay for them! And to what purpose, to what use could dead souls be put? And why is the governor's daughter mixed up in it? If he wanted to elope with her, why should he buy dead souls? If he wanted to buy dead souls, why should he run away with the governor's daughter? Does he want to make her a present of these dead souls or what? What nonsensical stories they do spread about the town. What are things coming to when you can hardly turn round before there is some scandal going about you, and not a word of sense in it either. . . . The story is going about though, so there must be some reason for it. What reason could there be for dead souls? There is positively no reason for it. It's all fiddlesticks, nonsense rhymes, soft-boiled boots! It's simply the deuce! . . ." In short, the discussions were endless, and all the town was talking of dead souls and the governor's daughter, of Tchitchikov and dead souls, of the governor's daughter and Tchitchikov, and everything was in a stir. The town that till then had been wrapped in slumber was boiling like a whirlpool. All the sluggards and lazybones who had been for years lounging at home in dressing-gowns abusing the shoemaker for making their boots too narrow, or the tailor or the drunken coachman, crept out of their holes; all who had dropped all their acquaintances years ago and whose only friends, to use the popular expression, were Mr. Slugabed and Mr. Sleepyhead (characters as well known all over Russia as the phrase, "visiting Mr. Snooze and Mr. Snore," which signifies to sleep like the dead on the side, or the back, or in any other position to the accompaniment of snoring, wheezing and so on); all those who could not have been lured out of their houses even by an invitation to taste a fish soup costing five hundred roubles, with sturgeon six feet long, and all sorts of fish-pasties which melt in the mouth, turned out now; in fact it seemed as though the town were busy and important and very well populated. A Sysoy Pafnutevitch and a Makdonald Karlovitch who had never been heard of before appeared in public. A long lanky gentleman with his arm in a sling, taller than any one who had been seen before, was conspicuous in the drawing-rooms. Closed chaises, unfamiliar waggonettes, all sorts of turn-outs, rattling and squeaking, appeared in the street—and there was soon a fine to-do. At another time and under other circumstances, such rumours would perhaps not have attracted attention, but it was a long time since the town of N. had heard any news at all. In fact for the last three months there had not been in the town of N. what in Petersburg is called *Commérages*,* which, as we all know, is as important for a town as the van that brings its provisions. Two quite opposite points of view were at once apparent in the discussions in the town, and two opposing parties, masculine and feminine, were immediately formed. The masculine party, the more irrational, concentrated their attention on the dead souls. The feminine party were completely absorbed by the abduction of the governor's daughter.

To the credit of the ladies, in the latter party there was far more discipline and watchfulness. It was evidently their vocation to be good managers and organisers. With them everything soon took a vivid, definite shape, and clothed in clear and distinct forms, was ex-

*Gossip (French).

plained and classified, and the result was a finished picture. It appeared that Tchitchikov had been in love for months, and that they used to meet in the garden by moonlight, that the governor would have given his consent to the match as Tchitchikov was as rich as a Jew, had it not been for his wife, whom he had abandoned (how they had learned that Tchitchikov was married no one could say), and that his wife, who was brokenhearted and hopelessly in love with him, had written the most touching letter to the governor, and that Tchitchikov, seeing that the father and mother would never give their consent, had determined on an elopement. In other houses the story was told a little differently: that Tchitchikov had not a wife at all, but as a subtle man, who liked to be sure of his ground, he had, in order to win the daughter, begun by laying siege to the mother, and had a secret amour with her, and that he had made a proposal for the hand of the daughter; but the mother, horrified at the thought of so criminal and impious a proceeding, and suffering from pangs of conscience, had refused point blank, and this was why Tchitchikov had planned an elopement. Many variations and additions were tacked on to this, as the rumours penetrated into the more remote corners of the town. In Russia, the lower ranks of society are very fond of discussing the scandals that take place among their betters, and so all this began to be talked about in little houses in which no one had ever set eyes on Tchitchikov, or knew anything about him, fresh complications were added and further explanations were made. The subject became more interesting every minute, and took a more definite form every day, and at last was brought to the ears of the governor's wife herself in its final shape. As the mother of a family, as the leading lady in the town, as a lady in fact quite unsuspicious of anything of the sort, she was deeply wounded by this tittle-tattle, and was moved to an indignation which was, indeed, perfectly justified. The poor schoolgirl had to endure one of the most unpleasant interviews to which a girl of sixteen has ever been exposed. A perfect torrent of questions, inquiries, upbraidings, threats, reproaches, admonitions were poured out, so that the girl burst into tears, sobbed, and could not understand a word. The porter received the strictest orders never on any pretext or under any circumstances to admit Tchitchikov.

Having done their duty by the governor's wife, the ladies attacked the men's party, trying to bring them over to their side, and maintaining that the dead souls were a mere pretext only made up to avert suspicion and to enable the elopement to be carried out more successfully. Many of the men were brought over and joined the ladies' party, although they were exposed to severe censure from their fellows, who called them old women and petticoats—names, as we all know, most insulting to the male sex.

But in spite of the defence and resistance put up by the men, there was by no means the same discipline in their party as in the women's. With them everything was crude, unpolished, inharmonious, untidy and poor; there was a discordance, a chaos, an incoherence, a muddle in their thoughts—in fact it exemplified the worthless character of man, his coarse dense nature, incapable of domestic management, and of genuine convictions, lacking in faith, slothful, always full of doubts and everlasting apprehensions. They said that this was all nonsense, that eloping with the governor's daughter was more in a Hussar's line than in a civilian's, that Tchitchikov would not do that, that women talked nonsense, that a woman was a sack—she would swallow anything; that the important point to take notice of was the purchase of the dead souls, and what the devil that meant there was no saying, though there was certainly something very nasty and unpleasant about it. Why the men thought there was something very nasty and unpleasant about it we shall learn immediately. A new governor-general had been appointed for the province, an event as every one knows that always throws the local officials into great perturbation: it is invariably followed by dismissals, reprimands, punishments, and the various official treats with which higher officers regale their subordinates. "Why," thought the local officials, "if he finds out that these stupid rumours are going about the town, his fury may be a matter of life and death." The inspector of the medical board suddenly turned pale: he imagined, God knows why, that the words "dead souls" might be a reference to the patients, who had died in considerable numbers in the hospitals and infirmaries of an epidemic fever, against which no proper precautions had been taken, and that Tchitchikov might have been sent by the governor-general to gather secret information. He mentioned this to the president of the court. The president answered that this was absurd, and then grew pale himself, as he wondered whether the souls bought by Tchitchikov were really dead, and he had allowed the deed of purchase to be drawn up and had even acted for Plyushkin in the matter, and if this were to come to the governor-general's knowledge, what would happen? He did no more than mention this to one or two others, and those one or two others instantly turned pale too; fear is more contagious than the plague and is instantly communicated. They all discovered in themselves even sins they had not committed. The phrase "dead souls" was so vaguely suggestive, that they began to suspect that there might be in it an allusion to corpses buried in haste, in consequence of two incidents which had occurred not long before. The first incident was connected with some merchants who had come from another district to the fair and, after selling their goods, had given to other merchants a banquet on the Russian scale with German concoctions: orgeats,* punches, balsams† and so on. The banquet ended as usual in a fight. The merchants who gave the entertainment beat their guests to death, though they suffered violent treatment at their hands, blows in the ribs, in the pit of the stomach and elsewhere, that testified to the size of the fists with which nature had endowed their deceased opponents. One of the successful party had his "beak broken off" as the combatants expressed it, that is, his nose was so completely smashed, that there was not more than a half finger's breadth left on his face. At their trial the merchants pleaded guilty, explaining that they had had just a drop. There were rumours that while on their trial they had offered four imperial notes each to the judges. The case was very obscure, however; from the inquiry and the report that was made, it appeared that the merchants had been suffocated by charcoal fumes and as such they were buried. The other event, which had taken place only recently, was as follows: the Crown peasants of the village of Vshivaya-Spyess in conjunction with the Crown peasants of the village of Borovka, otherwise Zadirailovo, were accused of having made away with the rural police in the shape of one Drobyazhkin, a tax-assessor; it was said that the rural police, that is Drobyazhkin, had taken to visiting their village with excessive frequency, which in some cases is as bad as a pestilence, and the reason of his doing so was that the "rural police," having a weakness for the fair sex, ran after the village girls

---

*Drinks made with almonds, sugar, and orange extract.
†Aromatic, resinated drinks.

and women. This was not known for certain, however, though in their evidence the peasants plainly stated that the "rural police" was as wanton as a tom-cat, and that they had lain in wait for him more than once and on one occasion had kicked him stark naked out of a hut where he lay hidden. The "rural police," of course, did deserve to be punished for his amatory propensities. But the peasants of both villages were on their side, too, certainly guilty of taking the law into their own hands, that is, if they really committed the murder. But the facts were not clear. The "rural police" was found on the road, the uniform or coat on the "rural police" was nothing but a rag, and even his face was unrecognisable.

The case went through the local courts and was brought at last before the high court, where it was at first deliberated on in private, to this effect: since it was not known which of the peasants had taken part in the crime, and since there were many of them; since Drobyazhkin was dead, so that it would not be much advantage to him, even if he did win the case, while the peasants were still alive, so that a decision in their favour was very important for them, it was therefore decided that Drobyazhkin was himself responsible, since he had been guilty of oppressive treatment of the peasants, and that he had died in his sledge of an apoplectic stroke. The case, it would seem, had been neatly settled; but the officials, for some inexplicable reason, began to think that these were the dead souls in question.

As ill luck would have it, just when the officials were in this difficult position, two communications to the governor arrived at the same time. The first informed him that, from evidence and reports received, it appeared that a forger of counterfeit notes was in their province, concealed under various aliases, and that a very strict search was to be made at once. The other was a despatch from the governor of a neighbouring province, and was concerned with the escape from justice of a brigand, and directed that if any suspicious person who could not produce a passport or give a good account of himself were to be found in the province, he was to be at once arrested. These two documents had a shattering effect on every one. Their previous conclusions and surmises were completely checkmated. Of course it could not be supposed that there was any reference to Tchitchikov; all of them, however, as they pondered, each from his own point of view, realised that they did not know what sort of man Tchitchikov was, that he had been very vague in his account of himself, that he had indeed said that he had suffered in the cause of justice, but that was all very indefinite, and when they remembered at the same time that he had actually said that he had many enemies who had attempted his life, they wondered all the more: his life, then, was in danger; he was, then, being pursued; so he must have done something. . . . And who was he in reality? Of course it could not be thought that he had forged counterfeit notes and still less that he was a brigand—his appearance was most respectable; but with all that, what sort of person could he be? And now the officials asked themselves the question which they ought to have asked themselves in the first chapter of my poem. It was decided to make inquiries of the persons from whom the dead souls had been bought, so as to find out at least what sort of transaction it was, and what was to be understood by dead souls, and whether he had not perhaps explained to some one casually in some chance word what was his real intention, and whether he had not told some one who he really was. First of all they went to Madame Korobotchka, but they did not get much out of her: he had bought them, she said, for fifteen roubles and was going to buy poultry feathers too, and had promised to buy a great many things, to take fat pork for a government contract, and so he was certainly a rogue, for she had a fellow before buy poultry feathers and fat pork for the government, and he took every one in and cheated the head priest's wife out of a hundred roubles. Everything else she said was almost a repetition of the same thing, and the officials gathered nothing from it but that she was a foolish old woman. Manilov replied that he was ready to answer for Pavel Ivanovitch as for himself, that he would give his whole estate for a hundredth part of Pavel Ivanovitch's good qualities, and altogether used the most flattering expressions of him, adding some reflections in regard to friendship, while his eyes almost closed with emotion. No doubt these reflections satisfactorily explained the tender emotions of his heart, but they threw no light on the matter in question. Sobakevitch replied that in his opinion Tchitchikov was a good man, and that he had sold him peasants to be settled in another province, and they were living in every respect; but that he could not answer for what would happen in the future, that if they were to die during transportation from the hardships of the journey, it would not be his fault, that was in

God's hands, and that there were plenty of fevers and dangerous illnesses, and that there were instances of whole villages dying of them
at once. The official gentlemen had recourse to one other method
which was not perfectly honourable perhaps, but which is however
sometimes employed, that is, through various acquaintances in the
servants' quarters to question privately Tchitchikov's serfs, and to find
out whether they knew anything of their master's past life or circumstances: but again they got very little. From Petrushka they got
nothing but the smell of a stuffy room, while from Selifan they heard
that: "he was engaged in the Imperial Service, and before that was in
the Revenue Department"—and nothing more. Persons of this class
have a very strange habit. If they are asked a direct question they are
utterly unable to remember anything, cannot put their thoughts in
order, and even answer simply that they do not know, but if they are
questioned about something different, they immediately complicate
it with ever so many details that you do not want to hear. All the investigations made by the officials revealed to them nothing but that
they did not know what Tchitchikov was, and at the same time that
Tchitchikov certainly must be something. They resolved at last to discuss the subject thoroughly, and to decide at least what they were to
do, how they were to act and what steps they were to take, and what
he was precisely, whether he was the sort of person who was to be
seized and detained as a suspicious character, or whether he was the
sort of person who might seize and detain all of them as suspicious
characters. To do all this it was proposed to meet together at the
house of the police-master, who is already known to the reader as the
father and benefactor of the town.

CHAPTER 10

When they met at the house of the police-master, already known to the reader as the father and benefactor of the town, the officials had the opportunity of observing of each other that they had actually grown thin through all these worries and anxieties. And, indeed, the appointment of a new governor-general, and the two documents of so serious a character, and these extraordinary rumours, had, all taken together, left a perceptible imprint on their faces, and the dress-coats of some of them had become noticeably looser. Everything was changed for the worse: the president was thinner, and the inspector of the medical board was thinner, and the prosecutor was thinner, and one Semyon Ivanovitch, who was never called by his surname, and wore on his first finger a ring which he used to show to ladies—even he was thinner. Of course there were some bold spirits, as there always are, who did not lose their presence of mind; but they were not many; in fact the postmaster was the only one. He alone was unchanged in his invariable composure, and always when such things happened was in the habit of saying: "We know all about you governor-generals! You may be changed three or four times over, but I have been for thirty years in the same place, my good sir." To this the other officials usually answered: "It's all very well for you, Sprechen Sie Deutsch, Ivan Andreitch: the post office is your job—receiving and dispatching the mails; the worst you can do is to close the post office an hour too early if you are in a bad temper, or to accept a late letter from some merchant at the wrong hour, or to send off some parcel which ought not to be sent off—any one would be a saint, of course, in your place. But suppose you had the devil at your elbow every day, so that even what you don't want to take he thrusts upon you. You have not much to fear, to be sure; you have only one son; while God has been so bountiful to Praskovya Fyodorovna, my boy, that not a year passes but she presents me with a little Praskovya or a little Petrushka; in our place, you'd sing a different tune, my boy." So said the officials, but whether it is really possible to resist the devil it is not for the author to decide. In the council assembled on this occasion, there was a conspicuous absence of that essential thing which among the common people is called good sense. We seem somehow not made for representative institutions. In all our assemblies, from the meetings of the peasants up to all kinds of learned and other committees, there is a pretty thorough muddle, unless there is some one at the head who is managing it all. It is hard to say why it is. Apparently the nature of the Russian people is such, that the only successful committees are those formed to arrange entertainments, or dinners, such as clubs, or pleasure gardens in the German style. Yet we are always ready at any minute for anything. We fly like the wind to get up benevolent and philanthropic societies and goodness knows what. The aim may be excellent but nothing ever comes of it. Perhaps it is because we are satisfied at the very beginning and consider everything has already been done. For instance, after organising a society for the benefit of the poor, and subscribing a considerable sum, we immediately spend half of the fund subscribed on giving a dinner to all the worthies of the town in celebration of our laudable enterprise; with what is left of our funds we promptly take a grand house with heating arrangements and porters for the use of the committee; after which five roubles and a half is all that is left for the poor, and over the distribution of that sum, the members of the committee cannot agree, each one urging the claims of some crony of his own. The committee that met on this occasion was of quite another kind: it was formed through urgent necessity. It was not a question of the poor or of outsiders at all: it concerned every official personally: the occasion was a calamity which threatened all alike, and so the meeting should have been more unanimous and more united. But for all that the result was awfully queer. To say nothing of the differences of opinion that crop up at every meeting, an inexplicable indecisiveness was apparent in the views of all present; one said that Tchitchikov was a forger of government notes, and then added, "Though perhaps he isn't a forger"; another declared that he was an official in the governor-general's office, and at once went on, "Though the devil only knows, it is not branded on his forehead." All were opposed to the suggestion that he was a brigand in disguise. They considered that besides his appearance, which was highly respectable, there was nothing in his conversation to suggest a man given to deeds of violence. All at once the postmaster, who had been standing for some minutes lost in meditation, cried out suddenly from some inspiration or from something else: "Do you know who he is, my friends?" There was something so striking in the voice in which he uttered this, that it made them all cry out with one voice: "Who?" "He is no other than Captain Kopeykin, gentlemen!" And when they all instantly asked with one voice, "Who is Captain Kopeykin?" the postmaster said: "Why, don't you know who Captain Kopeykin is?"

They all answered that they did not know who Captain Kopeykin was.

"Captain Kopeykin," said the postmaster, opening his snuffbox only a little way for fear that some of his neighbours should take a pinch with fingers in whose cleanliness he had no confidence—he was, indeed, in the habit of saying, "We know, my good sir, there is no telling where your fingers have been, and snuff's a thing that must be kept clean,"—"Captain Kopeykin," he repeated as he took a pinch: "why you know if I were to tell you, it would make a regular romance after a fashion, very interesting to any author."

Every one present expressed a desire to hear this story, or as the postmaster expressed it, a regular romance after a fashion, very interesting to any author, and he began as follows:

"After the campaign of 1812, my good sir"—so the postmaster began his story, regardless of the fact that not one but six gentlemen were sitting in the room—"after the campaign of 1812, Captain Kopeykin was sent back with the wounded. A hot-headed fellow, as whimsical as the devil, he had been punished in various ways and been under arrest—there was nothing he had not had a taste of. Whether it was at Krasnoe* or at Leipzig† I can't say but, can you fancy, he had an arm and a leg blown off. Well, at that time, no arrangements had been made, you know, about the wounded; that— what do you call it?—pension fund for the wounded was only set going, can you fancy, long afterwards. Captain Kopeykin saw that he would have to work, but he only had one arm, you understand, the left. He went home to his father's. His father said, 'I can't keep you,

---

*Or Krasny; town west of Moscow near Smolensk; site of a decisive 1812 battle during Napoléon's invasion of Russia, in which Russian troops resisted a French advance.
†City in eastern Germany; site of the 1813 "Battle of the Nations," in which Napoléon I was defeated and forced to retreat.

I can scarcely,' only fancy, 'get a crust of bread for myself.' So my Captain Kopeykin made up his mind to go to Petersburg, my good sir, to see whether he could get help from the authorities, to put it to them, in a manner of speaking, that he had sacrificed his life and shed his blood. . . . Well, in one way or another, on a train of wagons, you know, or on the government vans, he got at last to Petersburg, my good sir. Well, can you fancy, here what do you call him, I mean, Captain Kopeykin, found himself in the capital, the like of which, in a manner of speaking, there is not in the world! All at once a world, in a manner of speaking, lies before him, a certain plane of life, a fairy tale of Scheherazade,* you understand. All at once, can you fancy, the Nevsky Prospect or Gorohovaya,† dash it all, or Liteiny; there is a spire of some sort in the air; the bridges hang there like the devil, only fancy, without any support, that is, in short, a Semiramis,‡ sir, and that's the only word for it! He made some attempts to get lodgings, only it was all terribly dear: curtains, blinds, all sorts of devilry, you understand, carpets—Persia, sir, in short . . . in a manner of speaking, you trample fortunes under foot. You walk along the street and your very nose can sniff the thousands: and all my Captain Kopeykin's banking account consisted of some fifty roubles and some silver. . . . Well, you can't buy an estate with that, you know, you might buy one perhaps, if you added forty thousand to it, but you would have to borrow the forty thousand from the King of France; well, he found a refuge in a tavern for a rouble a day; dinner—cabbage soup, a piece of beef-steak . . . he sees it won't do to stay there long. He makes inquiries where he is to apply? 'Where are you to apply?' they say, 'the higher authorities are not in Petersburg yet.' They were all in Paris, you understand, the troops had not come back yet. 'But there is a temporary committee,' they tell him. 'You had better try there, maybe they can do something.' 'I'll go to the committee,' says Kopeykin. 'I'll say that I have, in a manner of speaking, shed my blood, that in a sense I have sacrificed my life.' So, sir, getting up early he combed his beard with his left hand, for to pay a barber would be in a certain sense to run up a bill, he pulled on

---

*Storytelling heroine in the Arabian tales *The Thousand and One Nights*.
†Prominent streets in St. Petersburg.
‡Legendary queen of Assyria said to have founded the city of Babylon.

his shabby uniform and stumped off, only fancy, on his wooden leg to the chief of the committee. He inquired where the chief lives. 'Over yonder,' they tell him, 'a house on the embankment': a poor hovel, you understand, glass panes in the windows, only fancy, mirrors ten feet across, marbles, footmen, my good sir, in fact, enough to turn you giddy. A metal handle on the door—a luxury of the highest class so that one would have to run to the shop, you know, and buy a ha'porth of soap and scrub away at one's hands for a couple of hours in a manner of speaking, and then perhaps one might venture to take hold of the handle. A porter at the door, you understand, with a stick in his hand, a face like a count's, a cambric collar, like some fat, over-fed pug dog. . . . My Kopeykin dragged himself somehow on his wooden leg to the reception room, squeezed himself into a corner for fear he might jerk his elbow against some American or Indian, only fancy, gilt china vase of some sort. Well, I need hardly say he had to wait till he had had enough, for he arrived at the hour when the chief was, in a manner of speaking, just getting out of bed, and his valet had just brought him a silver basin for washing and all that, don't you know. My Kopeykin waits for four hours, and then the clerk on duty comes in and says: 'The director will be here directly.' And the room was full up by then with epaulettes and shoulder knots, as many people as beans on a plate. At last, my good sir, the director comes in. Well . . . can you imagine . . . the director! In his face, so to say . . . well in keeping, you understand, . . . with his position and his rank . . . such an expression, you know. He had a tip-top manner in every way; he goes up first to one and then to another: 'What have you come about? What do you want? What is your business?' At last, my good sir, he goes up to Kopeykin. Kopeykin says one thing and another. 'I have shed my blood, I have lost my arms and legs, I can't work—I make bold to ask, will there not be some assistance, some sort of an arrangement in regard to compensation, so to speak, a pension or something, you understand. The director sees that the man has got a wooden leg and that his right sleeve is empty and pinned to his uniform. 'Very good,' he says, 'come again in a day or two.' My Kopeykin is highly delighted. 'Come,' he thinks, 'the matter's settled.' He hops along the pavement in such spirits as you can fancy, goes into the Palkinsky restaurant, drinks a glass of vodka, dines, my good sir, at the London restaurant, orders cutlets, with caper sauce, a chicken with all sorts of trimmings, asks for a bottle of wine, and in the evening goes to the theatre—in fact he has a jolly good time, so to say. In the street he sees a graceful English girl, floating along like a swan, only fancy. My Kopeykin—his blood was a little heated, you understand—was just about to run after her on his wooden leg, tap, tap along the pavement. 'But no,' he thought, 'to the devil with dangling after ladies for the time being! Better later on, when I get my pension. I have let myself go a little too much as it is.' And meanwhile he had spent almost half his money in one day, I beg you to observe. Three or four days later he goes to the committee to see the director. 'I have come,' he said, 'to hear what you have for me, owing to the illnesses and wounds I have sustained . . . I have in a sense shed my blood . . .' and that sort of thing, you understand, in the language suitable. 'Well,' said the director, 'I must tell you first of all that we can do nothing in your case without instructions from the higher command. You see yourself the position. Military operations are, in a manner of speaking, not completely over yet. You must wait till the minister arrives, you must have patience. Then you may be sure you won't be overlooked. And if you have nothing to live upon, here,' he said, 'here is something to help you. . . .' And what he gave him, you understand, was not very much, though with prudence it might have lasted till further instructions came. But that was not what my Kopeykin wanted. He had been reckoning on their paying him a thousand roubles down or something of the sort, with 'There you are, my dear boy, drink and make merry,' and instead of that, 'You can wait,' and no date fixed either. And already, you know, he had visions of the English girl and little suppers and cutlets. So he went down the steps as glum as an owl, looking like a poodle that has been drenched with water, with its ears drooping and its tail between its legs. Life in Petersburg had already got a hold on him, he had had some taste of it already. And now there was no knowing how he was to live, and he had no hope of any luxuries, you understand. And you know he was full of life and health and he had the appetite of a wolf. He passes some restaurant; and the cook there, only fancy, a Frenchman of some sort with an open countenance, with a linen shirt, an apron as white, in a manner of speaking, as snow, is

making fines-herbes* or cutlets with truffles, in fact all sorts of such
delicacies that it would give one appetite enough to eat oneself. He
passes Milyutinsky's shop, there is a salmon looking out of window,
in a manner of speaking, cherries at five roubles the measure. A huge
watermelon as big as an omnibus peeps out of window and seems
to be looking for some one fool enough to pay a hundred roubles
for it—in short, there is temptation at every step, his mouth water-
ing, so to speak, and he must wait. So imagine his position: here on
one side, so to say, there is salmon and watermelon, while on the
other side they present him with the bitter dish called 'to-morrow.'
'Well,' he thinks, 'they can do as they like, but I will go,' he says, 'and
rouse all the committee, every one in authority. I shall say, "do as you
like."' And he certainly was a persistent, impudent fellow, no sense
in his head, you understand, but plenty of bounce. He goes to the
committee: 'Well, what is it?' they say. 'Why are you back again? You
have been told already.' 'I can't scrape along anyhow,' he says. 'I want
to eat a cutlet, have a bottle of French wine, enjoy myself in the theatre too, you understand. . . .' 'Well, you must excuse me,' said the
director. 'For all that you must, in a manner of speaking, have patience. You have been given something to keep you for the time, till
instructions arrive, and no doubt you will be properly pensioned,
for it has never happened yet that among us in Russia a man who
has, in a manner of speaking, deserved well of his country should be
left without recognition. But if you want to pamper yourself with
cutlets and the theatre, then you must excuse me. In that case, you
must find the means and do what you can for yourself.' But my
Kopeykin, can you fancy, did not turn a hair. Those words bounced
off him like peas against a wall. He made such an uproar, he did let
them have it! He began going for them all and swearing at them, all
of them, the head clerks and the secretaries. 'You are this,' he said,
'you are that,' he said, 'you don't know your duties,' he said. He gave
them all a dressing. A general turned up, you know, from quite a different department; he went for him too, my good sir! He made such
a row. What's to be done with a beggar like that? The director sees
that they must have recourse, so to say, to stern measures. 'Very
good,' he says, 'if you won't be satisfied with what is given you, and

---

*Mixture of herbs used for seasoning (French).

wait quietly, in a manner of speaking, here in the capital for your case to be settled, I will find a lodging for you elsewhere. Call the attendant,' he said, 'take him to a place of detention!' And the attendant was there already, you understand, at the door, a man seven feet high, with a great fist made by nature for a driver, only fancy, a regular dentist, in fact. . . . So they put him, the servant of God, into a cart, with the attendant. 'Well,' thinks Kopeykin, 'I shan't have to pay my fare, anyway, that is something to be thankful for.' He goes in the cart, and as he goes he thinks: 'Very good,' he thinks, 'you told me I must find means for myself; very good, I will find them!' Well, how they took him to his destination and where he was taken, no one knows. All traces of Captain Kopeykin were lost, you understand, in the waters of oblivion, in Lethe,* or whatever the poets call it. But here, gentlemen, allow me to point out, begins the gist of the story. What became of Kopeykin no one knows, but before two months had passed, would you believe it, a band of robbers made their appearance in the forests of Ryazan and the chief of that band, my good sir, was no other than . . ."

"But excuse me, Ivan Andryevitch," said the police-master, suddenly interrupting him, "why, you said yourself that Captain Kopeykin lost an arm and a leg, while Tchitchikov has . . ."

The postmaster cried out, slapped himself on the forehead and called himself a calf publicly before them all. He could not understand how the circumstance had not occurred to him at the beginning of the story, and confessed that the saying, "The Russian is wise after the event," was perfectly true. A minute later, however, he began to be ingenious and tried to wriggle out of it, saying that mechanical limbs had been brought to a wonderful perfection in England, that it seemed from the papers that a man had invented artificial legs, that by merely touching an unseen spring would carry a man goodness knows where, so that he could never be found again.

But every one was extremely doubtful whether Tchitchikov really was Captain Kopeykin, and thought the postmaster was a little wide of the mark. However, they would not own themselves beaten either, and inspired by the postmaster's clever suggestion, made others that

---

*In classical mythology, the river in Hades whose waters caused forgetfulness in those who drank from it.

were almost more far-fetched. Among a number of sagacious theories there was one, strange to say, that Tchitchikov might be Napoleon in disguise, that the English had long been envious of the greatness and vast expanse of Russia—there had actually been on several occasions cartoons in which a Russian was represented talking to an Englishman, the Englishman was holding a dog on a cord behind him, and the dog of course stood for Napoleon: "Mind," he was saying, "if there is anything I don't like I will let the dog off." And now perhaps they really had let him out from the island of St. Helena,* and now here he was wandering about Russia got up as Tchitchikov, though he was really not Tchitchikov at all.

Of course the officials did not fully believe this, but they grew very thoughtful, and each separately thinking the matter over, decided that Tchitchikov, if he were turned round and looked at sideways, was very much like the portraits of Napoleon. The police-master, who had served in the campaign of 1812 and had seen Napoleon in person, could not but admit that he was no taller than Tchitchikov, and that in figure Napoleon could not be said to be too stout, though on the other hand he was far from thin. Perhaps some of my readers will call this improbable; the author is quite prepared to oblige them by confessing that it is most improbable; but unfortunately it all happened precisely as described, and what makes it the more astonishing is that the town was not far away in the wilds, but, on the contrary, no great distance from both capitals. But it must be remembered that all this happened very shortly after the glorious expulsion of the French. At that period all our landowners, officials and merchants and shopmen and every one that could read and write, and even illiterate peasants, became at least for eight years inveterate politicians. The *Moscow News* and the *Sun of the Fatherland* were read with merciless zeal, and reached the last reader in tatters quite useless for any purpose whatever. Instead of such questions as: "At what price were they selling the measure of oats, sir?" "Did you get any fun out of the snow we had yesterday?" they used to ask: "What news is there in the paper? Haven't they let Napoleon out of the Island again?" The merchants were in the greatest apprehension of this, for they put im-

*Remote island in the South Atlantic Ocean where Napoléon was exiled in 1815; he died there in 1821.

plicit faith in the predictions of a prophet who had been for three years in prison. No one knew where the prophet came from, he made his appearance wearing bark shoes, and an unlined sheepskin and smelling terribly of stale fish, and announced that Napoleon was Antichrist, and was bound by a stone chain behind six walls and seven seas, but later on would break his chain and gain possession of the whole world. The prophet was very properly put into prison for his predictions, but nevertheless he had done his work and completely confounded the merchants. Long afterwards, even at a time of most profitable transactions, the merchants talked of Antichrist when they went to the tavern to drink their tea. Many of the official class and of the gentry could not help thinking about it too, and infected by the mysticism which was, as is well known, all the fashion then, saw in every letter of the name Napoleon some peculiar significance, some even discovered Apocalyptic numbers in it. And so there is nothing surprising in the fact that the officials unconsciously thought on the same lines; but they soon pulled themselves together, realising that their imaginations were running away with them, and that all this was nonsense. They pondered and pondered and discussed and discussed and at last decided that it would not be amiss to question Nozdryov thoroughly again. Since he was the first to tell the story of the dead souls and was, so it was said, on very intimate terms with Tchitchikov, and therefore would undoubtedly know something about the circumstances of his life, it was decided to try again what Nozdryov could tell them.

Strange people were these official gentlemen, and so indeed are the gentlemen of all other callings too: they knew perfectly well that Nozdryov was a liar, that one could not believe a word he said, even about the merest trifle, and yet they had recourse to him! Explain man if you can! He doesn't believe in God but he believes that if the bridge of his nose is scratched he will die; he passes by the work of a poet clear as daylight, all bathed in harmony and the sublime wisdom of simplicity, and pounces eagerly on the work of some audacious fellow who muddles, twists, and distorts nature, and he is delighted with it and cries: "This is it, here is real comprehension of the mysteries of the heart!" All his life he has despised doctors and ends by consulting some peasant woman who cures him by muttering spells and using spittle, or better still invents for himself some de-

coction of goodness knows what rubbish, which he regards as a remedy for his complaints, God knows why. Of course the officials may
be to some extent excused by the really difficult position in which
they were placed. A drowning man will catch even at a straw, they say,
and he has not the sense at the moment to reflect that a fly could
scarcely save itself on a straw, while he weighs eleven if not twelve
stone; but that consideration does not occur to him at that moment,
and he clutches at the straw. So our friends clutched at Nozdryov. The
police-master immediately wrote a note to him, inviting him to an
evening party. And a policeman in big boots, with engagingly rosy
cheeks, ran off instantly, with his hand upon his sword, to Nozdryov's
rooms. Nozdryov was engaged upon something very important; it
was four whole days since he had kept his room, admitting no one,
and having his food passed in at his window, in fact he had actually
grown thin and sallow. It was a business that called for the closest attention; it consisted of making up out of several hundreds of cards a
complete suit of the most recognisable, upon which he could rely as
upon a faithful friend. He had at least another fortnight's work before
him. All this time, Porfiry had to brush a mastiff puppy with a special brush and to wash it with soap three times a day. Nozdryov was
very angry at his solitude being broken in upon; first of all, he sent
the policeman to the devil, but when he read in the letter that he
might reckon on winning something, as a novice at cards was expected at the party, he immediately locked the door of his room,
dressed himself after a fashion and set off. Nozdryov's statements, his
evidence and his suppositions were so completely the opposite of
those of the officials that every theory they had was confounded. He
was a man for whom doubt did not exist, and there was as much decision and certainty about his suppositions as there was hesitation
and timidity about theirs. He answered every question without fal-
tering: he declared Tchitchikov had bought thousands of roubles'
worth of dead souls, and that he, Nozdryov, had sold them, because
he did not see any reason why he shouldn't. To the question whether
he was a spy and whether he was trying to find out something,
Nozdryov answered that he was a spy; that even at school, where
Nozdryov was with him, they used to call him a tell-tale, and that his
schoolfellows, among them Nozdryov himself, had knocked him
about for it so much that he had had to have two hundred and forty

leeches put on his temples, that is, he meant to say forty but two hundred had somehow got said of itself. To the question whether he was a forger of counterfeit notes Nozdryov answered that he was, and thereupon told an anecdote of Tchitchikov's extraordinary dexterity; how it was found out that there were in his house counterfeit notes for two million roubles, a seal was put on the house, and two soldiers were set to keep guard at every door, and how Tchitchikov changed all the notes in a single night so that when the seal was taken off the next day, the notes were found to be all genuine. To the question whether Tchitchikov were designing to elope with the governor's daughter, and whether it were true that he had himself undertaken to assist him and to take part in arranging it, Nozdryov answered that he had helped him and that nothing would have come off without him. Here he pulled himself up, realising that he had told quite an unnecessary lie, and might get himself into trouble, but his tongue ran away with him. And it was particularly difficult to restrain it, for so many interesting details which he could not possibly sacrifice rose before his imagination. For instance, the very village in the parish church of which it was arranged that the wedding should take place was mentioned by name as Truhmatchevka, the priest, Father Sidor, was to be paid seventy-five roubles for the wedding, and he would not have agreed to do it even for that if Nozdryov had not scared him, threatening to inform the police that he had illegally married a corn-dealer called Mihail, to a girl who had stood godmother to a child of which the latter was the godfather; that he had offered the use of his carriage and had bespoken relays of horses at the posting stations. He went so far into details as even to mention the names of the drivers.

They tried dropping a hint about Napoleon, but regretted doing so afterwards, for Nozdryov went off into a rigmarole which not only had no semblance of truth, but had actually no semblance of anything whatever, so much so that the officials all walked away with a sigh; only the police-master went on listening to him, thinking that something might crop up later, but at last he too made a gesture of despair, saying: "What the devil is one to make of it!" And all agreed that, "do what you will with a bull you can never get milk out of him," and the officials found themselves in a worse position than before, and the upshot of it was that they could not possibly find out who Tchitchikov was. And what followed showed distinctly what a

strange sort of creature man is: he is wise, clever, sensible in everything that concerns other people but not in what concerns himself.
How well he is provided with resolute and prudent counsels in the
difficult crises of life! "How quick and resourceful a brain!" cries the
crowd, "what a resolute character!" But let some misfortune befall
that quick and resourceful man, let him be put in a difficult position
himself, and what becomes of his character! The resolute man is utterly distracted, and turns into a pitiful coward, a weak insignificant
baby or simply a muff, as Nozdryov called it.

All these discussions, opinions and rumours for some unaccountable reason affected the poor prosecutor more than any one
else. They had such an effect upon him that on reaching home he fell
to brooding, and suddenly, for no rhyme or reason as the saying is,
died. Whether it was a paralytic stroke or some other attack, anyway,
while he was sitting at the table he flopped forward on his face. As is
usual on such occasions, people cried out, "Good God!" and flinging
up their hands, sent for the doctor to bleed him, but saw that the
prosecutor was a soulless corpse. It was only then they recognised
with regret that he really had a soul, though he had always been too
modest to show it. And meanwhile death was as terrible in a small
man as in a great one: a man who had only lately been walking
about, moving, playing whist, and signing various papers, and who
had been so often seen among the other officials with his thick eyebrows and his winking eye, was now lying on the table; his left eye
did not wink now at all, but one eyebrow was still raised with questioning expression. What the dead man was inquiring about, why he
died or why he had lived—God only knows.

"But this is absurd though! It's out of the question! It's impossible that officials could scare themselves so, could make up such nonsense, could stray so far from the truth when a child could have seen
through it!" Many readers will say this, and will blame the author for
improbability, or will call the poor officials fools, for man is lavish in
the use of the word fool, and is ready to apply it to his neighbour
twenty times a day. It is quite enough if out of ten points in his character he has one stupid one, for him to be set down as a fool in spite
of his nine good points. It is easy for readers to criticise, looking
down from their comfortable niche on the heights from which the
whole horizon lies open, at all that is taking place below, where man

can only see the object nearest to him. And in the history of humanity there are many whole centuries which he would, I fancy, strike out and suppress as unnecessary. Many mistakes have been made in the world which now one would hardly think a child could make. How many crooked, narrow, impassable blind alleys, leading far off the track, has mankind chosen in the effort to reach the eternal verity, while before him the straight road lay open like the road that leads to a magnificent mansion destined to be a royal palace! It is broader and more splendid than all the other paths, with the sun lighting it up by day and many lights by night. But men have streamed past it in blind darkness. And how many times even when guided by understanding that has been given them from heaven, they have managed even then to halt and go astray, have managed in the light of day to get into the impassable jungle, have managed to throw a blinding fog again over one another's eyes, and lured by will-of-the-wisps have succeeded in reaching the brink of the abyss, only to ask one another with horror: "Where is the way out? Where is the road?" The present generation sees everything clearly, marvels at the errors and laughs at the follies of its forefathers, not seeing that there are streaks of heavenly light in that history, that every letter in it cries aloud to them, that on all sides a pointing finger is turned upon it, upon the present generation. But the present generation laughs and proudly, self-confidently, enters upon a series of fresh errors at which their descendants will laugh again in their turn.

Tchitchikov knew absolutely nothing of all this. As ill luck would have it, he had taken a slight chill and had a swollen face and a slight sore throat, in the distribution of which the climate of our provincial towns is extremely liberal. That his life might not—God forbid—be cut short without leaving descendants he thought it better to keep to his bed for three or four days. During those days he was continually gargling with a decoction of milk and figs which he afterwards ate, and bound a bag filled with camomile and camphor on his cheek. To occupy his time he made some new and detailed lists of all the peasants he had bought, read a volume of the Duchesse de la Vallière,* which he dug out of his trunk, looked through many notes and other

---

*Louise-Françoise de la Vallière (1644–1710), mistress of Louis XIV, became a nun and wrote *Reflections on God's Compassionateness*.

objects in his chest, read something over a second time, and all this bored him horribly. He could not make out how it was that none of the officials of the town had been to inquire after him, though a little while before there had always been a chaise standing before the hotel door—either the postmaster's, the prosecutor's or the president's. But he only shrugged his shoulders as he walked up and down the room. At last he felt better and was highly delighted when he saw that he could go out in the open air. Without delay he set to work to get ready, opened his case, poured some hot water into a glass, took out his shaving brush and his soap, and proceeded to shave, and indeed it was high time he did, for feeling his chin with his hand and looking into the glass he exclaimed: "Ough, what a forest!" And indeed though it was not a forest there was a very thick growth over his cheeks and under his chin. When he had shaved he began to dress rapidly, so much so that he almost jumped out of his trousers. At last he was dressed, sprinkled with eau-de-Cologne and, warmly wrapped up, made his way down into the street, keeping his cheek bandaged as a precaution. Going out was for him, as for every convalescent, like a holiday. Everything that caught his eye looked smiling,—the houses, and some passing peasants who however did in reality look glum, and one of whom had just boxed his brother's ears. He meant to pay his first visit to the governor. All sorts of ideas came into his mind on the road: the fair daughter was continually in his thoughts, and he indulged in flights of fancy, till at last he began to mock and laugh at himself. In such a frame of mind he reached the governor's door. He was on the point of hurriedly flinging off his overcoat in the entrance hall, when the hall porter astonished him by the utterly unexpected words: "I've orders not to admit you."

"What! what do you mean! I suppose you don't know me? You should look at one more carefully!" Tchitchikov said to him.

"Not know you indeed, it is not the first time I have seen you," said the porter. "Why it is just you I've orders not to let in, I may admit any one else."

"Well, upon my soul! Why? What for?"

"That's my orders; so I suppose that's right," said the hall porter, and added the word, "Yes," after which he stood facing him in the most free and easy attitude, completely dropping the ingratiating air with which on other occasions he had hastened to help him off with his coat. He seemed as he looked at him to think, "Aha, since their Excellencies kick you out of the door you must be a low rascal!"

"How inexplicable!" Tchitchikov thought to himself, and he set off at once to call upon the president of the court of justice, but the president was so overwhelmed with confusion on seeing him that he could not utter anything coherent, and talked such utter twaddle that they were both abashed. On leaving him Tchitchikov did his very utmost to understand what the president had meant and what his words could refer to, yet he could make nothing out of them. Then he went on to the others: to the police-master, to the deputy-governor, to the postmaster, but either they were not at home to him, or they received him so strangely, made such constrained and unaccountable observations, were so disconcerted, and the general effect of irrational incoherence was such that he began to have doubts of their sanity. He tried going on to some one else in the hope of finding out the reason anyway, but he could not get at the reason. Like a man half awake he wandered aimlessly about the town, unable to decide whether he had gone out of his mind or the officials had gone out of theirs, or whether it was all a dream or whether it was a reality more absurd than any dream. It was late, almost getting dusk, when at last he went back to his hotel which he had left that morning in such a pleasant state of mind, and feeling dull, he ordered tea to be sent up. Musing and absentmindedly brooding over the strangeness of his position, he began to pour out his tea when suddenly the door of his room was opened and Nozdryov most unexpectedly stood before him.

"As the proverb has it, 'to see a friend, five miles is not out of one's way,' " he said, taking off his cap. "I was passing and saw the light in the window. 'There,' I thought, 'I'll go in, no doubt he is still up.' And it is first rate that you have got tea on the table, I shall enjoy a cup: I ate all sorts of rubbish at dinner to-day, I feel as though there were a riot beginning in my stomach. Tell your man to fill me a pipe! Where is your pipe?"

"I don't smoke a pipe," said Tchitchikov drily.

"Nonsense, as though I don't know you are a smoker. Hi, what's your fellow's name? Hi, Vahramey, I say."

"Not Vahramey but Petrushka!"

"How is that? You did have a Vahramey?"

"I never had a man called Vahramey."

"Oh yes, it is at Derebin's that there is a Vahramey. Only fancy, what luck for Derebin: his aunt has quarrelled with her son because he has married a serf girl, and now she has left him all her property. I thought to myself if only one could have an aunt like that for the sake of the future! But how is it, old man, you have kept away from all of us and have not been near any one? Of course I know you are sometimes engaged in abstruse studies, you are fond of reading" (on what ground Nozdryov believed that Tchitchikov was engaged in abstruse subjects and was fond of reading we must own we cannot tell, and still less could Tchitchikov). "Ah, Tchitchikov, old man, if you had only seen . . . it really would have been a subject for your sarcastic wit" (why Tchitchikov was supposed to have a sarcastic wit is unknown also). "Only fancy, old boy, we were having a game of cards at the merchant Lihatchev's, and didn't we have fun there too! Perependev who was with me, 'If only Tchitchikov were here,' said he, 'it would be just the thing for him. . . .'" (Tchitchikov had never known any one called Perependev in his life.) "But you must own up, old boy, you did play me a nasty trick, do you remember, over that game of draughts? I won it, you know . . . Yes, old man, you simply did me over that. But there I don't know how the devil it is but I can't be cross. The other day at the president's . . . Ah, yes, I ought to tell you every one in the town is turned against you. They imagine you forge notes. They kept pestering me about you, I stood up for you like a rock—I told them I had been to school with you and knew your father; and there, there's no denying I pitched them a fine tale."

"I forge notes!" cried Tchitchikov, getting up from his seat.

"Why did you give them such a fright though?" Nozdryov went on. "They were terrified out of their wits, the devil knows why: they take you for a brigand and a spy. And the prosecutor has died of fright; the funeral is to-morrow. Won't you be there? To tell the truth they are afraid of the new governor-general, in case there may be trouble about you. But what I think about the governor-general is, that if he is stuck up and gives himself airs he certainly won't be able to do anything with the nobility. The nobility insist on hospitality, don't they? Of course he can shut himself up in his study if he likes and not give a single ball, but what's the use of that? There is no gain-

ing anything by that. But you know, Tchitchikov, it is a risky business
you are going in for."

"What risky business?" Tchitchikov asked uneasily.

"Why, eloping with the governor's daughter, I must own I expected it, I did, upon my soul. The first time I saw you together at the
ball I thought to myself: 'I'll be bound Tchitchikov is up to something. . . .' But you have made a poor choice, I see nothing in her.
Now there is one, a relation of Bikusov's, his sister's daughter—that
is something like a girl! a wonderful little bit of goods!"

"What do you mean? what are you talking about? Elope with the
governor's daughter? What do you mean?" said Tchitchikov, with his
eyes starting out of his head.

"Oh, drop that, old boy, you are a close one. I'll own I came to
you to tell you I am ready to help you. So be it: I'll hold the wedding
crown over your head, I'll provide the carriage and the changes of
horses, only on one condition: you must lend me three thousand
roubles. I must have it if I die for it."

While Nozdryov was rattling on, Tchitchikov several times
rubbed his eyes to make sure that he was not hearing all this in a
dream. The charge of forging counterfeit notes, the elopement with
the governor's daughter, the death of the prosecutor, of which
Tchitchikov was supposed to be the cause, the arrival of the new
governor-general—all this excited considerable alarm.

"Well, if it has come to this," he thought to himself, "it's no good
lingering on here, I must make haste and get away."

He tried to get rid of Nozdryov as quickly as he could, at once
sent for Selifan and told him to be ready at daybreak, so that they
could leave the town at six o'clock next morning without fail, to look
over everything, see that the carriage was greased and so on, and so
on. Selifan articulated, "Yes, Pavel Ivanovitch," but remained for some
minutes standing motionless at the door. Our hero bade Petrushka
pull the portmanteau, by now thickly covered with dust, from under
the bed and began packing indiscriminately stockings, shirts, under-
linen washed and unwashed, boot trees, a calendar. . . . All this was
packed anyhow: he wanted to make sure of being ready so that nothing could happen to detain him in the morning. Selifan after standing for two minutes at the door went slowly away. He went slowly, as
slowly as possible downstairs, leaving traces of his wet boots on the

steps worn hollow by long use, and he stood for a long time scratching the back of his head. What did that scratching signify? and what
does it indicate as a rule? Was it a vexation at missing the meeting
planned for the next day in some imperial tavern with a fellow
coachman, clad in an unattractive sheepskin with a sash tied round
the waist, or had some little affair of the heart developed in this new
place, and had he to give up standing in the evenings at the gate and
diplomatically holding white hands at the hour when twilight drops
upon the town, when a lad in a red shirt twangs on the balalaika before the assembled house serfs, and working people of all sorts after
their toil exchange quiet talk? Or was he simply sorry to leave the
snug place he had made for himself under a sheepskin by the stove
in the servants' kitchen, and the cabbage soup with the tender little
town-made pies, to go dragging again through the rain and the sleet
and all the hardships of the road? God knows,—there is no guessing.
Scratching the head signifies all manner of things among the Russian
people.

CHAPTER 11

Nothing happened however as Tchitchikov intended. To begin with, he woke later than he expected—that was the first mishap. As soon as he was up he sent to inquire whether the chaise had been packed and everything got ready; but they brought him word that the chaise had not been prepared and nothing was ready—that was the second mishap. He was very angry, and even made up his mind to give our friend Selifan something like a drubbing, and only waited with impatience to hear what explanation the latter would give to justify himself. Selifan soon made his appearance at the door, and Tchitchikov had the satisfaction of hearing from his lips the sayings usually heard from servants when one is in a hurry to set off.

"But the horses want shoeing, you know, Pavel Ivanovitch."

"Oh you pig's face! you post! Why did you not speak about it before? Surely you had plenty of time, hadn't you?"

"Why yes, I had time. And then there's the wheel too, Pavel Ivanovitch, there ought to be new tires for the road is all, ups and downs, there are such ruts everywhere now. . . . And if you will allow me to say so, the front part of the chaise is very rickety, so that maybe it would hardly last beyond two posting stations."

"You scoundrel!" cried Tchitchikov, flinging up his hands, and he went up to him so close that Selifan stepped back a little and ducked to one side, afraid he was going to get something from his master.

"Do you want to be the death of me, eh? Do you mean to bring me to my grave? Do you mean to murder me on the road, you ruffian, you damned pig's face, you sea monster, eh? Haven't you been doing nothing here for three weeks? If you had only dropped a hint, you senseless brute, but here you put it off till the last minute. When everything is almost ready for me to get in and set off, here you go and make a mess of it all, eh, eh? Didn't you know it before? You knew it, didn't you, didn't you? Answer. Did you know?"

"Yes, I did," answered Selifan, looking down.

"Then why didn't you tell me, eh?"

To this question Selifan made no reply, but looking down seemed to be saying to himself: " 'Pon my soul, it's a queer thing, I knew, but I didn't say anything."

"Well, now go and get the blacksmiths, and have everything ready in two hours' time. Do you hear? In two hours' time without fail, and if it isn't, I'll . . . I'll twist you into a horn and tie you in a knot."

Selifan was turning towards the door to retire and carry out these instructions, but he stopped and said: "And another thing, sir, that dappled horse ought to be sold, for he is a regular rascal, Pavel Ivanovitch, please God I never see his like again, he is nothing but a hindrance."

"So I am to go and run off to the market to sell him!"

"As God's above, Pavel Ivanovitch, to look at him he is a likely horse, but that's all, when it comes to work he is a sly brute; you'd never find another like him. . . ."

"You fool, when I want to sell him I'll sell him. Here you go maundering on about all sorts of things! I'll see to you; if you don't get the blacksmiths at once, and if everything is not ready in two hours from now, I'll give you such a dressing . . . you won't know whether you are on your head or your feet! Get along! Be off!" Selifan went out.

Tchitchikov felt thoroughly out of temper and threw down on the floor the sword that always travelled with him to inspire befitting terror wherever necessary. He was over a quarter of an hour bargaining with the blacksmiths before he could come to terms with them, for the blacksmiths, as usual, were arrant knaves, and seeing that the work was wanted in a hurry asked six times the proper price. Though he grew heated, called them swindlers and robbers who plundered travellers, and even referred to the Day of Judgment, he made no impression whatever on the blacksmiths, they stuck to their guns, not only refused to knock the price down but took five and a half hours over the work instead of two. During this time it was his pleasant lot to experience those agreeable moments, familiar to every traveller, when everything is packed and nothing but bits of string and paper and such rubbish is left lying about the room, when a man is neither on the road nor settled in one spot, when he looks out of window at the people passing up and down and talking of their gains and losses, and with a sort of vacant curiosity raising their eyes to stare at him and then going on their way, which further aggravates the ill humour of the poor traveller who cannot get off. Everything about him, everything he sees: the little shops opposite his windows and the head of the old woman opposite, as she goes up to the window with the short curtains—it is all distasteful to him, and yet he does not move away from the window. He stands there sometimes lost in oblivion, sometimes again paying a sort of dull attention to everything moving and unmoving about him, and in his vexation crushes a fly which buzzes and beats against the widow-pane under his finger.

But there is an end to everything and the longed-for moment arrived, everything was ready, the front part of the chaise had been properly repaired, the wheels had new tires, the horses had been brought back from the drinking place, and the rascally blacksmiths departed, counting over their roubles and wishing him a good journey. At last the chaise was packed and two fancy loaves, hot from the baker's, had been put in, and Selifan had stuffed something for himself in the pocket in the coachman's box, and finally, while the waiter in the same cotton shoddy coat waved his cap, while the assembled waiters from the restaurants and coachmen and other servants stood gaping at the departure of some one else's master, amid the various other circumstances attendant on departure, our hero got into his carriage, and the chaise—of the pattern favoured by bachelor gentlemen of the middling sort—which had so long been stationary in the town, and with which the reader is perhaps so bored, at last drove out of the gates of the hotel. "Thank God," thought Tchitchikov, and he crossed himself. Selifan cracked his whip, Petrushka after first hanging on for some time on the step, sat down beside him, and our hero, settling himself more comfortably in his Georgian rug and flattening the two hot loaves together, thrust the leather pillow behind his back, and the chaise fell to jolting and hopping up and down again, thanks to the cobble-stones which had, as the reader knows, wonderful resilient properties. With a vague, undefined feeling he looked at the houses, the walls, the fences and the streets, which seeming to dance up and down too, gradually retreated, and which there was no knowing whether he was fated to see again in his life.

At a turning in one of the streets the chaise had to pull up because an endless funeral procession was passing up the whole length of it. Tchitchikov, putting his head out, told Petrushka to inquire whose funeral it was, and learned that it was the prosecutor's. Overcome by an unpleasant feeling he hid himself in the corner, covered himself with the leather apron, and pulled the curtain over the window. While the chaise was held up, Selifan and Petrushka, devoutly taking off their hats, were looking to see who were driving or riding, and how and in or on what they were doing so, counting how many there were on foot and in carriages, and their master, bidding them not greet or recognise any of their acquaintances, began timidly looking too through the little pane in the leather curtain. All the officials walked bareheaded after the coffin. He began to be afraid that his carriage might be recognised, but no one noticed it. They were not even indulging in the trivial talk which is usually kept up by persons attending a funeral. At that moment all their thoughts were concentrated on themselves: they were wondering what the new governor-general would be like, how he would set to work and how he would take them. The officials who were walking were followed by carriages out of which peeped ladies in mourning caps. From the movements of their hands and lips, it could be seen that they were engaged in eager conversation: possibly they, too, were discussing the arrival of the governor-general, and speculating about the balls he would give, and were busily chattering about their everlasting festoons and frills. Then the carriages were followed by a file of empty droshkys, and at last there was nothing left to come, so that our hero could drive on. Drawing back the leather curtain, he heaved a sigh, and exclaimed from his heart: "So much for the prosecutor! He lived and lived and then he died! And now they will print in the newspapers that he has passed away to the grief of his subordinates and of all humanity, an honoured citizen, a devoted father, a faithful husband, and they will write all sorts of nonsense; they will very likely add that he was followed to the grave by the lamentations of widows and orphans; and yet if one goes into the facts of the case, it turns out on investigation that there was nothing special about you but your thick eyebrows." Here he told Selifan to drive faster, while he thought to himself, "Well, it is a good thing we met the funeral, they say meeting a funeral means happiness."

Meanwhile the chaise had turned into more deserted streets, and soon wooden fences stretching each side of the road showed the end of the town was near. And now the cobbled road ceased and the barrier and the town were left behind and nothing remained, and they were on the high road once more. Soon they saw again milestones, superintendents of posting stations, wells, strings of wagons, grey villages with samovars, with peasant women and a brisk bearded innkeeper, running out of his yard with oats in his arms, a wayfarer in frayed bark shoes who had wandered some six hundred miles, little towns run up in a hurry with wretched little wooden shops, flour barrels, bark shoes, fancy rolls and other such trifles, spotted barrier posts, patched up bridges, interminable fields on both sides of the road, old-fashioned country gentlemen's coaches, a soldier on horseback, carrying a green box with grapeshot, with a label on it of some Artillery Battery, green, yellow, and freshly dug black strips of land flashing by on the steppe, a song chanted in the distance, the crests of pine-trees in the mist, the jingle of bells in the distance, crows as thick as flies, and a boundless horizon. Russia! Russia! I behold thee, from my lovely faraway paradise, I behold thee! It is poor, neglected and comfortless in thee, no insolent marvels of nature crowned by insolent marvels of art, no towns with many-windowed lofty palaces piled in precipitous heights, no picturesque trees, no ivy-clad houses in the roar and everlasting spray of waterfalls rejoice the eye or strike awe into the heart; the head is not turned to gaze at the rocks piled up on the heights above it; no everlasting lines of shining mountains rising into the silvery pure skies gleam in the distance through dark arches, scattered one upon the other in a tangle of vines, ivy and wild roses beyond number. In thee all is open, desolate, flat; thy lowly towns lie scattered like dots, like specks unseen among thy plains; there is nothing to allure or captivate the eye. But what mysterious inexplicable force draws one to thee? Why does the mournful song that floats all over the length and breadth of thee from sea to sea echo unceasingly in the ear? What is in it, in that song? What is it that calls and sobs and clutches at my heart? What are these strains that so poignantly greet me, that go straight to my soul, that throb about my heart? Russia! what wouldst thou of me? What is the mysterious hidden bond between us? Why dost thou gaze at me thus, and why is everything within thee turning upon me eyes full of expectation? . . .

And still full of perplexity I stand motionless; and already a threatening cloud, heavy with coming rain, looms above my head, and thought is numb before thy vast expanse. What does that immense expanse foretell? Is it not here, is it not in thee that limitless thought will arise, since thou art thyself without limit? . . . Is it not here there should be giants where there is space for them to develop and move freely. And thy mighty expanse enfolds me menacingly, with fearful force reflected in the depths of me; with supernatural power light dawns upon my eyes. . . . Ah, marvellous, radiant horizons of which the earth knows nothing! Russia!

"Steady, steady, you fool!" Tchitchikov shouted to Selifan.

"I'll hang you," shouted a courier with moustaches a yard long, who was galloping towards them. "Don't you see a government carriage, the devil flay your soul?" and the troika vanished amid dust and rattle.

How strange, alluring, stimulating and wonderful is the sound of the words "on the road." And how marvellous that road is! The sunny day, the autumn leaves, the cold air. . . . Wrapped more closely in one's winter coat, cap over ears, one huddles more snugly into the corner. For the last time a faint shiver passes through the limbs and is followed by a pleasant warmth. The horses race along . . . how seductively drowsiness steals over one and the eyelids close, and through sleep one hears, "Not white were the snows," and the breathing of the horses and the rumble of the wheels, and one snores, squeezing one's neighbour into the corner. One wakes—five stations are left behind; moonlight; an unfamiliar town; churches with old-fashioned wooden cupolas and blackened spires; dark log houses and white brick ones; patches of moonlight here and there like white linen handkerchiefs hung upon the walls, the pavements, the streets; slanting, coal black shadows intersect them; the wooden roofs shine like gleaming metal in the moonlight and not a soul to be seen, everything is asleep. At most one solitary light glimmers at a window, is it a workman mending his boots, or a baker busy with his oven—what do they matter? And the night! . . . Heavenly powers! What a night is being enacted on high! And the air, and the sky, lofty, far away yonder, in its fathomless depths, stretching in all directions, so infinitely, so harmoniously, so radiantly! But the cold breath of the night blows fresh upon the eyes and lulls one to sleep, and one dozes, sinks into forgetfulness, and snores, and one's poor neighbour, squeezed into the corner, turns around angrily feeling a weight upon him. One wakes—and again, fields and plains before one; nothing to be seen, it is all deserted and open. A milestone with a number on it flies into sight; daybreak is near; on the cold whitening horizon there is a pale streak of gold; the wind grows colder and harsher: one pulls one's coat more closely round one! What delicious freshness! How delightful is the sleep that comes over one again! A jolt—and again one wakes. The sun is high up in the sky. "Gently, gently!" cried a voice, the chaise is going down a steep place, below, a broad dam and a broad shining pond gleaming like copper in the sun; a village; huts scattered on the slope; the cross of the village church glittering like a star on one side; the chatter of peasants and the ravenous appetite for breakfast. . . . My God, how glorious at times is the long, long road! How often have I, drowning and perishing, clutched at thee, and always thou hast rescued and preserved me! And how many wonderful plans and poetical dreams hast thou brought forth, what glorious impressions have I experienced on the road. And indeed our friend Tchitchikov was indulging in reveries not altogether prosaic. Let us see what he was feeling. At first he felt nothing at all, and simply kept looking back as though to make sure that he really had got out of the town; but when he saw that the town had long been out of sight, that neither smithy nor mill nor any of the objects usual on the outskirts of a town were visible, and that even the white spires of the white churches had long since melted into the landscape, his attention was absorbed by nothing but the road, he kept looking to right and left, and it seemed as though the town of N. had passed out of his memory, as though he had passed through it long ago in his childhood. At last the road too ceased to occupy his mind, and he began to half-close his eyes and lean his head on the pillow. The author confesses that he is glad of the opportunity of talking a little about his hero, for hitherto he has always been hindered from doing so either by Nozdryov or by balls or by ladies, or by the scandal of the town, in short, by the thousand and one trivialities which only seem trivialities when they are brought into a book, while in the world they pass for very important matters. But now we will lay aside everything else and go straight to the point.

It is very doubtful whether the reader will like the hero we have selected. That he will not please the ladies one may say with certainty, for ladies insist on a hero's being absolute perfection, and if he has some tiny spiritual or physical blemish then—there's trouble! However deeply the author gazes into his soul, and though he may reflect it more clearly than a mirror, they will give him no credit for it. Tchitchikov's very stoutness and middle age will do him great damage in their eyes: they will never forgive stoutness in a hero under any circumstances, and very many ladies will turn away, saying, Fie! what a horrid man! Alas! the author is very well aware of all this, and yet he cannot take a virtuous man for his hero. But . . . perhaps in this very novel some chords hitherto unstruck may be discerned, the infinite wealth of the Russian soul may be set forth, a man endowed with divine qualities, or a wonderful Russian maiden, such as cannot be found elsewhere in the world, with the marvellous beauty of a woman's soul made up of generous impulse and self-sacrifice, may emerge. And all the virtuous people of other races will seem dead beside them as a book is dead beside the living word! Russian emotions will arise. They will see how deeply what has only glided through the nature of other peoples has taken root in the nature of the Russians. . . . But what use or reason is there to speak of what is in the future? It is unseemly for the author, a man of full age, disciplined by a harsh inner life and the invigorating sobriety of solitude, to forget himself like a boy. There is a fitting time and place for everything! But all the same I have not taken a virtuous man for my hero. And I may even say why I have not. Because it is high time at last to let the poor virtuous man rest; because the phrase "virtuous man" is too often taken in vain, because they have made a regular hack of the virtuous man and there is not a writer who has not ridden him to death, lashing him on with whip or anything that comes to hand; because they have so overdone the virtuous man that there is not a shadow of virtue left about him, and he is nothing but skin and bone; because it is through hypocrisy they invoke the virtuous man; because the virtuous man is not respected. No, the time has come at last to trot out the rascal! And so let us trot out the rascal!

Our hero's origin was humble and obscure. His parents were of the nobility, but whether by birth or by merit—God only knows. He did not resemble them in face. Anyway, a female relation who was present at his birth, a short little woman, one of those intrusive fussy people commonly called "lapwings," cried out as she took the baby in her arms: "He is not a bit what I expected! He ought to have been like his granny on his mother's side, that would have been the best, but he reminds me of the saying: not like father nor like mother, but like a passing stranger." Life looked at him at first with sour inhospitality as through a dim snow-darkened window; he had no friend, no comrade in his childhood! A tiny room with tiny windows, never opened, summer or winter; his father, an invalid in a long lambswool-lined coat, with slippers on his bare feet, for ever sighing and wandering about the room and spitting into a spittoon full of sand in a corner; the boy, everlastingly sitting on a bench with a pen in his hand, ink on his fingers and even on his lips; the everlasting copy before his eyes, "Speak the truth, be obedient to your elders, and cherish virtue in your heart"; with the everlasting flap and shuffle of the slippers about the room, the familiar, always harsh voice calling out, "In mischief again," when the child, weary with the monotony of his work, drew some flourish or tail on a letter; and everlastingly the familiar and always unpleasant sensation when these words were followed by his ears being very painfully wrung by the long clawing fingers behind him: such is the pitiful picture of the early childhood of which he retained scarcely a faint memory. But in life everything changes rapidly, and one day with the first sunshine and rushing floods of spring, the father, taking his son with him, drove out in a little cart, drawn by a piebald nag with a white mouth, of the kind known among horse-dealers as magpies. She was driven by a little hunchback who performed almost all the duties in the house, and was the progenitor of the only family of serfs owned by Tchitchikov's father. With the magpie they were driving for over a day and a half; they stayed a night on the road, crossed a river, lunched on cold pie and roast mutton, and only reached the town on the morning of the third day. The streets of the town dazzled the boy with their unexpected splendour and made him gape with wonder. Then the magpie lurched with the cart into a big hole at the entrance of a narrow lane which ran downhill and was thick with mud. There she was a long time struggling her utmost and working her legs, urged on by the hunchback and the master himself, and at last she dragged them into a little yard standing on the slope of the hill, with two apple-trees in flower in front of the little old house, and with a humble little garden behind it, consisting of nothing but mountain ashes and elder-trees with a wooden summer-house hidden in its recesses, covered with trellis and with a narrow opaque window. Here there lived a relation, a decrepit old woman who still went to market every morning, and dried her stockings on the samovar afterwards. She patted the boy on his cheeks and admired his plumpness. Here he was to remain and to go every day to the town school. After staying the night, his father set off again next morning. At the parting no tears fell from the father's eyes; half a rouble in copper was given the boy for pocket money and to buy sweets, and what was far more important, a judicious admonition: "Mind now, Pavlushka: be diligent with your lessons, don't play the fool or get into mischief, and above all, satisfy your teachers and superiors. If you please your chief you'll get on and be ahead of all the rest, even if you don't do well in your lessons and God has given you no talent. Don't keep company with your schoolfellows, they'll teach you no good; but if you have to, keep company with those who are better off, who may be of use to you. Don't treat any one or offer any one anything, but manage so that you may be treated, and, what is most important of all, take care of your kopeks and save them up: money's the most reliable thing on earth. A schoolfellow or a friend will cheat you and be the first to fail you in trouble, but your kopek won't fail you whatever trouble you are in. You can do anything and smash anything in the world with a kopeck." After giving his son this advice, the father parted from him and was dragged home again by the magpie, and he never saw the boy again; but his words and his admonition sank deeply into Pavelushka's heart.

Next day he began going to school. He did not manifest any marked ability for any branch of study, he was more distinguished by diligence and neatness; on the other hand, he displayed a remarkable ability in another direction—in a practical direction. He instantly took in the situation and succeeded in behaving with his schoolfellows in such a way that they treated him, while he never treated them, and, indeed, sometimes concealed what they had given him and sold it to the very same boys afterwards. Even as a child, he was capable of denying himself anything. Of the half rouble his father had given him he did not spend a kopeck; on the contrary, that same year he added something to it, displaying a resourcefulness almost extraordinary; he moulded a goldfinch in wax and sold it very profitably. And after that he indulged for some time in other speculations, for instance, buying edibles of some sort in the market, he would sit down in class beside boys who were rather well off, and as soon as he noticed his companion showing signs of flagging, always a symptom of approaching hunger, he showed him under the bench as if by accident, the corner of a biscuit or a bun, and after tantalising him with it extorted a sum proportionate to his appetite. For two months he was unwearying in his attentions to a mouse which he kept in a little wooden cage, and succeeded at last in getting the mouse to stand on its hind legs, to lie down and get up at the word of command, and then sold it, also very profitably. When he had saved up five roubles he made a little bag for them and began saving up in a second one. He was even more discreet in his demeanour towards his teachers. No one could sit so quietly on a bench. It must be observed that the teacher made a great point of quietness and good conduct, and could not endure clever or witty boys. He fancied that they must be laughing at him. If one who had come under observation for display of wit merely stirred in his seat or twitched an eyebrow at the wrong moment, he would incur the teacher's displeasure at once. The latter would turn him out and punish him without mercy. "I'll knock the conceit and disobedience out of you, my lad!" he said. "I know you through and through as you don't know yourself, I'll make you go down on your knees to me! I'll let you go hungry!" And the poor boy wore out his knees and went hungry for days together without knowing what for. "Cleverness and talent are all nonsense," he used to say; "all I look at is conduct. I would give full marks on every subject to a boy who did not know his A B C if he behaved himself properly. And if I see a boy showing a bad spirit or turning things into ridicule, I'd give him a nought, even if he were wiser than Solon."* So said the teacher, who had a mortal hatred for Krylov because he said, "Better a drunkard who understands his job than a sober man who doesn't," and who always described with gratification in his face and in his voice, how the stillness in the school in which he used to teach was so great that they could hear a fly move, and that in the

---

*Statesman and poet (c.640–558 B.C.) who laid the foundations of Athenian democracy.

course of a whole year not one single pupil coughed or blew his nose
in class, and that until the bell rang one could not have told whether
there was any one in the room or not. Tchitchikov instantly perceived
the master's spirit and saw what good conduct meant. He never
blinked an eye or twitched an eyebrow in class, however much the
others might pinch him from behind; as soon as the bell rang, he
dashed to fetch the master his three-cornered hat (the teacher always
wore one); after handing him his hat he was the first to run out of
the schoolroom and tried to meet him two or three times on the
road, always taking off his hat when he did so. This strategy was completely successful. All the while he was at school he was in high
favour, and on leaving received a full class certificate in all branches,
a diploma and a book with the inscription, "For exemplary diligence
and excellent conduct," in gold letters. When he left school he was a
youth of rather attractive appearance, with a chin that already needed
shaving. It was then that his father died.

His inheritance turned out to be four hopelessly worn out vests,
two old coats lined with lamb's wool, and a trifling sum of money.
The father was evidently only competent to advise saving money, but
had himself saved very little. Tchitchikov instantly sold the dilapidated homestead with its wretched little bit of land for a thousand
roubles, and took his family of serfs to the town, purposing to settle
there and go into the service. It was about this time that the poor
teacher who so prized quietness and good conduct was dismissed for
stupidity, or some other failing. The teacher began to drown his sorrows in drink, but at last he had nothing left to buy drink with; ill,
helpless, without a crust of bread, he took refuge in some unheated,
abandoned shed. Some of his former pupils, clever and witty ones
whom he had always suspected of disobedience and impudent behaviour, hearing of his pitiful plight, got up a subscription for his
benefit, even selling many things they needed to do so; only one,
Pavlushka Tchitchikov, refused on the ground of lack of means, and
only offered a five kopeck piece, which his schoolfellows at once
flung back at him: "Ough, you screw!" The poor teacher hid his face
in his hands, when he heard what his old pupils had done, tears
gushed from his faded eyes, as though he were a helpless child. "The
Lord has made me weep on the brink of the grave," he murmured in
a feeble voice; and he heaved a bitter sigh when he heard about

Tchitchikov, adding: "Ah, Pavlushka! how people change! Why, what a well-behaved boy he was! Nothing unruly in him—soft as silk! I have been deceived in him, dreadfully deceived. . . ."

It cannot be said, however, that our hero was naturally hard and callous, or that his feelings were so blunted that he knew neither pity nor compassion. He was capable of feeling both; he would even have liked to help so long as no considerable sum was involved, so long as he had not to touch the money which he had determined not to touch; in short his father's admonition, "Be careful and save money," was bearing fruit, but he had no great love of money for its own sake: he was not governed by meanness and miserliness. No, those were not the motives that actuated him; he had a vision of a future of ease and comfort with enough of everything; carriages, a well-built house, good dinners—these were the ideals continually floating in his mind. It was to make sure of enjoying all this some day in the future, that the kopecks were saved, and for a time stingily denied himself and to others. When a rich man dashed by him in a light elegant droshky drawn by richly-harnessed trotting horses, he would stand still as though rooted to the spot, and then as though waking from a long sleep, would say: "Why, he was a counting-house clerk and wore his hair cut like a peasant's!" And everything suggestive of wealth and prosperity made an impression upon him that he could not himself explain. On leaving school he did not even want to take a holiday, so strong was his desire to set to work at once and get into the service. In spite, however, of his high testimonials, it was with great difficulty that he succeeded in getting a berth in the Palace of Justice; even in the remotest corners powerful patronage is just as necessary! The job he obtained was a wretched one, the salary a miserable thirty or forty roubles a year. But he resolved to set to work zealously, to conquer and overcome all difficulties. And, indeed, he displayed incredible self-sacrifice, patience and self-denial. From early morning till late in the evening, without flagging spiritually or physically, he was up to the ears in official papers. He did not go home, but slept at the office on the tables, had dinner sometimes with the porters, and with all that, succeeded in preserving his neat exterior, in dressing decently, in retaining an agreeable expression on his face, and even something of dignity in his movements. It must be said that the officials of the Palace of Justice were distinguished by their ugliness and unprepossessing appearance. Some had faces that looked like badly-baked bread, with a cheek swollen out on one side, and the chin bent in the other direction, with a pimple on the upper lip, which was cracked, moreover—in fact they were anything but pretty. They all spoke gruffly in a voice that sounded as if they were just going to hit some one; they frequently sacrificed to Bacchus,* so proving that there are many relics of paganism left in the Slovanic nature; they used even to come to the office sometimes the worse for liquor, as it is called, which made things very unpleasant and the air anything but fragrant. Tchitchikov, who was a complete contrast to them both in his looks, in the affableness of his voice and in his complete abstinence from strong drink, could not but be conspicuous and distinguished among such clerks. But, for all that, his progress was difficult. He was under the authority of a very old head clerk, who was the very incarnation of stony callousness and insensibility: everlastingly the same, unapproachable, he had never in his life displayed a trace of a smile on his face, he had never greeted any one even with an inquiry after his health. No one had ever seen him different from what he always was, either in the street, or at home. If only he had shown an interest in anything; if only he had got drunk and laughed in his cups; or if he had given himself up to the savage merriment of a drunken robber, but there was not a shadow of anything of the sort. There was absolutely nothing in him; neither wickedness nor goodness, and there was something terrible about this absence of anything. His coarsely marble-like face, free from any striking irregularity, did not suggest resemblance to anything; there was a morose harmony between his features. Only the pockmarks with which his face was pitted classified it with those faces on which, to use the popular expression, the devil has threshed peas at night. It seemed as though it were beyond human power to make up to this man and win his favour, but Tchitchikov made the attempt. At first he set to work to please him in all sorts of imperceptible trifles; he carefully considered the way he mended the pens with which he wrote, and preparing several on the same pattern, always put them ready to his hand; he blew or brushed away the sand and tobacco from his table, and brought a new rag to clean his inkstand; he looked for and

---

*In classical mythology, the god of wine.

found his hat, as wretched a hat as ever was seen in the world, and always laid it beside him before closing time; he brushed the back of the old man's coat if he chanced to rub against the whitewashed wall. But it remained absolutely unnoticed, exactly as though nothing had been done. At last he sniffed out something about his private life: he found out that he had a rather mature daughter whose face also looked as if the devil had threshed peas on it. He determined to make his attack on that side. He found out what church she went to on Sundays, and made a practice of standing just opposite her, neatly dressed, with a stiffly starched shirt-front. This strategy was crowned with success: the morose head clerk was shaken and invited him to tea! And before the clerks in the office had time to look round things had gone so far that Tchitchikov had moved into the old man's house, had become useful and indispensable to him, bought the flour and the sugar for the household, behaved to the daughter as though they were engaged, called the head clerk papa and kissed his hand. Every one in the office assumed that at the end of February, before Lent, there would be a wedding. The morose old head clerk even began trying to promote his interests with the higher powers, and in a short time Tchitchikov was himself appointed to a post as head clerk, which had just fallen vacant. This, it seemed, was the chief object of his connection with the old clerk, for the next day Tchitchikov secretly removed his trunk, and the following morning departed to another lodging. He left off calling the old head clerk papa, and never kissed his hand again, and the question of marriage dropped, as though it had never been thought of. Whenever he met the old man, however, he shook hands with him affably and invited him to tea, so that, in spite of the old clerk's invariable stoniness and gruff indifference, he always shook his head and muttered to himself: "You took me in, you took me in, you limb of Satan!"

This was the hardest stage in his upward journey. From that time forward, his advance was easier and more successful. He became a marked man. He turned out to possess everything necessary in that world: agreeable manners and deportment and briskness in business matters. With these qualifications, he succeeded within a short time in obtaining what is called a lucrative post and made the fullest possible use of it. It must be understood that just at that time very strict measures were being taken against bribes of all sorts. He was not afraid of these measures, but turned them to his own advantage, displaying that typical Russian resourcefulness that only comes to the surface in times of stress. The way things were managed was this: as soon as a petitioner came forward and thrust his hand into his pocket in order to extract therefrom the familiar letters of recommendation signed by Prince Hovansky, as the expression is among us in Russia—"No, no," he would say with a smile, stopping the petitioner's hand, "do you imagine that I . . . no, no! this is our duty, the work we are bound to do without any recompense! As far as that goes you may rest assured: everything will be done by to-morrow. Allow me to know your address, there is no need for you to trouble yourself, it shall be brought to your house."

The delighted petitioner would return home almost ecstatic, thinking: "Well, at last here's the sort of man we want more of! He's a precious jewel!" But the petitioner would wait one day, a second, the papers are not brought to the house; nor are they on the third day. He goes to the office—the business has not been touched—he applies to the precious jewel. "Oh, I beg your pardon," says Tchitchikov, taking both his hands. "We have had such a lot of work, but by to-morrow it shall be done, by to-morrow without fail! I really feel quite ashamed." And all this is accompanied by the most fascinating manners. If meanwhile the skirts of a coat fly open a hand is instantly trying to set things right and hold the skirt. But neither the next day, the day after, or the day after that are the papers brought to the house. The petitioner begins to put two and two together: "Why, hang it all, what's at the bottom of it?" He makes inquiries and is told: "You have to give something to the copying clerks." "Why not! I am ready to give a quarter of a rouble or two." "No, not a quarter, but a twenty-five rouble note." "Twenty-five roubles to the copying clerks!" the petitioner cries out. "Yes, why are you so excited," he is answered, "it's divided like this: the copying clerks get a quarter rouble each, and the rest goes to the heads." The slow-witted petitioner slaps himself on the forehead and swears for all he is worth at the new order of things, at the suppression of bribes, and the courteous refined manners of the officials. "In old days one did know what to do anyway: one brought the chief man ten roubles and the thing was done, and now they must have twenty-five roubles, and you have to wait a week before you guess what to do . . . the devil take all this disinterested honesty and official dignity!" The petitioner of course was right; but on the other hand, now there are no bribe-takers, all our higher officials are most honest and gentlemanly people, only the secretaries and copying clerks are scoundrels.

Soon a much wider field presented itself to Tchitchikov. A committee was formed to superintend the erection of a very expensive government building. He succeeded in getting on the committee, and became one of its most active members. The committee immediately set to work. They were busy over the building for six years, but either the climate hindered its progress, or the building materials were peculiar in some way, for the government building got no higher than the foundation. Meanwhile a handsome private residence made its appearance at the other end of the town for each member of the committee: apparently the character of the soil was more favourable there. The members of the committee began to grow prosperous and to rear families. It was only at this point that Tchitchikov began to relax a little the severity of his rules of abstinence and self-denial. Only now his long drawn-out fast was a little mitigated, and it appeared that he had by no means an aversion for various enjoyments which he had succeeded in denying himself in those years of ardent youth, when hardly any man is completely master of himself. Some superfluities made their appearance: he engaged a rather good cook, procured fine linen shirts. Already he had bought himself cloth such as no one in the province wore, and from that time forth took to wearing by preference clothes of a shot-brown or shot-reddish hue; already he obtained a fine pair of horses and held one rein himself, making the trace horse turn his head to one side: he had already adopted the habit of sponging himself over with water mixed with au-de-Cologne; already he had bought a special very expensive soap to preserve his complexion, already . . .

But all at once a new chief, a stern military man, the enemy of bribe-takers and of everything that is called injustice, was sent to replace the easy-going old fogey who had been in command. The next day he frightened every one of them, he called for accounts, detected inaccuracies and sums of money missing at every step, instantly noticed the handsome private residences and a severe inquiry followed. Officials were dismissed from their posts. The handsome private residences passed to the Treasury and were transformed into almshouses and schools for the sons of soldiers—everything was scattered to the winds and Tchitchikov suffered more than the others. The new chief suddenly—God only knows why, sometimes indeed it happens for no reason—took a dislike to his face in spite of its pleasantness, and conceived a mortal hatred for him. And the relentless chief was a terrible menace to every one. But as he was a military man and so did not understand all the subtleties of civilian strategy, within a short time another set of officials succeeded in worming themselves into his favour, thanks to an appearance of honesty and a capacity for pleasing, and the general soon found himself in the hands of still greater scoundrels, though he did not recognise them as such; he was even delighted that he had at last picked out the right men and even boasted of his keen powers of discriminating character. The officials instantly grasped his temper and character. Everything that was under his command was carried on by men who fiercely tracked down every delinquency; everywhere, in every case, they hunted it as a fisherman hunts some fat white salmon with a harpoon, and they hunted it with such success, that in a short time every one of them had saved up several thousands of roubles. Then many of the former officials returned to the paths of righteousness and were received into the service. But Tchitchikov could not worm his way in again anyhow, though the general's chief secretary, who completely led his chief by the nose, encouraged by Prince Hovansky's letters, espoused his cause and did his utmost, yet he could do nothing for him whatever. Though the general could be led by the nose (without being aware of it of course), yet if an idea once got into his head it was like an iron nail, there was no pulling it out again. All the intelligent secretary could obtain was the destruction of the record of his ignominy, and he only obtained this by appealing to the general's compassion, and painting in vivid colours the touching plight of the delinquent's children, though Tchitchikov fortunately had none.

"Well!" said Tchitchikov to himself, "I hooked a good thing, I was pulling it out when the line broke—don't keep on worrying. It's no good crying over spilt milk, I must set to work." And so he made up his mind to begin his career once more, once more to arm himself with patience, once more to deny himself everything although he had so greatly enjoyed his slackness just before. He had to move to another town, there to make himself a position again. Nothing he attempted succeeded. He had to pass from one job to another and then to a third in a very short time. The jobs were humble and degrading. It must be understood that Tchitchikov was one of the most refined men that ever existed on this earth. Though he had at first to rub along in coarse society, he always maintained his inward refinement; he liked the table in the office to be of polished wood, and everything to be on a gentlemanly scale; he never permitted himself an unrefined word and was always offended if he saw a lack of proper respect for rank or position in the words of others. I believe it will please the reader to hear that he changed his linen every alternate day, and in the heat of summer every day; the slightest offensive smell annoyed him, for this reason he always put cloves in his nose when Petrushka came to undress him and pull off his boots; and in many cases his nerves were as delicate as a girl's, and so it was hard to find himself again in those grades in which everything smelt of brandy and indecorum. However much he hardened his heart, he grew thin and even greenish in the face during this time of hardship. He had been beginning to grow plump and to develop those seemly rounded contours with which the reader found him when he met him last, and already when he looked in the looking-glass he had begun to meditate on many agreeable things—a wife and a nursery—and a smile followed such thoughts; but now when he glanced at some unlucky moment into the looking-glass he could not help crying out: "Holy Mother! how disgusting I have grown!" And for a long while afterwards he would not look at himself. But our hero endured it all, endured it with fortitude, endured it with patience, and—at last succeeded in getting into the Customs Office. It must be said that this department had long been the secret subject of his reveries. He saw what stylish foreign articles the customs house officials possessed, what pieces of china and of fine cambric they sent to their lady friends, aunts and sisters. More than once he said with a sigh: "That's what one ought to get into: the frontier is near, and enlightened people, and what fine linen shirts one can get hold of!"

I must mention that another thing he used to dream of was a special sort of French soap which imparted an extraordinary whiteness to the skin and freshness to the complexion; what it was called, God only knows, but he imagined he would certainly come upon it at the frontier. And so he had for years been longing to get into the customs department, but he had been restrained by the various advantages connected with the building committee, and he justly argued that the customs was far away and that a bird in the hand was worth two in the bush. Now he determined at all costs to get into the customs—and he got into the customs. He attacked his duties with extraordinary zeal. It seemed as though fate itself had marked him out to be a customs house official. Such promptitude, penetration, and sharpsightedness had never before been seen or even heard of. In three or four weeks he had become so completely at home in the work that he knew absolutely everything about it. He did not even weigh or measure but found out from the invoice how many yards of cloth or other material there was in the piece; lifting a parcel in his hand he could tell at once how many pounds it weighed. As for searches, in that, as his colleagues expressed it, he simply had the scent of a hound; one could not but be amazed at the patience with which he felt every button, and all this was done with killing *sang-froid** and incredible courtesy. And while the victims were furious and beside themselves with anger, conscious of a malignant impulse to slap his suave countenance, he would only say, without the slightest change in his face or his courteous manners: "May I trouble you to be so kind as to stand up?": or, "Will you kindly walk into the other room, madam, there the wife of one of our clerks will interview you?": or, "Allow me to unpick the lining of your coat with my penknife," and saying this he would extract from within the lining shawls and kerchiefs, as coolly as though he were taking them out of his own trunk. Even his superiors declared that he was not a man but a fiend: he found contraband goods in wheels and shafts of carriages and the ears of horses, and in all kinds of places in which it would never occur to the author to peep, and into which no one but a customs house official would venture to peep, so that the unfortunate traveller after crossing the frontier could not recover for quite a long time, and as he mopped up the beads of perspiration that came out all over him, could only cross himself and say: "Well, well!" The victim's position was very much like that of a schoolboy who has escaped from a private room, to which he has been summoned by a master to receive a lecture, instead of which he has quite unexpect-

---

*Cold blood (French); coolness, composure.

edly received a thrashing. For a brief period there was no peace for the smugglers of contraband goods. He was the menace and despair of all the Polish Jews. Nothing could overcome his honesty and incorruptibility, they were almost unnatural. He did not even amass a small fortune from the confiscated goods and various articles which instead of being passed on to the Treasury, were retained to avoid unnecessary correspondence. Such zealous, disinterested service could not but be the subject of general admiration, and was bound in the end to attract the attention of the authorities. He was promoted, and immediately drew up a scheme for catching all smugglers, only asking for the means of carrying it out himself. He was immediately entrusted with the commission and unlimited authority to conduct searches. This was all that he wanted. Just at that time a regularly organised society of smugglers was formed. The audacious enterprise gave promise of a profit of millions. Tchitchikov had long been aware of its existence and refused the offers of an emissary sent to bribe him, saying drily: "It's not time for that yet." When he had received full control he sent word to the society saying: "The time has come now." His calculation was only too correct. Now he could gain in one year what he could not have made by twenty years of the most zealous service. He had not before been willing to enter into relations with them because he had been nothing but a humble pawn and so could not have got much; but now . . . now it was quite a different matter: he could make any terms he liked. That the thing might go through without hindrance he brought into it another man, a colleague of his, who could not resist temptation although his hair was grey. The terms were fixed and the society set to work. The enterprise began brilliantly. The reader has no doubt often heard the story of the clever journey of the Spanish sheep who, crossing the frontier in two sheep-skins, carried over Brabant lace to the value of millions of roubles under their fleeces. This incident took place at the time when Tchitchikov was in the customs. Had he not had a hand in this enterprise no Jews in the world could have succeeded in carrying out such an undertaking. After three or four flocks of sheep had crossed the frontier the two customs house officials found themselves in possession of a capital of four hundred thousand roubles. Tchitchikov is said to have made five hundred thousand because he was a little sharper. Goodness knows to what immense figure their gains might have swelled, had not an unlucky chance in an evil hour ruined everything. The devil confounded the two officials. To speak plainly the officials lost their temper and quarrelled about nothing. In some heated conversation, possibly after too much to drink, Tchitchikov called his colleague a priest's son, and, though he really was a priest's son, the latter, why I cannot say, was bitterly offended and answered him at once forcibly and extremely cuttingly in these words: "That's a lie, I'm a civil councillor and not a priest's son, but you are a priest's son," and added to annoy him further: "so that's all about it." Though he did score off him in this way, throwing the offensive epithet back at him, and though the expression, "So that's all about it!" may have been a strong one, he was not satisfied with that, he gave secret information against him. Though indeed they do say that they were at loggerheads already over some woman as fresh and firm as a juicy turnip, to use the expression of the customs officials, that men had even been bribed to waylay our hero some evening in a dark alley and beat him within an inch of his life, but that she made fools of both the officials and really bestowed her favours on a staff-captain, called Shamsharev. How it really was, God only knows; the reader who cares to may complete the story for himself. The chief point is that their secret relations with the smugglers were discovered. Though the civil councillor was himself ruined, he certainly brought his colleague to grief also. The officials were brought to justice, an inventory was made of everything they had and all was confiscated, and all this fell like a thunderbolt on their heads. They came to themselves as after delirium, and saw with horror what they had done. The civil councillor had not the fortitude to endure his fate and perished in obscurity, but the collegiate councillor faced his troubles bravely. He succeeded in concealing part of the money in spite of the keen scent of the officials who were tracking him; he brought into play all the subtle wiles of a brain of much experience and deep understanding of men; with one he tried his agreeable address, with another pathetic appeal, with one he employed flattery, which never comes amiss, into another's hands he slipped money, in short he managed things so far successfully at least, as to get off with less ignominy than his colleague, and to escape trial on a criminal charge. But both his fortune and all his foreign treasures were lost: other amateurs of such things turned up to secure them. All he managed to keep was a paltry ten thousand, carefully put away for a rainy day, two dozen linen shirts, a small chaise such as bachelor gentlemen drive about in, and two serfs, the coachman Selifan and the footman Petrushka; and the customs house officials, moved by genuine sympathy, left him five or six pieces of soap for preserving the freshness of the complexion— that was all! This was the position in which our hero found himself again! Such was the immensity of the catastrophe that overtook him. This was what he called suffering in a good cause. It might have been expected that after such storms, such trials, such fluctuations of destiny and troubles in life, he would retire with his precious ten thousand to the peaceful seclusion of some little district town and there vegetate for ever in a chintz dressing-gown at the window of a little low-pitched house, watching on Sundays the peasants fighting under his window, or for fresh air and exercise walking into the poultry yard to feel with his own hands the hen destined for soup, and so lead an inglorious but not altogether useless existence. But this did not happen. One must do justice to the invincible strength of his character. After misfortunes that were enough if not to kill, at least to cool and subdue a man for ever, his indomitable passion was not quenched. He was plunged in grief and vexation, he murmured against the whole world, was wroth with the injustice of destiny, indignant at the injustice of men, and yet he could not resign himself to abandoning all effort. In short, he displayed a patience compared with which the wooden patience of a German, due to the sluggish, languid circulation of his blood, is nothing. Tchitchikov's blood on the other hand circulated vigorously, and he needed a great deal of good sense and strong will to keep a tight rein on all the impulses that were longing to break bounds and enjoy themselves in freedom. He argued, and there was some justice in the argument, "Why me? Why should misfortune have overtaken me? Who wastes his time in the service nowadays? They all make what they can. I have never brought trouble on any one: I haven't robbed the widow, I have reduced no one to beggary; I have made use of what was to spare; I took where any one would have taken; if I had not made use of it, others would have. Why are other people prosperous and why should I be crushed like a worm? And what am I now? What use am I? How can I look any respectable father of a family in the face? How can I help feeling stings of conscience when I know that I am a useless burden on the earth? And what will my children say one day? 'Our father is a beast,' they will say, 'he has left us no property!' "

As the reader is already aware, Tchitchikov was much troubled about his descendants. It was such a touching subject! He would not have set to work so vigorously if it had not been for the question, which for some unknown reason spontaneously occurred to him: "What will my children say?" And so our future founder of a family was like a cautious tomcat who, looking out of the corner of one eye to see whether his master is watching him from somewhere, hurriedly grabs whatever is nearest to him: soap, candles, salt pork, or a canary if he can get it in his claws, in fact, lets nothing escape him. So our hero wept and lamented, but meanwhile his active brain did not flag; there everything was longing to build up something and only waiting for a plan. Once more he drew himself in, once more he began to lead a hard life, once more restricted himself in every way, once more from an elegant decorous existence sank into degradation and low life. And while waiting for better times he was even obliged to adopt the calling of a legal agent, a calling which is not recognised as creditable among us, he was jostled out of the way on all sides, treated with scant respect by all the small fry of the attorneys' offices, and even by those who employed him, doomed to cool his heels hanging about in entries, to put up with rudeness and so on, but poverty forced him to accept anything. Among the jobs he got was one to arrange for the mortgaging of several hundred of peasants to the Trustee Committee. The estate on which they existed was hopelessly ruined. It had been ruined by the cattle plague, rascally stewards, bad harvests, infectious diseases, which carried off the best of the workmen, and lastly the folly of the landowner himself, who had furnished a house for himself in Moscow in the latest fashion, and wasted upon this the whole of his property to the last kopeck, so that he had literally nothing to eat. At last the only thing left to do was to mortgage his last remaining estate. Mortgaging to the government was at that time a new scheme and people resorted to it with some uneasiness. Tchitchikov acting as agent, after first propitiating every one (as we all know, without a preliminary consideration no one can obtain a simple piece of information or verification, at least a bottle of Madeira must be poured down every throat) and so after propitiating every one concerned, he pointed out one circumstance—that half the peasants had died—in order that there might be no difficulties made afterwards. . . . "But they are all on the census list, aren't they?" said the secretary. "They are," answered Tchitchikov. "Well, why are you troubled about them? One dies, another's born, and all are just as good to pawn." The secretary, as the reader perceives, could talk in rhyme. And meanwhile the most brilliant inspiration that ever entered the mind of man suddenly dawned upon Tchitchikov. "Ough, I am a Simple Simon," he said to himself: "I look for my gloves and they are both in my belt! Why, suppose I buy all who are dead, before the new census lists are sent out, if I get, let us say, a thousand of them, and suppose the Trustee Committee gives me two hundred roubles a soul: why there's a fortune of two hundred thousand! And now is a good time, there has just been an epidemic, the peasants have died, thank goodness, in great numbers. The owners have been losing at cards, carousing and squandering their money most appropriately; they are running to Petersburg to go into the service, their estates are deserted and managed anyhow, and it is more and more difficult every year to pay the taxes. So every one will be delighted to let me have them if only to escape paying the tax on them; and perhaps in some cases I may get a kopeck for taking them. Of course it is a difficult and troublesome business, and there is a danger of getting into trouble again, of some scandal arising. Well, but man has been given a brain to make use of it. And the best of it is that the project will seem incredible to every one, no one will believe in it; it is true that one cannot buy peasants without land, nor mortgage them either. But I will buy them for resettlement; nowadays you can get land in the Taurida* or Kherson provinces for nothing if only you settle peasants on them. And that is where I will settle them all! To Kherson with them! Let them live there! The resettlement can be done properly, in the legal way through the courts. If they want to verify the peasants—by all means, I have nothing against it. Why not? I'll present the verification with a signature of the captain of the police in his own handwriting. The village might be called Tchitchikov's Settlement or from my Christian name, the hamlet of Pavlovskoe."

And so this was how our hero's mind reached this strange idea, for which I cannot tell whether my readers will be grateful to him,

---

*Province in Crimea and southern Ukraine.

though it would be hard to say how grateful the author is, for had this idea not entered Tchitchikov's head, this poem would not, in any case, have seen the light.

Crossing himself after the Russian fashion he proceeded to carry it out. On the pretence of looking for a place to settle and other pretexts, he went off to look at various corners of our empire, especially those which had suffered more than others from various misfortunes, such as bad harvests, high rate of mortality and so on, where in fact he might most conveniently and cheaply buy the sort of peasants he wanted. He did not apply to every landowner indiscriminately, but selected those who were most to his taste, or those with whom he found less difficulty in making such bargains, trying first to make their acquaintance and gain their good-will, so as to obtain the peasants through friendship rather than by purchase. And so the reader must not be indignant with the author if the characters who have hitherto appeared are not to his taste, that is Tchitchikov's fault; here he is completely master and where he thinks fit to take us there we must go. If, however, we do incur censure for the colourlessness and unattractiveness of our characters, we will only say for ourselves that the full scope and magnitude of anything is not to be seen at first. The approach to any town whatever, even to the capital, is always dull and uninteresting; at first everything is grey and monotonous; there are endless strings of smoke-begrimed factories and workshops, and only afterwards the corners of six-storied houses, shops, signboards, great vistas of streets begin to appear, all with belfrys, columns, statues, and turrets, with the splendour, noise and uproar of the town, and everything that the brain and hand of man has so marvellously devised.

How his first purchase took place my readers have seen already. They will see later how things go afterwards, what successes and failures our hero meets with, how he has to overcome more difficult obstacles, how titanic forms appear, how the hidden springs of our great novel move as its horizon spreads wide in the distance, and it takes a grand lyrical direction. The travelling party, consisting of a middle-aged gentleman, a chaise such as bachelors drive in, the valet Petrushka, the coachman Selifan, and the three horses already known to the reader, from the Assessor to the rascally dappled grey, have a long way still to go.

And so here we have the full-length portrait of our hero, just as he was! But perhaps the reader will insist on a definite answer in regard to one particular: what sort of man was he as regards moral qualities? That he was not a hero filled with virtues and perfections is evident. What was he then? He must have been a scoundrel, I suppose. Why a scoundrel? Why be so severe to others? There are no scoundrels among us nowadays: there are well-intentioned, agreeable people, but you will scarcely find above two or three men who would risk the public ignominy of a slap in the face, and even those talk about virtue nowadays. It would be more just to call him a good manager, a man bent on making money. Making money is the universal vice: things have been done which the world describes as not very honest for the sake of it. It is true that there is something repellent in such a character, and the very readers who on their way through life would make friends with such a man, would entertain him in their house and spend their time agreeably with him, will look at him askance if he is made the hero of a drama or a poem. But wise is he who does not disdain any character, but probing it with searching eye investigates its primary elements. Everything is rapidly transformed in a man; before you have time to look round, a terrible worm has grown up within him and is sucking all his vital sap. And more than once some passion—not merely a great passion, but some insignificant little propensity for something petty—has sprung up in a man born for better things, has made him forget great and sacred duties and see something great and holy in insignificant baubles. Innumerable as the sands of the sea are the passions of man and all are different, and all, base and noble alike, are first under a man's control, and afterwards cruel tyrants dominating him. Blessed is the man who has chosen from among them a noble passion: it grows and with every hour and minute increases his immense happiness, and he enters further and further into the infinite paradise of his soul. But there are passions, the choice of which lies not in a man's hands. They are born with him at the moment of his birth into the world, and he has not been given the strength to turn away from them. They work upon some higher plan, and there is in them something that for ever calls to one and is never silent all one's life. They are destined to complete the grand pageant of the earth, whether they appear in gloomy, sinister form, or as a bright apparition that rejoices the world—they are equally called up for some good unknown to man. And maybe in this very Tchitchikov, the passion that led him on was not due to him, and in his cold existence there lies hidden what will one day reduce a man to ashes and to his knees before the wisdom of the heavens. And it is another mystery why this type has appeared in the poem that is now seeing the light.

But what weighs upon me is not that my readers will be displeased with my hero. What weighs upon me is the conviction which nothing can shake in my soul, that my readers would have been delighted with the same hero, this same Tchitchikov, if the author had not looked too deeply into his soul, had not stirred up in its depths what slips away and hides from the light, had not displayed the most secret thoughts which a man does not trust to any other, but had shown him such as he appeared to all the town, to Manilov and others; then every one would have been delighted with him, and would have welcomed him as an interesting man. It would not have mattered that neither his face nor his whole figure would have moved as though living before their eyes; on the other hand, when they had finished the book, their souls would have been untroubled and they could go back to the card table, which is the solace of all Russia. Yes, my gentle readers, you would rather not see the poverty of human nature exposed. "What for?" you say; "what is the use of it? Do you suppose we don't know that there is a great deal that is stupid and contemptible in life? We often have to see what is by no means cheering, apart from you. You had better show us what is noble and attractive. Better let us forget."

"Why do you tell me that my estate is in a bad way, my lad?" says the landowner to his steward, "I know that, my dear fellow, without your telling me; have you nothing better than that to say? Let me forget it; let me not know it, then I shall be happy." And so the money which might to some extent have saved the situation is wasted on all sorts of ways of inducing forgetfulness. The mind from which, perhaps, great resources might have sprung sleeps; and the estate is knocked down at auction and the owner is cast adrift to forget his troubles with his soul ready in his extremity for base deeds at which he would once have been horrified.

The author will incur censure also from the so-called patriots who as a rule sit quietly at home and busy themselves about quite other matters, making money, making their fortunes at the expense of others; but as soon as anything happens which they regard as insulting to their country, if a book appears in which some bitter truth is told, they run out of every corner like spiders, when they see a fly caught in their web, and immediately raise outcries: "Is it right to bring such a thing to light, to proclaim it aloud? Why, all the things that are described here are our private affairs—is it right? What will foreigners say? Is it pleasant to hear a low opinion of oneself? Do they imagine that it isn't painful? Do they imagine that we are not patriots?" I must confess that I cannot find a fitting answer to these sage observations, especially the one concerning the opinion of foreigners. Unless perhaps this. Two citizens lived in a remote corner of Russia. One whose name was Kifa Mokievitch was the father of a family, and a man of mild disposition, who passed his life in a dressing-gown and slippers; he did not trouble his head about his family; his time was devoted rather to speculative inquiries and engrossed with the following philosophical—as he called it—questions: "Now for instance the animal is born naked," he would say as he walked up and down the room. "Why is it that he is naked? Why isn't he born like a bird: why isn't he hatched out of an egg? It really is . . . er . . . The more you look into nature the harder it is to understand! . . ." Such were the meditations of the worthy citizen Kifa Mokievitch. But that is not what matters. The other citizen was Moky Kifovitch, his son. He was what is called in Russia a *bogatyr*,* and while his father was absorbed in the question of the problem of the birth of animals, this muscular young man of twenty craved for self-expression. He could not do anything by halves: somebody's arm was always broken or somebody else had a bump on his nose. Every one in the house or the neighbourhood—from the serf girl to the yard dog—fled at the sight of him: he even smashed his own bedstead into fragments. Such was Moky Kifovitch, but yet he had a kind heart. But that is not the point either. The point really is this: "Mercy on us, kind sir, Kifa Mokievitch," said all the servants of his own and the neighbouring households to his father, "your Moky Kifovitch is too much for us. Nobody has any peace for him, he is such a pestering fellow!" "Yes, he is mischievous, he is mischievous," his father usually replied: "but

---

*Legendary Russian hero in medieval poems and songs.

there, what's to be done? It's too late to knock him about, besides every one would blame me for cruelty; and he is sensitive; reproach him before two or three other people, he'll be meek, but then the publicity! That is what is so dreadful! All the town would be calling him a cur. Do you really imagine that would not be painful—am I not his father? Because I am absorbed in philosophy and have not time to attend to my family, do you suppose I am not a father? No, indeed, I am his father! his father, hang it all, his father. Moky Kifovitch is very near and dear to me!" At this point Kifa Mokievitch smote himself on the chest with his fist and became greatly excited. "If he is to remain a cur, don't let people learn it from me, don't let me give him away!" And having thus displayed his paternal sentiments, he left Moky Kifovitch to persevere in his heroic exploits and returned again to his favourite subject, asking himself some such question as: "Well, if an elephant were hatched out of an egg I expect the shell would be pretty thick, you wouldn't break it with a cannon ball, they would have to invent some new explosive." So thus they went on living, these two citizens who have so unexpectedly peeped out of their quiet retirement as out of a window into the end of our poem, in order to furnish a modest answer to the censures of some ardent patriots who have hitherto been quietly engaged in philosophical pursuits or in increasing their fortunes at the expense of the finances of the country they love so dearly, not caring about avoiding wrongdoing, but very anxious that people should not talk of their wrongdoings. But no, not patriotism, nor genuine feeling is at the root of their censure. Another feeling lies concealed under it. Why hide the truth? Who if not an author is bound to speak the holy truth? You are afraid of any one's looking deeply below the surface, you dread looking below the surface yourselves, you like to glide over everything with heedless eyes. You even laugh heartily at Tchitchikov, perhaps you will even praise the author—and will say: "He has neatly hit it off, though, he must be an amusing fellow!" And after saying that you look at yourself with redoubled pride, a self-satisfied smile comes on to your face and you add: "There is no denying that there are very queer and funny people in some provinces and thorough rogues too!" And which of you, full of Christian meekness, not in public, but alone in private, at the moment of solitary inward converse, asks in the depths of your own soul, this painful question: "Is there not a bit of Tchitchikov in me too?" And it is pretty sure to be so indeed! And if some friend, not of too low or too high a grade in the service, should chance to pass by at that moment, you will immediately nudge your neighbour and will say almost guffawing: "Look, look, there goes Tchitchikov, there's Tchitchikov!" And then like a child, forgetting all decorum befitting your age and position, you will run behind him, mimicking and repeating: "Tchitchikov! Tchitchikov! Tchitchikov!"

But we have begun talking too loudly, forgetting that our hero who was asleep all the while we have been telling his story, is by now awake and might easily hear his name so frequently repeated. He easily takes offence, and will be annoyed if any one speaks disrespectfully about him. It is no great matter to the reader whether Tchitchikov is angry with him or not, but an author ought never under any circumstances to fall out with his hero—they have still to go a long way hand in hand together; two long parts are to come, that is no trifling matter.

"Hey, hey! What are you about?" said Tchitchikov to Selifan.

"What's the matter?" said Selifan in a deliberate voice.

"What's the matter indeed, are you a goose! How are you driving? Come, get on!"

And, indeed, Selifan had for a long time been driving with closed eyes, only occasionally shaking the reins about the sides of the horses who were also dozing; and Petrushka's cap had fallen off long ago, and he had sunk back with his head poking Tchitchikov's legs so that the latter was obliged to give him a nudge. Selifan pulled himself together, and giving the dappled grey a few switches on the back, after which the latter fell into a trot, and flourishing the whip over them all, cried in a thin sing-song voice: "Never fear." The horses bestirred themselves and carried the chaise along as though it were as light as a feather.

Selifan brandished the whip and kept shouting, "Ech! ech! ech!" smoothly rising up and down on the box, as the three horses darted up or flew like the wind down the little hills which dotted the high road that sloped scarcely perceptibly down hill. Tchitchikov merely smiled as he lightly swayed on his leather cushion, for he loved rapid driving. And what Russian does not love rapid driving? How should his soul that craves to be lost in a whirl, to carouse without stint, to say at times, "Damnation take it all!"—how should his soul not love it? How not love it when there is a feeling in it of something ecstatic and marvellous? One fancies an unseen force has caught one up on its wing and one flies oneself, and everything flies too: milestones fly by, merchants on the front seats of their tilt-carts fly to meet one, the forest flies by on both sides with dark rows of firs and pines, with the ring of the axe and caw of the crows; the whole road flies into the unknown retreating distance; and there is something terrible in this rapid flitting by, in which there is no time to distinguish the vanishing object and only the sky over one's head and the light clouds and the moon that struggles through them seem motionless. Ah! troika,* bird of a troika! Who was it first thought of thee? Sure, thou couldst only have been born among a spirited people,—in that land that does not care to do things by halves, but has spread, a vast plain, over half the world, and one may count its milestones till one's eyes are dizzy! And there is nothing elaborate, one would think, about thy construction; it is not held together by iron screws—no, a deft Yaroslav† peasant fitted thee up and put thee together, hastily, roughly, with nothing but axe and drill. The driver wears no German top boots: he has a beard and gauntlets, and sits upon goodness knows what; but when he stands up and swings his whip and sets up a song—the horses fly like a whirlwind, the spokes of the wheels are blended into one revolving disc, the road quivers, and the pedestrian cries out, halting in alarm—and the troika dashes away and away! . . . And already all that can be seen in the distance is something flinging up the dust and whirling through the air.

And, Russia, art not thou too flying onwards like a spirited troika that nothing can overtake? The road is smoking under thee, the bridges rumble, everything falls back and is left behind! The spectator stands still struck dumb by the divine miracle: is it not a flash of lightning from heaven? What is the meaning of this terrifying onrush? What mysterious force is hidden in this troika, never seen before? Ah, horses, horses—what horses! Is the whirlwind hidden under your manes? Is there some delicate sense tingling in every vein? They hear the familiar song over their heads—at once in uni-

---

*Russian carriage drawn by three horses abreast.
†Or Yaroslavl; city about 150 miles northeast of Moscow.

son they strain their iron chests and scarcely touching the earth with their hoofs are transformed almost into straight lines flying through the air—and the troika rushes on, full of divine inspiration. . . . Russia, whither flyest thou? Answer! She gives no answer. The ringing of the bells melts into music; the air, torn to shreds, whirs and rushes like the wind, everything there is on earth is flying by, and the other states and nations, with looks askance, make way for her and draw aside.

PART II

CHAPTER 1

Why depict the poverty of our life and our melancholy imperfection, digging people out from the wilds, from the most secluded corners of the empire? What is to be done, if such is the character of the author; if he is so sick at heart over his own imperfection, and if his talent is formed to depict the poverty of our life, digging people out from the wilds and the remotest corners of the empire! And here we are again in the wilderness, again we have come upon an out-of-the-way corner. But what a wilderness and what a corner!

The hills run zig-zagging for over eight hundred miles. Like the gigantic rampart of some unending fortress they rise above the plain, here a yellowish cliff like a wall with ravines and hollows, here a green, round cushion covered, as with lamb's wool, with young foliage springing from the stumps of cut-down trees, and here dark forests untouched by the axe. The river, faithful to its high banks, makes with them many a crook and turn across the whole expanse, but sometimes it escapes from them altogether into the meadows, then after taking several twists it flashes like fire in the sun, hides in a copse of birch-trees, aspens and alders, and races out of it in triumph accompanied by bridges, water mills and dams which seem to be pursuing it at every turn.

In one place the steep side of the hill rises higher than the rest, and is covered from top to bottom in the green of the thickly crowded trees. Here there is everything together, maples, pear-trees, low-growing willows, brooms, birch-trees, firs and mountain ash entwined with hops; here . . . glimpses of red roofs of farm buildings, the tops of the huts hidden behind them, the upper part of a mansion, and above all this mass of trees and roofs, an old-fashioned church lifts its five flashing cupolas. On each one of them is a carved gilt cross fastened to the cupola by carved gilt chains, so that the gold glitters in the distance as though hanging in the air unfastened to anything. And all this mass of trees and roofs together with the church are reflected upside down in the river where picturesque and misshapen old willows, some standing on the bank, others right in the water, dipping into it their branches and leaves, seem to be gazing at that reflection which they have not wearied of admiring through all the long years of their life.

It was a very fine view, but the view from the house over the plain and the distance was finer still. No guest or visitor could stand unmoved upon the balcony: there was a thrill at his heart and he could only exclaim, "My God, what a vista!" A boundless expanse lay open below. Beyond the water meadows, dotted with copses and water mills, there were green and dark-blue patches of forest, like the sea or like mist flooding the distance. Beyond the forest through the hazy atmosphere could be seen yellow sand. Beyond the sand on the distant horizon lay a ridge of chalk hills, gleaming with dazzling whiteness even in cloudy weather as though lighted up by eternal sunshine. Dark purplish patches were faintly visible here and there upon them. These were far-away hamlets, but the eye could hardly distinguish them, only a golden church spire, flashing like a spark, betrayed the presence of a big, populous village. All this was wrapped in an unbroken stillness which even the scarcely audible notes of the feathered songsters that filled the air could not disturb. In short the visitor or guest could never stand unmoved upon the balcony, and after contemplating it for an hour or two he would exclaim again as at the first moment: "My God, what a vista!"

Who was it that lived in this village which like an invincible fortress could not be approached from the front, but could only be reached from the other side by meadows, cornfields and at last through a copse of oak-trees, dotted picturesquely on the green turf, right up to the huts and the mansion? Who was the inhabitant, the master and owner of this village? To what happy man did this secluded nook belong?

To Andrey Ivanovitch Tyentyetnikov, a landowner of the Tremalahansky district, a young unmarried man of thirty-three, by rank a collegiate secretary.

What sort of man was Andrey Ivanovitch Tyentyetnikov, what was his disposition, what were his qualities and his character?

We ought, of course, to inquire of his neighbours. A neighbour who belonged to the class of retired officers, old martinets, summed him up in the laconic expression, "A regular beast." A general, living some eight miles away, said: "The young man is not a fool, but he has too many notions in his head. I might have been of use to him because I have in Petersburg even . . ." The general did not finish his observation. The police captain remarked: "Why, his rank in the service is wretched, contemptible; and I have to go to him to-morrow for arrears of taxes!" If a peasant in the village was asked what his master was like, he made no answer. In fact the general opinion of him was rather unfavourable than favourable.

Yet Andrey Ivanovitch was neither good nor bad in his life and actions—he simply vegetated. Since there are not a few people in this world who do vegetate, why should not Tyentyetnikov vegetate?

Here, however, in a few words is a full chronicle of his day, and from it the reader may judge for himself of his character.

He woke up very late in the morning and would sit for a long time on his bed, rubbing his eyes. His eyes were unfortunately rather small and so the rubbing of them lasted a long time. All this time his man Mihailo was standing at the door with the washing basin and a towel. This poor Mihailo would stand waiting for an hour or two, then would go off to the kitchen and come back again—and his master was still sitting on the bed, rubbing his eyes. At last he got up from his bed, washed himself, put on his dressing-gown and went into the drawing-room, there to drink tea, coffee, cocoa, or even milk, sipping a little of each, crumbling up his bread in a merciless way and making a shameless mess everywhere with his tobacco ash. He would spend a couple of hours over his morning tea; and that was not all, he would take a cup of cold tea and go to the window looking out into the yard. The following scene took place every day before the window.

The unshaven butler Grigory would begin it by bawling at Perfilyevna the housekeeper, in the following terms: "You paltry soul! You nonentity! You had better hold your tongue, you nasty woman."

"I am not going to take my orders from you, anyway, you guzzling glutton!" the nonentity, alias Perfilyevna, would shout in reply.

"Nobody could get on with you: you quarrel even with the steward, you store-room trash," bawled Grigory.

"Yes, and the steward is as great a thief as you are!" shouted the nonentity, so that she could be heard in the village. "You are both drunkards, wasting your master's substance, barrels without a bottom! You think that the master does not know you? Why, he is there, he hears it all."

"Where is the master?"

"Why, he is sitting at the window, he sees it all."

And indeed the master was sitting at the window and seeing it all.

To complete the picture, a brat whose mother had just boxed his ears, was screaming at the top of his voice, and a borzoi hound squatting on the ground whined pitifully, for the cook had just looked out of the kitchen and splashed it with scalding water; the hubbub and uproar were insufferable. Their master saw and heard it all and not till it became so unendurable that it even hindered him in doing nothing did he send to tell them to be a little quieter in their noise.

About two hours before dinner Andrey Ivanovitch went off to his study to set to work seriously, and serious his occupation certainly was. It consisted in thinking over a work which had been continually thought over for a long time past. This work was to deal with all Russia from every point of view—civic, political, religious, philosophical, to solve the difficult questions and problems that beset her, and define clearly her great future; in short, it was a work of wide scope. But so far it had not got beyond the stage of meditation: the pen was bitten, sketches made their appearance on the paper and then it was all pushed aside; a book was taken up instead and not put down till dinner-time. The book was read with the soup, the sauce and the roast, and even with the pudding, so that some dishes got cold and others were removed untasted. Then came sipping a cup of coffee, with a pipe; then he played a game of chess with himself. What was done afterwards till supper-time it is really hard to say. I believe that simply nothing was done.

So all alone in the wide world this young man of thirty-three passed his time, sitting indoors in a dressing-gown without a cravat. He did not go out to amuse himself, he did not walk, he did not even care to go upstairs to look at the distance and the views, he did not care to open the windows to let the fresh air into the room; and the lovely view which no visitor could gaze upon without delight seemed not to exist for the owner.

From this record of his day, the reader can gather that Andrey Ivanovitch Tyentyetnikov belonged to that class of people, numerous in Russia, who are known as idlers, sluggards, lazy-bones, and so on.

Whether these characters are born such or are made so by life—is still another question. I think, instead of answering it, I had better tell the story of Andrey Ivanovitch's childhood and education.

As a child he was a clever talented boy, lively and thoughtful by turns. By a lucky or unlucky chance he was sent to a school, the head master of which was a remarkable man in his way, though he had some eccentricities. Alexandr Petrovitch had the gift of divining the nature of the Russian, and knew in what language to speak to him. No boy ever left his presence downcast; on the contrary, even after the sternest reprimand he felt buoyed up and eager to efface his nasty or mischievous action. The mass of his pupils were on the surface so full of mischief, so lively and free and easy in their manners, that one might have taken them for a disorderly gang under no control, but one would have been mistaken; the authority of one man was too powerful in that gang. There was no boy, however mischievous or naughty, who would not come of himself to tell the head master of his pranks. He knew everything that was going on in their minds. His method was unusual in everything. He used to say that what was most important was to arouse ambition—he called ambition the force that urged men onwards—without which there is no moving him to activity. A great deal of mischief and wild spirits he did not restrain at all: in the pranks of childhood he saw the first stage of the development of character. They enabled him to discern what was hidden in the child, as a skilful physician looks calmly at the temporary symptoms, at rashes coming out on the body, and does not try to suppress them, but watches them intently to find out what is going on inside the patient.

His teachers were few in number: he taught most of the subjects himself, and it must be said that without any of the pedantic terminology and sweeping theories which young professors pride themselves upon, he could in few words convey the very essence of his subject, so that it was evident even to the youngest why he needed to understand it. He used to declare that what a man needed most of all was the science of life, that in understanding that he would understand himself and know to what he ought principally to devote himself.

This science of life he made into a separate course of study to which only the most promising of his pupils were admitted. The less

gifted boys he allowed to enter the government service straight from
the first class, saying it was no use to worry them too much: it was
enough for them if they learnt to be patient and diligent workers free
from conceit and ulterior motives. "But the clever boys, the gifted
boys, keep me busy a long time," he used to say, and in this last
course Alexandr Petrovitch became a different man, and from the first
informed them that he had hitherto expected only simple intelligence, but that now he would expect from them a higher intelligence, not the intelligence that can jeer and mock at fools, but that
which can bear every insult, and suffer fools without irritation. At
this stage he required from them what others require from children.
That he called the highest stage of intelligence. To preserve in the
midst of any troubles that lofty calm in which man ought to dwell
for ever—that was what he called intelligence. In this course Alexandr
Petrovitch showed that he did understand the science of life. Of subjects only those were selected for study which were calculated to turn
a man into a true citizen. A great part of the lectures consisted of descriptions of what lay before them in various careers, in the government service or in private callings. He laid before them in all their
nakedness, concealing nothing, all the mortifications and obstacles
which would confront a man on his path through life, all the dangers
and temptations that would beset him. He knew all about them as
though he himself had practised every calling and held every office.
In fact he pictured anything but a joyful future. Strange to say, either
because ambition had already been aroused in them, or because there
was something in the very eye of that exceptional teacher that uttered
the word, forward!—that marvellous word that works such miracles
with the Russian—these lads actually sought positions of difficulty,
thirsting for action just where action was hardest, where there was
need to show a stout heart. There was a kind of sobriety in their lives.
Alexandr Petrovitch put them to all sorts of proofs and tests, inflicted
on them painful mortifications by his own action and also through
their schoolfellows; but seeing through it they were all the more on
their guard. Those who passed through the course were few in number, but those few were strong men, were like men who had been
through fire. In the service they kept their footing even in the most
precarious position when many others, cleverer perhaps than they,
could not hold out, but gave up the service on account of the most

trivial annoyances, or without being aware of it got into the hands of rogues and bribe-takers. But Alexandr Petrovitch's pupils did not merely hold on steadily but, trained in the knowledge of man and nature, exerted a lofty influence, even upon the corrupt and the depraved.

But poor Andrey Ivanovitch was not destined to enjoy this teaching. Just when he had been approved for that higher course as one of the best among the boys—there was a sudden calamity; the rare teacher, from whom one word of approval threw him into a delicious tremor, was all at once taken ill and died. Everything in the school was transformed. Alexandr Petrovitch's place was filled by a certain Fyodor Ivanovitch, a kindhearted and conscientious man whose views however were entirely different. He saw something unbridled in the free and easy manners of the pupils of the first class. He began to introduce an external discipline, insisted that the young creatures were to maintain a mute stillness, that they should never under any circumstances walk out except in twos; and even began with a yard measure fixing the distance between one pair and the next. For the sake of appearance he placed them at a table according to height instead of according to intelligence, so that the asses got all the best pieces and the clever ones all the bones. All this raised murmurings, especially when the new head master, as though intentionally slighting his predecessor, announced that a boy's intelligence and success in his studies were of no account in his eyes, that what he prized was good conduct, that if a boy were not good at his lessons but behaved well he preferred him to the clever ones. But Fyodor Ivanovitch did not succeed in getting just what he aimed at. Mischief went on in secret, and secret mischief, as we all know, is worse than what is open; the strictest discipline was observed by day, but at night there were orgies.

In the top class everything was turned upside down. With the best of intentions he set up all sorts of unsuitable innovations. He engaged new teachers with new ideas and points of view. They lectured in a learned way and flung a mass of new terms and expressions at their audience; they were learned and acquainted with the latest discoveries, but alas! there was no life in their teaching. It all seemed dead to listeners who had just begun to understand. Everything went wrong. But what was worst of all was that the boys lost all respect for the school authorities: they took to laughing both at the head master and at the teachers, they used to call the head master Fedka, the bun, and various other nicknames; things came to such a pass that a good many boys had to be expelled.

Andrey Ivanovitch was of a gentle disposition. He did not take part in the nightly orgies of his companions, who in spite of the strictest supervision had set up a mistress in the neighbourhood, one for eight of them, nor in their other evil courses which went as far as sacrilege and jeering at religion, just because the head master insisted upon their attending church very frequently. But he lost heart. His ambition had been stirred, but there was no activity, no career for him. It would have been better if it had never been aroused at all. He listened to the professors who grew hot in the lecture hall, and thought of his old master, who without getting hot, knew how to speak intelligibly. He heard lectures on chemistry, on the philosophy of law, and listened to the professors, as they went deeply into the subtleties of political science and the universal history of man conceived on such a vast scale that the professor only succeeded in treating of the introduction and development of guilds in some German towns in three years; but only some shapeless scraps of all this remained in his head. Thanks to his natural good sense, he saw that this was the wrong way to teach, but what was the right way he could not tell. And he often thought of Alexandr Petrovitch, and he used to be so sad that he did not know what to do for misery.

But youth has a future before it. As the time of leaving school drew nearer his heart began to throb. He said to himself: "This is not life of course, but only a preparation for life, real life is to be found in the service, there are great things to be done there." And like all ambitious youths he went to Petersburg, to which, as we all know, our ardent young men flock from all parts of Russia—to enter the service, to distinguish themselves, to gain promotion or simply to gather a smattering of our sham, colourless, icy cold "society" education. Andrey Ivanovitch's ambitious yearnings were, however, dampened at the outset by his uncle Onufry Ivanovitch, an actual civil councillor. He informed him that the only thing that mattered was a good handwriting, that without that there was no becoming a minister or statesman, while Tyentyetnikov's handwriting was of the sort which is popularly described as a "magpie's claw, not a man's

hand." After having lessons in calligraphy for two months he succeeded with great difficulty, through his uncle's influence, in obtaining a job of copying documents in some department. When he went
into the well-lighted hall in which gentlemen, with their heads on
one side, sat at polished tables, writing with scratchy pens, and when
he was seated beside them and a document was set before him to
copy—he experienced a very strange sensation. He felt for a time as
though he were at a school for small boys learning his A B C again.
The gentlemen sitting round him seemed to him so like school-boys!
Some of them read novels which they hid between the big pages of
their work, pretending to be busy in the work itself, and at the same
time they were in a twitter every time the head of the department appeared. The time at school suddenly rose up before him as a paradise
lost for ever: his studies seemed something so much above this paltry work of copying! That preparation for the service seemed to him
now far superior to the service itself. And all at once his incompara-
ble wonderful teacher whom no one could replace rose vividly before his mind, and tears suddenly gushed from his eyes, the room
began to go round, the tables grew misty, his fellow-clerks were a
blur, and he almost swooned. "No," he thought, when he came to
himself, "I will set to work, however petty it may seem at first!" Hardening his heart he determined to do his work as the others did.

Is there any place where there are no enjoyments? They exist even
in Petersburg in spite of its grim forbidding aspect. There is a cruel
frost in thirty degrees in the street, a witch's hurricane howls like a
despairing devil, flapping the collars of men's fur coats against their
heads, powdering their moustaches and the noses of beasts: but there
is a hospitable gleam from some little window even on the fourth
storey; in a cosy room a conversation that warms both heart and soul
is carried on to the hiss of the samovar, in the humble light of
stearine* candles; an inspired and uplifting page is read from one of
the poets with whom God has enriched His Russia, and the youthful
heart throbs with a lofty ardour unknown in other lands and under
the voluptuous skies of the south.

Tyentyetnikov soon grew used to his office work, but it never be-

---

*Waxlike, solid substance used to make candles.

came his prime interest and object as he had at first expected; it always took a second place. It served as the best means of filling up his time, making him appreciate more thoroughly the moments that were left him. His uncle, the actual councillor, began to think that his nephew would be of some use, when suddenly his nephew spoilt it all. It must be mentioned that among Andrey Ivanovitch's friends were two who belonged to the class known as disappointed men. They were those strange uncomfortable characters who not only cannot endure injustice but cannot endure anything which to their eyes appears to be injustice. Fundamentally good, though somewhat irresponsible in their own conduct, they were full of intolerance for others. Their heated talk and lofty indignation had a great effect upon him. Working upon his nerves and exciting his irritability, they made him begin to notice all sorts of trivialities to which he would never have dreamt of paying attention in the past. He took a sudden dislike to Fyodor Fyodorovitch Lyenitsyn, the chief of the department in which he served, a man of very prepossessing appearance. He began looking for a mass of defects in him, and detested him on the ground that he displayed too much sweetness in his face when he talked to his superiors and was all vinegar at once when he turned to his inferiors. "I could forgive him," said Tyentyetnikov, "if the change did not take place so quickly in his face: but on the spot, before my eyes, he is sugar and vinegar all in a minute!" From that time forward he began to watch him at every step. He fancied that Fyodor Fyodorovitch stood on his dignity to excess, that he had all the ways of petty Jacks-in-office, that he noticed unfavourably all those who did not come to pay their respects on holidays, and that he even revenged himself on those whose names did not appear on the list of visitors kept by his porter, and a number of other shortcomings from which no man good or bad is entirely free. He felt a nervous aversion for him. Some evil spirit prompted him to do something unpleasant to Fyodor Fyodorovitch. He sought an opportunity for doing this with peculiar satisfaction and succeeded in finding one. On one occasion he spoke so rudely to him that a message was sent him from the higher authorities that he must either beg his pardon or leave the service. He sent in his resignation. His uncle, the actual civil councillor, came to him, imploring and panic-stricken: "For Christ's sake, upon my word, Andrey Ivanovitch, what's this you have been about?

To throw up a career after such a good beginning, just because your
chief isn't quite to your liking? What do you mean by it? Why, with
that way of looking at things there would be no one left in the service. Think better of it, think better of it, there's still time. Swallow
your pride and your *amour propre*,* go and see him!"

"That's not the point, uncle," said the nephew. "There's no difficulty about my asking his pardon, especially as I really am to blame.
He is my chief and I ought not in any case to have spoken to him as
I did. But the real point is this: you have forgotten that I have other
duties: I have three hundred peasants, my estate is in disorder and my
steward's a fool. It will be no great loss to the state if some one sits
in my place copying papers, but it will be a great loss if three hundred men don't pay their taxes. I am a landowner: there's plenty to
do in that position also. If I concern myself with the preservation,
care and improvement of the people entrusted to me and present the
state with three hundred sober, hardworking subjects, in what way
will my work be inferior to that of some chief of a department like
Lyenitsyn?"

The actual civil councillor was open-mouthed with astonishment: he had not expected such a flood of words. After a moment's
reflection he began after this style: "But all the same . . . however can
you? . . . How can you vegetate in the country? What society will you
have among peasants? Here anyway a general or prince may pass you
in the street, if you like you can walk by the beautiful public buildings, or can go and look at the Neva,† but there, whoever you pass
will be a peasant. Why condemn yourself to rustic ignorance all your
life?"

So spoke his uncle, the actual civil councillor. He had never
walked down any street but that which led to the office, and there
were no beautiful public buildings in it; he did not notice any of the
people he met, whether they were princes or generals, knew nothing
of the temptations by which people prone to incontinence are allured
in cities, nor did he even go to the theatre. He had said all that he did
to stir the ambition and work upon the imagination of the young
man. He did not succeed in doing so however. Tyentyetnikov stuck to

---

*Self-love (French).
†River that runs through St. Petersburg.

his decision. He had begun to be bored with official work and Petersburg. The country began to seem to him a haven of freedom, fostering thought and meditation and the one career of useful activity. A fortnight after this conversation he was approaching the places where his childhood had been spent.

How his heart beat, how many memories came back to him when he felt that he was near the village of his fathers! Many places he had completely forgotten and he looked with curiosity at the glorious views as though they were new to him. When the road passed by a narrow ravine into the recesses of an immense tangled forest, when he saw above, below, over his head and beneath his feet, oaks three hundred years old, which it would take three men to span, silver firs, elms, black poplars, and when in answer to the question, "Whose forest is this?" he was told, "Tyentyetnikov's"; and when, leaving the forest, the road ran through meadows, by aspen copses, willows old and young, and twining creepers, in sight of the heights stretching in the distance, and in various places passed over several bridges across the same river, having it sometimes on the right and sometimes on the left, and when in answer to the question, "Whose prairies and water meadows are these?" he was told "Tyentyetnikov's"; when the road mounted a hill and passed along a high plateau with fields of standing corn, wheat, rye and barley on one side, while on the other lay all the part they had driven through already, which suddenly seemed to be in a picturesque distance; and when, gradually overshadowed, the way dived into and afterwards emerged from the shade of huge spreading trees dotted here and there on the green turf right up to the village, and he caught a glimpse of the brick huts and the red roofed buildings surrounding the big house; when his eagerly throbbing heart knew without question where he had arrived, all the thoughts and sensations that had been accumulating within him burst forth in some such words as these: "Well, haven't I been a fool! Fate made me the owner of an earthly paradise, a prince, and I bound myself as a copying clerk in an office! After being educated and enlightened and accumulating a decent store of just that knowledge which is needed for the ruling of men, for the improvement of a whole region, for performing the duties of a landowner who has to be at once a judge and an organiser and a guardian of order—to entrust the task to an ignorant steward!

And to choose in place of it what?—the copying of papers which a cantonist who has learnt anything could do incomparably better," and Andrey Ivanovitch called himself a fool once more.

And meanwhile, another spectacle was awaiting him. Hearing of the master's arrival the population of the whole village had gathered at the entrance. Bright-coloured kerchiefs, sashes, headbands, full-skirted coats, beards of all shapes—shovel, spade, wedge-shaped, red, fair, and white as silver, covered the whole court in front of the house. The peasants boomed out: "Our dead master, we have lived to see you again!" The women chanted: "Thou golden one, silver of our hearts!" Those who stood further off actually began fighting to get nearer. A decrepit little old woman who looked like a dried pear, darted between the legs of the others, stepped up to him, clasped her hands and shrieked: "Our nurseling! But how thin you are! the accursed foreigners have worn you out!" "Get away, woman!" the beards, shovel, spade, and wedge-shaped, shouted to her. "Where are you shoving to, you shrivelled thing?" Some one added to this an expression at which only a Russian peasant could help laughing. Andrey Ivanovitch could not refrain from laughter, but nevertheless he was deeply touched at heart. "How much love, and what for?" he thought to himself, "in return for my never having seen them, never having troubled about them! I swear from to-day that I will share your labours and your toils! I will do everything to help you to become what you ought to be, what the goodness innate in you meant you to be—that your love for me may not be for nothing, that I really may be a good master to you!"

And Tyentyetnikov really did set to work looking after his estate and his peasants in earnest. He saw at once that the steward really was an old woman and a fool with all the characteristics of a thoroughly bad steward—that is, he accurately kept an account of hens and eggs, of the yarn and the linen brought by the peasant women, but he knew absolutely nothing of harvest and sowing, and in addition suspected all the peasants of designs upon his life. He dismissed the foolish steward and engaged another, a smart fellow, in his place: without going into trivial matters he turned his attention to the points of most importance, diminished the dues, took off some of the days of labour for himself, giving the peasants more time to work on their own account, and thought that now things would go swimmingly. He went into everything himself and began to show himself in the fields, at the threshing floor, in the sheepfolds, at the mills and at the landing stage when barges and punts were being loaded and sent off.

"My word, but he is a sharp one!" the peasants began to say, and they even scratched their heads a bit, for under the feeble control that had lasted so long they had all grown lazy. But this did not go on for very long. The Russian peasant is clever and shrewd: they soon realised that though the master was zealous and eager to undertake a great deal, he had no idea as yet how to set to work, that he talked somehow too learnedly and fancifully, beyond the grasp and understanding of the peasants. It came about that the master and the peasants, though they did not completely misunderstand each other, could not, so to speak, sing in unison, were incapable of producing the same note. Tyentyetnikov began to notice that everything somehow turned out worse on the master's land than on the peasants'. His fields were sown earlier and the crops came up later. Yet they seemed to be working well: he himself was present, and even ordered them to be given a mug of vodka for their diligent work. The peasants' rye had already long been in ear, their oats were dropping, their millet was growing into a tuft, while his corn had scarcely begun to push up into a stem, the base of the ear had not yet formed. In fact he began to notice that the peasants were simply taking him in, in spite of all their flatteries; he tried reproaching them, but received some such answer, "How could we neglect the master's profit, your honour? you saw yourself, sir, how we did our best when we were ploughing and sowing, you ordered us to be given a mug of vodka"; what reply could he make to that? "But why has it come up so badly?" he persisted. "Who can tell! It seems the worms have eaten it below! And look what a summer it has been, no rain at all." But he saw that the worms had not eaten the peasants' corn, and that the rain must have fallen queerly in streaks—it had favoured the peasants' land, and not a drop had trickled on the master's fields. He found it still more difficult to get on with the women. They were continually asking to be let off their work, complaining of the heavy burden of the labours they had to perform for him. It was strange! He had abolished all the dues of linen, fruit, mushrooms and nuts, and had taken off half of their other forced labour, expecting the women to employ their free time attending to their households, sewing and making clothes for their husbands and enlarging their kitchen gardens. But nothing of the sort happened. Such idleness, squabbling, scandal-mongering prevailed among the fair sex that their husbands were continually coming to him, saying: "Master, will you bring this fury of a woman to her senses, she is a regular devil, there is no living with her!" Sometimes, hardening his heart, he attempted to resort to severity. But how could he be severe? The woman came, so hopelessly womanish, made such a shrill outcry, was so sick and ailing, and had got herself up in such wretched filthy rags! (where she had picked them up, goodness only knows). "Go away, go where you like as long as it is out of my sight," said poor Tyentyetnikov, and immediately afterwards had the satisfaction of seeing the woman at once, on going out of the gate, come to blows with a neighbour over a turnip and in spite of her ailing condition give her as sound a leathering as any sturdy peasant could have done.

He had an idea of setting up a school among them, but this led to such a ridiculous fiasco that he hung his head and felt that it would have been better not to have thought of it. All this perceptibly cooled his zeal for looking after his estate as well as for the judicial and moral duties of his position, in fact for activity generally. He was present at the field labours almost without noticing them; his thoughts were far away, his eyes sought extraneous objects. During the mowing he did not watch the rapid rising and falling of the sixty scythes, and the regular fall of the high grass into long rows beneath them; he looked away at some bend in the river, on the bank of which some red-beaked, red-legged martin was walking—a bird of course, not a man; he watched how the martin having caught a fish held it crossways in his beak, hesitating whether to swallow it or not, and at the same time looked up the river where another martin could be seen who had not yet caught a fish, but was watching intently the martin who had. When the corn was being cut he did not watch how the sheaves were being laid in cocks or ricks or sometimes simply in a heap; he did not care whether they threw the sheaves up and made the cornstacks lazily or vigorously. Screwing up his eyes and gazing upwards at the vast expanse of the sky, he let his nostrils drink in the scent of the fields and his ears marvel at the voices of the numberless singers of the air when from all sides, from heaven and earth alike they unite in one chorus, without jarring on one another. The quail lashes its whip, the landrail utters its harsh grating cry among the grass, the linnets twitter and chirrup as they flit to and fro, the trills of the lark fall drop by drop down an unseen airy ladder, and the calls of the cranes, floating by in a long string, like the ringing notes of silver bugles, resound in the void of the melodiously vibrating ether. If the work were going on near by, he was far away; if it were far away, his eyes sought something near by. And he was like an inattentive schoolboy who looks into a book but sees his schoolfellow making a long nose at him. At last he gave up going out to look at the work altogether, abandoned his judicial duties, settled indoors and even left off seeing his steward and receiving reports from him.

At times some of the neighbours would come to see him—a retired lieutenant of the Hussars, an inveterate pipe-smoker and saturated through and through with tobacco smoke, or an old martinet colonel, a great hand at small talk about everything. But this too began to bore him. Their conversation began to strike him as superficial; their brisk sprightly manner, their way of slapping him on the knee, and their free and easy behaviour generally, seemed to him too blunt and unreserved. He made up his mind to drop their acquaintance and did so rather curtly. When Varvar Nikolaitch Vishnepokromov, the most typical martinet among all colonels, and most agreeable of all small talkers, called upon him expressly to converse to his heart's content, touching upon politics, philosophy, literature and morality and even the financial position of England, he sent word that he was not at home and at the same time was so incautious as to show himself at the window. The visitor's eyes met his. One of course muttered between his teeth, "Beast!" while the other threw some epithet like "Pig!" after him. So the acquaintance ended. From that time no one else came to see him. Complete solitude reigned in the house. The young man got into his dressing-gown for good, abandoning his body to inactivity and his mind to meditating upon a work on Russia. The reader has seen already how he meditated upon it. The days came and went, uniform and monotonous. It cannot be said, however, that there were not moments when he seemed as it were to awaken from sleep. When the post brought him newspapers, new books and magazines, and when he saw in print the familiar name of some old schoolfellow who had already been successful in a distinguished career in the government service, or who had made some modest contribution to science and universal culture, a quiet secret melancholy crept over his heart, and a quiet dumbly-sorrowful aching regret at his own inactivity rose up in spite of himself. Then his life seemed to him hateful and loathsome. His school-days rose up before him extraordinarily vividly, and Alexandr Petrovitch seemed to stand before him. . . . Tears streamed from his eyes, his sobs lasted almost all day.

What did those sobs mean? Did his sick soul betray in them the sorrowful secret of its sickness—that the fine inner man, that had begun to be formed within him, had not had time to develop and grow strong; that unpractised in the struggle with failure he had never attained the precious faculty of rising to higher things and gaining strength from obstacles and difficulties; that the rich treasure of lofty feelings that had glowed within him like molten metal had not been tempered like steel, and now his will had no elasticity and was impotent; that his rare, marvellous teacher had died too soon, and now there was no one in the whole world who could rouse and awaken his forces, flagging from continual hesitation, and his weak, impotent will—who could cry to the soul in a living, rousing voice, the rousing word: "Forward!" which the Russian, at every stage, in every condition and calling, thirsts to hear?

Where is the man who can utter that all-powerful word "Forward," in the language of our Russian soul, who knowing all the strength and quality and all the depth of our nature can, with one wonder-working gesture, spur the Russian on to the higher life? With what tears and what love would he be repaid! But centuries after centuries pass by; half a million sluggards and idlers lie plunged in unwaking slumber, and rarely is the man born in Russia that can utter that all-powerful word.

Something happened, however, that almost roused Tyentyetnikov from his apathy, and almost brought about a transformation in his character. It was something almost like love, but it too came to nothing. In the neighbourhood, some eight miles away, there lived the general who, as we have seen, gave a rather doubtful opinion of Tyentyetnikov. The general lived like a general, was hospitable and liked people to come and pay their respects to him; he did not himself pay visits, talked in a husky voice, was fond of reading, and had a daughter, a strange unique creature who was more like a fantastic apparition than a woman. Sometimes a man sees something of the sort in a dream, and all his life afterwards is brooding on that vision (and reality is lost to him for ever), and he is good for nothing. Her name was Ulinka. Her education had been rather unusual, she had been brought up by an English governess who did not know a word of Russian. She had lost her mother early in childhood. Her father had no time to look after her, and indeed, loving his daughter passionately, he could have done nothing but spoil her. It is uncommonly hard to draw her portrait. She was as full of life as life itself. She was more charming than any beauty; she was more than intelligent; more graceful and ethereal than the classical antique. It was impossible to say what country had put its imprint on her, for it would be hard to find such a profile and features anywhere, except perhaps in antique cameos. Everything in her was original as in a child brought up in freedom. If any one had seen how sudden anger would bring stern lines in her lovely forehead, and how passionately she disputed with her father, he would have thought that she was a most ill-humoured creature. But her wrath was only aroused when she heard of some injustice, whatever it might be, or of some cruel action. And how instantly that anger would have passed if she had seen the very person, who had excited it, in trouble! How immediately she would have flung him her purse without considering whether it was wise or foolish to do so, and would have torn up her dress to make bandages if he were wounded! There was something impulsive in her. When she spoke, everything in her seemed to be rushing after her thoughts—the expression of her face, the tone of her voice, the movement of her hands; the very folds of her dress seemed flying in the same direction, and it seemed as though she herself would fly away after her own words. Nothing in her was concealed. She was not afraid to lay bare her thoughts before any one, and no force could have made her be silent when she wanted to speak. Her fascinating individual gait, which belonged to her only, was so fearlessly free that every one involuntarily made way for her to pass. An evil man could not help being confused and dumb in her presence, while any one good, however shy, could talk to her at once as though she were a sister, and, strange illusion!—from the first minute it seemed as though he had somewhere, sometime, known her already, that they had met in days of unremembered infancy in their own home, on some happy evening, among the joyous shouts of a crowd of children, and after that the years of discretion seemed dull and dreary.

Andrey Ivanovitch Tyentyetnikov could never have said how it was that from the first day they were as though they had known each other all their lives. A new inexplicable feeling came into his heart. His life was for an instant lighted up. His dressing-gown was for a time laid aside. He did not linger so long in bed in the morning, and Mihailo did not have to stand so long with a washing basin in his hands. The windows were thrown open in the rooms, and the owner of the picturesque estate spent a long while wandering about the dark winding paths of his garden, and stood for hours gazing at the enchanting view into the distance. At first the general received Tyentyetnikov fairly cordially, but they could not get on really well together. Their conversations always ended in an argument and in a rather unpleasant feeling on both sides. The general did not like contradiction or controversy, though on the other hand he was very fond of talking even of subjects of which he knew nothing at all. Tyentyetnikov, too, was rather ready to take offence. For the sake of the daughter, however, much was forgiven to the father, and the peace was kept between them until some relations, Countess Boldyrev and Princess Yuzyakin, came to stay with the general: one was a widow, the other an old maiden lady, both had been maids of honour in earlier days, were somewhat given to gossip and talking scandal, and not particularly distinguished by their amiability, but they had important connections in Petersburg, and the general almost grovelled before them. It struck Tyentyetnikov that from the very day of their arrival the general became more frigid, scarcely noticed him, treated him as though he were a nonentity or the very humblest sort of clerk employed for copying. He addressed him as "my lad," or "my good man," and on one occasion even used the second person singular* in speaking to him. Andrey Ivanovitch was furious; the blood rushed to his head. Controlling himself and setting his teeth, he had, however, the presence of mind to say in a particularly soft and courteous voice, while patches of colour came into his face and he was inwardly boiling: "I ought to thank you, general, for your warm feeling; you invite me by

---

*Form of the verb used to address servants.

your familiar form of address to the closest friendship, obliging me to address you in the same way, but allow me to observe that I do not forget the difference in our ages, which absolutely forbids such familiarity in our manners." The general was abashed. Collecting his thoughts he began to say, though rather incoherently, that he had not meant it in that sense, that it is sometimes permissible for an old man to address a young man in that informal way (he did not make the faintest allusion to his rank). Their acquaintance was of course cut short from that time. Love ended as soon as it began; the light that had gleamed before him for one instant was quenched, and the gloom that followed it was darker than ever. The sluggard got back into his dressing-gown again. His life was again spent in lying about and doing nothing. Dirt and disorder reigned in the house: the broom remained in the room together with the dust for days together; his trousers even made their way into the drawing-room; on the elegant table in front of the sofa lay a pair of greasy braces as though it were a tit-bit for a guest. And his life became so drowsy and abject that not only his servants ceased to respect him, but even the hens almost pecked at him. For hours at a time he would scribble feebly, drawing crooked trees, little houses, huts, carts, sledges, or he would write "Honoured Sir!" with an exclamation mark after it in all sorts of handwritings and characters. And sometimes while he was still plunged in forgetfulness, his pen would of itself, without his knowledge, sketch a little head that seemed to be taking flight, with delicate pointed features, with a light tress of hair raised and falling from under the comb, in long, delicate curls, with bare youthful arms—and with amazement he saw that it had turned into a portrait of her whose portrait no artist could paint. And he was even more sorrowful after that, and believing that there was no happiness on earth he was depressed and hopeless for the rest of the day.

Such were the circumstances of Andrey Ivanovitch Tyentyetnikov. Suddenly one day, on going to the window as usual with his cup of tea and his pipe, he noticed some commotion and bustle in the yard. The kitchen boy and the woman who scrubbed the floors were running to open the gate, and in the gate appeared three horses exactly as they are carved or moulded on triumphal arches, that is, one horse's head to the right, one to the left and one in the middle. On the box above them were a coachman and a footman wearing a full frock-coat, girt round the waist with a pocket-handkerchief; behind them sat a gentleman in a cap and greatcoat, wrapped in a shawl of rainbow hues. When the carriage turned before the front door it appeared that it was nothing more than a light chaise on springs. A gentleman of exceptionally decorous exterior skipped out on to the steps with the swiftness and agility almost of a military man.

Andrey Ivanovitch was scared; he thought he might be a police officer. It must be explained that in his youth he had been mixed up in rather a foolish affair. Some philosophers among the Hussars, and a student who had not completed his studies, and a spendthrift gambler got up a philanthropic society under the sole direction of an old rogue, freemason and cardsharper, who was a drunkard and a very eloquent person. The society was formed with an extremely grandiose object—to secure the happiness of all humanity. The funds required were immense. The amount of money subscribed by the generous members was incredible. Where it all went no one knew but the sole director. Tyentyetnikov was drawn into this society by two friends who were disappointed men, good-natured fellows, who became habitual drunkards through continually drinking toasts to science, enlightenment and progress. Tyentyetnikov quickly realised the position and got out of the circle. But the society succeeded in getting mixed up with other doings rather below the dignity of gentlemen, so that it even attracted the notice of the police. . . . So that it was no wonder that even though he had left the society and broken off all relations with the benefactor of mankind, Tyentyetnikov could not help feeling some anxiety, for his conscience was not quite at ease. And now he looked, not without alarm, at the door which was about to open.

His fears were, however, soon dispelled when his visitor made his bows with incredible elegance, keeping his head respectfully bent on one side. In brief but definite phrases he explained that for some time past he had been travelling about Russia, both on business of his own and for the purpose of gathering information, that our empire abounded in objects of inherent interest apart from the beauties of nature, the number of industries, and the variety of soils; that he had been carried away by the beautiful scenery of Tyentyetnikov's estate; that in spite of the beautiful scenery of his village he would not have ventured to disturb him by his ill-timed visit, but that something had happened to his chaise, which called for the skilled hand of black-smiths and wheelwrights; but that, for all that, even if nothing had happened to his chaise, he could hardly have denied himself the pleasure of calling to pay his respects in person. As he finished his speech the visitor with fascinating courtesy scraped with his foot, making a little skip backwards as he did so, with the lightness of an india-rubber ball.

Andrey Ivanovitch thought that this must be some learned pro-fessor in search of knowledge, who was travelling about Russia to collect plants or possibly even geological specimens. He protested his readiness to assist him in every way, offered him the services of his workmen, his wheelwrights and his blacksmiths for the repair of the chaise and begged him to make himself at home; he made his affa-ble visitor sit down in a big Voltairean armchair,* and prepared him-self to listen to his conversation, which he did not doubt would deal with learned or scientific subjects.

The visitor, however, touched rather upon the incidents of the inner world. He spoke of the mutability of destiny, compared his life to a ship in midocean, driven before the winds; referred to the fact that he had frequently had to change his appointments and his du-ties, that he had suffered a great deal in the cause of justice, that his life even had more than once been in danger from his enemies, and he said a great deal more from which Tyentyetnikov could gather that his visitor was rather a practical man. In conclusion he brought out a white cambric handkerchief and blew his nose more loudly than An-drey Ivanovitch had ever heard any one do. Sometimes in an orchestra there is a rascally trumpet which, when it gives a blast, seems to be blaring right in one's ear: such was the sound which echoed through the awakened rooms of the slumbering house, and it was immedi-ately followed by an agreeable fragrance of eau-de-cologne, invisibly diffused by the deft flourish of the cambric pocket-handkerchief.

The reader will have perhaps guessed already that the visitor was no other than our honoured and long-deserted Pavel Ivanovitch Tchitchikov. He was a little older; evidently this interval had not been free from storms and agitations. It seemed as though even the coat he

---

*Padded armchair associated with French author Voltaire (1694–1778), who was the embodiment of eighteenth-century enlightenment.

wore were rather older, and the chaise, and the coachman and the groom and the horses, and the harness seemed as though they were a little worn and shabby. It seemed as though his finances too were not in a condition to be envied. But the expression of his face, his propriety, his affability were unchanged. It seemed as though he were even more agreeable in his manners and deportment. He crossed his legs even more elegantly when he sat down in an armchair; there was a still greater softness in the utterance of his words and circumspect moderation in his sayings and his looks, more discretion in his behaviour and more tact in everything. His collar and cuffs were cleaner and whiter than snow, and although he came straight from the road there was not a speck on his coat; he might have been going to a nameday party. His cheeks and chin were so smoothly shaven that only a blind man could fail to admire their agreeable curves.

A transformation took place in the house at once. Half of the house, which had been in darkness with its shutters closed, looked out on the light again. They began bringing in the luggage from the chaise, and arranging it in the rooms now flooded with light; soon in the room that was destined for a bedroom all the things essential for the toilet were installed; in the room destined for the study . . . But first of all it is essential that the reader should know that there were three tables in the room: one a writing-table in front of the sofa, another a card-table against the wall between the windows, and the third a corner table in the corner between the door into the bedroom and the door into an uninhabited room full of invalid furniture. On this corner table the clothes taken from the portmanteau were placed, that is: one pair of old and one pair of new trousers to wear with his dress-coat, a pair of trousers to go with the frock-coat, a pair of grey trousers, two velvet waistcoats and two satin ones, a frock-coat and two dress-coats (the white piqué* waistcoats and the summer trousers had gone with the under-linen into the chest of drawers in the bedroom). These were all piled one upon another in a pyramid and covered with a silk pocket-handkerchief. In another corner between the door and the window the boots were stored in a row, a pair of top boots, not quite new, a pair perfectly new, a pair of top boots with new uppers and a pair of low patent leather boots. They too

---

*Cotton or silk fabric with raised cords.

were modestly veiled with a silk pocket-handkerchief, so that they might not have been there at all. On the table between the two windows lay the writing-case. On the table before the sofa lay his portfolio, a bottle of eau-de-cologne, sealing-wax, tooth brushes, a new calendar and two novels, both second volumes. The clean linen was all put away in the chest of drawers which was already in the bedroom; the linen that was to go to the laundress was done up into a bundle and thrust under the bed. The portmanteau being empty was also stored under the bed. The sword too was taken into the bedroom and hung on a nail not far from the bed. Both the rooms acquired an extraordinary air of neatness and tidiness, nowhere was there a scrap of paper, a feather or litter of any kind, the very air seemed to have become more refined. The agreeable odour of a fresh healthy man who changed his linen frequently, visited the bathhouse and sponged himself all over on Sunday mornings was permanently installed in the room. The odour of Petrushka, the footman, made an effort to establish itself in the vestibule adjoining, but Petrushka was soon banished to the kitchen, which was indeed a more suitable place for him.

For the first few days Andrey Ivanovitch was apprehensive for his independence, fearing that the visitor might be a constraint and might involve changes in his manner of life, and might disturb the order of his day so satisfactorily established. But his apprehensions were groundless. The guest displayed an unusual capacity for adapting himself to everything. He applauded his host's philosophical leisureliness, saying that it gave him promise of living to be a hundred. He expressed himself very felicitously about solitude, also saying that it fostered great ideas in a man. Glancing at the bookcase, he spoke with approval of books in general, observing that they preserved a man from idleness. In short, he dropped few words, but they were weighty ones. In his conduct he was even more tactful; appeared at the right minute and at the right minute retired; did not pester his host with questions when he was disinclined for conversation; was pleased to play chess with him, and was pleased to sit silent. While his host was puffing out tobacco smoke in curly clouds the visitor, who did not smoke, bethought himself of an occupation in keeping with it; he would for instance take his black and silver snuffbox from out of his pocket, and holding it between two fingers of his left hand, twirl it round rapidly with one finger of his right hand, just as the terrestrial globe rotates on its own axis, or simply drummed upon it with his fingers, whistling some undefined tune. In short, he did not hinder his host in any way. "For the first time in my life I've met a man with whom I could live," Tyentyetnikov said to himself. "As a rule that gift is rare amongst us. There are plenty of people among us, intelligent, cultured, good-natured, but people who are always agreeable, always good-tempered, people with whom one might live all one's life without quarrelling, I don't know whether many such people could be found in Russia! This is the first and only man I have seen." So Tyentyetnikov characterised his visitor.

Tchitchikov for his part was very glad to be settled for a time in the house of so peaceful and inoffensive a man. He was sick of a gipsy's life. To rest if only for a month in a beautiful country place, in view of the fields and the coming spring was beneficial even from the point of view of his digestion. It would have been hard to find a better retreat to rest in. The spring decked it out with inexpressible beauty. What brilliance there was in the green! What freshness in the air! What bird notes in the woods! Paradise, joy and exaltation everywhere! The country resounded with singing as though born to new life.

Tchitchikov walked about a great deal. Sometimes he took his walks about the flat plateau that crowned the heights, keeping to the edges of it from which he had a view of the valleys in the distance where big lakes still remained from the flooded river; or he went out into the ravines, where the trees, just beginning to be green with leaves and weighed down with birds' nests, and the narrow strip of blue between them were darkened by the continual flitting to and fro of flocks of crows and resounded with the harsh cries of the crows, the chatter of the jackdaws and the cawing of the rooks; or he went down hill to the water meadows and the broken-down dam, watching the water as it rushed to fall upon the mill wheels with a deafening sound; or he made his way further to the landing-stage from which the first boats laden with peas, oats, barley or wheat were setting off as the river thawed; or he went off to the fields where the first labours of spring were beginning, to see the ploughed land lie like a black streak across the green, or the deft sower scatter the seed from the hollow of his hand, evenly, accurately, not letting a single grain fall to one side or the other. He talked to the steward and the peasants and the miller, discussing how and why and what sort of crops were to be expected, and how the ploughing was going, and at what price wheat was being sold, and what they charged in spring and autumn for the grinding of the flour, and what each peasant's name was, and which was related to which, and who bought the cows and what they fed the pigs on—in fact everything. He found out too how many of the peasants had died. It appeared that they were few in number. Being an intelligent man he saw at once that Tyentyetnikov's land was not being well managed, on every hand he saw omissions, neglect, thieving, and a good deal of drunkenness. And inwardly he said to himself: "What a brute that Tyentyetnikov is! To neglect an estate that might bring in at least fifty thousand roubles a year!" And unable to restrain his just indignation, he repeated, "He certainly is a brute!" More than once during these walks the idea occurred to him that he might, not now of course, but later on when his great enterprise had been accomplished and he had the means, become a peaceful owner of a similar estate. At this point there usually rose up before his mind the image of its youthful mistress, a fresh white-skinned young woman, of the merchant class perhaps, though with the breeding and education of a girl of noble birth, so that she might know something of music; music of course was of no great consequence, but since it was considered the proper thing, why run counter to public opinion? He pictured also the younger generation, destined to perpetuate the name of Tchitchikov: a rogue of a boy and a beautiful little daughter, or even a couple of urchins and two or even three little girls that every one might know that he had really lived and existed, that he might not have seemed to have passed through life like a shadow or a phantom, and might be able to hold up his head feeling he had done his duty to his country. It occurred to him also that it might not be amiss to obtain a higher grade in the service; that of a civil councillor for instance, a grade held in honour and respect. . . . And many things came into his mind such as often carry a man away from dreary actuality, disturb, stir and tantalise him and are sweet to him even when he knows that they will never come to pass.

Pavel Ivanovitch's servants liked the place too. Like him they felt at home in it. Petrushka was very quickly friends with Grigory, though at first they tried to impress each other and gave themselves insufferable airs. Petrushka scored off Grigory by having been in Kostroma,* Yaroslavl, Nizhni and even Moscow: Grigory completely floored him with Petersburg, where Petrushka had never been. The latter tried to recover his prestige by enlarging on the great remoteness of the places which he had visited, but Grigory mentioned a locality, the name of which could not be found on any map, and reckoned up journeys of more than twenty thousand miles, so that Petrushka was staggered, and stood gaping, while all the servants laughed at him. It ended in their becoming the closest friends, however: bald-headed Uncle Pimen kept a celebrated tavern, the name of which was "Akulka," at the farther end of the village: every hour of the day they were to be seen in this establishment, there they became bosom friends, or what is called among the peasants—pothouse inseparables.

Selifan found other allurements. Every evening was spent in singing, games, and country dances in the village. Fine, graceful girls, such as it would be hard to find elsewhere, made him for some hours gape in astonishment. It was hard to say which was the finest of them, they were all white-bosomed and white-throated, they all had eyes like turnips—languishing eyes; they had the step of a peacock and their plaits reached to their waists. When he held their white hands and slowly moved with them in the figures of the dance, or when in a row with other young fellows he advanced like a wall to meet them, and the warmly glowing evening died away, and the country all around was slowly wrapped in darkness, and far away beyond the river there sounded the faithful echo of the always melancholy chant, he did not know himself what was happening to him. Long afterwards he dreamed both sleeping and waking that white hands lay in his, and he was moving with them in the dance. . . . With a wave of his hand he would say: "Those damned girls won't let me alone!"

Tchitchikov's horses were also pleased with their new abode. Both the shaft horse and the bay-coloured trace horse, known as Assessor, as well as the dappled grey, whom Selifan called "the rascally horse," found their sojourn at Tyentyetnikov's anything but tedious.

---

*City about 40 miles northeast of Yaroslavl.

The oats were excellent, and the arrangements of the stables exceptionally convenient, each one had a stall partitioned off, yet through this partition he could see the other horses, so that if any one of them, even the furthest, took a fancy to neigh he could be answered at once.

In short they all felt at home. The reader may be surprised that Tchitchikov had not yet breathed a word in regard to his favourite subject. No, indeed! Pavel Ivanovitch had become very cautious in regard to that subject. Even if he had had to deal with absolute fools he would not have begun upon it quite immediately, and Tyentyetnikov, whatever he might be, read books, talked philosophy and tried to find an explanation of everything that happened and the why and wherefore of everything. . . . "No, the devil take him! perhaps I had better begin from another side," thought Tchitchikov. Chatting from time to time with the servants he learned among other things from them that their master used pretty often to visit his neighbour the general, that there was a young lady at the general's, that their master had been "taken" with the young lady and the young lady had been "taken" with their master . . . but that afterwards they had fallen out about something and parted. He noticed himself that Andrey Ivanovitch was always with pen or pencil drawing little heads, one like the other. One day soon after dinner, as he sat making his silver snuffbox rotate on its axis as usual, he spoke as follows: "You have got everything, Andrey Ivanovitch, there is only one thing wanting." "What's that?" asked the other, letting off coils of smoke. "A partner to share your life," said Tchitchikov. Andrey Ivanovitch said nothing; and with that the conversation ended. Tchitchikov was not disconcerted. He chose another moment, this time just before supper, and after talking of one thing and another, said suddenly: "You know really, Andrey Ivanovitch, it wouldn't be at all amiss for you to get married." Tyentyetnikov said not a word in reply, as though he disliked any talk on the subject. Tchitchikov was not disconcerted. For the third time he chose a moment, this time after supper, and spoke thus: "It's all very well but the more I turn over your circumstances in my mind, the more clearly I see that you must get married: you will fall into hypochondria." Either Tchitchikov's words were so convincing, or Andrey Ivanovitch's mood was particularly favourable for openness—he heaved a sigh and said, blowing tobacco smoke into the air: "You need to be born lucky for everything, you know, Pavel Ivanovitch." And he told him the whole story of his acquaintance with the general and their rupture, exactly as it had all happened.

When Tchitchikov heard the whole story, word for word, and saw that the trouble had entirely originated from the word "thou," he was aghast. For some minutes he looked steadily into Tyentyetnikov's face and inwardly concluded: "Why, he is a perfect fool!"

"Andrey Ivanovitch, upon my soul!" said he, gripping both his hands: "Where is the insult? What is there insulting in the word 'thou'?"

"There is nothing insulting in the word itself," answered Tyentyetnikov, "but in the significance of the word, in the voice in which it was uttered, that is where the insult lies. Thou! that means 'Remember that you are of no importance; I receive you only because there is no one better, but if some Princess Yuzyakin comes, you know your place and stand at the door!' That's what it means." As the mild and gentle Andrey Ivanovitch said this his eyes flashed, and a thrill of angry resentment could be heard in his voice.

"Well, even if it were said in that sense, what of it?" said Tchitchikov.

"What?" said Tyentyetnikov, gazing intently at Tchitchikov, "you would have me visit him again after such an action?"

"What do you mean by action, it's not an action at all," said Tchitchikov.

"What a strange fellow this Tchitchikov is!" thought Tyentyetnikov to himself.

"What a strange fellow this Tyentyetnikov is!" thought Tchitchikov to himself.

"It's not behaviour, Andrey Ivanovitch. It's simply a habit with generals: they say thou to everybody. Besides why not allow it in an honourable and distinguished man?"

"That's a different matter," said Tyentyetnikov. "If he were a poor old man, not proud and stuck up, not a general, I would allow him to call me thou, and even accept it with respect."

"He's a perfect idiot," thought Tchitchikov to himself. "He would allow some ragged fellow but not a general!" and upon this reflection he retorted aloud: "Very good, let us suppose he did insult you, but you were quits with him anyway, you insulted him and he insulted you. But to part for ever on account of a trifle, upon my word, it is beyond everything. How could you give things up when they were only just beginning? Once you have set an object before you you must persist in spite of all obstacles. What's the use of minding whether a man's insulting! people are also insulting. You won't find any one in the world nowadays that isn't insulting."

Tyentyetnikov was completely nonplussed by this observation. He was disconcerted, he looked into Pavel Ivanovitch's face and thought to himself: "A very strange fellow this Tchitchikov!"

"What a queer creature this Tyentyetnikov is!" Tchitchikov was thinking meanwhile.

"Allow me to set things right," he said aloud. "I can go to his Excellency's and say that it happened through a misunderstanding on your part, owing to your youth and your ignorance of life and the world."

"I don't intend to grovel before him!" said Tyentyetnikov emphatically.

"God forbid, grovel!" said Tchitchikov, and crossed himself. "To influence him by advice like a prudent mediator, but to grovel . . . excuse me, Andrey Ivanovitch, I did not expect that in return for my good will and devotion . . . I did not expect you to take my words in such an offensive sense!"

"Forgive me, Pavel Ivanovitch, I was to blame!" said Tyentyetnikov, genuinely touched, taking both his hands gratefully. "Your kind sympathy is precious to me, I assure you! But let us drop this subject, let us never speak of it again!"

"In that case I'll simply go to the general's without any reason," said Tchitchikov.

"What for?" asked Tyentyetnikov, looking at Tchitchikov with surprise.

"To pay him my respects," said Tchitchikov.

"What a strange fellow this Tchitchikov is!" thought Tyentyetnikov.

"What a strange fellow this Tyentyetnikov is!" thought Tchitchikov.

"As my chaise is not yet in fit condition," said Tchitchikov, "allow me to borrow a carriage from you. I will go and call upon him about ten o'clock to-morrow morning."

"Good heavens, what a thing to ask! Everything here is at your disposal, take any carriage you like, everything is at your service."

They said good-night and went off to bed, not without reflecting each on the other's queerness.

Strange to relate, however, next morning when the carriage was brought round for Tchitchikov and he jumped into it with the lightness almost of a military man, wearing his new dress-coat, white cravat and waistcoat, and rolled off to pay his respects to the general, Tyentyetnikov was thrown into an agitation such as he had not experienced for a long time. The whole current of his ideas which had been slumbering and had grown dull were awakened to restless activity. All the feelings of the idler, who had hitherto been plunged in careless sloth, were suddenly caught up in a nervous tumult. At one moment he sat down on the sofa, then he went to the window, then he took up a book, then he tried to think. A fruitless attempt! A thought would not come into his head. Then he tried to think of nothing at all. A fruitless effort. Fragments of something like thought, shreds and ends of thoughts forced themselves on him and pecked at his brain from all sides. "What a strange condition!" he said, and moving towards the window, looked out at the road which was intersected by the oak copse, and at the end of it he saw still floating in the air the dust raised by the carriage.

CHAPTER 2

In a little over half an hour the horses had borne Tchitchikov over the seven or eight miles, at first through an oak copse, then by cornfields just beginning to turn green in the midst of the freshly ploughed land, then along the edge of the hillside from which fresh views over the distant plain came into sight every minute, and finally by a wide avenue of spreading lime-trees leading up to the general's village. The avenue of limes was followed by an avenue of poplars, protected below by hurdles, and ended in openwork iron gates, through which peeped the ornately magnificent carved façade of the general's house, supported by eight columns with Corinthian capitals. Everywhere there was a smell of oil paint, with which everything was continually renewed, so that nothing could fall into decay. The courtyard was like a parquet floor for cleanliness. Driving up to the front door Tchitchikov mounted the steps deferentially, sent in his name, and was conducted straight to the study.

He was impressed by the general's majestic appearance. He was attired at the moment in a crimson satin dressing-gown. He had a frank glance, a manly face, grizzled whiskers and big moustaches, his hair was closely cropped, and especially so at the back. His neck was stout and thick, a neck in three storeys, as it is called (that is in three lateral folds with a crease at right angles to them), his voice was a somewhat husky bass, his gestures and deportment were those of a general. General Betrishtchev was, like all of us sinful mortals, possessed of many good qualities, and also of many defects; both were mixed up together in him in a sort of picturesque disorder, as is apt to be the case with Russians: he was capable of self-sacrifice, magnanimity, valour at critical moments, and was possessed of intelligence, and with all there was a considerable mixture of conceit, ambition, egoism, a petty readiness to take offence, and a very liberal portion of the weaknesses all flesh is heir to.* He disliked all who rose above

---

*Allusion to Shakespeare's *Hamlet* (act 3, scene 1): "the thousand natural shocks / That flesh is heir to."

him in the service, and spoke of them in biting, sardonic epigrams. He was particularly severe upon a former colleague whom he regarded as his inferior in intelligence and abilities, although he had risen to a higher grade in the service, and was now governor-general of two provinces, in one of which General Betrishtchev had estates, so that he was in a sense dependent on his rival. In revenge he derided him, criticised every measure he took, and considered everything he said or did as the height of imbecility. In spite of his good heart the general was given to malicious mockery. Altogether he liked to be first, he liked applause and flattery, he liked to shine and to show off his cleverness, he liked to know what other people did not know, and did not like people who knew things he did not know. Though his education had been half foreign he wanted at the same time to play the part of a Russian grand gentleman. With such incongruous elements, with such great and glaring contradictions in his character, he was inevitably bound to meet with a number of unpleasant incidents, in consequence of which he retired from the service. He ascribed this to the intrigues of a hostile party, and had not the magnanimity to blame himself for anything. In retirement he still kept up the same picturesque majestic deportment. Whether he was in his frock-coat, his dress-coat or his dressing-gown, he was always the same. Everything in him, from his voice to his slightest gesture, was commanding, peremptory, and inspired in his inferiors if not respect at least awe.

Tchitchikov was conscious of both feelings, both respect and awe. Inclining his head respectfully on one side, he began as follows: "I thought it my duty to present myself to your Excellency. I cherish the deepest respect for the distinguished men who have saved our country on the field of battle, and I thought it my duty to present myself in person to your Excellency."

The general evidently did not dislike this mode of approach. With a gracious inclination of his head, he said: "Very glad to make your acquaintance. Pray sit down. Where have you served?"

"My career in the service," said Tchitchikov, sitting down, not in the middle of the chair but on the edge of it, with one hand holding on to the arm, "began in the Treasury, your Excellency; I passed the later years of it in various departments: I have been in the Imperial Court department, and on the Buildings Committee and in the Customs. My life may be compared to a vessel in mid-ocean, your Excellency. In suffering, I may say, I was reared, in suffering I was fostered, in suffering I was swaddled and I am, so to say, nothing but an embodiment of suffering. And what I have endured at the hands of my enemies no words could depict. Now in the evening, so to speak, of my life I am seeking a nook in which to spend the remnant of my days. I am staying for the time with a near neighbour of yours, your Excellency . . ."

"With whom?"

"At Tyentyetnikov's, your Excellency."

The general frowned.

"He deeply regrets, your Excellency, that he did not show fitting respect . . ."

"Respect for what?"

"For the distinguished merits of your Excellency," answered Tchitchikov. "He cannot find words, he does not know how to atone for his conduct. He says: 'If only I could in some way . . .' he says. 'I know how to honour the men who have saved their country. . . .'"

"Upon my soul, what does he mean? . . . Why, I am not angry with him," said the general, mollified. "At heart I have a genuine affection for him, and I am sure that in time he will become a very useful person."

"Most useful," Tchitchikov assented. "He has the gift of words and a ready pen."

"But he writes, I expect, rubbish, trashy verses?"

"No, your Excellency, not rubbish."

"Why not?"

"He is writing . . . a history, your Excellency."

"A history! A history of what?"

"A history . . ." at this point Tchitchikov paused, and either because there was a general sitting before him or to give more importance to the subject, added, "A history of generals, your Excellency."

"Of generals? What generals?"

"All kinds of generals, your Excellency, that is, to be more exact . . . the generals of our country."

"Excuse me, I don't quite understand. . . . How do you mean? Is it the history of some period, or separate biographies, and is it of all Russian generals or only those that took part in the campaign of 1812?"

"That is just it, your Excellency, the history of those that took part in the campaign of 1812."

"Then why does he not come to me? I could give him a great deal of new and very interesting material."

"He does not dare, your Excellency."

"What nonsense! For the sake of a foolish word. . . . I am not at all that sort of person. I am ready to go and call on him myself, if you like."

"He would not think of allowing that, he will come himself," said Tchitchikov, while he thought to himself, "the generals came in pat; though I was gagging away quite at random."

There was a rustling sound. The walnut door of a carved cupboard flew open, and on the further side of the open door, a living figure appeared, clutching with her lovely hand at the handle of the door. If a transparent picture, lighted up by a lamp behind it, had suddenly gleamed upon a dark room, it would not have been so startling as that figure, radiant with life, which seemed to have suddenly appeared to light up the room. It seemed as though a ray of sunlight, suddenly lighting up the ceiling, the cornice and the dark corners, had flown into the room together with her. She seemed to be remarkably tall. But it was an illusion, and was due to her exceptional slenderness and the harmonious symmetry of all parts of her from her head to her finger tips. The dress all of one colour, hastily flung on, had been flung on with such taste, that it seemed as though the dressmakers of both capitals had consulted together how to attire her to the best advantage. That was an illusion. She made her own dresses and made them anyhow; a piece of uncut material was caught up in two or three places, and it hung and draped round her in such folds, that a sculptor would have at once chiselled them in marble, and young ladies, dressed in the fashion, looked like gaudy dolls beside her. Although her face was almost familiar to Tchitchikov from Andrey Ivanovitch's sketches he stared at her as though he were dazed, and only afterwards realised that she had a defect, that is, a lack of plumpness.

"Let me introduce my spoilt darling," said the general, introducing Tchitchikov. "But I don't know your name and your father's."

"But is there any need to know the name of a man who has done nothing to give it distinction?" said Tchitchikov.

"But still one must know a man's name."

"Pavel Ivanovitch, your Excellency," said Tchitchikov, with a slight inclination of his head to one side.

"Ulinka! Pavel Ivanovitch has just told us a very interesting piece of news. Our neighbour Tyentyetnikov is by no means so stupid as we supposed. He is engaged on rather important work—a history of the generals of the year 1812."

Ulinka seemed at once to fire up and grow eager. "Why, who thought he was stupid?" she said quickly. "Nobody could think such a thing except Vishnepokromov, whom you believe in, papa, though he is an empty-headed and contemptible person!"

"Why is he contemptible? He is an empty-headed fellow, that is true," said the general.

"He is mean and disgusting as well as empty-headed," Ulinka put in hastily. "Any one who could treat his brothers as he did and turn his own sister out of the house is a disgusting person."

"But that is only talk."

"People wouldn't talk for nothing. You are kindness itself, papa, and no one has such a heart, but sometimes you do things that might make any one believe the opposite. You will welcome a man though you know he is bad just because he has a ready tongue and knows how to get round you."

"My love, I could not kick him out," said the general.

"No need to kick him out, but why like him!"

"Well, your Excellency," said Tchitchikov to Ulinka, with a slight inclination of his head and an agreeable smile, "as Christians it is just those we ought to love," and then turning to the general, he said smiling, this time rather slily, "Did you ever hear, your Excellency, of the saying—'Love us dirty, for any one will love us clean'?"

"I have never heard it."

"It is a very interesting anecdote," said Tchitchikov, with a sly smile. "On the estate, your Excellency, of Prince Gukzovsky, whom no doubt your Excellency knows . . ."

"I don't know him."

". . . There was a steward, your Excellency, a young man and a German. He had to go to the town about the levy of recruits and other business, and of course he had to grease the hands of the court officials. They liked him however and entertained him. So one day when he was at dinner with them, he said: 'Well, gentlemen, I hope one day you will come and see me on the prince's estate.' They said: 'We'll come.' It happened not long afterwards that the court had to conduct an examination on the estate of Count Trehmetyev, whom no doubt your Excellency knows also."

"I don't know him."

"They didn't make the examination, but all the officials of the court betook them to the quarters of the count's steward, an old man, and for three days and three nights they played cards without stopping. The samovar and punch of course were on the table all the time. The old man got sick of them. To get rid of them he said to them: 'You had better go and see the prince's German steward, gentlemen, he lives not far from here.' 'Oh, to be sure,' they said, and half drunk, unshaven as they were and drowsy, they got into a cart and went off to the German's. . . . And the German, I must tell your Excellency, had only just got married; he had married a boarding-school miss, quite young and very genteel—(Tchitchikov expressed her gentility in his face). They were sitting at tea, the two of them, thinking of nothing at all, when the door opened, and the whole crew of them came reeling in."

"I can fancy—a nice set!" said the general laughing.

"The steward was so taken aback that he said: 'What do you want?' 'Ah,' said they, 'so that's your line!' And with that they put on quite a different face and countenance. . . . 'We have come on business! How much spirit is being distilled on the estate? Show us your books.' The German did not know what to do. They called in witnesses. They bound his arms and took him away to the town, and for a year and a half he lay in prison."

"Upon my soul!" said the general.

Ulinka clasped her hands.

"His wife did all she could," Tchitchikov went on. "But what can an inexperienced young woman do? Luckily some kind people turned up who advised her to settle it amicably. He got off for two thousand roubles and a dinner to the officials. And at the dinner when they were all rather exhilarated, and he also, they said to him— 'Aren't you ashamed now of the way you treated us? You wanted us shaven and well got up in our dress-coats: no, you love us dirty, for any one will love us clean.' "

The general went off into a roar of laughter, Ulinka gave a moan of distress.

"I don't understand how you can laugh!" she said quickly. Her lovely brow was darkened by wrath. . . . "It was a most disgraceful action for which they ought all to have been sent, I don't know where. . . ."

"My dear, I don't in the least justify them," said the general, "but what's to be done if it is funny? How did it go? 'Love us clean'? . . ."

"Dirty, your Excellency," Tchitchikov prompted him.

" 'Love us dirty, for any one will love us clean.' Ha, ha, ha, ha!" And the general's huge frame began quivering with laughter. His shoulders which had once worn fringed epaulettes shook as though they were still wearing fringed epaulettes.

Tchitchikov permitted himself also a peal of laughter, but out of respect for the general he pitched it on the letter *e*: "He, he, he, he, he!" and his frame too began quivering with laughter, though his shoulders did not shake, for they had never worn fringed epaulettes.

"I can fancy what a nice set the unshaven fellows were!" said the general, still laughing.

"Yes, your Excellency, in any case three days sitting up without sleep is like keeping a fast: they were exhausted, they were exhausted, your Excellency," said Tchitchikov still laughing.

Ulinka sank into a low chair and put her hand before her lovely eyes; as though vexed that there was no one who could share her indignation, she said: "I don't know, but it merely makes me angry."

And indeed the feelings in the hearts of the three persons were extremely strange in their incongruity. One was amused by the uncompromising tactlessness of the German; another was amused at the funny trick the rogues had played; the third was distressed that an injustice had been committed with impunity. All that was lacking was a fourth to ponder over these words which aroused laughter in one and sadness in the other. For what is the significance of the fact that even in his degradation, a man besmirched and going to his ruin claims still to be loved? Is it an animal instinct or the faint cry of a soul stifled under the heavy burden of base passions, still breaking through the hardening crust of vileness, still wailing: "Brother, save me!" There was no fourth for whom the ruin of a brother's soul was bitterest of all.

"I don't know," said Ulinka, taking her hands from her face, "all I can say is that it makes me angry."

"Only please don't be angry with us," said the general. "We are not to blame for it. Give me a kiss and run away, for I am just going to dress for dinner. You'll dine with me of course," said the general, suddenly addressing Tchitchikov.

"If only, your Excellency . . ."

"No ceremony. There will be cabbage soup."

Tchitchikov bowed his head affably, and when he raised it again he did not see Ulinka, she had vanished. A gigantic valet with thick whiskers was standing in her place, holding a silver ewer and basin in his hands.

"You'll allow me to dress before you, won't you?" said the general, flinging off his dressing-gown, and tucking up his shirt sleeves over his heroic arms.

"Upon my word, your Excellency, you may do whatever you like before me," said Tchitchikov.

The general began to wash, snorting and splashing like a duck. Soapy water was flying all over the room.

"How does it go?" he said, rubbing his thick neck from both sides, 'Love us clean . . .' "

"Dirty, your Excellency. 'Love us dirty, for any one will love us clean.' "

"Very good, very."

Tchitchikov was in unusually good spirits, he was conscious of a sort of inspiration. "Your Excellency," he said.

"Well?" said the general.

"There is another story."

"What is it?"

"It's an amusing story too, only it is not amusing for me. So much so indeed that if your Excellency . . ."

"Why, how's that?"

"This is how it is, your Excellency." At this point Tchitchikov looked round and seeing that the valet with the basin had gone, began as follows: "I have an uncle, a decrepit old man. He has three hundred souls and no heirs except me. He can't look after the estate himself, for he is too feeble, and he won't hand it over to me either. And the reason he gives for not doing so is very queer: 'I don't know my nephew,' he says; 'perhaps he is a spendthrift, let him prove that he is a reliable person, let him get three hundred souls on his own account first, the I'll hand him over my three hundred too.' "

"What a fool!"

"That is a very just observation, your Excellency. But imagine my position now." Here Tchitchikov, dropping his voice, began saying as though it were a secret, "He has a housekeeper, your Excellency, and the housekeeper has children. If I don't look out it will all go to them."

"The silly old man has outlived his wits and that is all about it," said the general. "But I don't see how I can help you."

"What I thought of was this: now until the new census lists are given in, owners of large estates must have accumulated besides their living serfs, a great number who have passed away and died. . . . So, your Excellency, if you were to transfer them to me, just as though they were living, by a regular deed of purchase, I could show the purchase deed to the old man, and he couldn't get out of giving me my inheritance."

At this the general burst into a roar of laughter such as is rarely heard, he rolled into an armchair just as he was, hung his head back and almost choked. The whole household was alarmed. The valet appeared. His daughter ran into the room in a fright.

"Papa, what has happened to you?"

"Nothing, my dear, ha, ha, ha! Run along, we'll come into dinner directly. Ha, ha, ha!"

And several times after a rest the general's laughter broke out again with renewed violence, resounding from the entrance hall to the furthest room in the general's lofty echoing apartments.

Tchitchikov awaited with some uneasiness the end of this extraordinary mirth.

"Come, my dear fellow, you must excuse me! The devil must have put you up to such a trick! Ha, ha, ha! To humour the old gentleman and to foist dead ones on him. Ha, ha, ha! Your uncle, your uncle! What a fool you will make of him!"

Tchitchikov found himself in a somewhat embarrassing position; facing him stood the valet, with his mouth open and his eyes staring out of his head.

"Your Excellency, what makes you laugh costs me tears,"* he said.

"Forgive me, my dear fellow! You have nearly been the death of me. Why, I'd give five hundred thousand to see your uncle's face

---

*Russian poet Alexander Pushkin (1799–1837) characterized Gogol's art as laughter "through tears of sadness."

when you show him the deed of purchase for three hundred serfs. But is he very aged? How old is he?"

"Eighty, your Excellency. But it is a private matter. I should be . . ." Tchitchikov looked significantly at the general, and at the same time glanced out of the corner of his eye at the valet.

"You can go, my good man. You can come back presently." The whiskered giant withdrew.

"Yes, your Excellency. . . . It's such a queer business, your Excellency, that I should prefer to keep it quiet. . . ."

"Of course, I quite understand that. What a fool the old man is! To think of such foolishness at eighty years old! What's he like to look at? is he strong and hearty? does he still keep on his legs?"

"He does get about but with difficulty."

"What a fool! Has he got any teeth?"

"He has only two teeth, your Excellency."

"What an ass! You mustn't be vexed at my saying so, you know, but he is an ass!"

"Quite so, your Excellency. Though he is a relation and it is painful to admit it, he certainly is an ass." However, the reader may surmise for himself, the admission was by no means painful to Tchitchikov, especially as it is doubtful whether he ever had an uncle. "So that, if your Excellency would be so kind . . ."

"As to give you my dead souls? Why, for such an idea, I'd give you them land and all! You may take the whole cemetery. Ha, ha, ha, ha! To think of the old man! Ha, ha, ha, ha! What a fool! Ha, ha, ha, ha!" And the general's laugh went echoing through his apartments again.

(Here there is a gap in the manuscript.)

CHAPTER 3

N o," thought Tchitchikov, when he found himself once more in the midst of fields and open country, "as soon as I get it all done satisfactorily and really become a man of means and property, I shall not manage things like that. I will have a good cook and a house well provided in every way, but it shall all be managed properly too. I shall make both ends meet and little by little I shall lay by a sum for my children if only, please God, my wife brings me offspring. . . . Hey, you great stupid!"

Selifan and Petrushka both looked round from the box.

"Where are you driving to?"

"Why, as you were pleased to tell us yourself, Pavel Ivanovitch—to Colonel Koshkaryov's," said Selifan.

"And did you inquire the way?"

"Why, Pavel Ivanovitch, as your honour can see for yourself, since I was busy looking after the carriage all the while, well . . . I saw nothing but the general's stable, but Petrushka inquired of the coachman."

"Well, you are a fool! You have been told not to rely upon Petrushka: Petrushka's a blockhead."

"There is nothing very difficult about it," said Petrushka, with a sidelong glance at him, "excepting when we go down hill, we are to keep straight on, there was nothing more at all."

"And excepting brandy I'll be bound you have not put a drop to your lips. And you are drunk now, I shouldn't wonder."

Seeing the turn the conversation was taking, Petrushka simply wrinkled up his nose. He was on the point of saying that he had never touched it, but he felt somehow ashamed to say so.

"It's pleasant driving in the carriage," said Selifan, turning round.

"What's that?"

"I say, Pavel Ivanovitch, it is pleasant for your honour driving in the carriage, it's better than the chaise, it's not so jolting."

"Get on, get on, nobody asked you about that."

Selifan switched the horses' sides and addressed his remarks to

Petrushka: "Did you hear, they say this gentleman, Koshkaryov, dresses up his peasants like Germans; you wouldn't know what they were at a distance, they strut along like cranes, just as Germans do. And the women don't tie kerchiefs round their heads like a pie or wear a head-band, but some sort of German kapor,* as German women, you know, go about in kapors. A kapor, that's what it's called, you know, kapor— it's some sort of German thing, you know, a kapor."

"I should like to see you dressed up like a German and in a kapor!" said Petrushka, by way of a gibe at Selifan, and he grinned. But a queer face he made when he grinned! And there was not the slightest semblance of a grin, he looked like a man who has caught a bad cold and is trying to sneeze but cannot sneeze, and remains with a fixed expression of trying to sneeze.

Tchitchikov looked up into his face from below to see what was going on and said to himself: "He is a pretty fellow and thinks he is handsome too!" Pavel Ivanovitch, it must be explained, was genuinely convinced that Petrushka was in love with his own looks, though as a matter of fact the latter at times completely forgot that he had a face at all.

"You ought, Pavel Ivanovitch," said Selifan, turning round from the box, "to have thought to ask Andrey Ivanovitch to give you another horse in exchange for the dappled grey here; he is so friendly disposed to you he wouldn't have refused you, and this horse is simply a rascally beast, and only a hindrance."

"Get on, get on, don't chatter," said Tchitchikov, while he thought to himself, "Yes, it really is a pity I didn't think of it."

The lightly moving carriage raced along easily meanwhile. It ran lightly up the hills, though the road was rough in parts, and lightly down hill, though there were steep descents in the cross roads. They were going down hill. The road passed by meadows, across bends of the river, by water mills. In the distance there were glimpses of sand; one aspen copse stood out picturesquely behind another; close beside them willow bushes, alders and silver poplars flew rapidly by, hitting Selifan and Petrushka in the face with their twigs. They were continually knocking off the latter's cap. The surly servant clambered down from the box, swore at the stupid tree and the man who had planted

---

*Bonnet.

it, but never thought to tie his cap on or even to keep hold of it, hoping all the while that perhaps it might not happen again. As they went on, the trees were more numerous and closer together. Here there were birch-trees as well as aspens and alders, and soon they were in a regular forest. The sunlight was hidden. There were dark pines and fir-trees. The impenetrable darkness of the boundless forest grew thicker and seemed turning into the blackness of night. And all at once between the trees the light glittered here and there like quicksilver or looking-glass through the trunks and branches. The forest began to grow lighter, the trees were more scattered, they heard shouts and all at once a lake lay before them. There was an expanse of water three miles across, with trees around it and huts behind it. Some twenty men up to their waists, their shoulders, or their throats in the water were dragging a net towards the opposite bank. In the midst of them a man almost as broad as he was long, perfectly round, a regular watermelon, was swimming rapidly, shouting and giving orders to every one. He was so fat that he could not under any circumstances have drowned, and however he had tumbled and turned trying to dive the water would have always borne him on the surface; and if a couple of men had set on his back he would have remained floating like an obstinate bubble, though he might have snorted a bit and blown bubbles from his mouth and nose.

"Pavel Ivanovitch," said Selifan, turning round on the box, "that must be Colonel Koshkaryov."

"Why do you think so?"

"Because his body's whiter than the others, and he is more corpulent and dignified, like a gentleman."

The shouts meanwhile were becoming more distinct. The watermelon gentleman was shouting rapidly in a ringing voice:

"Hand it to Kozma, Denis, hand it to him, Kozma, take the tail from Denis. Big Foma, shove there where Little Foma is. Keep to the right, keep to the right. Stay, stay, the devil take you both! You've caught me round the navel. You have tangled me in it, I tell you, confound you, you have caught me in it!"

Those who were dragging on the right side of the net stopped, seeing that an unforeseen accident had occurred: their master was caught in the net.

"I say," said Selifan to Petrushka, "they have caught their master like a fish."

The gentleman floundered about and trying to disentangle himself, turned on his back, belly upwards, and became more entangled than ever. Afraid of breaking the net he swam together with the fish that had been caught, telling them to tie a cord round him. Tying him with the cord they flung the end of it on to the bank. Some twenty fishermen standing on the bank caught hold of the end and began carefully hauling it in. When he reached shallow water the gentleman stood up, covered with the meshes of the net like a lady's hand covered with her openwork summer glove, glanced upwards and caught sight of the visitor driving along the dam in the carriage. Seeing a visitor he nodded to him. Tchitchikov took off his cap and politely bowed from the carriage.

"Have you dined?" shouted the gentleman, scrambling with the fish on to the bank, holding one hand over his eyes to shield them from the sun, the other in the attitude of the Medici Venus* stepping out of the bath.

"No," said Tchitchikov.

"Well, you may thank God then."

"Oh why?" asked Tchitchikov with curiosity, holding his cap above his head.

"Why, look at this," said the gentleman, who stood on the bank together with the carp and crucians† which were struggling at his feet and leaping up a yard from the ground. "These are nothing, don't look at these, that is the prize over there, yonder. Show the sturgeon, Big Foma." Two sturdy peasants pulled a monster out of a tub. "Isn't he a little prince? we have got him out of the river."

"Yes, that is a regular prince!" said Tchitchikov.

"To be sure he is. You drive on ahead and I will follow you. Coachman, you take the lower road through the kitchen garden, my man. You run, Little Foma, you booby, and take down the barrier, and I'll be with you in a trice, before you have time to look round."

"The colonel's a queer fish," thought Tchitchikov, as after driving

---

*This famous statue of the classical goddess of love, once owned by the Medici family, is now exhibited in the Uffizi Gallery in Florence, Italy; it is a Roman copy (first century B.C.) of a Greek original.

†Or crucian carp; freshwater fish found in central Europe.

across the endless dam he approached the huts, of which some were scattered about the slope of the hillside like a flock of ducks, while others stood below on piles like herons. Creels, nets and fishing tackle were hung about everywhere. Little Foma removed the barrier, the carriage drove through the kitchen garden, and came out into an open space near an ancient wooden church. A little further, beyond the church, the roofs of the manor house and its outbuildings could be seen.

"Well, here I am again," cried a voice from one side. Tchitchikov looked round and saw that the stout gentleman was already driving in a droshky beside him, clothed—a grass-green nankeen* coat, yellow breeches, and a bare neck without a cravat like a Cupid. He was sitting sideways on the droshky, which he completely filled. Tchitchikov was about to say something to him, but the fat man had already vanished. The droshky appeared on the other side and the voice rang out again: "Take the pike and the seven crucians to my booby the cook, but hand me the sturgeon here; I'll take it myself on the droshky." Again there were shouts: "Big Foma and Little Foma, Kozma and Denis!"

When Tchitchikov drove up to the front door, to his intense astonishment the fat gentleman was already on the steps, and received him with open arms. It was inconceivable how he could have managed to fly there in the time. They kissed each other three times, first on one cheek and then on the other.

"I have brought you greetings from his Excellency," said Tchitchikov.

"From what Excellency?"

"From your kinsman, from the General Alexandr Dimitrievitch."

"Who is Alexandr Dimitrievitch?"

"General Betrishtchev," answered Tchitchikov, with some surprise.

"I don't know him, he is a stranger."

Tchitchikov was still more astonished.

"How's that? I hope anyway I have the pleasure of addressing Colonel Koshkaryov?"

"Pyotr Petrovitch Pyetuh," the stout gentleman caught him up.

Tchitchikov was dumfounded.

---

*Yellowish cotton fabric made in Nanking, China.

"Well, upon my soul! What have you done, you fools?" he said, turning to Selifan, who was sitting on the box and Petrushka, who was standing at the carriage door, both with their mouths wide open and their eyes starting out of their heads with astonishment. "What have you done, you fools? You were told Colonel Koshkaryov's . . . and this is Pyotr Petrovitch Pyetuh!"

"The fellows have done splendidly," said Pyotr Petrovitch. "I'll give you each a mug of vodka for it and a fish pasty into the bargain. Take out the horses and run along at once to the servants' quarters!"

"I am really ashamed," said Tchitchikov, bowing. "Such an unexpected mistake."

"Not a mistake," Pyotr Petrovitch Pyetuh declared eagerly, "it is not a mistake. You try what the dinner's like first and then say whether it is a mistake. Pray come in," he said, taking Tchitchikov's arm, and leading him into the inner rooms.

Tchitchikov from politeness went in at the door sideways so as to allow the master of the house to pass in with him; but this courtesy was thrown away, the stout gentleman could not have got through the door with him, moreover he had already disappeared, he could only hear his remarks in the yard.

"Why, what's Big Foma about? Why isn't he here yet? Emelyan, you sluggard, run to booby the cook and tell him to make haste and stuff the sturgeon. Put the soft roe and the hard roe, the insides and the bream into the soup, and the crucians into the sauce. And the crayfish, the crayfish! Little Foma, you sluggard, where are the crayfish? The crayfish, I say the crayfish?" And for a long time afterwards he still heard shouts "Crayfish, crayfish."

"Well, the master of the house is busy," said Tchitchikov, sitting in an easy-chair, and looking round at the walls and corners.

"Here I am again," said the fat gentleman, coming in and bringing two lads in light summer coats, as slender as willow bands and almost a full yard taller than Pyotr Petrovitch.

"My sons, high-school boys, they are home for the holidays. Nikolasha, you stay with the visitor, and you, Alexasha, follow me." And Pyotr Petrovitch Pyetuh disappeared again.

Tchitchikov was entertained by Nikolasha. The lad was talkative. He told him that they were not very well taught at their high-school, that the teachers favoured those whose mammas sent the richest presents, that there was a regiment of the Inkermanlandsky Hussars stationed in the town; that Captain Vyetvitsky had a better horse than the colonel himself, though Lieutenant Vzyomtsev rode far better than he did.

"And tell me in what condition is your father's estate?" Tchitchikov asked.

"It's mortgaged," the father himself replied, reappearing again in the drawing-room, "It's mortgaged."

Tchitchikov felt inclined to make that movement of the lips which a man makes when a thing is no good, and is ending in nothing.

"Why did you mortgage it?" he asked.

"Oh, no particular reason; everybody goes in for mortgaging nowadays, so why shouldn't I do the same as the rest? They tell me it's profitable. Besides I have always lived here, so I may as well try living in Moscow."

"The fool, the fool!" thought Tchitchikov, "he will spend everything and make his children spendthrifts too. You had better stay at home in the country, you fish pie."

"I know what you are thinking," said Pyetuh.

"What?" asked Tchitchikov, embarrassed.

"You are thinking, 'He is a fool, he is a fool, this Pyetuh! He has invited me to dinner and there is no dinner all this time.' It will soon be ready, my good sir, in less time than it takes a cropped wench to plait her hair, it will be here."

"Father, Platon Mihailovitch is coming," said Alexasha, looking out of the window.

"On a roan horse," Nikolasha put in, stooping down to the window. "Do you think it's a better horse than our grey, Alexasha?"

"Better, no, but its paces are different."

A dispute sprung up between them about the merits of the roan and the grey. Meanwhile a handsome man of graceful figure, with fair shining curls and dark eyes, walked into the room. A ferocious-looking dog with powerful jaws came in behind him, jingling its copper collar.

"Have you dined?" asked the fat man.

"Yes, I have," said the visitor.

"Why, have you come to make fun of me or what?" said Pyetuh, getting angry. "What do I want with you after dinner?"

"Well, Pyotr Petrovitch," said the visitor smiling, "I can assure you I ate nothing at dinner, if that's any comfort."

"Such a catch we have had, you should have seen it. Such a monstrous sturgeon was landed, and there was no counting the carp."

"It makes me envious to hear you," said the visitor. "Do teach me to enjoy myself as you do."

"But why be dull? Upon my soul!" said the fat gentleman.

"Why be dull? Because it is dull."

"You don't eat enough, that is all. You should just try having a proper dinner. It's a new fashion they have invented, being bored; in old days no one was bored."

"Don't go on boasting! Do you mean to say you have never been bored?"

"Never! And I don't know how it is, but I have not time to be bored. One wakes up in the morning—one has to have one's morning tea, you know, and then there is the steward to see, and then I go fishing and then it is dinner-time; after dinner you have hardly time for a snooze before supper's here, and after that the cook comes up—I have to order dinner for to-morrow. When could I be bored?"

All the while he was talking, Tchitchikov was looking at the visitor.

Platon Mihailovitch Platonov was an Achilles* and Paris† in one, a graceful figure, picturesque height, freshness—everything was combined in him. A pleasant smile with a faint expression of irony, as it were, accentuated his beauty, but, in spite of all that, there was something lifeless and drowsy about him. No passions, no sorrows, no agitations had traced lines on his virginal fresh face, but the absence of them left him lifeless.

"I must confess," Tchitchikov pronounced, "I too cannot understand how with an appearance like yours—if you will allow me to say so—you can be bored. Of course there may be other reasons—lack of money or vexations due to evil-minded persons, for indeed there are some such as are ready to attempt one's life."

---

*Greek hero in the Trojan War, celebrated in Homer's *Iliad*.
†Trojan prince who carried off Helen and brought about the Trojan War.

"But the point is that there is nothing of the sort," said Platonov. "Would you believe it that sometimes I could wish that it were so, that I had some anxiety and trouble, well, even for instance that some one would make me angry, but no, I am bored and that is all about it!"

"I don't understand it, but perhaps your estate is insufficient and you have only a small number of souls?"

"Oh no. My brother and I have thirty thousand acres of land and a thousand souls of peasants on them."

"And with all that to be bored, it is incomprehensible! But perhaps your estate is in disorder? Perhaps your crops have failed, or a great many of your serfs have died?"

"No, on the contrary, everything is in the best of order and my brother is an excellent manager."

"I don't understand it," said Tchitchikov, and shrugged his shoulders.

"Well, we'll drive away his boredom directly," said their host. "Run quickly to the kitchen, Alexasha, and tell the cook to send in the fish pies as soon as she can. But where's that sluggard Emelyan and that thief Antoshka? Why don't they bring the savouries?"

But the door opened. The sluggard Emelyan and the thief Antoshka made their appearance with table napkins, laid the table, set a tray with six decanters of various coloured homemade wines; soon round the trays and decanters there was a necklace of plates—caviare, cheese, salted mushrooms of different kinds, and something was brought in from the kitchen covered with a plate, under which could be heard the hissing of butter. The sluggard Emelyan and the thief Antoshka were quick and excellent fellows. Their master gave them those titles because to address them without nicknames seemed tame and flat, and he did not like anything to be so; he was a kind-hearted man, but liked to use words of strong flavour. His servants did not resent it, however.

The savouries were followed by dinner. The good-hearted fat gentleman showed himself now a regular ruffian. As soon as he saw one piece on a visitor's plate he would put a second piece beside it, saying: "It is not good for man or bird to live alone." If the visitor finished the two pieces, he would foist a third on him, saying: "What's the good of two, God loves a trinity." If the guest devoured all three he would say: "Where's the cart with three wheels? Who built a three-cornered hut?" For four he had another saying and for five, too.

Tchitchikov ate nearly a dozen slices of something and thought: "Well, our host won't force anything more upon me." But he was wrong, without a word the master of the house laid upon his plate a piece of ribs of veal roasted on a spit, the best piece of all with the kidney, and what veal it was!

"We kept that calf for two years on milk," said the fat gentleman. "I looked after him as if he were my son!"

"I can't," said Tchitchikov.

"You try it, and after that say you can't!"

"It won't go in, there's no room for it."

"Well, you know, there was no room in the church, but when the mayor arrived, room was made; and yet there was such a crush that an apple couldn't have fallen to the floor. You just try it: that morsel's like the mayor."

Tchitchikov did try it, it certainly might be compared with the mayor; room was made for it though it had seemed that it could not have been got in.

It was the same thing with the wines. When he had received the money from the mortgage of his estate Pyotr Petrovitch had laid in a supply of wine for the next ten years. He kept on filling up the glasses; what the guests would not drink he poured out for Alexasha and Nikolasha, who simply tossed off one glass after another, and yet got up from the table as though nothing had happened, as though they had only drunk a glass of water. It was not the same with the visitors. They could hardly drag themselves to the verandah, and were only just able to sink into armchairs; as soon as the master of the house had settled himself in his, an armchair that would have held four, he dropped asleep. His corpulent person was transformed into a blacksmith's bellows: from his open mouth and from his nose he began to emit sounds such as are not found even in the newest music. All the instruments were represented, the drum, the flute, and a strange abrupt note, like the yap of a dog. . . .

"Isn't he whistling!" said Platonov. Tchitchikov laughed.

"Of course if one dines like that," said Platonov, "how can one be bored? one falls asleep."

"Yes," said Tchitchikov languidly. His eyes seemed to be becoming very small. "All the same, if you will forgive my saying so, I can't understand how you can be bored. There are so many things you can do to keep off boredom."

"Such as?"

"Why there are all sorts of things a young man can do! You can dance, you can play some instrument . . . or else you can get married."

"Married! To whom?"

"Surely there must be some attractive and wealthy young ladies in the neighbourhood."

"No, there are not."

"Well, look for them in other places. Go about." At this point a happy thought flashed upon Tchitchikov's brain; his eyes grew wider. "Well, here's a capital remedy," he said, looking into Platonov's face.

"What do you mean?"

"Travel."

"Where could I go?"

"Why if you are free, come with me," said Tchitchikov, and to himself he thought, looking at Platonov, "and that would be a good thing, we could go halves over the expenses; and the repair of the carriage I could put down entirely to him."

"Why, where are you going then?"

"Oh, how shall I say? I am travelling not so much on my own affairs as on other people's. General Betrishtchev, my intimate friend, and I may say my benefactor, has asked me to visit his relations. . . . Of course, relations are all very well, but I am partly travelling on my own account too; for seeing the world and what people are doing, is—say what you like—a book of life, a second education."

Platonov pondered.

Tchitchikov meanwhile reflected: "It really would be a good thing. I might manage that he should undertake all the expenses. I might even so arrange as to set off with his horses, and to leave mine to be kept in his stables, and to take his carriage for the journey."

"Well, why not go for a trip?" Platonov was thinking meanwhile; "maybe it would cheer me up. I have nothing to do at home, my brother looks after everything as it is; so it would not be disarranging things. After all why shouldn't I amuse myself?"

"And would you agree," he said aloud, "to stay two days at my brother's? He won't let me go without."

"With the greatest pleasure, three if you like."

"In that case here's my hand on it! We'll go," said Platonov, becoming more animated.

"Bravo!" cried Tchitchikov, clapping his hands, "we'll go!"

"Where? where?" asked their host, waking up and staring at them with wide-open eyes. "No, gentlemen, orders have been given for the wheels to be taken off your carriage, and your horse, Platonov Mihailitch, is ten miles away by now. No, tonight you will stay here, and tomorrow you can go home after an early dinner."

"Upon my soul!" thought Tchitchikov. Platonov made no answer, knowing that Pyetuh had his own ways, and could not be turned from them. They had to remain. They were rewarded however by a marvellous spring evening. Their host arranged a row on the river for them. Twelve rowers with twenty-four oars rowed them, to the accompaniment of singing, over the smooth surface of the mirror-like lake. From the lake they were borne along into an immense river with sloping banks on each side. Not an eddy stirred the surface of the water. They had tea too and rolls on the boat, passing continually under ropes stretched across the river for catching fish. Before tea their host undressed and jumped into the water, where he floundered about for half an hour, and made a great noise with the fishermen, shouting to Big Foma and Kozma, and after having shouted and having fussed about to his heart's content, and got thoroughly chilled in the water, he returned to the boat with an appetite for tea which made the others envious to look at him. Meanwhile the sun had set; the sky remained clear and transparent. There was the sound of shouting. In place of the fishermen there were groups of boys bathing on the banks; splashing and laughter echoed in the distance. The oarsmen after plying their twenty-four oars in unison, suddenly raised them all at once into the air and the long-boat, light as a bird, darted of itself over the motionless, mirror-like surface. A fresh-looking sturdy lad, the third from the stern, began singing in a clear voice; five others caught it up, and the other six joined in and the song flowed on, endless as Russia; and putting their hands to their ears the singers themselves seemed lost in its endlessness. Listening to it one felt free and at ease, and Tchitchikov thought: "Ah, I really shall have a country place of my own one day."

"Oh, what is there fine in that dreary song?" thought Platonov, "it only makes me more depressed than ever."

It was dusk as they returned. In the dark the oars struck the water which no longer reflected the sky. Lights were faintly visible on both sides of the river. The moon rose just as they were touching the bank. On all sides fishermen were boiling soups of perch and still quivering fish on tripods. Everything was at home. The geese, the cows and the goats had been driven home long before, and the very dust raised by them was laid again by now, and the herdsmen who had driven them were standing by the gates waiting for a jug of milk and an invitation to partake of fish soup. Here and there came the sound of talk and the hum of voices, the loud barking of the dogs of their village and of other villages far away. The moon had risen and had begun to light up the darkness; and at last everything was bathed in light—the lake and the huts; the light of the fires was paler; the smoke from the chimneys could be seen silvery in the moonlight. Alexasha and Nikolasha flew by them, racing after each other on spirited horses; they raised as much dust as a flock of sheep.

"Oh, I really will have an estate of my own one day!" thought Tchitchikov. A buxom wife and little Tchitchikovs rose before his imagination again. Whose heart would not have been warmed by such an evening!

At supper they over-ate themselves again. When Pavel Ivanovitch had retired to the room assigned to him, and had got into bed, he felt his stomach: "It's as tight as a drum!" he said; "no mayor could possibly get in." As luck would have it, his host's room was the other side of the wall, the wall was a thin one and everything that was said was audible. On the pretence of an early lunch he was giving the cook directions for a regular dinner, and what directions! It was enough to give a dead man an appetite. He licked and smacked his lips. There were continually such phrases as: "But roast it well, let it soak well." While the cook kept saying in a thin high voice: "Yes sir, I can, I can do that too."

"And make a four-cornered fish pasty; in one corner put a sturgeon's cheeks and the jelly from its back, in another put buckwheat

mush, mushrooms and onions and sweet roe, and brains and something else—you know . . ."

"Yes sir, I can do it like that."

"And let it be just a little coloured on one side, you know, and
let it be a little less done on the other. And bake the underpart, you
understand, that it may be all crumbling, all soaked in juice, so that
it will melt in the mouth like snow."

"Confound him," thought Tchitchikov, turning over on the other
side, "he won't let me sleep."

"Make me a haggis and put a piece of ice in the middle, so that
it may swell up properly. And let the garnishing for the sturgeon be
rich. Garnish it with crayfish and little fried fish, with a stuffing of
little smelts, add fine mince, horse radish and mushrooms and
turnips, and carrots and beans, and is there any other root?"

"I might put in kohlrabi and beetroot cut in stars," said the cook.

"Yes, put in kohlrabi, and beetroot, and I'll tell you what garnish
to serve with the roast . . ."

"I shall never get to sleep," said Tchitchikov. Turning over on the
other side, he buried his head in the pillow and pulled the quilt up
over it, that he might hear nothing, but through the quilt he heard
unceasingly: "And roast it well," and "Bake it thoroughly." He fell
asleep over a turkey.

Next day the guests over-ate themselves to such a degree, that
Platonov could not ride home; his horse was taken back by one of
Pyetuh's stable boys. They got into the carriage: Platonov's dog Yarb
followed the carriage lazily, he too, had over-eaten himself.

"No, it is really too much," said Tchitchikov, as soon as the carriage had driven out of the yard. "It's positively piggish. Aren't you
uncomfortable, Platon Mihailovitch? The carriage was so very comfortable and now it seems uncomfortable all at once. Petrushka, I suppose you have been stupidly rearranging the luggage? There seem to
be baskets sticking up everywhere!"

Platonov laughed. "I can explain that," he said, "Pyotr Petrovitch
stuffed them in for the journey."

"To be sure," said Petrushka, turning round from the box. "I was
told to put them all in the carriage—pasties and pies."

"Yes indeed, Pavel Ivanovitch," said Selifan, looking round from
the box in high good humour. "A most worthy gentleman, and most

hospitable! He sent us out a glass of champagne each, and bade them let us have the dishes from the table, very fine dishes, most delicate flavour. There never was such a worthy gentleman."

"You see he has satisfied every one," said Platonov. "But tell me truly, can you spare the time to go out of your way to a village some seven or eight miles from here? I should like to say good-bye to my sister and my brother-in-law."

"I should be delighted," said Tchitchikov.

"You will not be the loser by doing so; my brother-in-law is a very remarkable man."

"In what way?" asked Tchitchikov.

"He is the best manager that has ever been seen in Russia. It's only a little more than ten years since he bought a neglected estate for which he gave barely twenty thousand, and he has brought it into such a condition that now he gets two hundred thousand from it."

"What a splendid man! The life of a man like that ought to be held up as an example to others. It will be very, very agreeable to make his acquaintance. And what's his name?"

"Skudronzhoglo."

"And his Christian name and father's name?"

"Konstantin Fyodorovitch."

"Konstantin Fyodorovitch Skudronzhoglo. Very agreeable to make his acquaintance. One may learn something from knowing such a man." And Tchitchikov proceeded to ask questions about Sku-dronzhoglo, and everything he learned about him from Platonov was surprising indeed.

"Look," said Platonov, pointing to the fields, "his land begins here. You will see at once how different it is from other people's. Coachman, here you take the road to the left. Do you see that copse of young trees? They were all sown. On another man's land they wouldn't have been that height in fifty years, and they have grown up in eight. Look, there the forest ends and the cornfields begin, and in another one hundred and fifty acres there will be forest again, also raised from seed, and then cornland again. Look at the corn, how much heavier it is than anywhere else."

"Yes, I see. But how does he do it?"

"Well, you must ask him that. There is nothing he hasn't got. He knows everything, you would never find another man like him. It is not only that he understands what soil suits anything, he knows what ought to be next to what, what grain must be sown near which kind of trees. With all of us the land is cracking through the drought, but his land is not. He calculates how much moisture is needed and plants trees accordingly: with him everything serves two purposes, the forest is timber, and it also improves the fields by its leaves and its shade."

"A wonderful man!" said Tchitchikov, and he looked with curiosity at the fields.

Everything was in extraordinarily good order. The forest was fenced in; there were cattleyards, also with good reason enclosed and admirably kept up; the stacks of corn were gigantic. There was abundance and fertility on every side. It could be seen at once that here there was a prince among managers. Going a little up hill they saw a big village facing them, scattered upon three hillsides. Everything in it was prosperous; the roads were well made; the huts were solid; if a cart was standing anywhere, that cart was new and strong; if they met a horse the horse looked well fed and spirited. The horned cattle also looked picked specimens, even a peasant's pig had the air of a nobleman. It was evident that here were living those peasants who dig silver with their spades as the song says. There were here no English parks, no arbours, no bridges, nothing fantastic, no landscape gardening. From the huts to the big house stretched a row of fishermen's yards. On the roof was a watch tower, not for the sake of the view, but to see how and where the work was going on.

They drove up to the house. The master was not at home; they were met by his wife, Platonov's sister, fair-haired, white-skinned, with a specially Russian expression, as handsome but also as listless as he. It seemed as though she cared little for the things that were most cared for, either because the all-devouring activity at her side left nothing for her to do, or because by her very nature she belonged to that class of philosophical people, who, having feelings and intelligence only, as it were, half alive, look at life with their eyes half closed and seeing its fierce struggle and agitation, say: "Let them rave, the fools! So much the worse for them."

"Good-day, sister," said Platonov. "Where is Konstantin?"

"I don't know, he ought to have been here long ago. No doubt he has been kept by something."

Tchitchikov took little notice of the lady of the house. He was interested in looking at the habitation of this remarkable man. He scrutinised everything in the room; he expected to find traces of its owner's character, as from the shell one can judge what the oyster or the snail that lived in it was like; but there was nothing of the sort. The room was absolutely characterless, it was spacious and nothing else. There were no pictures or frescoes on the walls, nor bronzes on the tables, no what-nots with china and cups on them, no vases, no flowers, no statues—in fact it was somewhat bare, there was simple furniture, and a piano standing on one side, and even that was shut, evidently the lady of the house did not often sit down to it. A door opened from the drawing-room into the master's study, but there too it was as bare—simple and bare. It could be seen that the master of the house came home only to rest and not to live in it, that he did not need a study with well-upholstered easy-chairs and all the comforts in order to think over his plans and ideas, and that his life was not spent in seductive dreams by a glowing fireside but in actual work: his ideas sprang at once from the circumstance itself, at the moment when it arose, and passed at once into action without any need of written records.

"Ah, here he is. Here he comes!" cried Platonov. Tchitchikov too rushed to the window. A man of about forty, with a swarthy face and alert appearance, walked up to the steps. He had on a serge cap. Two men of a lower class were walking with their caps in their hands, one on each side of him, talking and discussing something with him. One appeared to be a simple peasant, the other in a blue Siberian coat, seemed to be a close-fisted and knavish dealer who had come to buy something.

"So you'll bid them take it, sir," said the peasant, bowing.

"No, my good man, I have said to you twenty times already: don't bring any more, I have so much material already that I don't know where to put it."

"But it all turns to profit with you, Konstantin Fyodorovitch. One couldn't find another man as clever anywhere. Your honour will find a place for everything. So do bid them take it."

"I need hands; get me workmen, not material."

"But you wouldn't have any lack of workmen either. All our village goes out to work: no one remembers our being so short of bread as now. It's only a pity you won't take us on altogether, we'd serve you well and truly, by God we would. One can learn the way to do everything from you, Konstantin Fyodorovitch. So bid them take it for the last time."

"But last time you said it was the last time, and here you have brought the stuff again."

"But this is for the last time, Konstantin Fyodorovitch. If you won't take it no one will. So do tell them to take it, sir."

"Well, listen, this time I will take it, but I am only taking it because I am sorry for you, and don't want you to have it carted here for nothing. But if you bring me any more, I won't take it, not if you go on worrying me for three weeks."

"Certainly, Konstantin Fyodorovitch; you may be sure I won't bring any more. I most humbly thank you." The peasant walked away gratified. He was lying however, he would bring some more: "try your luck" is a saying of great power.

"Then be so good, Konstantin Fyodorovitch, . . . make it a little less," said the travelling merchant in the blue Siberian coat, who was walking on the other side of him.

"Why, I told you my price at first, I am not fond of bargaining. I tell you again: I am not like other landowners to whom you go just the day the interest is due on their mortgage. I know you well. You have a list of them and put down when each has to pay his interest. He is pressed for money and he will sell at half price. But what's your money to me? For all I care my things can lie unsold three years; I have no interest to pay."

"That's the fact, Konstantin Fyodorovitch. But you know I only . . . so that I may have dealings with you in the future and not from greed. Take three thousand as deposit." The dealer took out of the bosom of his coat a bundle of greasy notes.

Skudronzhoglo took it coolly, and without counting them, thrust them into the back pocket of his coat.

"H'm," thought Tchitchikov, "just as though it were a pocket handkerchief."

A minute later Skudronzhoglo appeared at the door of the drawing-room.

"Hullo, brother, you here?" he said on seeing Platonov. They embraced and kissed each other. Platonov introduced Tchitchikov.

Tchitchikov went reverently towards him, kissed him on the cheek and received an imprint of a kiss from him.

Skudronzhoglo's face was very striking. It betrayed its southern origin. His hair and his eyebrows were thick and dark, his eyes were speaking and of intense brilliance. Every expression of his face was sparkling with intelligence, and there was nothing drowsy about him. But an element of something choleric and irritable could be detected. He was not of pure Russian descent. There are in Russia numbers of Russians not of Russian descent, but quite Russians at heart. Skudronzhoglo took no interest in his origin, thinking that it made no practical difference, and he knew no language but Russian.

"Do you know, Konstantin, what I am thinking of?" said Platonov.

"Why what?"

"I have thought of going for a driving tour in several provinces, perhaps it would cure me of my depression."

"Well, very likely it will."

"In company with Pavel Ivanovitch here."

"Excellent. What districts," asked Skudronzhoglo, addressing Tchitchikov cordially, "do you purpose visiting now?"

"I must own," said Tchitchikov, putting his head on one side and grasping the arm of his chair, "for the moment I am not travelling so much on my own affairs as upon somebody else's. General Betrishtchev, my intimate friend, and I may say my benefactor, asked me to visit his relations. Relations of course are relations, but to some extent I may say I am going on my own account, for apart from the benefit that may accrue from the point of view of the digestion, the mere fact of seeing the world and what people are doing . . . say what you will, is a living book, a second education."

"Yes, to have a look at different places is not a bad thing."

"Your observation is most just," replied Tchitchikov, "it certainly is not a bad thing. You see things that otherwise you would not see, and meet people you would not otherwise meet. Talk with some people is as precious as gold. Teach me, honoured Konstantin Fyodorovitch, teach me, I appeal to you. I await your precious words as heavenly manna."

Skudronzhoglo was embarrassed. "But what, teach you what? I have had a very second-rate education myself."

"Wisdom, honoured sir, wisdom! The wisdom that will enable me to manage an estate as you do, and like you to succeed in making it yield a revenue not in dreams but in real fact; to obtain like you, possessions that are not visionary, but are real and actual, and so performing the duty of a citizen to win the respect of my countrymen."

"Do you know what?" said Skudronzhoglo, "stay a day here with me. I will show you all my work and tell you all about it. There is no particular wisdom about it as you will see."

"Brother, do stay for the day," said Madame Skudronzhoglo, turning to Platonov.

"I don't mind," said the latter indifferently, "what does Pavel Ivanovitch say?"

"I shall be delighted. . . . But there is one point. . . . I must pay a visit to General Betrishtchev's relations. There is a certain Colonel Koshkaryov . . ."

"But don't you know that he is a fool, a madman?"

"I have heard that; I have nothing to do with him. But since General Betrishtchev is my intimate friend, and so to say my benefactor . . . it would be awkward not to go."

"In that case," said Skudronzhoglo, "do you know what you had better do? drive over to him now. I have a racing droshky standing ready. It's not more than seven miles to his place, so you will be there in no time. You will be back before supper in fact."

Tchitchikov gladly availed himself of this suggestion. The droshky was brought round, and he drove off at once to see the colonel, who amazed him more than any one he had seen before. Everything at the colonel's was unusual. The whole village was upside down; building, rebuilding, heaps of mortar, bricks, and beams were about all the streets. Some houses were planned like government buildings. On one was inscribed in golden letters: "Depot for Agricultural Implements," on another, "Principal Counting House," on the third, "Committee of Rural Affairs," "School of Normal Education for Villagers"; in fact there was no telling what there was. He wondered whether he had not driven into the district town. The colonel himself was a rather stiff individual. His face was somewhat prim-looking and of the shape of a triangle. The whiskers were drawn stiffly down each cheek, his hair, his nose, his lip and his chin all looked as though they had been kept under a press. He began talking

like a sensible man. From the first word he began complaining of the
lack of culture among the surrounding landowners, of the great difficulties that lay before him. He received Tchitchikov cordially and affably, and quite took him into his confidence, describing with
self-complacency what immense labour it had cost him to bring his
estate into its present prosperous condition: how difficult it was to
make the simple peasant understand that there are higher pleasures
which enlightened luxury provides for man, that there is such a thing
as art; how necessary it was to struggle with the ignorance of the
Russian peasant, to dress him in German breeches and to make him
at least to some extent sensible of the higher dignity of man; that in
spite of all his efforts he had, so far, been unable to make the peasant
women put on corsets, while in Germany, where he had stayed with
his regiment in 1814, a miller's daughter could even play on the
piano, speak French and make a curtsey. He deplored the terrible lack
of culture of the neighbouring landowners, telling him how little
they thought about their subjects; how they even laughed when he
tried to explain how necessary for the management of an estate it was
to establish a secretary's office, counting houses and even committees, so as to prevent all sorts of stealing, and so that everything
should be known; that the clerk, the steward and the book-keeper
ought not to be educated just anyhow, but ought to complete their
studies at the university, that in spite of all his persuasions he could
not convince the landowners of the benefit it would be to their estates if every peasant were so well educated that he could read a trea-
tise on lightning conductors while following the plough.

Upon this, Tchitchikov reflected, "Well I doubt if there'll ever be
such a time. Here I have learnt to read and write but I haven't finished
reading the Countess de la Vallière, yet."

"The ignorance is awful," Colonel Koshkaryov said in conclusion, "the darkness of the Middle Ages, and there is no possibility of
remedying it, believe me there is not! Yet I could remedy it all; I know
the one means, the certain means of doing so."

"What is that?"

"To dress all, every one in Russia, as they are in Germany. Do absolutely nothing but that and I warrant you all will go swimmingly;
the level of education will rise, trade will improve, the golden age
will come to Russia."

Tchitchikov looked at him intently and thought: "Well, it's no use standing on ceremony with him." Without putting things off he informed the colonel on the spot that he was in need of certain souls with the completion of purchase and all the formalities.

"As far as I can see from your words this is a request, isn't it?"

"Yes, certainly."

"In that case put it in writing, it will go to the committee for all sorts of petitions. The committee for all sorts of petitions, after making a note of it, will bring it to me. From me it will go to the committee for rural affairs, there they will make all sorts of inquiries and investigations concerning the business. The head steward together with the counting-house clerks will pass their resolution in the shortest possible time and the business will be completed."

Tchitchikov was aghast. "Excuse me," he said, "like that it will take a long time."

"Ah!" said the colonel with a smile, "that is just the advantage of doing everything on paper. It takes a little time certainly, but on the other hand nothing escapes notice, every detail will be seen."

"But excuse me. . . . How can one treat of this in writing! You see, it is rather a peculiar business . . . the souls are . . . you see . . . in a certain sense . . . dead."

"Very good. So you write then that the souls are in a certain sense dead."

"But how can I write dead? One can't write it like that, you know, though they are dead, they must seem as though they are alive."

"Very good. So you write then: 'But it is necessary or it is required, that it should seem as though they are alive.' "

What was to be done with the colonel? Tchitchikov decided to go himself and see what these various boards and committees were like, and what he found was not merely astonishing, but was really beyond all conception. The committee for all sorts of petitions existed only on its signboard. The president of it, a former valet, had been transferred to the newly formed Board of Rural Affairs. His place was filled by the counting-house clerk, Timoshka, who had been dispatched to make an inquiry—to settle a dispute between a drunken clerk and the village elder, who was a rogue and a thief. There were no officials anywhere.

"But where is one to go then? How is one to get at anything sensible?" said Tchitchikov to his companion, a clerk for special commissions, whom the colonel had sent to escort him.

"You won't get any sense anywhere," said his escort, "it's all at sixes and sevens. Everything among us is managed, you see, by the Committee of Rural Construction, they take every one from his work and send him where they like. The only ones who are well off are those who are on the Committee of Construction (he was evidently displeased with the Committee of Construction). What happens here is that every one leads the master by the nose. He thinks that everything is as it should be, but it's all only in name."

"I must tell him that, though," thought Tchitchikov, and on getting back to the colonel, he told him that everything was in a muddle, and that there was no making head or tail of it, and the Committee was stealing right and left.

The colonel boiled over with righteous indignation; he immediately wrote off eight severe inquiries: on what grounds the Committee of Construction without authorisation disposed of officials who were not in their department? How could the chief steward allow the president to go off to an investigation without giving up his post? And how can the Board of Rural Affairs see with indifference that the Committee for All Sorts of Petitions doesn't even exist?

"Now there will be a fine to-do," thought Tchitchikov, and he began to take his leave.

"No, I am not going to let you go. In two hours at the utmost you will be satisfied about everything. I will put your business into the hands of a special man who has only just finished his studies at the university. Sit down in my library. Here there is everything you can want, books, papers, pens, and pencils—everything. Make use of them, make use of everything, you are master."

So said the colonel as he opened the door into his library. It was an immense apartment, the walls of which were lined with books from the floor to the ceiling. There were even stuffed animals in it. There were books on every subject—on forestry, cattle-rearing, pig-breeding, gardening, thousands of all sorts of magazines, handbooks and masses of journals representing the very latest development and perfection in horse breeding and the natural sciences. There were titles such as *Pig-breeding as a Science*. Seeing that these were all subjects that did not offer an agreeable way of passing the time, he turned to other bookcases. It was out of the frying-pan into the fire: there all the books were on philosophy. The title of one was *Philosophy as a Science*. There were six volumes in a row, entitled *Preliminary Introduction to the Theory of Thought in its General Aspect as a Whole, and in its Application to the Interpretation of the Organic Principles of the Mutual Distribution of Social Productivity*. Wherever Tchitchikov opened the book, on every page he found "phenomenon," "development," "abstract," "cohesion" and "combination"; and the devil only knows what. "No, all that's not in my line," thought Tchitchikov, and he turned to the third bookcase, where all the books related to art. Here he pulled out a huge volume of somewhat free mythological pictures, and began looking at them. That was to his taste. Middle-aged bachelors always like such pictures. It is said that of late years old gentlemen have acquired a taste for them excited by the ballet. There is no help for it. Man is fond of spices. When he had finished looking through this book Tchitchikov was about to pull out another of the same class, when Colonel Koshkaryov made his appearance with a beaming face, holding a paper in his hand.

"It is all finished and finished admirably. That man really does understand, he is the one that makes up for all the rest. For this I'll promote him above all the rest: I'll make a special board of control and make him president of it. This is what he writes . . ."

"Well, thank the Lord," thought Tchitchikov, and prepared to listen.

" 'In reference to the commission that your honour has entrusted to me I have the honour herewith to report as follows: 1. In the very petition of the collegiate councillor and cavalier, Pavel Ivanovitch Tchitchikov, there is some misunderstanding: inasmuch as souls are required that have been assailed by various sudden calamities, and died. Thereby, doubtless, he signifies those on the point of death, not actually dead; seeing that the dead cannot be obtained. How can a thing be purchased if it does not exist. Logic itself tells us that and evidently the gentleman has not gone very far in the study of the humanities.' " Here for a moment Koshkaryov stopped and said: "In this passage the rogue certainly scores off you. But he has a smart pen, hasn't he, and yet he has only been three years at the university, in fact he did not finish his education." Koshkaryov continued: " 'He has not gone far, as is evident, in the study of the humanities . . . for he has used the expression "dead souls," while every one who has completed a course of humane studies, knows for a fact that the soul is immortal. 2. Of the aforementioned souls, acquired by purchase or otherwise, or, as the gentleman incorrectly expresses it, dead, there are none that have not only been mortgaged, seeing that all without exception have been not only mortgaged but re-mortgaged for an additional hundred and fifty roubles a soul, except the little village of "Gurmailovka," which is in a doubtful position owing to the lawsuit with the landowner, Predishtchev, and so cannot be sold or mortgaged.' "

"Then why did you not tell me before? Why have you delayed me over these trifles?" said Tchitchikov angrily.

"Why, how could I tell that at first? That's the advantage of putting everything on paper, that everything now is perfectly clear."

"You are a fool, a silly ass," thought Tchitchikov to himself. "He has rummaged about in books, but what has he learned?" Regardless of all the rules of propriety and politeness, he seized his cap and rushed out of the house. The coachman was standing with the racing droshky in readiness: feeding them would have involved a petition in writing, and the resolution to give the horses oats would only have arrived next day. Rude and uncivil as Tchitchikov was, Koshkaryov was nevertheless courteous and refined. He shook his hand warmly and pressed it to his heart (just as Tchitchikov was getting on to the droshky) and thanked him for having given him an opportunity of seeing the working of his system in practice, that he certainly must give them a severe reprimand, for everything was apt to be slack and the springs of the rural mechanism to grow rusty and weak; that in consequence of this incident the happy thought had occurred to him to establish a new committee, which would be called the Committee for the Supervision of the Committee of Construction, so that then no one would dare to steal.

"Ass! fool!" thought Tchitchikov, feeling angry and out of humour all the way back. He drove back by starlight. Night had come on. There were lights in the villages. When he arrived at the steps he saw through the windows that the table was already laid for supper.

"Why are you so late?" asked Skudronzhoglo, when he appeared at the door.

"What have you been discussing with him for so long?" asked Platonov.

"He bored me to death!" said Tchitchikov. "I have never seen such a fool in my life."

"Oh! that's nothing," said Skudronzhoglo. "Koshkaryov is a comforting phenomenon. He is of use because the follies of the intellectual people are reflected and caricatured in him and so are more apparent. They have set up offices, counting-houses and directors and works and factories, and schools and committees, and the devil only knows what, as though they had got an empire to govern! How do you like this, I ask you? A landowner has arable land and not enough peasants to work it, and he goes and sets up a candle factory; he gets candlemakers from London and goes into the trade! Then there is another fool better still: he sets up a silk factory."

"Well, but you have factories too," observed Platonov.

"But who set them up? They started themselves: the wool accumulated and I had nowhere to get rid of it, so I began weaving cloth, and stout plain cloth too; it is bought freely at my market here at a low price. The refuse from fish was flung on my bank for six years together; well, what was I to do with it? I began making glue of it and get forty thousand for it. Everything is like that with me, you know."

"What a devil!" thought Tchitchikov, looking him full in the face. "What a paw for raking in the roubles."

"And I don't build edifices for it; I have no grand buildings with columns and façades. I don't send abroad for workmen, and I don't take the peasant off the land for any consideration; all my hands are men who came for the sake of bread in a famine year. I have lots of such factory workers. Only look carefully after the management and you'll see that every rag may be turned to account, every bit of refuse may yield a profit, so that at last you can only reject it and say, I want no more."

"That's amazing," said Tchitchikov, full of interest: "amazing! amazing! What's most amazing is that every bit of refuse yields a profit."

"H'm, but that's not all." Skudronzhoglo did not finish his sentence; his spleen was rising and he wanted to abuse the neighbouring landowners. "There's another clever fellow, what do you suppose he has started? Alms-houses, brick buildings in the village. An act of Christian charity! . . . If you want to help, help every peasant to do his duty, and don't turn him away from his Christian duty. Help the son to keep his father comfortable in his own home, and don't help him to throw off his responsibility. Give him the possibility of sheltering his brother or his neighbour in his own house, give him money to do that, help him as much as you can, but don't separate him, or he will throw off every Christian duty. There are Don Quixotes simply in every direction. . . . Every man in the almshouses costs two hundred roubles a year! . . . Why, I could keep ten men in the village for that." Skudronzhoglo spat with anger.

Tchitchikov was not interested in alms-houses: he wanted to turn the conversation on the way in which every bit of refuse yielded an income. But Skudronzhoglo was thoroughly roused by now, his spleen was excited, and his words flowed freely.

"And here another Don Quixote of enlightenment has founded a school. Well, what can be more useful for a man than to know how to read or write? But this is how he manages things. The peasants from his village come to me, 'What's the meaning of this, sir?' they say, 'our sons have got completely out of hand, they won't help us on the land, they all want to be clerks, but you know there is only one clerk wanted.' So that's what it comes to."

Tchitchikov had no use for schools either, but Platonov took up the subject.

"But one must not be stopped by the fact that clerks are not wanted now; there will be a need for them hereafter. We must work for posterity."

"Oh, brother, do you at least be sensible; what do you want with that posterity? Every one seems to think that he is Peter the Great. But you look at what's under your feet, and don't gaze away at posterity; work to make the peasant competent and well off, and to let him have leisure to study as he likes instead of saying to him, stick in hand: 'Learn!' They begin at the wrong end! . . . Here, listen; come, I ask you to judge. . . ." At this point Skudronzhoglo moved closer to Tchitchikov, and to make him attend more closely to the matter, took possession of him, or, in other words, put his finger through the buttonhole of his coat. "Come, what could be clearer. You have peasants in order that you may protect them in their peasant existence. And what does it consist of? What is the peasant's occupation? Growing corn. So you must try and make him a good husbandman. Is that clear? There are wiseacres who say: 'We can raise him out of that condition. He leads too coarse and simple an existence. We must make him acquainted with objects of luxury.' It is not enough for them that through this luxury they have themselves become rags instead of men, and the devil only knows what diseases they have contracted from it, and now there is not a wretched boy of eighteen who hasn't tried everything and has lost all his teeth and is bald,—and so now they want to infect the peasants too. But thank God we have one healthy class left which hasn't got to know these vices. For that we ought simply to thank God. Yes, the man who tills the land is to my mind more worthy of honour than any. God grant that we may all be tillers of the land."

"So you think that growing corn is the most profitable occupation?" inquired Tchitchikov.

"It's the most righteous, but that's not to say it is the most profitable. 'Till the land in the sweat of thy brow'*—that is said to all of us, that's not said in vain. The experience of ages has shown that it is in the agricultural class that morals are purest. Where agriculture is the basis of the social structure, there is abundance and plenty. There is neither poverty nor luxury, but there is plenty. 'Till the land, labour,' man has been told. . . . What could be plainer? I say to the peasant: 'For whomever you are working, whether it is for me, for yourself, or for a neighbour—work. I'll be the first to help you in what you want to do. If you haven't cattle, here's a horse for you, here's a cow for you, here's a cart. I am ready to provide you with whatever you need, but work. It breaks my heart if your land is neglected and I see disorder and poverty in your household, I can't endure idleness: I am over you to make you work.' H'm, they think to increase their income by setting up factories and institutions of all sorts. But you ought first to think of making every one of your peasants well off, for then you'll be well off yourself without any factories or works and without foolish whims."

"The more I listen to you, honoured Konstantin Fyodorovitch,"

---

*Paraphrase of the Bible, Genesis 3:19: "In the sweat of thy face shalt thou eat bread" (King James Version).

said Tchitchikov, "the greater my desire to listen; tell me, my honoured friend, if for instance I formed a design to become a landowner, in this province, let us suppose, what ought I to turn my attention to chiefly, what am I to do, how am I to set to work to get rich as quickly as possible, thereby fulfilling the duty of a citizen to my country."

"How set to work to get rich? Why, I'll tell you . . ." said Skudronzhoglo.

"It's supper-time," said the lady of the house, getting up from the sofa, stepping into the middle of the room, and wrapping her chilled young limbs in a shawl.

Tchitchikov leaped up from his chair with the agility of a military man; he flew up to the lady with a soft expression, with the politeness of a refined civilian made his arm into a loop, offered it to her and led her in state across two rooms to the dining-room, keeping his head agreeably on one side all the time. The servant took the cover off the soup tureen; they all moved their chairs nearer to the table and began upon the soup.

When he had finished his soup and drunk a glass of home-made cordial (it was excellent cordial), Tchitchikov said to Skudronzhoglo: "Allow me, honoured sir, to bring you back to the point at which our conversation broke off. I was asking you: what to do, how to proceed, how best to set to work. . . ."

* * * * * * * * * *

(*Two pages of the manuscript are missing here.*)

"If he asked forty thousand for the estate I would pay it him down on the spot."

"H'm!" Tchitchikov pondered. "Then why don't you buy it yourself?" he brought out with some diffidence.

"Well, one must know one's limits. I have a great deal to do with my own estates without that. As it is, the gentry of the neighbourhood are all crying out against me, declaring that I take advantage of their difficulties and their ruined position, buying up land for a song. I am sick of it at last."

"Country gentlemen are fond of backbiting," said Tchitchikov.

"Yes, especially among us in our province. . . . You can't imagine what they say about me. They never speak of me except as the skinflint and a money-grubber of the worst kind. They don't blame themselves for anything. 'I have run through my money of course,' they say, 'but that's because I had higher needs. I must have books. I must live luxuriously to encourage trade; one needn't be ruined if one lived the life of a pig like Skudronzhoglo.' You see that's how they go on."

"I should like to be such a pig," said Tchitchikov.

"And you know all that's because I don't give dinners, and don't lend them money. I don't give dinners because it would bore me, I am not used to them; but if you like to come and see me and eat what I eat, you are very welcome! That I won't lend money is nonsense. If you come to me really in want and tell me your circumstances and what use you will make of my money, if I see from your words that you'll make a sensible use of it and that it will be of some real benefit to you—I would not refuse you, and would not even take the interest. But I am not going to throw my money away. No, you must excuse me! He'll give a dinner to his mistress, or furnish his house on an insane scale, and I'm to lend him the money! . . ."

Here Skudronzhoglo spat and was almost uttering some unseemly and violent language in the presence of his wife. A shade of gloomy melancholy darkened his lively face. Lines that betrayed the wrathful ferment of his rising spleen furrowed his brow vertically and horizontally.

Tchitchikov emptied a glass of raspberry cordial and said: "Allow me, my honoured friend, to bring you back again to the point where our conversation broke off. Supposing I were to obtain the estate to which you kindly referred, how long a time or how quickly could I grow as rich as——"

"If you want to grow rich quickly," Skudronzhoglo caught him up suddenly and abruptly, for he was still full of ill-humour, "you'll never get rich at all: if you want to get rich without caring how long it takes, you'll get rich quickly."

"You don't say so!" said Tchitchikov.

"Yes," said Skudronzhoglo abruptly, as though he had been angry with Tchitchikov himself. "You must have a love for the work: without that you can do nothing. You must like farming. Yes! and believe me it is anything but dull. They have got up an idea that it is depressing in the country . . . but I should die of depression if I had to spend one day in town as they spend their time. A farmer has no time to be bored. There is no emptiness in his life, it is all fullness. You have only to look at the varied round of the year's work—and what work! Work that does truly elevate the spirit, to say nothing of its variety. In it a man goes hand in hand with nature, with the seasons of the year, and is in touch and in sympathy with everything that is done in creation. Before the spring is here our labours are already beginning: there is carting and getting in timber, and while the roads are impassable, there is the getting ready the seed, the sifting and measuring of the corn in the granaries and the drying of it and distributing the tasks among the peasants. As soon as the snows and floods are over, work begins in earnest; by the river there is loading the boats, then there is thinning trees in the wood and planting trees in the garden, and in every direction the men are turning up the ground. The spade is at work in the vegetable garden, the ploughs and harrows in the fields. And the sowing begins—that's a trifling matter of course: they are sowing the future harvest! When summer has come there's the mowing, the husbandman's first holiday—that's a trifling matter too! One harvest comes after the other, after the rye the wheat, after the barley the oats, and then the pulling of the hemp. They throw the hay into cocks, they build the stacks. And when August is half over there is the carting of it all to the threshing barns. Autumn comes, there is the ploughing and the sowing of the winter corn, the repair of the granaries, the barns and the cattle-sheds, sampling the corn, and the first threshing. Winter comes and even then work does not flag: the first wagonloads setting off for the town, threshing in all the barns, the carting of the threshed grain from the barns to the granaries; in the woods the chopping and sawing of timber, the carting of bricks and materials for the building in the spring. Why, I am simply incapable of dealing with it all. Such variety of work! One goes here and there to look: to the mill, to the workyard, and to the factory and to the threshing floor; you go to have a look at the peasants, too, how they are working for themselves—that's a trifling matter, too, I suppose! But it's a festival for me to see a carpenter using his axe well; I could stand for a couple of hours watching him, the work delights me so. And if you see too with what object all this is created, how everything around you is multiplying and multiplying, bringing fruit and revenue, why, I can't tell you what a pleasure it is. And not because your money's growing—money is only money—but because it is all the work of your hands; because you see that you are in a way the cause and creator of it all, and you, like some magician, are scattering abundance and welfare on every side. Where will you find me a delight equal to that?" said Skudronzhoglo, and he looked up; all the lines in his face had vanished. He beamed like a triumphant emperor on the day of his coronation. "Why, you couldn't find anything so delightful in the whole world! It's in this, just in this, that a man imitates God. God chose for Himself the work of creation as the highest delight, and requires the same of man, that he should be the creator of prosperity and the harmonious order of things. And they call that dull work!"

Tchitchikov drank in the sweet sound of his host's words like the singing of a bird of paradise. His mouth positively watered. His eyes shone with sugary sweetness, and he could have listened for ever.

"Konstantin, it is time to get up," said his wife, getting up from the table. Platonov rose, Skudronzhoglo got up, Tchitchikov got up, though he would have liked to go on sitting still and listening. Making a loop of his arm, Tchitchikov led the lady of the house back. But his head was not ingratiatingly on one side and there was not the same sprightly politeness in his movements. His mind was absorbed in more substantial movements and considerations.

"You can say what you like, but it is dull all the same," said Platonov, who was walking behind them.

"Our visitor seems quite a sensible fellow," thought Skudronzhoglo, "and not a boastful fool." And upon this reflection he became still more cheerful, as though his own talk had warmed him up, as though he were delighted at having found a man capable of taking good advice.

Afterwards when they were all settled in a snug little room lighted by candles, facing a big glass door into the garden, Tchitchikov felt happier than he had for a very long time, as though after long wandering he had been welcomed home, and to crown it all had gained the object of his desires, and had flung away his pilgrim's staff, saying: "Enough!" Such was the enchanting state of mind induced in him by his host's sensible words. There are for every heart certain words which are nearer and more akin than any others; and often in some remote, forgotten out-of-the-way place, in some lonely nook, we unexpectedly meet a man whose warming discourse makes us forget the hardships of the road, the comfortless night lodging and the contemporary world, full of the follies of mankind, and of deceptions that cloud men's vision; and an evening spent in that manner remains with us for ever, and a distinct memory is kept of everything that happened in it, who was present, and at what spot each person was standing, and what was in his hand—the walls, the corners, and every trifle in the room.

So Tchitchikov noticed everything that evening: the little plainly furnished room, and the good-natured expression on the face of his clever host, and the pipe with the amber mouthpiece that was handed to Platonov, and the smoke which he blew in Yarb's broad face and Yarb's snorting, and his pretty hostess's laugh, interrupted by the words, "That's enough, don't tease him," and the cheerful candlelight and the cricket in the corner, and the glass door and the spring night which looked in at them from without, over the tops of the trees among which the nightingales were singing.

"Your words are sweet to me, honoured Konstantin Fyodorovitch," Tchitchikov brought out. "I may say that in all Russia I have not met your equal in intelligence."

Skudronzhoglo smiled. "No, Pavel Ivanovitch," he said, "if you want to know an intelligent man, we really have one man whom one might call an intelligent man, and I am not worth the sole of his old shoe."

"Who is that?" Tchitchikov asked with surprise.

"It is our government contractor, Murazov."

"This is the second time I have heard of him."

"He is a man who could administer not merely an estate but a whole kingdom. If I had a kingdom I should immediately make him the minister of finance."

"I have heard it said that he is a man of abilities beyond all belief: he has made ten millions."

"Ten millions, it must be more than forty. Soon half Russia will be in his hands."

"What do you mean?" cried Tchitchikov, amazed.

"It certainly will be. His wealth must be increasing now at a terrible rate. That's evident. A man gets rich slowly if he has a few hundred thousands; but when a man has a million he has a wide range: whatever he takes up is soon doubled and trebled. His field of action is so wide. And he has no rivals in it either: there is no one to compete with him. Whatever price he fixes stands: there is no one to knock it down."

Tchitchikov gazed into Skudronzhoglo's face with his mouth open and his eyes starting out of his head as though he were moon-struck. He held his breath.

"Inconceivable," he said, when he had recovered himself a little, "the mind is petrified with awe. People are amazed at the wisdom of Providence as they scrutinise a beetle; to my mind it is even more overwhelming that such vast sums can find their way into a mortal's hands! Allow me to put a question to you in regard to one point: tell me, all this was surely not obtained in the first place quite honestly, was it?"

"Absolutely irreproachably and by the most straightforward means!"

"I can't believe you, most honoured friend, I really can't believe you. If it were a case of thousands perhaps, but millions . . . no, pardon me, but I can't believe it."

"On the contrary, it is difficult to get thousands honestly, but millions are easily piled up. A millionaire has no need to resort to crooked ways. The road is straight, you have but to go along it and take whatever lies before you. Another man would not pick it up, not every one has the capacity."

"It's incredible! And what is most incredible is, that it all started from a farthing."

"That's how it always is. That's the natural order of things," said Skudronzhoglo. "A man who has been brought up on thousands will never make money; he will have already formed luxurious habits and goodness knows what. One must start from the beginning and not from the middle. One must begin from the bottom, quite from the bottom. It is only there that one gets a thorough knowledge of life and men with whom you have to deal later on. When you have to put up with this and that in your own person, and when you find out that you must take care of the kopecks before you can get to the roubles, and when you have been through all sorts of ups and downs, it does train you and teach you sense, so that you are not likely to make a false move and come to grief in any enterprise. Believe me, that's the truth. One must start from the beginning and not from the middle. If any one were to say to me: 'Give me a hundred thousand and

I'll get rich directly,' I shouldn't believe him; he is counting on luck and not a certainty. One must begin with a farthing."

"In that case I shall get rich," said Tchitchikov, "because I am beginning almost, so to say, from nothing." He meant, of course, his dead souls.

"Konstantin, it is time for Pavel Ivanovitch to rest and sleep," said his wife, "and you keep chattering."

"And you will certainly get rich," said Skudronzhoglo, not heeding his wife. "Rivers and rivers of gold will flow into your hands. You won't know what to do with your income."

Pavel Ivanovitch sat spellbound in the golden realm of mounting visions and daydreams. His thoughts were in a whirl. . . .

"Really, Konstantin, it is time to let Pavel Ivanovitch go to bed."

"Why, what is it? Well, go to bed yourself if you want to," said her husband, and he stopped; there came the loud sound of Platonov's snoring, and after him Yarb snored still more loudly. The far-away tap of the watchman on a sheet of iron had been audible for a long while past. It was past midnight. Skudronzhoglo realised that it really was bedtime. They separated, wishing each other sound sleep, and their wishes were quickly realised.

Only Tchitchikov could not sleep. His thoughts were wide awake. He kept pondering how to become the owner, not of an imaginary, but of a real estate. After his conversation with Skudronzhoglo, everything had become so clear; the possibility of becoming rich seemed so evident, the difficult work of managing an estate seemed to have become so easy and intelligible, and seemed so well suited to his temperament, that he began to think seriously of obtaining not an imaginary but a real estate. He at once determined with the money he would get by mortgaging the imaginary souls to obtain an estate that would not be imaginary. He already saw himself managing his estate and doing everything as Skudronzhoglo had instructed him, promptly, carefully, introducing nothing new until he had thoroughly mastered everything old, looking into everything with his own eyes, getting to know all his peasantry, rejecting all superfluities, devoting himself to nothing but work, and looking after his land. . . . He had already a foretaste of the delight that he would feel when he had introduced harmonious order, when every part of the organisation was moving briskly and working well together. The work would go merrily, and just as the flour is swiftly ground out of the grain in the mill, it would grind all sorts of rubbish and refuse into ready money. His marvellous host rose before his imagination every moment. He was the first man in all Russia for whom he had felt a personal respect: hitherto he had always respected men either for their high rank in the service, or for their great possessions; simply for his brains he had never respected any man; Skudronzhoglo was the first. Tchitchikov realised that it was useless to talk dead souls with a man like this, and that the very mention of them would be out of place. He was absorbed now by another project—that of buying Hlobuev's estate. He had ten thousand, another ten thousand he purposed borrowing from Skudronzhoglo, since he had said he was ready to help any one who wanted to grow rich and to take up farming. The remaining ten thousand it might be possible to put off paying till after he had mortgaged the souls. It was not possible yet to mortgage all the souls he had bought, because he had not yet the land on which he must settle them. Though he did assert that he had land in the Kherson province, its existence was somewhat hypothetical. He had proposed to buy the estate in the Kherson province because land was sold there for a mere song, and was even given away on condition that peasants were settled upon it. He thought, too, he ought to make haste to buy what runaway and dead souls any one had left, for the landowners were one after another hurrying to mortgage their estates, and soon there would not be a spot left in Russia that was not mortgaged to the Government. All these ideas one after another filled his mind and prevented him from sleeping. At last slumber, which had, as the saying is, held all the household in its embrace for the last four hours, embraced Tchitchikov also. He slept soundly. . . .

CHAPTER 4

The next day everything was arranged most successfully. Sku-dronzhoglo was delighted to lend ten thousand roubles with-out interest or security, simply upon a signed receipt: so ready was he to help any one on to the way of prosperity. That was not all: he undertook to accompany Tchitchikov to Hlobuev's, in order to look over the latter's estate with him. After a substantial breakfast they set off all three in Pavel Ivanovitch's carriage; Skudronzhoglo's racing droshky followed empty. Yarb ran on ahead, chasing the birds off the road. They did the twelve miles in a little over an hour and a half and then caught sight of a small village with two houses—a big new one that was unfinished and had remained in the rough for many years, and a little old one. They found the owner very untidy and sleepy, as he was only just awake; there was a patch on his coat and holes in his boots.

He was as delighted at their visit as though it were a great piece of good fortune: as though he were seeing brothers from whom he had long been parted.

"Konstantin Fyodorovitch! Platon Mihailovitch!" he cried. "My dear friends, it is good of you to come! Just let me rub my eyes. I really thought no one would ever come and see me again. Every one avoids me like the plague: they think I am going to ask them to lend me money. Oh, it's hard, it's hard, Konstantin Fyodorivitch! I see that I am to blame for everything. There's no help for it . . . I am living like a pig. Excuse me, gentlemen, for receiving you in such an attire; my boots as you see are in holes. But what will you take? Tell me."

"Please let us come straight to the point. We have come to you on business," said Skudronzhoglo. "Here is a purchaser for you, Pavel Ivanovitch Tchitchikov."

"Sincerely glad to make your acquaintance. Let me shake hands with you."

Tchitchikov gave him both hands.

"I should be delighted, honoured Pavel Ivanovitch, to show you my estate, which is deserving of attention. . . . But, gentlemen, allow me to ask you, have you dined?"

"We have, we have," said Skudronzhoglo, anxious to get off at once.

"In that case, let us start."

Hlobuev picked up his cap. The visitors put on their caps too, and they all set off to look at the estate.

"Come and look at my disorder and neglect," said Hlobuev. "Of course you did well to have your dinner. Would you believe it, Konstantin Fyodorovitch, I haven't a hen in the place—that's what I've come to. I'm behaving like a pig, a regular pig!"

He heaved a deep sigh, and apparently thinking that he would not get much sympathy from Konstantin Fyodorovitch, and that his heart was rather hard, took Platonov's arm and went on ahead with him, pressing closely up to him. Skudronzhoglo and Tchitchikov remained behind and followed them at some distance, arm-in-arm.

"It's hard, Platon Mihailovitch, it is hard," said Hlobuev to Platonov. "You can't imagine how hard it is! No money, no bread, no boots! I should snap my fingers at all that if I were young and alone. But when all these hardships come upon one in old age and with a wife and five children at one's side, one is distressed, one can't help being distressed. . . ."

Platonov felt sorry for him. "Well, if you sell the estate won't that set you right?" he asked.

"Set me right indeed," said Hlobuev, with a gesture of despair. "It will all go to pay pressing debts, and I shan't have a single thousand left for myself."

"Well, what will you do then?"

"God knows," said Hlobuev, shrugging his shoulders.

Platonov was amazed. "How is it you are not taking steps to extricate yourself from such a position?"

"What steps could I take?"

"Haven't you any other means?"

"None at all."

"Well, try and get some work, take a post."

"Why, you know I am provincial secretary. What sort of good job could be given me? They would pay me a wretched salary, and you see I have a wife and five children."

"Well, take some private situation. Go in for being a steward."

"Who would trust me with his estates? I have squandered my own."

"Yes, but if one is threatened with hunger and death one must take some steps. I'll ask whether my brother could not get you a place through some one in the town."

"No, Platon Mihailovitch," said Hlobuev, sighing and pressing his hand warmly, "I am no use for anything now. I have grown decrepit before I am old, and I am paying for my weakness in the past by a pain in my back and rheumatism in my shoulders. What could I do? Why should I plunder the government? Without me there are plenty of men in the government service who are there simply to make money. God forbid that to get myself a salary I should help increase the taxes for the poorer class: it's hard enough for them to live as it is with such masses of blood-suckers. No, Platon Mihailovitch, I'll have nothing to do with them."

"Here's a position," thought Platonov, "it's worse than my ennui!"

Meanwhile Skudronzhoglo and Tchitchikov, walking at a considerable distance behind, were talking together.

"He has neglected the place beyond everything," said Skudronzhoglo. "He has brought his peasants to such poverty! When the cattle plague comes it is no use thinking of what belongs to you. You must sell everything you have to get your peasants cattle so that they shouldn't be left a single day without the means of going on with their work. Now it would take years to reform them; the peasants have grown lazy and taken to drink."

"So it is not very profitable to buy this estate now?" inquired Tchitchikov.

At that point Skudronzhoglo looked at Tchitchikov, as though he would have said: "What an ignoramus you are; must one teach you everything from the A B C?"

"Not profitable? Why, in three years I would get an income of twenty thousand from that estate—that's how unprofitable it is. Ten miles across—is a trifle, it seems! And the land, look what the land's like! It's all water meadows. I'd sow flax, and for flax alone I'd get five thousand; I'd sow turnip, and get four thousand for turnip. And now look, the rye has come up; it was all self sown. He did not sow any corn, I know that. Why, that estate is worth a hundred and fifty thousand, not forty."

Tchitchikov began to be afraid that Hlobuev might overhear, and so dropped even further behind.

"You see how much land has run to waste," said Skudronzhoglo, beginning to get angry. "If he had only let people know beforehand, some one might have been glad to cultivate it. If he has nothing to plough with, he might dig it up and turn it into a market garden; he would have got something for the vegetables! He has made his peasants sit idle for four years—that's no matter, of course! Why, by that alone you have corrupted them and ruined them for ever; they have grown used to rags and vagrancy!"

Skudronzhoglo spat with anger as he said this, and his features were overshadowed by a cloud of gloom.

"I can't stay here any longer: it makes me ill to see this neglect and waste. You can settle with him without me now. Get this treasure away from that fool as soon as you can. He simply dishonours God's gifts." Saying this Skudronzhoglo said good-bye to Tchitchikov, and overtaking Hlobuev, began saying good-bye to him too.

"Upon my word, Konstantin Fyodorovitch," cried Hlobuev in astonishment, "you have only just come and you are going!"

"I can't stay, it is very urgent for me to be at home," said Skudronzhoglo, and taking leave, got on his racing droshky and went off.

It seemed as though Hlobuev understood the reason of his departure. "Konstantin Fyodorovitch couldn't endure it," he said. "I feel that it can't be cheering for a farmer such as he is, to look at such senseless mismanagement. Would you believe it, Pavel Ivanovitch, that I cannot, that I am not able . . . that I have hardly sown any wheat at all this year! As I am an honest man I had no seed, let alone the fact that I have nothing to plough with. Your brother is an extraordinary manager I am told, Platon Mihailovitch: but Konstantin Fyodorovitch, there is no denying it, is a Napoleon in that line. I often think indeed: 'Why is it that there is so much sense in one head? if only there were one drop of it in my silly brain, just enough to know how to manage my household.' I don't know how to do anything: I am no use for anything. Oh, Pavel Ivanovitch, take my land under your care. I feel most sorry for my poor peasants, I feel that I am incapable. . . . I don't know how to be strict and exacting. And, indeed, how could

I train them in order and regularity when I am so disorderly and irregular myself. I should like to give them all their freedom at once, but a Russian's so made that he can't do without a purchaser. . . . As he drowses so he drowns."

"Why, that is really strange," said Platonov. "Why is it in Russia that if you don't look sharply after the peasant he becomes a drunkard and good-for-nothing?"

"From lack of culture," said Tchitchikov.

"Well, God knows why. Here we are cultured, and see how we live. I have been to the university and have listened to lectures on all sorts of subjects, but I did not learn the art and right way of living, and what's more I did, so to say, learn the art of spending money on all sorts of new refinements and comforts, and became more familiar with the objects for which money is necessary. Was that because I did not study sensibly? No, my comrades were all the same. Two or three of them perhaps did get real benefit from the lectures and that was perhaps because they were intelligent anyway, but the others did nothing but try to learn what spoils health and wastes money. Yes, indeed! They came to the lectures simply to applaud the professors, to bestow laurels upon them, and not to gain anything from them, so that we take from culture only its worst side; we snatch at the surface of it, but don't take the thing itself. No, Pavel Ivanovitch, it's from some other cause that we don't know how to live, but what it is, upon my word I don't know."

"There must be a cause," said Tchitchikov.

Poor Hlobuev heaved a deep sigh and said: "It sometimes seems to me that the Russian is a lost man. He has no strength of will, no courage to persevere. One wants to do everything and one can do nothing, one is always thinking that from to-morrow one will begin a new life, that from to-morrow one will set to work as one ought, that from to-morrow one will put oneself on a diet; but not a bit of it, on the evening of that very day one will over-eat oneself, so that one can only blink one's eyes and can't say a word—yes really; and it's always like that."

"One must keep a store of common sense," said Tchitchikov, "and consult one's common sense at every minute, have a friendly conversation with it."

"Well!" said Hlobuev. "Really it seems to me that we are not cre-

ated for common sense. I don't believe any one of us is sensible. If I
do see that some one is actually living respectably and making and
saving money I don't trust even him: the devil will confound him in
his old age, he will suddenly let it all go! And every one is like that
among us, the gentry and the peasants, the cultured and the uncul-
tured. There was a clever peasant who, starting from nothing, made a
hundred thousand, and when he had made a hundred thousand he
took a silly craze into his head to have a bath of champagne, and he
did bathe in champagne. But now I believe we have looked over
everything. There is nothing more. I don't know whether you would
like to look at the mill. It has no wheel, though, and its works are
good for nothing."

"What's the use of looking at it then?" said Tchitchikov.

"In that case let us go home."

And they all turned their steps homeward.

The sights that met them on their way back were of the same nature. Slovenliness and disorder seemed to show their ugliness on
every side. Everything was neglected and had run to waste. An angry
peasant woman in greasy rags was beating a poor little girl till the
child was half dead, and was calling on all the devils. One philosophic bearded peasant gazed out of window with stoical indifference at the wrath of the drunken woman; another bearded one was
yawning. Another was scratching the lower part of his back, while yet
another yawned. Yawning was visible in the buildings and in everything: the roofs too gaped. Platonov looking at them gave a yawn.
"My future property—the peasants," thought Tchitchikov, "hole
upon hole, and patch upon patch."

And in fact a whole gate had been put bodily on the top of one
hut instead of a roof; the falling windows were propped up with
beams dragged out of the master's barn. Indeed, the system of
Trishka's coat seemed to prevail; the cuffs and the tails were cut off to
patch the elbows.

They went indoors. Tchitchikov was somewhat surprised by the
mingling of poverty with some splendid nicknacks of the latest fashion in luxury. In the middle of broken ornaments and furniture there
were new bronzes. A Shakespeare sat on the inkstand, an ivory hand
for scratching the back lay on the table. Hlobuev introduced his wife.
She was a fine specimen; she could have held her own in Moscow.

She was tastefully and fashionably dressed. She liked talking about the town and the theatre that was being set up in it. It was evident that she liked the country even less than her husband did, and that she yawned more even than Platonov when she was left alone. The room was soon filled with children, charming girls and boys. There were five of them, the sixth was still a baby in arms. They were all delightful: the boys and girls were a joy to look at. They were dressed prettily and with taste, they were full of play and gaiety, and that made it all the sadder to look at them. It would have been better if they had been badly dressed, in simple homespun skirts and smocks, if they had been running about the yard and had been in no way different from the peasant children! A friend came to call on the lady of the house. The ladies went off to their own domain. The children ran after them and the gentlemen were left alone.

Tchitchikov approached the subject of the purchase. Like all purchasers he began depreciating the estate he wanted to buy, and after running it down on all sides, said: "What price are you asking for it?"

"You see," said Hlobuev, "I don't ask too much and I don't like to do so: it would be shameful on my part. I won't conceal from you either that on my estate out of every hundred souls reckoned on the census list only fifty are left, the rest have either died of an epidemic or have run away without a passport, so that you may reckon them as dead. So I only ask you thirty thousand."

"Oh, thirty thousand! A neglected estate, dead peasants and thirty thousand! Take twenty-five."

"Pavel Ivanovitch, I could mortgage it for twenty-five thousand: do you understand that? Then I should get twenty-five thousand and the estate would still be mine. I am selling it simply because I need money at once, and there would be a lot of delay over mortgaging it; I should have to pay the clerks, and I haven't the money to do it."

"Oh well, but you might let me have it for twenty-five thousand!"

Platonov felt ashamed of Tchitchikov. "Buy it, Pavel Ivanovitch," he said. "Any one would give that price for the estate. If you won't give thirty thousand for it my brother and I will club together and buy it."

Tchitchikov was frightened. "Very well," he said, "I will give thirty thousand. Here I will give you a deposit of two thousand at once, eight thousand in a week's time, and the remaining twenty thousand in a month."

"No, Pavel Ivanovitch, I only sell it on condition of receiving the money as soon as possible. Give me now fifteen thousand at least, and the rest not later than in a fortnight's time."

"But I haven't got fifteen thousand! Ten thousand is all I have with me now. Let me get the money together." This was a lie: he had twenty thousand.

"No, please, Pavel Ivanovitch! I tell you that I absolutely must have fifteen thousand at once."

"But I really have not got the five thousand and I don't know where to get it."

"I will lend it to you," put in Platonov.

"Well, perhaps, if you will!" said Tchitchikov, and thought to himself, "well, it really is very handy that he should lend it me: in that case it will be possible to bring the money to-morrow."

The writing-case was brought from the carriage for Hlobuev, and ten thousand was at once taken from it; the other five thousand was promised for the next day. It was promised, but Tchitchikov inwardly proposed to bring three thousand; the rest later, in two or three days, or if possible to put off the payment somewhat longer. Pavel Ivanovitch had a peculiar dislike for letting money go out of his hands. If it were absolutely inevitable to make a payment it still seemed to him better to pay the money to-morrow and not to-day. In fact he behaved as we all do: we all like to keep a man dangling about when he is asking for his money. Let him hang about in the passage! As though he could not wait a little! What does it matter to us that every hour may be precious to him and that his business is suffering from his absence!

"Come to-morrow, my good man," we say. "I have no time to attend to you to-day."

"Where are you going to live?" Platonov asked Hlobuev. "Have you some other estate?"

"No, I haven't, but I am going to move to the town. I should have had to do that in any case, not on my own account, but for the children. They must have teachers for scripture, music, and dancing. You can't get that in the country, you know."

"Hasn't a crust of bread, but wants his children to be taught dancing!" thought Tchitchikov.

"Queer!" thought Platonov.

"Well, we must have something to sprinkle the bargain with," said Hlobuev. "Hey, Kiryushka! bring us a bottle of champagne, my lad."

"Hasn't a crust of bread, but has champagne!" thought Tchitchikov. Platonov did not know what to think.

The champagne was brought in. They drank three glasses each and grew livelier. Hlobuev unbent and became clever and charming; witticisms and anecdotes were continually dropping from him. Much knowledge of men and the world was apparent in his talk! He had seen many things so well and so truly; he sketched in a few words the neighbouring landowners so aptly and smartly; he saw the failings and mistakes of all of them so clearly; he knew so well the history of the spendthrift gentry—and why and how and through what they had come to ruin; he could reproduce their most trifling habits with such originality and insight, that they were both fascinated by his talk and were prepared to declare that he was a very intelligent man.

"Listen," said Platonov, taking him by the hand, "how is it that with your cleverness, your experience, and your knowledge of life, you can't find some way of escape from your difficult position?"

"But I can," answered Hlobuev, and thereupon he poured out a perfect avalanche of projects. They were all so absurd, so odd, and were so little the result of a knowledge of men and the world that there was nothing for it but to shrug one's shoulders and say: "Good Lord, what a fathomless gulf there is between knowledge of the world and the capacity for making use of it!" Almost all his projects rested upon the possibility of obtaining at once by some means a hundred or even two hundred thousand roubles. Then, so he fancied, everything could be settled satisfactorily and the estate would be properly run and the rents would be patched, and the revenues would be quadrupled, and it would be in his power to pay all his debts. And he ended his talk by saying: "But what would you have me do? There isn't any benefactor who would venture to lend me two hundred or even one hundred thousand roubles! It seems it is not God's will."

"As though God would send two hundred thousand roubles to such a fool!" thought Tchitchikov.

"I have got an aunt, indeed, who is worth three million," said Hlobuev, "a devout old lady, she gives to churches and monasteries, but is stingy about helping relations. She is a remarkable old woman—an aunt of the old-fashioned type who is well worth seeing. She has four hundred canaries; she has pug dogs and lady companions and servants such as can't be found nowadays. The youngest of her servants must be sixty, though she always calls to him: 'Hey, boy!' If a visitor does not behave himself, she will tell the servant to leave him out when handing the dishes at dinner. And they actually do miss him out."

Platonov laughed.

"And what is her name, and where does she live?" asked Tchitchikov.

"She lives in our town, Alexandra Ivanovna Hanasarov."

"Why don't you apply to her?" Platonov asked sympathetically. "I think if she were to get a closer insight into the position of your family, she would not be capable of refusing you, however stingy she may be."

"Oh no, she is capable! My aunt has a tough character. She is one of those old women that are like flint, Platon Mihailovitch! Besides there are other people making up to her apart from me. Among them there is one who is aiming at being a governor. He claims to be a relation. God bless him, perhaps he will succeed. God bless the lot of them! I never have been able to make up to people, and less than ever now; I can't stoop to it."

"Idiot!" thought Tchitchikov. "Why, I'd look after an aunt like that like a nurse looking after a baby!"

"Well, talking like this is dry work," said Hlobuev. "Hey, Kiryushka! bring us another bottle of champagne."

"No, no, I can't drink any more," said Platonov.

"Nor can I," said Tchitchikov, and both refused resolutely.

"Well, anyway you must give me your word that you will come and see me in town: on the 8th of June I am giving a little dinner to our local magnates."

"Upon my word!" cried Platonov. "In such a position, completely ruined, and now a dinner-party."

"There's no help for it, it must be: it's a debt," said Hlobuev. "They have entertained me too."

"What is to be done with him?" thought Platonov. He was not aware that in Russia, in Moscow and many other towns, there are numbers of these clever people whose life is an enigma. A man has lost everything it seems, he is in debt all round, he has no means whatever and the dinner he gives, one would think, must be the last; and those who dine with him imagine that next day their host will be hauled off to prison. Ten years pass and he is still extant; he is more deeply in debt than ever, and again he gives a dinner and every one believes it is his last and every one is convinced that their host will be hauled off to prison next day.

Hlobuev was almost one of these wonderful people. It is only in Russia that one can exist in that way. Though he had nothing he entertained and kept open house, and was even a patron of the fine arts, encouraging artists of all sorts who visited the town, giving them board and lodging in his house. If any one had looked into the house he had in town, he could not have told who was the master of it. One day a priest in a chasuble would be holding a service in it; next day some French actors would be having a rehearsal; on one occasion some one who was a complete stranger to almost every one in the house installed himself with his papers in the drawing-room, of all places, and turned it into an office for himself, and no one in the house was troubled by this, but seemed to regard it as in the ordinary course of events. Sometimes for days together there was not a crumb in the house, sometimes they gave a dinner that would have satisfied the most refined gourmand, and the master of the house appeared festive and lively, with the deportment of a wealthy nobleman, and the carriage of a man whose life has been spent in the midst of plenty and prosperity. On the other hand, at times there were moments so bitter that another man in his place would have hanged or shot himself. But he was saved by a religious temperament which in him was strangely combined with his reckless manner of life. In these bitter painful moments he would turn over the pages of a book and read the lives of the saints and martyrs, who disciplined their souls to be superior to misfortunes and sufferings. His soul at such times completely melted, his spirit was softened and his eyes were filled with tears. And, strange to say, unexpected help almost always came to him from one quarter or another at these times; either some of his old friends would think of him and send him some money; or a wealthy lady, a generous Christian soul, a stranger to him personally, casually heard his story on a visit to the town, and with the impulsive generosity of the female heart, sent him a handsome present; or some law-suit of which he had never even heard would be settled to his advantage. Reverently and gratefully he recognised at such times the incomprehensible mercy of Providence, had a thanksgiving service celebrated, and began the same reckless life as before.

"I am sorry for him, I am really sorry for him!" said Platonov to Tchitchikov, as they were driving away.

"A prodigal son!"* said Tchitchikov. "It is no use being sorry for people like that."

And soon they both left off thinking about him: Platonov, because he took an indolent and a pathetic view of every one's position as of everything in the world, indeed. His heart was touched and ached at the sight of the sufferings of others, but his impressions did not cut deeply into his heart. He did not think of Hlobuev for he did not think even of himself. Tchitchikov did not think of Hlobuev because all his thoughts were absorbed in his new purchase. He was reckoning and calculating and considering all the advantages of the estate he had bought. And however he looked at it, from every point of view he saw that it was a profitable purchase. He might mortgage the estate. Or he might merely mortgage the dead and runaway serfs. Or he might first sell the best pieces of land and then mortgage the remainder. Or he might decide to manage the land himself, and become a landowner after the pattern of Skudronzhoglo, profiting by his advice, as Konstantin Fyodorovitch would be his neighbour and benefactor. Or he might even adopt the course of selling the estate into private hands (always supposing that he did not himself care to undertake the management of it), while keeping the dead and runaway serfs for his own purposes. Then other advantages presented themselves; he might disappear from these parts altogether without repaying Skudronzhoglo the money he had lent him. In fact, however he looked at the matter, it was evident that it was a profitable one. He

---

*Reference to the Bible, Luke 15:13: "[The prodigal son] wasted his substance with riotous living" (King James Version).

felt delighted, delighted because he had now become a landowner, an owner not of an imaginary but of a real estate with land and all appurtenances and serfs—serfs not creatures of a dream, existing only in imagination, but real and substantial. And at last he began prancing up and down and rubbing his hands, and humming and murmuring, and putting his fist to his mouth blew a march on it as on a trumpet, and even uttered aloud a few encouraging words and nicknames addressed to himself, such as "bulldog" and "little cockerel." But then remembering that he was not alone he subsided and tried to suppress his untimely outburst of delight, and when Platonov, mistaking these vague sounds for words addressed to him, asked him, "What?" he answered, "Nothing."

Only then looking about him he noticed that they were driving through a beautiful copse. An enclosure of charming birch-trees stretched to left and to right. Between the trees a white brick church appeared. At the end of the road a gentleman came into sight walking towards them, wearing a cap and carrying a gnarled stick in his hand. A long-legged English hound was running ahead of him.

"Stop!" cried Platonov to the coachman, and he jumped out of the carriage. Tchitchikov did the same. They walked to meet the gentleman. Yarb had already succeeded in greeting the English dog who was evidently an old acquaintance, for he received on his thick nose the eager licking of Azor (that was the name of the English dog) with complete indifference. The agile dog called Azor, after licking Yarb ran up to Platonov and jumped up with the intention of licking him on the lips, but did not succeed in doing so and, repulsed by him, bounded off to Tchitchikov and licking his ear, dashed back to Platonov again, hoping to lick at least his ear.

Platonov and the gentleman coming towards them met at this moment and kissed each other.

"Upon my word, Platon! What do you mean by treating me like this?" the gentleman asked quickly.

"Like what?" Platonov answered apathetically.

"Why, it's too bad really! For three days there has been no sight or sound of you! Pyetuh's groom brought your horse. 'He has driven away with a gentleman,' he said. But he didn't say a word as to where, with what object, or for how long. Upon my word, brother, how can you go on like this? Goodness knows what I have been imagining these days!"

"Well, I can't help it. I forgot," said Platonov. "We went to see Konstantin Fyodorovitch. He sends you his greetings and so does sister. Let me introduce Pavel Ivanovitch Tchitchikov. Pavel Ivanovitch, brother Vassily: I beg you to like him as you do me."

"Brother Vassily" and Tchitchikov taking off their caps kissed each other.

"What sort of man is this Tchitchikov?" thought "brother Vassily." "Brother Platon is not very discriminating in his acquaintances, and probably has not found out what sort of a man he is." He scrutinised Tchitchikov so far as was consistent with good manners. Meanwhile Tchitchikov stood with his head a little on one side, and maintained an agreeable expression on his countenance.

Tchitchikov for his part scrutinised "brother Vassily" so far as good manners would permit. He was shorter than Platonov, had darker hair, and was altogether far less handsome; but there was a great deal of life and animation in his face. It was evident that he did not spend his time in lethargy and depression.

"Do you know what I am going to do?" said Platonov.

"What?" asked Vassily.

"Going for a tour about holy Russia with Pavel Ivanovitch here, and perhaps it will rouse me and distract me from my depression."

"How did you come to settle it so quickly?" Vassily was beginning, genuinely puzzled at such a decision, and he was almost adding: "And settled to go too with a man you have never seen before, who may be a rascal, and goodness knows what!" And filled with mistrust he looked askance at Tchitchikov, and saw that he was still standing with perfect decorum, still politely holding his head a little on one side and still maintaining the respectfully affable expression on his face, so that it was impossible to say what kind of a man he was.

In silence the three gentlemen walked along the road, on the left of which was the white church of which they had caught glimpses between the trees, and on the right, the buildings of a gentleman's homestead began to come into sight through the trees. At last the gates too came into view. They walked into the yard where there was an old-fashioned high-roofed house. Two immense lime-trees standing in the middle of the yard wrapped almost half of it in their shade. The walls of the house could scarcely be seen through their luxuriant drooping branches. Under the lime-trees there were several long seats. Vassily Platonov asked Tchitchikov to sit down. Tchitchikov sat down and so did the younger brother. The whole yard was flooded with the fragrance of flowering lilacs and bird-cherries, which hanging over the pretty birch hedge from the garden on all sides into the yard looked like a flowery chain or a bead necklace wreathed about it.

A smart deft youth of seventeen in a handsome pink cotton shirt brought a decanter of water and bottles of kvass* of various kinds and colours, fizzing like effervescent lemonade. After setting the decanters before them he went up to a tree and, picking up a spade that was leaning against it, went off into the garden. At the Platonovs' all the house serfs worked in the garden, all the servants were gardeners, or to put it more correctly, there were no servants, but the gardeners sometimes performed their duties. Vassily Platonov always maintained that one could do without servants at all: any one, he said, could hand things, and it was not necessary to have a separate class of people to do it; and that a Russian is only nice and alert and handsome and unconstrained and works well so long as he wears a shirt and jerkin, but that as soon as he gets into a German coat he becomes ungainly and ugly and lazy and dawdling. He even declared that the peasants' cleanliness was only preserved so long as they wore the Russian shirt and jerkin, and that as soon as they got into a German coat they gave up changing their shirts and going to the bath, and took to sleeping in their coats and that bugs, fleas and God knows what besides began to breed under their coats. Perhaps he was right in this. In their villages the peasants dressed with peculiar neatness and smartness, and one might have looked far to find such handsome shirts and jerkins.

"Won't you take a little refreshment?" said Vassily Mihailovitch to Tchitchikov, indicating the decanters. "The kvass is our own make; our house has long been famous for it."

Tchitchikov poured out a glass from the first decanter. It was like the effervescent beverage he had sometimes drunk in Poland, fizzing like champagne, and the gas mounted with an agreeable stinging sen-

---

*Mildly alcoholic Russian beer made from fermented grain.

sation from the mouth into the nose. "Nectar," said Tchitchikov. He drank a glass from another decanter, it was better still.

"In what direction and into what parts do you propose to make your tour?" asked Vassily Mihailovitch.

"I am going," said Tchitchikov, rubbing his knee with his hand, while he gently swayed his whole person and leaned his head affably on one side, "not so much on my own affairs as on other people's. General Betrishtchev, my intimate friend, and I may say benefactor, asked me to visit his relations. Relations of course are relations, but in a sense I am going for my own sake too—since apart from the advantages from the point of view of digestion—to see the world and what people are doing is, so to say, the book of life and a second education. . . ."

Vassily Mihailovitch pondered. "The man speaks in rather a stilted way," he thought, "but there is a great deal of truth in what he says. My brother Platon has no knowledge of the world or of men or of life." After a brief silence he said aloud: "Do you know what, Platon? Travelling really may shake you up a bit. You are suffering from a lethargy of the soul. You are simply asleep, and not asleep from satiety or fatigue, but from lack of vivid impressions or sensations. Now I am quite the opposite. I should be very glad not to feel so keenly and not to take everything that happens so much to heart."

"Well, why do you take things so much to heart?" said Platonov. "You are only asking for trouble and you make worries for yourself."

"How can I help it when there is something unpleasant at every turn?" said Vassily. "Have you heard the trick that Lyenitsyn has played on us while you have been away? He has seized our waste land up by the Red Hill."

"He doesn't know, that's why he has taken it," said Platonov. "He is a new man, he has only just come from Petersburg. We must talk with him and explain."

"He knows, he knows perfectly well; I sent to tell him but he answered with rudeness."

"You ought to have gone and explained it to him yourself. Talk it over with him."

"Well, no. He is too stuck up. I'm not going to see him. You can go yourself if you like."

"I would go; but I am of no use. He may take me in and deceive me."

"Well, if you like, I will drive over," said Tchitchikov.

Vassily glanced at him and thought: "He is fond of driving about!"

"You must only give me an idea what sort of man he is," said Tchitchikov, "and what the business is about."

"I am ashamed really to impose such a disagreeable commission on you, for even an interview with such a man is to me an unpleasant commission. I must tell you that he comes of a simple family of small landowners of our province, has risen in the service in Petersburg, has managed to get into aristocratic society by marrying somebody's illegitimate daughter and has begun to give himself airs. He behaves like a grand gentleman. In our province, thank God, people have some sense. Fashion is not the law for us, and Petersburg is not our holy place."

"Of course not," said Tchitchikov. "But what's the point at issue?"

"Well, it is really a nonsensical business. He hasn't got land enough, so—well he has seized our waste land, that is, he reckoned on the land being of no use, and the owners . . . and as luck would have it the peasants have from time immemorial assembled there to celebrate the 'Red Hill.' On that account I would rather sacrifice other better lands than give it up. Tradition is for me sacred."

"So you are ready to let him have other land?"

"Yes, if he hadn't behaved like this; but as far as I can see, he wants to bring it into court. Very well, we shall see which wins the case. Though it is not very clear on the map, there are old men still living who know about it."

"H'm," thought Tchitchikov, "they are both a bit touchy." But aloud he said: "It seems to me that the business might be arranged amicably. Everything depends on the arbitrator. By letter . . ."

(Here two pages of the manuscript are lost.)

. . . "that for you too it will be very advantageous to transfer, for instance, to my name all the dead souls that are still reckoned on the old census lists as belonging to your estates, so that I should pay the taxes for them. And to avoid giving any cause of offence, you would make the transfer by means of a regular deed of purchase as though the souls were living."

"Well, upon my word!" thought Lyenitsyn, "this is something very queer," and he drew a little back, chair and all, for he was completely nonplussed.

"I have no doubt you will readily agree to this," said Tchitchikov, "for it is a transaction of precisely the class of which you have been speaking. It will be a private affair between thoroughly trustworthy people, and there will be no harm to any one."

What was to be done? Lyenitsyn found himself in a difficult position. He could not have foreseen that the views he had just expressed would expose him to carrying them into action so quickly. The proposition was utterly unexpected. Of course there was nothing calculated to injure any one about this proceeding: landowners would in any case mortgage those dead souls together with their living ones; so that there could be no loss to the Treasury from it; the only difference was that they would all be in one man's hands, instead of being in the hands of several different persons. But, nevertheless, he was troubled. He was a law-abiding man and a business man, in a good sense. He would never have decided any case unjustly for the sake of a bribe, however large. But on this occasion he stood uncertain what to call this action, just or unjust. If any one else had come to him with such a proposition he might have said: "That's nonsense, ridiculous! I don't care for playing with dolls or any other sort of foolery." But his guest had made such a good impression on him already, they were so thoroughly in agreement in their views on the progress of science and enlightenment—how could he refuse? Lyenitsyn found himself in a very difficult position.

But at that moment, as though to relieve his distress, his wife, a young woman with a turn-up nose, thin and pale like all Petersburg ladies, and tastefully dressed like all Petersburg ladies, came into the room. She was followed by a nurse carrying in her arms a baby, the first fruits of a tender passion of the young married couple. Tchitchikov, of course, went up to the lady at once, and the agreeable way in which he held his head on one side was enough alone, even apart from his courteous greeting, to dispose her in his favour. Then he ran up to the baby, who was on the point of breaking into a howl; Tchitchikov, however, succeeded by the words, "Agoo, agoo, little darling!", by snapping his fingers and dangling the sardonyx seal on his watch-chain, in luring him into his arms. As soon as he had him in his arms, he began tossing him up in the air and succeeded in evoking a gleeful smile on the baby's face, which delighted both his parents. But either from delight or from some other motive, the baby suddenly misbehaved himself. Madame Lyenitsyn cried out: "Oh good gracious! he has ruined your coat!"

Tchitchikov looked: the sleeve of his quite new dress-coat was completely spoilt. "Plague take you, you confounded little imp!" he muttered to himself in his wrath.

Lyenitsyn, his wife and the nurse all ran for eau-de-cologne; they began wiping him down on all sides.

"It's of no consequence," said Tchitchikov, "it is absolutely of no consequence. As though an innocent babe could do harm." And at the same time he was thinking to himself, "But how well he aimed, the confounded little beast!" "It's the golden age!" he said, when he had been thoroughly cleansed and the agreeable smile had come back into his face.

"Yes, indeed," said Lyenitsyn, turning to Tchitchikov also with an agreeable smile, "what is more to be envied than the age of infancy? No anxieties, no thought of the future."

"A state into which one would willingly change at any moment," said Tchitchikov.

"Without thinking twice about it," said Lyenitsyn.

But I fancy both were lying; if such a transformation had been offered them, they would have changed their views pretty quickly. And indeed what fun is there sitting in a nurse's arms and spoiling people's coats!

The young wife retired with her firstborn and the nurse, for he too needed a little setting to rights: though he had been so liberal to Tchitchikov he had not spared himself.

This insignificant circumstance disposed Lyenitsyn still more favourably to Tchitchikov. Indeed, how could he refuse such an agreeable and tactful guest, who had lavished such caresses on his little one, and who had so magnanimously paid for it with his coat?

Lyenitsyn thought: "After all why should I not grant his request if that is what he wants. . . ."

(*Here there is a considerable hiatus in the manuscript.*)

CHAPTER 5

Tchitchikov was lolling on the sofa dressed in a new Persian dressing-gown of gold-coloured brocade, and bargaining with a dealer in contraband goods, of Jewish extraction and German accent; before them lay a piece of the very finest Dutch linen for shirts, and two cardboard boxes of excellent soap of the finest quality (it was the same sort of soap that he used to get hold of when he was in the Customs; it really had the property of imparting an incredible freshness to the complexion, and a surprising whiteness to the cheeks). While he was, like a connoisseur, purchasing these products so indispensable for a man of culture, he heard the rumble of an approaching carriage which set the walls and windows of the room faintly vibrating, and his Excellency Alexey Ivanovitch Lyenitsyn walked into the room.

"I appeal to your Excellency's judgment: what do you say to this linen and to this soap, and what do you think of this thing I bought yesterday?" As he spoke Tchitchikov put on his head a cap embroidered with gold and beads and looked like a Persian Shah, full of stateliness and dignity.

But without answering his question, his Excellency said:

"I have to speak to you about something important." His face looked troubled. The worthy dealer with the German accent was at once dismissed, and they were left alone.

"Do you know, something unpleasant has happened. Another will has been found which the old lady made ten years ago. Half the property is left to a monastery and the other half to her two protégées, to be equally divided between them and nothing else to any one."

Tchitchikov was aghast.

"But that will is all nonsense. It means nothing, it is cancelled by the second."

"But it is not stated in that second will that it cancels the first."

"That's a matter of course: the second cancels the first. It's nonsense. That first will is of no consequence. I know the deceased's intentions perfectly. I was with her. Who signed this will? Who were the witnesses?"

"It was witnessed in the regular way at the court. The witnesses were Havanov and Burmilov, the former judge."

"That's bad," thought Tchitchikov, "Havanov's said to be honest. Burmilov is a canting old hypocrite, he reads the lessons in church."

"Come, it is nonsense, nonsense," he said aloud, and all at once he felt that he had determination enough to deal with any emergency. "I know better; I was present at the deceased lady's last moments. I know all about it better than any one. I am ready to take my oath in person."

These words and the air of decision with which they were uttered reassured Lyenitsyn.

He had been much perturbed and had almost been suspecting there might have been something underhand on Tchitchikov's part in regard to the will (though of course he could never have conceived what had really happened). Now he reproached himself with being suspicious. His readiness to take an oath seemed a clear proof that Tchitchikov . . . We cannot say if Pavel Ivanovitch would really have had the hardihood to take a solemn oath about it, but he had the hardihood to say that he would.

"Don't worry yourself and set your mind at rest, I will go and discuss the matter with some lawyers. You ought not to be brought into the matter at all. You ought to be entirely outside it. I can stay in the town now as long as I like."

Tchitchikov immediately ordered his carriage and set out to visit a lawyer. This lawyer was a man of exceptional experience. He had been on his trial for the last fifteen years, and he had somehow managed to make it impossible that he should be dismissed from his post. Every one knew that he deserved, six times over deserved, to be sent to a penal settlement for his exploits. He was suspected on all sides, but it was never possible to bring complete proof and evidence against him. There really was something mysterious about it, and we might confidently have called him a sorcerer if our story had been cast in the dark ages.

The lawyer impressed Tchitchikov by the coldness of his expression and the greasiness of his dressing-gown, which was in striking contrast to the very good mahogany furniture, the gold clock under a glass shade, the chandelier that peeped through a muslin cover, put on to preserve it, and in fact to all the objects round them which bore the unmistakable imprint of enlightened European culture.

Not baulked by the sceptical air of the lawyer, Tchitchikov proceeded to explain the difficult points of the case, and drew an alluring picture of the gratitude that would inevitably reward his kind advice and interest.

The lawyer replied to this by pointing out the uncertainty of all things earthly, and subtly suggested that a bird in the hand was worth two in the bush.

There was nothing for it, he had to give him the bird in the hand. The philosopher's sceptical frigidity vanished instantly. It turned out that he was the most good-natured of men, very ready to talk and a most agreeable talker, no less tactful in his manners than Tchitchikov himself.

"Instead of making a long business of it, allow me to suggest that you have very likely not examined the will properly: probably there is some little note in it. You should take it home for the time. Although of course it is against the law to take such things into one's own keeping, yet if you ask certain officials in the proper way . . . I will use my influence too."

"I understand," thought Tchitchikov, and said, "I really don't quite remember whether there is a note in it or not," just as though he had not written the will himself.

"The very best thing is for you to look into that. However, in any case," he added very good-naturedly, "set your mind completely at rest and don't be bothered by anything, even if something worse happened. Never despair of anything: there is nothing in the world that can't be set right. Look at me, I am always calm. Whatever charges are brought against me my composure is never disturbed."

There certainly was an extraordinary composure on the face of the lawyer-philosopher.

"Of course that's of the first importance," Tchitchikov said. "But you must admit that there may be cases and circumstances, and such false charges made by one's enemies and such difficult positions that all composure is destroyed."

"Believe me, that is weakness," the philosophical lawyer replied very calmly and good-naturedly. "Only take care that the statement of the case should always rest on documentary evidence, that nothing should be left to verbal evidence. And as soon as you see the case is approaching a *dénouement** and likely to be settled, try, not to justify and defend yourself, but simply to complicate it by introducing new facts, and thus . . ."

"You mean so as to . . . ?"

"Complicate it and nothing more," answered the philosopher, "introduce into the case other extraneous circumstances which will bring other people into it; make it complicated and nothing more, and then let some official from Petersburg unravel it, let him unravel it, let him unravel it!" he repeated, looking into Tchitchikov's eyes with peculiar pleasure, as a teacher looks at a pupil while explaining to him a tricky passage in the Russian grammar.

"Yes, it is very well if one can get hold of circumstances which are calculated to throw dust in their eyes," said Tchitchikov, also looking with pleasure into the philosopher's eyes like a pupil who has grasped the tricky passage explained to him by the teacher.

"The circumstances will turn up, they will turn up! Believe me: by constant practice the brain becomes apt at finding them. First of all remember that you will be helped. A complicated case is a godsend for many people: more officials are required, and they are paid more for it. . . . In short, we must drag into the case as many people as possible. There is no harm in some coming into it for nothing: it's for them to defend themselves, you know. . . . They have to draw up their answers in writing. They have to ransom themselves. . . . All that is bread and butter. Believe me that as soon as things begin to be critical, the first resource is complicating them. You can complicate things and muddle them, so that no one can make head or tail of it. Why am I so calm? Because I know that as soon as things begin to go badly, I'll involve every one in it, the governor and the vice-governor and the police-master and the treasurer—I'll bring them all into it. I know all their circumstances: who is on bad terms with whom and who wants to score off whom. Then let them all get out of it, and while they are doing it other people will have time to make their fortunes. You can only catch crayfish in troubled waters, you know. They are all only waiting to trouble them." Here the philosophic lawyer

---

*Final resolution of a plot (French).

gazed into Tchitchikov's eyes again with the satisfaction of a teacher who explains a still more tricky passage in the Russian grammar.

"Yes, this is a wise man, certainly," thought Tchitchikov, and parted from the lawyer in the happiest and most cheerful frame of mind.

Completely reassured and fortified, he flung himself with careless agility on the resilient cushions of the carriage, told Selifan to draw back the hood of the carriage (he had had the hood up and even the leather covers buttoned on his way to the lawyer's) and settled himself like a retired colonel of the Hussars, or even like Vishnepokromov himself, jauntily crossing one leg over the other, turning affably towards the people he met, and beaming under his new silk hat which was tilted a little over one ear. Selifan was told to turn in the direction of the bazaar. Both the travelling dealers and the local shopkeepers standing at their doors took off their hats respectfully, and Tchitchikov not without dignity lifted his in response. Many of them he knew already; others, though strangers, were so charmed by the smart air of the gentleman who knew so well how to deport himself, that they greeted him as though they too were acquaintances. There was a continual fair going on in the town of Tfooslavl. As soon as the horse fair and the agricultural fair were over, there followed one for the sale of drapery for gentlemen of the utmost refinement. Dealers who arrived in wheeled carriages stayed on till they had to depart in sledges.

"Pray walk in!" a shopkeeper, in a German coat of Moscow cut, with a round shaven chin, and an expression of the most refined gentility, said at the cloth shop, with a polite swagger, as he held his hat in his outstretched hand.

Tchitchikov went into the shop. "Show me some cloth, my good man."

The agreeable shopkeeper promptly lifted the flap of the counter and so making way for himself, stood with his back to his wares and his face to his customer. So standing and still holding his hat in his hand he greeted Tchitchikov once more. Then putting his hat on his head and leaning over with both hands on the counter, said: "What sort of cloth? Do you prefer it of English make or of home manufacture?"

"Home manufacture," said Tchitchikov, "but of the best sort that goes under the name of English."

"What colours do you desire?" asked the shopkeeper, still agreeably swaying with his two hands pressed on the table.

"Some dark colour, olive or bottle green, shot with something approaching the cranberry colour," said Tchitchikov.

"I may say that I can give you a first-class article as good as anything in Petersburg or Moscow," said the shopkeeper, clambering up to get a roll of cloth; he flung it lightly on the counter, unrolled it from the other end, and held it up to the light. "What a sheen! The most fashionable, the latest style!" The cloth shone as though it were of silk. The shopkeeper divined that he had before him a connoisseur in cloth and did not care to begin with the ten rouble quality.

"Very fair," said Tchitchikov, barely glancing at it. "Look here, my good man, show me now what you are keeping to show me last, and a colour that has more . . . more red sheen in it."

"I understand: you really desire the colour that is just coming into fashion. I have got a cloth of the very finest quality. But I must warn you that it is a very high price, but there, it is of the very highest quality."

The roll fell from above. The shopkeeper unrolled it with still greater dexterity; he caught hold of the other end and displayed a really silky-looking material, and held it up to Tchitchikov, so that the latter could not only see but also sniff at it, merely saying:

"Here is a bit of cloth! the colour of the smoke and flame of Navarino!"*

They came to terms over the price. The arshin† rod like an enchanter's wand promptly cut off enough for a coat and breeches for Tchitchikov. Making a nick with the scissors the shopkeeper with both hands neatly tore the cloth right across the whole width of the stuff, at the conclusion of which operation he bowed to Tchitchikov with the most ingratiating affability. The cloth was promptly rolled up and neatly wrapped in paper; the parcel was tied up with fine twine. Tchitchikov was about to put his hand in his pocket, but he was aware of a very refined arm agreeably encircling his waist, while his

---

*Greek port, site of a major sea battle in 1827 during the Greek War of Independence, when the Russian, French, and English fleets defeated the Egyptians and Turks.
†Or arsheen; unit of length in Russia.

ears were greeted with the words: "What are you buying there, my good friend?"

"Oh, a most agreeable and unexpected meeting!" cried Tchitchikov.

"An agreeable encounter," said the voice of the person whose arm was round his waist. It was Vishnepokromov.

"I was just going to pass the shop without noticing, when suddenly I saw a familiar face—I couldn't deny myself the pleasure! There is no doubt that the cloth is ever so much better this year. It used to be a shame, a disgrace! I never could find anything decent. . . . I am ready to pay forty roubles, fifty even, but give me something good. . . . What I think is: either have a thing that really is the best, or else have nothing at all. Isn't that right?"

"Perfectly right!" said Tchitchikov. "Why give oneself a lot of trouble if not to have really good things?"

"Show me some cloth at a moderate price," they heard a voice say behind them, which seemed to Tchitchikov familiar. He turned round and saw Hlobuev. It did not seem that he was buying cloth from extravagance, for the coat he had on was very shabby.

"Ah, Pavel Ivanovitch! Do let me have a talk with you at last. There's no meeting with you anywhere. I have been to find you several times; you were never at home."

"My good friend, I have been so busy that upon my soul I have had no time." He looked from side to side as though trying to escape from an interview, and he saw Murazov coming into the shop. "Afanasy Vassilyevitch! Ah, upon my word!" said Tchitchikov. "What a delightful meeting!" and after him Vishnepokromov repeated, "Afanasy Vassilyevitch!" Hlobuev repeated, "Afanasy Vassilyevitch!" And last of all the well-bred shopkeeper, taking his hat from his head and flourishing it with his arm stretched out at full length, brought out, "Afanasy Vassilyevitch, our humble respects!" On all the faces appeared that doglike ingratiating servility which sinful man exhibits before a millionaire.

The old man greeted all of them and turned at once to Hlobuev:

"Pardon me, I saw you from a distance going into the shop and ventured to disturb you. If you will be free in a little while and will be passing by my house, do me the favour to come in for a few minutes. I want to have a talk with you."

Hlobuev answered, "Very good, Afanasy Vassilyevitch."

And the old man bowing to all of them again, went out.

"It makes me feel quite giddy," said Tchitchikov, "when I think that that man has ten millions. It's positively incredible."

"It isn't the right state of things though," said Vishnepokromov, "capital ought not to be in one man's hands. That is the subject of ever so many treatises all over Europe nowadays. If you have money, well, share it with others: entertain, give balls, keep up a beneficent luxury that gives bread to tradesmen and artisans."

"I can't understand it," said Tchitchikov. "Ten millions and he lives like a humble peasant! Why, goodness knows what one might do with ten millions! Why, one might so arrange one's affairs as to keep no company but that of princes and generals."

"Yes," the shopkeeper put in, "it really is a lack of refinement. If a merchant becomes distinguished, he is no longer a merchant but is in a way a financier. In that case I would take a box at the theatre and wouldn't marry my daughter to a humble colonel! I'd marry her to a general or nobody. I shouldn't think much of a colonel. I should have to have a confectioner to get my dinner, not a cook."

"Yes, upon my word," said Vishnepokromov, "there is no denying that one could do anything with ten millions. Just give me ten millions and you would see what I would do with it." "No," thought Tchitchikov, "you wouldn't do much good with ten millions. But if I were given ten millions, I really should do something."

"And if I only had ten millions!" thought Hlobuev, "I would not do as I have done in the past, I wouldn't spend it so insanely. After such a terrible experience one learns the value of every farthing. Ah, I should do differently now . . ." And then after a few moments' reflection he inwardly asked himself, "Would you really manage more sensibly now?" and with a gesture of despair, he added, "The devil! I expect I should squander it just the same as before," and going out of the shop he set off to Murazov's, wishing to know what the latter had to tell him.

"I was waiting for you, Pyotr Petrovitch!" said Murazov, seeing Hlobuev as he came in. "Please come into my room," and he drew Hlobuev into the room with which the reader is already familiar, less luxurious than that of a government clerk with a salary of seven hundred roubles a year. "Tell me, I suppose your circumstances are easier now? I suppose you must have got something from your aunt anyway?"

"What shall I say, Afanasy Vassilyevitch? I don't know whether my position is any better. All that came to me was fifty serfs and thirty thousand roubles, with which I shall have to pay part of my debts, and then I shall have absolutely nothing again. And the worst of it is there has been a dirty business about this will. There has been such dishonesty, Afanasy Vassilyevitch! I'll tell you all about it and you will be amazed at the things that have been done. That Tchitchikov . . ."

"Excuse me, Pyotr Petrovitch; but before we talk about that Tchitchikov let me talk about you. Tell me how much in your opinion would be necessary and sufficient to get you out of your difficulties?"

"Why, to get out of my difficulties, to pay off all my debts and to be able to live on the most moderate scale, I should need at least a hundred thousand or more."

"Well, and if you had that how would you arrange your life?"

"Why then I should take a modest flat, devote myself to my children's education, for it is no good for me to go into the service, I am not fit for anything."

"And why are you fit for nothing?"

"Why, what am I fitted for? You can see for yourself that I can't very well begin as a copying clerk. You forget that I have a family. I am forty, already my back aches, I have grown lazy; and they wouldn't give me more important positions; I am not in their good books, you know. I confess that I wouldn't accept what is called a profitable post. I am a good-for-nothing person and a gambler, perhaps, and anything you like, but I am not going to take bribes. I couldn't get on with the Krasnonosovs and the Samosvitovs!"

"All the same, pardon me, I can't understand how one can exist without some path in life; how can you go forward except on a road; how can you advance without the earth under your feet; how can you float when your boat is not in the water? Life, you know, is a journey. Pardon me, Pyotr Petrovitch, but the gentlemen of whom you were speaking are, anyway, on some sort of a road, at any rate they are working. Well, suppose they have turned aside from the straight way, as happens to every simple mortal; still there is hope that they will wander back again. He who goes forward is bound to arrive; there is hope that he may find the road. But how can he who stands idle come upon any road? The road will not come to me, you know."

"Believe me, Afanasy Vassilyevitch, I feel that you are perfectly right . . . but I must tell you that all capacity for action is dead in me; I cannot see that I can be of any service to any one in the world. I feel that I am an absolutely useless log. In old days when I was younger I used to think that it was all a question of money, that if I had had hundreds of thousands, I might have made hundreds of people happy; that I might have helped poor artists, might have founded libraries and made collections. I have some taste and I know that in many respects I could have managed better than those of our own rich men who do all that sort of thing so stupidly. But now I see that that too is vanity and that there is not much sense in it. No, Afanasy Vassilyevitch, I am good for nothing, absolutely nothing, I tell you. I am not fit for any sort of work."

"Listen, Pyotr Petrovitch! You pray and go to church, you miss neither matins nor vespers, I know that. Though you are not fond of early rising you get up early and go to service—you go at four o'clock in the morning when no one is getting up."

"That is a different matter, Afanasy Vassilyevitch. I do that for the salvation of my soul, because I am convinced that thereby I do to some extent make up for my idle life, that however bad I may be, yet humble prayer and some self-denial has a value in the eyes of the Lord. I tell you that I pray, without faith,—but still I pray. I have a feeling that there is a Master on whom everything depends, just as horses and cattle feel they have a rightful master."

"So that you pray to please Him to whom you pray and to save your soul, and that gives you strength and energy to get out of bed. Believe me, that if you would undertake your duties in the same way as you serve Him to whom you pray, you would develop a capacity for action, and nobody would be able to turn you from it."

"Afanasy Vassilyevitch! I tell you again, that's a different thing. In the first case I see anyway what I am doing. I tell you I am ready to go into a monastery, and I would perform the hardest tasks that could be laid upon me because I see for whom I am doing it. It is not for me to reason. In that case I am convinced that those who have set me the task will be called to account; in that case I am obeying, and I know that I am obeying God."

"And why don't you reason in the same way in worldly affairs? You know in the world too we ought to serve God and no one else. If we serve any other it is only because we believe that it is God's will, and except for that we should not. What else are all the capacities and gifts which differ in every man? Why, they are the instruments of our prayer: in the one case in words, and the other in work. You cannot go into a monastery, you know: you are bound to the world, you have a family."

Here Murazov paused. Hlobuev too was silent.

"So you think that if for instance you had two hundred thousand roubles your living would be secure and you could live more prudently in the future?"

"Yes, anyway I should occupy myself with what I should be able to do: I should look after the education of my children, I should have the possibility of getting them good teachers."

"And shall I say to that, Pyotr Petrovitch, that in two years' time you'll be in bondage to debt again as though you were in cords?"

Hlobuev did not speak for a while, then he began hesitatingly:

"Well, after such experiences, though . . ."

"What's the use of arguing about it!" said Murazov. "You are a man with a good heart: if a friend comes to you and asks for a loan—you'll give it to him; if you see a poor man you will want to help him; if a pleasant guest visits you, you will want to entertain him handsomely, and you will give way to your first impulse of kindness, and will forget your prudence! And last of all, allow me to tell you in all sincerity that you are not capable of bringing up your children. Only the father who has not failed in his own duty can educate his children. And your wife too . . . She has a good heart too, but she has not had at all the right education for bringing up children. I even doubt—pardon me, Pyotr Petrovitch—whether it will not be bad for your children to be with you!"

Hlobuev pondered; he began mentally looking at himself from every point of view, and felt that Murazov was to some extent right.

"Do you know what, Pyotr Petrovitch; put all that, the care of your children and your affairs into my hands. Leave your wife and your children, I will take care of them. Your circumstances are such, you know, that you are really in my hands; if things go on like this you'll starve. In your position you must be ready to do anything. Do you know Ivan Potapitch?"

"And I have a great respect for him even though he does go about in a peasant's coat."

"Ivan Potapitch was a millionaire, he married his daughters to officials and lived like a king; when he went bankrupt—what could he do?—he became a clerk. It wasn't pleasant for him to change from a silver dish to a humble bowl: he felt as though he couldn't touch anything. Now Ivan Potapitch could eat from a silver dish but he doesn't care to. He could gather it all together again, but he says: 'No, Afanasy Vassilyevitch, now I serve not myself nor for myself, but because it is God's will. . . . I don't want to do anything to please myself. I listen to you because I want to obey God and not men, and because God speaks only by the lips of the best men. You are wiser than I, and therefore it is not for me to say but for you.' That is what Ivan Potapitch says, but to tell the truth he is many times wiser than I am."

"Afanasy Vassilyevitch! I too am ready to accept your authority over me . . . to be your servant and what you will; I give myself up to you. But do not give me work beyond my strength: I am no Potapitch, and I tell you I am not fit for anything good."

"It is not I, Pyotr Petrovitch, sir, that lay it upon you, but since you would like to be of service as you say yourself, here is a godly work for you. There is a church being built by the voluntary offerings of good people. There is not enough money, it must be collected. Put on the humble coat of a peasant. . . . You know you are a humble man now, a ruined nobleman is no better than a beggar: what's the use of standing on your dignity—with a book in your hand get into a humble cart and go about the towns and the villages; from the bishop you will receive a blessing and a book with the numbered pages, and so God be with you."

Pyotr Petrovitch was amazed at this perfectly new occupation. For him, who was anyway a nobleman of ancient lineage, to set off with a book in his hands, begging for a church and jolting in a cart! But it was impossible to refuse and get out of it; it was a godly work.

"You hesitate?" said Murazov. "You'll be doing two services in this: one a service to God, and another a service to me."

"What is the service to you?"

"This is it. Since you will be travelling about those parts where I have not been, you will find out everything on the spot, how the peasants are living, where they are better off, where they are in need, and in what condition they all are. I must tell you that I love the peasants, perhaps because I've come from the peasantry myself. But the trouble is that all sorts of wickedness have become common among them. The heretics and vagrants of all sorts confound them, and some are even rising up in rebellion against those in authority over them, and if a man is oppressed he will readily rebel. Indeed it is not hard to incite a man who is really ill treated. But the fact is that reforms ought not to begin from below. It's a bad business when men come to blows: there never will be any sense from that—it's a gain to none but the thieves. You are a clever man, you will look about you, you will find out where a man is really suffering from the fault of others, and where from his own restless character, and afterwards you will tell me all about it. In case of need I'll give you a small sum for distribution among those who are really suffering through no fault of their own. It will be serviceable also if you, on your part too, comfort them with words and explain well to them that God has bidden us bear our burdens without repining, and pray when we are unhappy, and not rebel or take matters into our own hands. In fact, speak to them without stirring up one against another and make peace between them. If you see in somebody hatred against any one whatever, do your very utmost."

"Afanasy Vassilyevitch, the work which you entrust to me is holy work," said Hlobuev, "but do think to whom you are entrusting it. You might entrust it to a man of holy life who has himself known how to forgive."

"Well, and I am not saying that you should do all that, but so far as possible do all that you can. Anyway you will come back knowing a great deal about those parts and will have an idea of the condition of that district. An official never gets into personal contact, and the peasant will not be open with them. While you, begging for the church, will have a look at every one,—at the artisan, at the merchant, and will have the chance of questioning every one. I tell you this because the governor-general particularly needs such men; and passing by all official posts you will be receiving one in which your life will not be useless."

"I will try, I will do my best as far as in me lies," said Hlobuev. And there was a perceptible note of confidence in his voice, he straightened his back and held his head up like a man on whom the light of hope has dawned. "I see that God has blessed you with understanding, and you know some things better than we short-sighted people."

"Now allow me to ask you," said Murazov, "what about Tchitchikov, and what's the meaning of this business?"

"I can tell you the most unheard-of things about Tchitchikov. He does such things. . . . Do you know, Afanasy Vassilyevitch, that the will was forged? The real one has been found, in which everything was left to her protégées."

"You don't say so? But who forged the false will?"

"The fact is that it was an abominable business! They say it was Tchitchikov, and that the will was signed after her death: they dressed up some woman to take the place of the deceased, and she it was signed it. It was a scandalous thing in fact. It's suspected that government officials had a hand in it too. They say the governor-general knows about it. They say that thousands of petitions have been sent in. Suitors have turned up for Marya Yeremyevna already; two official persons are fighting over her. So that's what's going on, Afanasy Vassilyevitch!"

"I've heard nothing about it, and it certainly is a shady business. Pavel Ivanovitch Tchitchikov is certainly a most enigmatical person," said Murazov.

"I sent in a petition for myself, too, to remind them that there is a near kinsman . . ."

"They may all fight it out together for me," thought Hlobuev as he went out. "Afanasy Vassilyevitch is no fool. No doubt he has given me this commission with intention. I must carry it out, that's all."

He began thinking about the journey while Murazov was still repeating to himself: "Most enigmatical man, Pavel Ivanovitch Tchitchikov. If only such will and perseverance were devoted to a good object!"

Meanwhile petition after petition poured into the law-courts. Relations turned up of whom nobody had heard before. Just as carrion birds flock about a dead body, so everybody pounced upon the immense property left by the old lady: there were secret reports upon Tchitchikov, upon the forgery of the last will, upon the forgery of the first will also, evidence of the theft and concealment of sums of money. Evidence was even produced incriminating Tchitchikov for the purchase of dead souls and for the smuggling of contraband goods at the time when he was in the Customs. They dug up everything and found out all his previous history. God knows how they scented it out and how they learned it. Evidence was even produced regarding matters of which Tchitchikov supposed that no one knew but himself and four walls. For a time all this was a judicial secret, and had not reached his ears, though a trustworthy note, which he very soon received from his lawyer, gave him some idea that a fine mess was brewing. The note was brief: "I hasten to inform you that there is going to be a great scrimmage; but remember that it never does to be agitated. The great thing is to be calm. We will manage everything." This note completely reassured Tchitchikov. "That man's a real genius," he said when he had read the note. To complete his good humour at that moment the tailor brought his new suit. Tchitchikov conceived an intense desire to behold himself in his new dress-coat of the "flame and smoke of Navarino." He pulled on the breeches which set wonderfully upon him, so that it was a perfect picture. . . . Such thighs . . . it was such a splendid fit, the calves too, the cloth brought out every detail and made them look even more resilient. When he drew the buckle behind him, his stomach was like a drum. He beat on it with a brush, saying: "What a fool he is and yet he completes the picture!" The coat seemed to be even better than the breeches, there was not a wrinkle, it fitted tightly on both sides and flared out at the waist, showing off the smart curve of his figure. On Tchitchikov's remarking that it cut him a little under the left armpit, the tailor immediately smiled: that made it set still better on the figure.

"Set your mind at rest as regards the cut, set your mind at rest," he repeated with undisguised triumph, "there is not a cut like that anywhere in Petersburg."

The tailor himself came from Petersburg and had put upon his sign-board: "Foreign tailor from London and Paris." He was not fond of doing things by halves, and wanted to ram both cities at once down the throats of the other tailors, so that for the future no one should display those names, but might simply write themselves down as coming from some paltry "Carlsruhe" or "Copenhagen."

Tchitchikov paid the tailor with magnanimous liberality, and left alone, began scrutinising himself at his leisure in the looking-glass with the eye of an artist, with aesthetic emotion and *con amore*.* It seemed to make everything even better than before: his cheeks looked more interesting, his chin more alluring, the white collar gave a tone to the cheeks, the dark-blue satin cravat gave a tone to the collar; the new-fashioned fold of the shirt-front gave a tone to the cravat, the rich velvet waistcoat gave a tone to the shirt-front, and the coat of the "smoke and flame of Navarino," shimmering like silk, gave a tone to everything. He turned to the right—it was good! He turned to the left—that was better still! He had the figure of a *kammerherr*,† or of an attaché on a foreign diplomatic mission, or of a gentleman who speaks French so beautifully that a Frenchman is nothing to him, and who even in a rage never demeans himself with a Russian word, but swears in French. Such refinement! Putting his head a little on one side he tried to assume the attitude in which he would address a lady of middle age, and of the most modern culture: it made a perfect picture. Painter, take a brush and paint him! In his delight he cut a little caper after the fashion of an *entrechat*. The chest of drawers shook and a bottle of eau-de-cologne fell on the floor; but this did not trouble him in the least. He very naturally called the bottle a silly thing, and began wondering: "To whom shall I pay my first visit? The best of all . . ."

When all at once in the passage there was a clanking of spurs and behold! a gendarme, fully armed, as though he had been a whole troop of soldiers. "You are commanded to appear before the governor-general this instant!" Tchitchikov was aghast; before him loomed a whiskered monster with a horse's tail on his head, a bandolier over his right shoulder, a bandolier over his left shoulder, a huge sabre hanging at his side. He fancied that on the other side was hanging a gun and God knows what else besides. He was like a whole regiment in himself. Tchitchikov was beginning to protest. The monster said roughly: "You are commanded to come at once!" Through the door

---

*With love (Italian); enthusiastically.
†Chamberlain (German).

in the hall he caught a glimpse of another monster; he looked out of window, there was a carriage. What could he do? Just as he was, in his coat of the "smoke and flame of Navarino" he had to get into it, and trembling all over he drove off with the gendarmes beside him.

They did not even let him get his breath in the hall. "Go in! the prince is expecting you," said the clerk on duty. He caught glimpses, as through a mist, of the hall with the couriers receiving envelopes, then of a big room which he crossed, thinking: "This is how men are seized and without trial, without anything, sent straight to Siberia." His heart beat more violently than the most passionate lover's. At last a door was thrown open before him: and he was confronted with a study, with portfolios, shelves and books, and the prince, the embodiment of anger.

"The author of my ruin!" thought Tchitchikov, "he'll be the ruin of my life," and he almost fell fainting: "he will slay me as a wolf slays a lamb!"

"I spared you, I allowed you to stay in the town when you ought to have been in prison, and you have disgraced yourself again with the foulest dishonesty with which a man has ever disgraced himself." The prince's lips trembled with anger.

"What foul action and dishonesty, your Excellency?" asked Tchitchikov, trembling in every limb.

"The woman who signed the will at your instigation," said the prince, coming closer and looking Tchitchikov straight in the face, "has been arrested and will stand beside you."

Tchitchikov turned as pale as a sheet. "Your Excellency! I will tell you the whole truth of the matter; I am to blame, I am truly to blame, but not so much to blame, my enemies have traduced me."

"No one can traduce you, because your infamy is many times worse than any slander could invent. I believe you have never done anything in your life that was not dishonest. Every farthing you have gained has been gained in some dishonest way, by thieving and dishonesty that deserves the knout and Siberia! No, enough! You will be removed to prison this minute and there, side by side with the lowest scoundrels and robbers, you must wait for your fate to be decided. And even that is too merciful, for you are far worse than they are: they are in smock and sheepskin while you . . ." He glanced at the coat of the "smoke and flame of Navarino," and, taking hold of the bellpull, rang.

"Your Excellency," shrieked Tchitchikov, "be merciful! You are the father of a family. Me I do not ask you to spare, I have an old mother!"

"You are lying," cried the prince wrathfully. "Last time you besought me for the sake of your wife and children, though you haven't any; now it is your mother!"

"Your Excellency! I am a scoundrel and the meanest wretch," said Tchitchikov. "I was lying indeed, I had neither wife nor children; but God is my witness I have always longed to have a wife and to fulfill the duties of a man and a citizen, that I might really deserve the respect of my fellows and my superiors . . . But what a calamitous concatenation of circumstances! With my heart's blood, your Excellency, I have had to earn a bare subsistence. At every step snares and temptation, enemies, and men ready to ruin and plunder me. My whole life has been like a ship on the ocean waves. I am a man, your Excellency!"

Tears suddenly gushed from his eyes. He fell at the prince's feet, just as he was, in his coat of the "smoke and flame of Navarino," in his velvet waistcoat and satin cravat, in his marvellously cut breeches and well-arranged hair that diffused a scent of eau-de-cologne.

"Do not come near me! Call the soldier to take him!" said the prince to the attendant who entered.

"Your Excellency!" cried Tchitchikov, clasping the prince's boot in both arms.

A shudder of repulsion ran through every fibre of the prince.

"Get away, I tell you!" he said, trying to pull his leg out of Tchitchikov's embrace.

"Your Excellency! I will not move from the spot till you have mercy on me!" said Tchitchikov, not letting go his hold but pressing the prince's boot to his bosom, and together with it moving over the floor in his coat of the "smoke and flame of Navarino."

"Get away, I tell you!" said the prince, with that inexplicable feeling of repulsion which a man experiences at the sight of a hideous insect which he cannot bring himself to stamp upon. He shook himself so violently that Tchitchikov got a kick on his cheek, his agreeably rounded chin and teeth; but he did not let go of the foot, but pressed the boot still more warmly in his embrace. Two stalwart gendarmes dragged him away by force, and taking him under the arms led him through all the rooms. He was pale, shattered, in that numbly terrified condition in which a man is thrown who sees before him the black form of inevitable death, that monster so terrible and alien to our nature. . . .

Just in the doorway on the stairs he met Murazov. A ray of hope instantly gleamed upon him. In one instant he tore himself with unnatural force out of the hands of the two gendarmes and fell at the feet of the astounded old man.

"My good sir, Pavel Ivanovitch, what is the matter?"

"Save me! they are taking me to prison, to death. . . ." The gendarmes seized him and led him away, without letting him have a hearing.

A damp stinking cell, smelling of soldiers' boots and leg wrappers, an unpainted table, two wretched chairs, a window with iron gratings, a dilapidated stove which smoked through a crack but gave no heat, this was the abode in which our Tchitchikov, who had just begun to taste the sweets of life and to attract the attention of his countrymen, found himself in his delicate new coat of the "smoke and flame of Navarino." They had not even let him arrange to take the most necessary articles, to take his case in which he had his money, his portmanteau in which he had his wardrobe. His papers relating to his purchase of dead souls, all were now in the hands of the officials! He grovelled on the floor, and the gnawing worm of terrible, hopeless grief coiled about his heart. With increasing rapidity, it began corroding his heart, which was utterly defenceless. Another such day, another day of such misery and there would have been no Tchitchikov left. But some one was keeping vigilant watch over Tchitchikov and holding out a hand to save him. An hour after he had reached his terrible plight, the doors of the prison opened, and old Murazov walked in.

If a draught of spring water were poured down the throat of a man tortured by burning thirst he would not have been so revived as poor Tchitchikov.

"My saviour!" said Tchitchikov, jumping up from the floor on which he had flung himself in heartrending grief; instantly he kissed his hand and pressed it to his bosom. "God will reward you for visiting the unhappy!"

He burst into tears.

The old man looked at him with an expression of pain and distress and said only: "Ah, Pavel Ivanovitch! Pavel Ivanovitch, what have you done!"

"I have done everything that the basest man might have done. But judge, judge, can I be treated like this? I am a nobleman. Without trial, without inquiry I have been flung into prison, everything has been taken from me: my things, my case . . . there is money in it, property, all my property, Afanasy Vassilyevitch, the property I have acquired by blood and sweat. . . ."

And unable to restrain the rush of fresh grief that flooded his heart he sobbed loudly on a note which carried through the thick walls of the prison and resounded with a hollow echo in the distance, he tore off his satin cravat and gripping himself near his collar tore his coat of the "flame and smoke of Navarino."

"Pavel Ivanovitch, anyway you must take leave of your property and of everything in the world: you have fallen under the sway of implacable law and not under the authority of any man."

"I have been my own ruin, I feel that I have been my own ruin. I could not stop in time. But what is such a fearful punishment for, Afanasy Vassilyevitch! Am I a robber? Have I made any one unhappy? By toil and sweat, by bloody sweat I have made my hard-earned kopecks. What have I made my money for? To live out the remnant of my days in comfort, to leave something to my wife and the children whom I had intended to have for the welfare, for the service of my country. I have not been straightforward, I admit it . . . what could I do? for I saw that I could never get there by the straight road, and that the shortest way was by the crooked path. But I have toiled, I have exerted myself. While those blackguards who take thousands in the courts—and not as though it were from the government—they rob poor people of their last kopeck, they fleece those who have nothing! Afanasy Vassilyevitch, I have not been profligate, I've not been drunken. . . . And what toil, what iron endurance I have shown! Yes I have, I may say, paid for every kopeck I have gained by suffering, suffering! Let any one of them endure what I have! What, what has all my life been? A bitter struggle, a ship tossing in the waves. And all at once to be deprived of what I have earned, Afanasy Vassilyevitch, of what I have won by such struggles . . ." He could not finish but broke into loud sobs with an unbearable ache in his heart. He sank on to a chair and tore the rent skirt of his smart coat completely off, flung it to a distance and putting both hands up to his hair, of which he had always taken such scrupulous care, tore it mercilessly, taking pleasure in the pain by which he hoped to stifle the insufferable ache in his heart.

"Ah, Pavel Ivanovitch, Pavel Ivanovitch!" said Murazov, looking mournfully at him and shaking his head. "I keep thinking what a man you might have made if with the same energy and patience you had applied yourself to honest labour and for a better object! If only any one of those who care for what is good had used as much energy in its service as you have to gain your kopecks! . . . And had been capable of sacrificing personal vanity and pride, without sparing himself, for a good cause as you have done to gain your kopecks!"

"Afanasy Vassilyevitch!" said poor Tchitchikov, and he clutched the old man's hands in both of his. "Oh, if I could but be set free and could regain my property! I swear to you that I would lead a very different life from this hour! Save me, benefactor, save me!"

"What can I do? I should have to fight against the law. Even supposing I brought myself to do that, the prince is a just man, nothing would induce him to transgress it."

"Benefactor! you can do anything. It is not the law that terrifies me—I can find means for outwitting the law—but the fact that . . . I have been flung into prison, that I am lying here abandoned like a dog, while my property, my papers, my case . . . save me!"

He embraced the old man's feet and watered them with his tears.

"Ah, Pavel Ivanovitch, Pavel Ivanovitch!" said the old man, shaking his head. "That property has blinded you! For the sake of it you have not thought of your poor soul."

"I will think of my poor soul too, but save me!"

"Pavel Ivanovitch!" said Murazov, and he paused. "To save you is not in my power, you see it yourself. But I will do everything I can to alleviate your lot and set you free. I don't know whether I shall succeed in doing that, but I will try. If I should succeed beyond my expectation, Pavel Ivanovitch, I beg of you a favour in return for my trouble; abandon all these crooked means of making gain. I tell you on my honour that if I were deprived of all my property—and I have more than you—I should not weep. Aie, aie, it is not those possessions which can be confiscated that matter, but those which no one can steal or take away from us! You have lived in the world long enough. You yourself call your life a ship tossing in the waves. You have already enough to last you for the rest of your days. Settle in a quiet corner near to a church and to good simple people, or if you are possessed by a great desire to leave descendants, marry a good girl, not rich but accustomed to moderation and simple housekeeping (and truly you will not regret it). Forget this noisy world and all its alluring luxuries, let it forget you too. There is no peacefulness in it. You see that all in it are enemies, tempters or traitors."

Tchitchikov pondered. Something strange, feelings hitherto unknown to him which he could not account for, rose in his heart: it seemed as though something were trying to awaken in him, something suppressed from childhood by the harsh, dead discipline of his dreary boyhood, by the desolateness of his home, his solitude, the niggardliness and poverty of his first impressions, and as though something, in bondage to the stern fate that looked mournfully at him as through a window darkened by the snowstorms of winter, were trying to break its chains.

"Only save me, Afanasy Vassilyevitch!" he cried, "and I will lead a different life, I will follow your advice! I give you my word."

"Mind, Pavel Ivanovitch, there is no going back from your word," said Murazov, holding his hand.

"I might go back from it perhaps, had it not been for this terrible lesson," said poor Tchitchikov with a sigh, and he added: "but the lesson is bitter; a bitter, bitter lesson, Afanasy Vassilyevitch!"

"It is a good thing it is bitter. Thank God for it, and pray to Him. I will go and do my best." Saying this the old man withdrew.

Tchitchikov no longer wept or tore his coat and hair; he was calm.

"Yes, it is enough!" he said at last, "a different life, a different life! It is high time indeed to become a decent man. Oh, if only I can somehow get out of this and go off with only a little capital, I will settle far away. . . . If I can but get back my papers . . . and the deeds of purchase . . ." he mused a little: "well? why abandon that which I have gained with such labour? I won't buy any more but I must mortgage those. Getting them cost me such labour! I shall mortgage them so as to buy an estate with the money. I shall become a landowner, because one can do a great deal of good in that position."

And the feelings which had taken possession of him when he was at Skudronzhoglo's rose up in his heart again, and he recalled the latter's charming clever talk about the fruitfulness and usefulness of work on the land as he sat in the warm evening light. The country suddenly seemed to him delightful, as though he had been able at the moment to feel all its charms.

"We are foolish, we race after vanity!" he said at last. "Really it is from idleness! Everything is near, everything is at hand, but we run to the ends of the earth. Is not life as good if one is buried in the wilds? Pleasure is really to be found in work. Skudronzhoglo is right. And nothing is sweeter than the fruit of one's own labours. . . . Yes, I will work, I will settle in the country, and I will work honestly so as to have a good influence on others. Why, I am not utterly good-for-nothing, am I? I have the very abilities for making a good manager; I have the qualities of carefulness, promptitude, good sense and even perseverance. I have only to make up my mind. Only now I feel truly and clearly that there is a duty which a man ought to perform on earth, without tearing himself away from the place and the niche in which he has been placed."

And a life of toil, away from the noise of cities and from all the temptations that man has devised in his idleness, rose up before him in such vivid colours that he almost forgot all the horror of his position, and perhaps was even ready to thank providence for this bitter trial, if only they would release him, and let him have at least a part of his property. But . . . the door of his filthy prison opened and there walked in a certain official, one Samosvitov, an epicure, a capital companion, a rake and a sly beast as his colleagues said of him. In time of war this man would have performed marvels: he would have been sent to make his way through impassable dangerous places, to steal a cannon from under the very nose of the enemy, that would have been the very task for him. But lacking a military career he had thrown his energies into civil life, and, instead of feats for which he would have been with good reason decorated, he did all sorts of nasty and abominable things. Incredible to relate, he was quite good to his comrades, he never sold them to any one, and when he had given a promise he kept it; but those in authority over him he regarded as something like the battery of the enemy through which he had to make his way, taking advantage of every weak spot or gap in their defences. . . .

"We know all about your position, we've heard all about it!" he said, when he saw that the door was close shut behind him. "Never mind, never mind! Don't be downcast, everything will be put right. We will all work for you and are your servants! Thirty thousand for all and nothing more!"

"Really," cried Tchitchikov, "and shall I be entirely acquitted?"

"Entirely! And you will get compensation too for damages."

"And for your trouble? . . ."

"Thirty thousand, that's for all together—for our fellows and for the governor-general's and for the secretary."

"But excuse me, how can I—all my things, my writing-case. . . . It's all been sealed up now, under guard. . . ."

"Within an hour you shall have it all. You shake hands on it, eh?"

Tchitchikov gave his hand. His heart was throbbing, and he could not believe that it was possible. . . .

"Farewell for the time then! Our mutual friend commissioned me to tell you that the great thing is calm and presence of mind."

"H'm!" thought Tchitchikov. "I understand, the lawyer!"

Samosvitov withdrew. Tchitchikov left alone was still unable to believe what he had said, when, less than an hour after their conversation, his case was brought him, with papers, money and everything in perfect order. Samosvitov had gone as though armed with authority, he had scolded the sentinels for not being careful enough, had ordered the man in charge to put more soldiers on watch for greater security, had not only taken the case, but had even removed from it all papers that could have compromised Tchitchikov in any way; he had tied all this up together, put a seal on it and commanded the very same soldier to take it promptly to Tchitchikov himself under cover of necessaries for the night, so that Tchitchikov received together with his papers all the warm things needed for covering his frail body. It delighted him unutterably to receive this so quickly. He was buoyed up by fresh hopes and already beginning again to dream of certain things; an evening at the theatre, a dancer after whom he was dangling. The country and a peaceful life began to seem duller while the town with its noise and bustle was more full of colour and brighter again. . . . Oh, life!

Meanwhile the case was developing into unlimited proportions in the courts and legal offices. The clerks' pens were busily at work and the legal bigwigs were deeply engaged, as they took their snuff with the feelings of an artist admiring their own crooked handiwork. Tchitchikov's lawyer was working the whole mechanism unseen, like a hidden magician; before any one had time to look round he had them all in a complete tangle. The case grew more and more complicated. Samosvitov excelled himself in his incredible audacity and the boldness of his schemes. Having found out where the woman who had been arrested was in custody, he went straight to the place and walked in with such swagger and authority, that the sentry saluted him and stood at attention.

"Have you been standing here long?"

"Since the morning, your honour."

"Is it long before you are relieved?"

"Three hours, your honour."

"I shall want you. I'll tell the officer to send another to take your place."

"Certainly, your honour."

And going home without a minute's delay he dressed up as a gendarme himself, repaired to the house where Tchitchikov was under guard, seized the first woman he came across and handed her over to two bold young officials who were also adepts and went off himself in his whiskers, with a gun in his hand, to the sentinel:

"You can go, the commanding officer sent me to take your place." He changed guns with the sentry. That was all that was wanted. Meanwhile the place of the first woman arrested was filled by another who knew nothing about the case, and did not understand what was said to her. The first was hidden away so effectually that it was never discovered what had become of her.

While Samosvitov was hard at work disguised as a warrior, Tchitchikov's lawyer was working miracles on the civilian side. He let the governor know in a roundabout way that the prosecutor was writing a secret report about him; he let the gendarmes' clerk hear that an official staying secretly in the town was writing a report against him, while he assured this secret official that there was a still more secret official who was giving information about him, and he brought them all into such a position that they were obliged to come to him for advice.

A regular chaos followed: there was one report on the top of another, and things were on the way of being discovered, such as the sun has never looked upon, and, indeed, such as did not exist at all. Everything was turned to account and brought into the case: the fact that so-and-so was an illegitimate son, and that so-and-so was of such an origin and calling, that so-and-so had a mistress, and whose wife was flirting with whom. Scandals, moral lapses and all sorts of things were so mixed up and intertwined with the story of Tchitchikov and of the dead souls, that it was utterly impossible to make out what was most nonsensical: it all seemed equally absurd. When the papers relating to the case began at last to reach the governor-general, the poor prince could make nothing of them. A very clever and efficient clerk who was commissioned to make a synopsis of them almost went out of his mind; it was utterly impossible to get a connected view of the case. The prince was worried at the time by a number of other matters, one more unpleasant than the other. There was famine in one part of the province. The officials sent to distribute bread had not carried out the relief work properly. In another part of the province heretics began to be active. Some one had spread a rumour among them that an Antichrist had appeared who would not leave even the dead in peace and was buying up dead souls. They did penance and sinned, and on the pretext of catching the Antichrist they made short work of persons who were not the Antichrist. In another district the peasants were revolting against the landowners and the police captains. Some vagrants had spread rumours among them that the time was at hand when the peasants were to become landowners and wear dress-coats, while the landowners were to wear sheep-skins and become peasants, and the whole district, without reflecting that there would be far too many landowners and police captains, refused to pay their taxes. Forcible measures had to be resorted to. The poor prince was greatly distracted. Just then word was brought him that Murazov had come.

"Show him in," said the prince.

The old man walked in. . . .

"So this is your Tchitchikov! You stood up for him and defended him. Now he is mixed up in a crime at which the lowest thief would hesitate."

"Allow me to say, your Excellency, that I don't quite understand the case."

"To forge a will and in such a way. . . . A public flogging is a fit punishment for such a crime."

"Your Excellency—I do not say it to defend Tchitchikov—but you know it is an unproved charge: the case has not yet been investigated."

"There is evidence: the woman who was dressed up to personate the deceased has been arrested, I will question her in your presence to show you."

The prince rang the bell and ordered the woman to be brought—"The one who was arrested," he said to the attendant.

Murazov was silent.

"It's a most disgraceful affair! And shameful to say, the leading officials of the town and the governor himself are mixed up in it. He ought not to be among the thieves and vagabonds," said the prince with warmth.

"Well, the governor is a kinsman, he has a right to make a claim; and as for the others who are grabbing at it on all sides, that, your Excellency, is the way of mankind. A wealthy woman has died without making a just and sensible disposition of her property, men have rushed in on all sides eager to get something; that is the way of mankind. . . ."

"But why do such dirty things? . . . The scoundrels!" said the prince, with indignation. "I haven't a single good official, they are all blackguards."

"Your Excellency! but which of us is as good as we should be? All the officials of our town are men, they have their qualities, and many are very capable at their work, but every one is liable to err."

"Listen, Afanasy Vassilyevitch, tell me—you are the only man I know to be an honest man—how is it you have this passion for defending every sort of scoundrel?"

"Your Excellency," said Murazov, "whoever the man may be whom you call a scoundrel, still he is a man. How can one help defending a man when half the evil deeds that he commits are due to coarseness and ignorance. We do unjust things at every step and not with evil intention. Why, your Excellency, you too have been guilty of great injustice."

"What!" cried the prince in amazement, completely taken aback by this unexpected turn in the conversation.

Murazov paused as though considering something, and said at last: "Well, in the case of Derpennikov for instance."

"Why, do you mean to say that I was unjust? a crime against the fundamental laws of the realm, equivalent to a betrayal of his country! . . ."

"I am not justifying him. But is it just to condemn a youth who has been seduced and led astray by others through inexperience, as though he were one of the instigators? Why, the same punishment has been given to Derpennikov as to Voronov-Dryanov; and yet their crimes are not the same."

"For God's sake," said the prince with visible emotion. "Do you know something about it? Tell me. I have only lately sent to Petersburg to mitigate his punishment."

"No, your Excellency, I am not speaking because I know something you don't know. Though indeed there is one circumstance which would be in his favour, but he will not himself agree to make use of it, because it will bring trouble on another man. All I think is that your Excellency may have been in too great a hurry then. Pardon me, but to my weak understanding it seems as though a man's previous life should also be taken into consideration, for if one does not look into everything coolly, but makes an outcry from the first, one only terrifies him and gets no real confession; while, if one questions him with sympathy as man to man, he will tell everything of himself and not even ask for mitigation of his sentence, and will feel no bitterness against any one, because he sees clearly that it is not I that am punishing him but the law."

The prince pondered. At that moment an official came in and stood waiting respectfully with his portfolio. There was a look of hard work and anxiety on his still young and fresh face. It could be seen that it was not for nothing that he served on special commissions. He was one of those few officials who do their work *con amore*. Not excited by ambition nor desire of gain, nor imitation of others, he worked simply because he was convinced that he ought to be here and in no other place, and that this was the object of his life. To investigate, to analyse, and after extricating all the threads of a tangled case, to make it clear was his task. And his toil and his efforts and his sleepless nights were abundantly rewarded if the case at last began to grow clear before his eyes, and its hidden causes to be laid bare, and he felt he could present it all clearly and distinctly in full words. One may say no schoolboy rejoices more when some difficult sentence is unravelled and the real meaning of a great writer's thought becomes apparent to him, than he rejoiced when an intricate case was disentangled. On the other hand . . .

(A page of the manuscript was torn out at this point and a gap appears in the narrative.)

. . . "with bread in the parts where there is famine, I know that region better than the officials do: I will find out personally what each one needs. And if you will permit me, your Excellency, I will talk with the heretics too. They will talk more readily with a plain man like me, so God knows, maybe I shall help to settle things with them peacefully. And I will take no money from you because, upon my word, I am ashamed to think of my own gain at such a time when men are dying of hunger. I have a store of bread in readiness, and I have sent to Siberia, and they will bring me more again the coming summer."

"God only can reward you, Afanasy Vassilyevitch, I will not say one word to you, for—you may feel it yourself—no word is strong enough for it. But let me say one thing in regard to your request. Tell me yourself: have I the right to leave this case uninvestigated, and will it be honest on my part to forgive the scoundrels?"

"Your Excellency, indeed you must not call them that, for many among them are worthy men. A man's circumstances are often very difficult, your Excellency, very, very difficult. It sometimes happens that a man seems to blame all round and when you go into it, he is not the culprit at all."

"But what will they say to themselves if I drop it? You know there are some among them who will give themselves more airs than ever after that, and will even say that they have frightened me. They will be the last to respect . . ."

"Your Excellency, allow me to give you my opinion: gather them all together, let them understand that you know all about it, and put before them your own position in exactly the same way as you have graciously done just now before me, and ask them to tell you what each of them would do in your place."

"But do you imagine that they will be capable of an impulse towards anything more honourable than legal quibbling and filling their pockets? I assure you they will laugh at me."

"I don't think so, your Excellency. Every Russian, even one worse than the average, has right feelings. Perhaps a Jew might do so, but not a Russian. No, your Excellency, there is no need for you to be reserved. Tell them exactly as you graciously told me. You know they speak ill of you as a proud, ambitious man who believes in himself and will listen to nothing,—so let them see how it really is. Why need you be afraid of them? You are in the right. Tell them as though you were making your confession, not to them but to God Himself."

"Afanasy Vassilyevitch," said the prince hesitatingly, "I will think about that, and meanwhile I thank you very much for your advice."

"And bid them release Tchitchikov, your Excellency."

"Tell that Tchitchikov to get out of the place as quickly as possible, and the further he goes the better. Him I could never forgive."

Murazov bowed and went straight from the prince to Tchitchikov. He found Tchitchikov with cheerfulness already restored, very placidly engaged upon a fairly decent dinner, which had been brought him on china dishes from a very respectable kitchen. From the first sentences of their conversation the old man at once perceived that Tchitchikov had already succeeded in making a secret plan with some one of the tricky officials. He even divined that the unseen hand of the sharp lawyer had some share in this.

"Listen, Pavel Ivanovitch," he said: "I have brought you freedom on condition that you leave the town at once. Collect all your belongings and go in God's name, without putting it off for a minute, for something worse is coming. I know there is a man who is behind you; so I must tell you in secret that there is something else being discovered, and that no power will save that man now. He of course is glad to drag others down for company and to share the blame. I left you in a very good frame of mind, better than your present one. I am advising you in earnest. Aie, aie, what really matters is not the possessions over which men dispute and for which they murder each other, exactly as though it were possible to gain prosperity in this life without thinking of another life. Believe me, Pavel Ivanovitch, that until men reject everything for which men rend and devour each other on earth, and think of the welfare of their spiritual possessions, it will not be well even with their earthly possessions. Days of hunger and poverty are coming for all the people, and each one severally . . . that is clear. Whatever you say, you know, the body depends on the soul, how then can you expect things to thrive as they ought? Think not of dead souls but of your own living soul, and in God's name take a different path! I too am leaving the town on the morrow. Make haste or when I am gone there will be trouble."

Saying this the old man went out. Tchitchikov sank into thought. Again the significance of life seemed to him something worthy of consideration. "Murazov is right," he said to himself, "it is time to take another path!" Saying this he went out of his prison. The sentry carried his case after him. Selifan and Petrushka were indescribably delighted at their master's release.

"Well, my good lads," said Tchitchikov, addressing them graciously, "we must pack up and set off."

"We'll drive in fine style, Pavel Ivanovitch," said Selifan. "The road's firm I'll be bound, snow enough has fallen. It certainly is high time to get out of the town. I am so sick of it I can't bear the sight of it."

"Go to the carriage-maker's and get the carriage put on runners instead of wheels," said Tchitchikov. He himself went off to the town, not that he was anxious to pay farewell visits to any one. It would have been rather awkward after all that had happened, especially as there were the most discreditable stories going about the town concerning him. He even avoided meeting any one and only went as stealthily as possible to the merchant's from whom he had bought the cloth of the "flame and smoke of Navarino," he took four yards for a coat and breeches, and went off with it himself to the same tailor. For double the price the latter undertook to work at the highest pressure, and set the tailoring population plying their needles, their irons and their teeth all night by candle-light, and the coat was ready next day, though a little late. The horses were all harnessed and waiting. Tchitchikov tried on the coat, however. It was splendid, exactly like the first. But alas! he noticed a smooth white patch upon his head, and murmured sorrowfully: "What reason was there to abandon myself to such despair? I oughtn't to have torn out my hair anyway." After settling with the tailor he drove out of the town at last in a strange frame of mind. This was not the old Tchitchikov; this was a sort of wreck of the old Tchitchikov. The inner state of his soul might be compared with a building that has been pulled down to be rebuilt into a new one, and the new one has not yet been begun, because no definite plan has come from the architect, and the workmen are left in suspense.

An hour earlier old Murazov had set off together with Potapitch in a covered cart, and an hour after Tchitchikov's departure an order went forth that the prince wished to see all the officials, every one of them, on the eve of his departure for Petersburg.

In the big hall of the governor-general's house, all the officials of the town were gathered together, from the governor to the humblest titular councillor, chiefs of offices and of departments, councillors, assessors, Kisloyedov, Samosvitov, those who had not taken bribes, and those who had taken bribes, those who had disregarded their conscience, those who had half disregarded it, and those who had not disregarded it at all—all awaited the prince's appearance with a curiosity that was not quite free from uneasiness. The prince came out to them neither gloomy nor severe; there was a calm determination in his step and his glance. All the assembled officials bowed, many making a deep bow from the waist. Acknowledging their greeting with a slight bow, the prince began:

"On the eve of my departure for Petersburg I have thought it proper to have an interview with all of you and even to some extent to explain to you the cause of my departure. A very scandalous affair has been set going among us. I imagine that many of those present know of what affair I am speaking. That affair led to the discovery of others no less dishonourable, in which persons, whom I had hitherto regarded as honest, were actually mixed up. I am aware, indeed, that it was the secret aim in this way to make the affair so intricate that it might turn out to be absolutely impossible to deal with it in the regular way. I know, indeed, who was the chief agent in this, though he very skilfully concealed his share in it. But I beg to inform you that I intend to deal with this matter not by the regular method of investigation through documentary evidence, but by direct court martial as in time of war, and I trust that the Tsar will give me the right to do so, when I lay this case before him. In such circumstances as these, when there is no possibility of conducting a case in accordance with civil law, when boxes of papers have been burned and when efforts are made by a vast mass of false evidence and lying reports to obscure a case which was somewhat obscure originally—I imagine that a court martial is the only resource left, and I should like to know your opinion."

The prince stopped, as though expecting an answer. All stood with their eyes on the floor, many were pale.

"I know, too, of another crime, though those who committed it are fully convinced that it can be known to no one. This case will not be conducted in writing, for I myself shall be the defendant and petitioner, and shall bring forward convincing evidence."

Some one shuddered among the officials, several of the more timorous were overcome with confusion.

"It goes without saying that those principally responsible must be punished by deprivation of rank and property, and the rest by dismissal from their posts. It goes without saying, that a number of the innocent will suffer, too. It cannot be helped, the case is too disgraceful and cries aloud for legal justice. Though I know that it will not even be a lesson to others, because others will come to take the place of those dismissed, and the very ones who have hitherto been honest will become dishonest, and the very ones who will be deemed worthy of trust will sell and betray that trust—in spite of all that, I must act cruelly, for justice cries aloud, and so you must all look upon me as the callous instrument of justice."

A shudder involuntarily passed over all their faces.

The prince was calm, his face expressed neither wrath nor indignation.

"Now the very man in whose hands the fate of many lies and whom no supplications could have softened, that very man flings himself now at your feet and entreats you all. All will be forgotten, effaced and forgiven, I will myself be the advocate for all if you grant my request. Here it is. I know that by no means, by no terrors, by no punishments can dishonesty be eradicated. It is too deeply rooted. The dishonest practice of taking bribes has become necessary and inevitable, even for such who are not born to be dishonest. I know that it is almost impossible for many to run counter to the general tendency. But I must now, as at the decisive and sacred moment when it is our task to save our country, when every citizen bears every burden and makes every sacrifice—I must appeal to those at least who still have a Russian heart and who have still some understanding of the word 'honour.' What is the use of discussing which is the more guilty among us! I am perhaps the most guilty of all; I perhaps received you too sternly at first: perhaps by excessive suspicion I repelled those among you who sincerely wished to be of use to me. If they really cared for justice and the good of their country, they ought not to have been offended by the haughtiness of my manner, they ought to overcome their own vanity and sacrifice their personal dignity. It is not possible that I should not have noticed their self-denial and lofty love of justice and should not at last have accepted useful and sensible advice from them. It is anyway more suitable for a subordinate to adapt himself to the character of his chief than for a chief to adapt himself to the character of a subordinate. It is more lawful anyway and easier, because the subordinates have only one chief, while the chief has hundreds of subordinates. But let us lay aside the question of who is most to blame. The point is that it is our task to save our country, that our country is in danger now, not from the invasion of twenty foreign races, but from ourselves; that, besides our lawful government, another rule has been set up, far stronger than any lawful one. Its conditions are established, everything has its price, and the prices are a matter of common knowledge. And no ruler, though he were wiser than all the legislators and governors, can cure the evil however he may curtail the activity of bad officials, by putting them under the supervision of other officials. All will be fruitless until every one of us feels that just as at the epoch of the rising up of all the peoples he was armed against the enemy, he must now take his stand against dishonesty. As a Russian, as one bound to you by ties of birth and blood, I must now appeal to you. I appeal to those among you who have some conception of what is meant by an honourable way of thinking. I invite you to remember the duty which stands before a man in every position. I invite you to look more closely into your duty and the obligation of your earthly service for we all have as yet but a dim understanding of it, and we scarcely. . . ."

THE END

INSPIRED BY DEAD SOULS

> I am interested only in "nonsense"; only in that
> which makes no practical sense. I am interested in
> life only in its absurd manifestations.
>
> —Daniil Kharms

Russian Literature

French literary historian Melchior de Vogüé once wrote, "We have all come out of Gogol's 'Overcoat.' " The metaphor, which refers to one of Nikolai Gogol's best-known stories, expresses the widespread belief that Gogol (and his renowned contemporary Alexander Pushkin [1799–1837], sometimes referred to as the Russian Shakespeare) are the forefathers of modern Russian literature.

Gogol was a popular author in his own lifetime: By the time his play *The Government Inspector* (1836) and his novel *Dead Souls: A Poem* (1842) were published, the reading public was clamoring for his works, and later progenitors of Russian literary realism—such as Ivan Turgenev (1818–1883), Leo Tolstoy (1828–1910), and Anton Chekhov (1860–1904), all often held up as antitheses of Gogol— were obliged to respond to the fabulist's ubiquitous influence. As translator Constance Garnett wrote, "The influence of Gogol may be traced in all the great writers that came after him. His realism, his humanity and irony, his 'laughter through tears' have given to all that is best in Russian literature its distinctive character."

One of the first writers to exemplify Gogol's influence was Fyodor Dostoevsky (1821–1881), author of many of Russia's greatest novels: *Crime and Punishment* (1866), *The Idiot* (1868), *The Possessed* (1871–1872), and *The Brothers Karamazov* (1879–1880). Dostoevsky's *Notes from Underground* (1864) exhibits many parallels with Gogol's "Diary of a Madman" (1835), which, along with "The Nose," is one of Gogol's best-known stories. The sympathy with which the impoverished, somewhat repellent czarist clerk Akaky Akakievitch is depicted in "The Overcoat" (1842) so compelled Dostoevsky that he attempted similar characterizations in Poor Folk, his first novel and the work that brought Dostoevsky to the public eye. The novel's main character, Makar Dyevushkin, in the words of Dostoevsky biographer Joseph Frank, "is a humble, socially and emotionally downtrodden clerk in the vast Russian bureaucracy of St. Petersburg, frightened to death at his temerity in questioning, even in thought, the supreme virtues of the God-ordained order in which he lives." In other words Dyevushkin—who in the course of the novel reads "The Overcoat," as well as Pushkin's "The Stationmaster"—in many ways resembles Akaky Akakievitch. The major change Dostoevsky rang on Gogol's work was getting inside Dyevushkin's head—that is, Dostoevsky had the ability to convey the psychology of his hero in addition to his outward appearance. When Nikolai Nekrasov, a poet and friend of Dostoevsky's, presented the Poor Folk manuscript to the critic Vissarion Belinsky, Belinsky declared, "A new Gogol has appeared!"

Russian novelist Ivan Aleksandrovitch Goncharov (1812–1891), whom Dostoevsky referred to in his diary as "one of my favorite writers," is best remembered for Oblomov (1859), a satirical and darkly humorous indictment of the aristocracy. The work finds its roots in Dead Souls. Serving as a government official for almost thirty years, Goncharov was no doubt keenly aware of such passages by Gogol as:

> "We must have witnesses, two at least for each party. Send now to the prosecutor: he is a man of leisure and no doubt he is at home now. Zolotuha the attorney, the most grasping scoundrel on earth, does all his work for him. The inspector of the medical board is another gentleman of leisure and sure to be at home, unless he has gone off somewhere for a game of cards; and there are lots of others, too, somewhat nearer, Truhatchevsky, Byegushkin—they all cumber the earth and do nothing" (p. 147).

Now regarded as one of Russia's paradigmatic novels, Oblomov is steadfast in its condemnation of nineteenth-century Russia's feudal society; in many ways it complements Gogol's critique of serfdom. Much of Goncharov's legacy is also the stuff of grim irony. For more than ten years—including the time when he was writing Oblomov—the author worked as a censor, a highly paid post with the benefit of an annual holiday.

Russian novelist and dramatist Mikhail Bulgakov (1891–1940) carried Gogol's sensibilities into the twentieth century, although many of his works were bowdlerized under Stalin's repressive regime. Bulgakov's affinity with Gogol was first evidenced by his 1922 story "The Adventures of Tchitchikov," and a theme that runs through his works is the kind of corruption at which Gogol's Tchitchikov excelled. Much of Bulgakov's writing is highly critical of Stalin's government; nevertheless, throughout the latter half of his literary career he enjoyed a singularly intimate relationship with Stalin, and many of his plays were revived by the state-run Moscow Art Theater.

Bulgakov's masterpiece is The Master and Margarita. Bulgakov wrote the novel between 1928 and 1940—a period during which he also produced a stage adaptation of Dead Souls. This was a dark era of Russian history, during which the intelligentsia was systematically intimidated and silenced. Bulgakov kept his novel a secret during his lifetime. It was posthumously serialized by the monthly Moskva in 1966 and 1967 in a severely censored form. The first unexpurgated edition of The Master and Margarita was finally published in 1973. A work of astonishing originality—it is a comic satire both of 1930s Moscow and of the corruption present at the birth of Christianity in Jerusalem—it is the most "Gogolesque" work written in the twentieth century.

Most often described as a fantasy, The Master and Margarita revolves around three characters: Professor Woland, a stranger to Moscow who, it becomes clear, is Satan himself; the master, an unnamed writer who pens a novel about the strange, apocryphal relationship between Jesus and Pontius Pilate; and Margarita, based on Bulgakov's third wife, Elena Sergeevna. The novel begins with the arrival of Woland, attended by a retinue of over-the-top demons. His picaresque frolics—baffling to average Muscovites—are intercut with scenes of the master's novel, which, finally, he burns. But, as Woland famously argues, "manuscripts don't burn." Other explicitly theatrical supernatural elements featured in The Master and Margarita include witch-style broom-flying, a magic show in which bank notes that later alchemize into worthless paper deluge the audience, a vampire attack, and what amounts to teleportation and time travel.

Bulgakov's paramount accomplishment, aside from drawing audacious parallels between Stalin and Caesar—tantamount to a death wish in the Soviet era of official erasure and dreaded gulag sentences—was his improvement upon the narrative voice Gogol employed in Dead Souls. As acclaimed translator Richard Pevear wrote: "There is no multiplicity of narrators in [The Master and Margarita]. The voice is always the same. But it has unusual range, picking up, parodying, or ironically undercutting the tones of the novel's many characters, with undertones of lyric and epic poetry and old popular tales." In the face of soul-crushing totalitarianism, Bulgakov's masterful novel elevates the artist's position above those who blindly push bureaucratic papers, but stops short of consigning artists to sainthood.

Bulgakov's contemporary Daniil Kharms (1905–1942) is another literary descendant of Gogol's absurd humor and grotesqueries. Many critics acknowledge Kharms's debt to Gogol and commonly compare the two for, among other things, their humor, their irreverence, and their suspicion of government. Kharms is widely considered the most important figure in twentieth-century Russian absurdism, a movement categorized as "leftist art" during the Soviet Era. The rise of Stalinism increasingly resulted in the denigration, shunning, and attempted obliteration of the experimentalist art movement. In 1941 Kharms was arrested and died in prison the following year. Though he published only a handful of poems and sketches during his lifetime, he left a substantial body of highly original work. Kharms's writing is pointedly and brilliantly irreverent toward national customs, government, and literary tradition. In his hilarious sketch "Pushkin and Gogol," the two progenitors of modern Russian literature are portrayed as the clumsiest oafs that ever walked onto a stage; indeed, only one stands upright at any given time. The duo continually fumble about, stumble over one another, and fall to the floor; all the while, the silver-tongued writers blurt oaths such as "Vile abomination!" and "Hooliganism! Sheer hooliganism!"

Another of Gogol's strange legacies to Kharms is the former's inability to complete Dead Souls, which Gogol intended to be a trilogy following the same trajectory as Dante's *Inferno*. Gogol burned various manuscripts of the second part of *Dead Souls*, and Kharms often intentionally undermines his writing by cutting it short with a halting and contradictory phrase, or allowing it to unravel altogether. In one of his best-known "incidences," "Blue Notebook No. 10, or 'The Red-Haired Man'," Kharms concludes his physical description of a man—which self-destructs midway through—by saying "There's no knowing whom we are even talking about. In fact it's better that we don't say any more about him."

Opera

Russian composer Rodion Shchedrin (born 1932) spent ten years of his life adapting *Dead Souls* into a three-act opera. The result, which premiered at Moscow's Bolshoi Theater in 1977, features Shchedrin's signature mélange of neoclassicism, pop, jazz, and traditional Soviet symphonic music (exemplified by Sergey Prokofiev and Dmitry Shostakovitch). This tapestry of styles lends itself perfectly to the various misadventures of the insidious, oft-slandered Tchitchikov. Shchedrin wrote his own libretto for the opera. His music is by turns somber, bombastic, and dissonant—but always concise and forward-moving. Shchedrin also adapted Tolstoy's novel *Anna Karenina* and Chekhov's play *The Seagull* and story "Lady with the Lapdog" as ballets.

Illustrative Art

Russian-born painter Marc Chagall (1887–1985), who anticipated surrealism, is best known for his large murals commissioned by the Jewish State Theater and New York's Metropolitan Opera House. Much of his work is derived from folklore and fairy tales and from village life in his native Russia; he was thus an ideal candidate to illustrate such a book as *Dead Souls*. Chagall did his black-and-white etchings for Gogol's novel between 1923 and 1927 while living in France; they were printed in 1927 and published in 1950. The plates range from the skeletal "On the Way to Sobakevitch's," which pictures a chortling Tchitchikov in a chaise driven by a cubist horse, to the drunken sumptuousness of "Révélations de Nozdryov," to the fragmentary "The Registry of Deeds," which depicts the dehumanizing strains of bureaucracy with chilling exactitude. Many of Chagall's panels represent busy scenes filled with dancing figures and dramatic life, while many others exhibit near-calligraphic minimalism. The varied presentation beautifully translates Gogol's honeycombed narrative. Indeed, Franz Meyer's description of the etchings in *Mark Chagall: His Graphic Work* could have been written by Gogol himself. He writes of Chagall painting his "native Russia with its wind-swept vastness and, for all its bitter misery born of unreason and inertia . . . its inexhaustible, wholesome, joyous vitality as well." A museum of Marc Chagall's work opened in Nice, France, in 1973.

COMMENTS & QUESTIONS

In this section, we aim to provide the reader with an array of perspectives on the text, as well as questions that challenge those perspectives. The commentary has been culled from sources as diverse as reviews contemporaneous with the work, letters written by the author, literary criticism and literary appreciations of later generations. Following the commentary, a series of questions seeks to discuss Nikolai Gogol's Dead Souls from various points of view and bring about a richer understanding of this enduring work.

Comments

NIKOLAI GOGOL

Within a week after this letter you will receive the printed *Dead Souls*— the rather pale threshold of the great poem which is being formed within me and will finally solve the riddle of my existence.

—translated by Carl R. Proffer,
from a letter to A. S. Danilevsky (May 9, 1842)

NEW YORK TIMES

If there had been no Gogol there might never have been a Turgenieff, for the strong influences of the former undoubtedly gave the author of the "Annals of a Sportsman" his peculiar bias. Turgenieff is a refinement on Gogol, but the theme they both sang was the same. It is a tender minor on the part of Turgenieff, exquisite in its delicacy, intoned with a broken heart, while Gogol howls it, if you like, in the major key, with many a joke and quibble; but the lesson is none the less apparent for that.

—December 19, 1886

VALERY BRYUSOV

[Gogol] created his own special world and his own special people; and what he found just hinted at in real life, he developed to the ultimate in his art. And such was the power of his talent, the power of his art, that he not only gave life to these fictions, but made them, as it were, more real than reality itself. He compelled generations of readers after him to forget real life and remember only the imaginary world that he had created. For many years we have all looked at the Ukraine and the Russia of Nicholas I through the Gogolian prism.

—translated by Robert A. Maguire, from *Vesy* (1909)

INNOKENTIJ ANNENSKIJ

Pushkin and Gogol. Our two-faced Janus. Two mirrors on the door that separates us from our past.

—translated by Victor Erlich, from *Apollon* (1911)

THE NATION

Gogol is of all Russian writers the nearest akin to Mark Twain or O. Henry. He has the same command of the grotesque, the same blending of fantastic humor with the occasional homely pathos, the same lack of any intellectual, philosophic insight into the depths of human character such as lends distinction to the work of his great successors. This very likeness to our American humorists has hindered Gogol from winning the wide fame he deserves. He is no master of plot; the subjects of both "The Inspector" and "Dead Souls" were suggested to him by Pushkin. His whole narrative art lies in stringing together, around some central figure, a succession of amusing incidents. His genius is in the creation of clear, distinct characters. These characters, however, are not types of universal significance, like Don Quixote and his squire, but rather local, Russian oddities. His humor and pathos are expressed through an unfamiliar medium that in our eyes dims their brilliancy. His grafters are like our own, but, like O. Henry, Gogol emphasizes not their souls but the tools of their trade, and those tools were emphatically made in Russia. Hence the humorous portraits that are so rich in suggestion to Gogol's countrymen may lose their savor in a translation. The difficulty is the same with other humorists, say, with Aristophanes. But no one attempts to read Aristophanes who has not a certain elementary knowledge of Athenian life, while a similar knowledge of Russian conditions is not yet a necessary part of even the most finished literary education. . . .

As time passes and Russian history and life become more familiar to outside nations, "Dead Souls" may after all prove to be a world classic. Rascality and meanness are independent of political barriers. A writer who can depict [his characters] as nothing but meanness and rascality, yet with a charity that does not refuse a handshake to the sneak and the rascal, with the light of humor that makes all men brothers, deserves a place among the great satirists and fun-makers of all ages.

—November 18, 1915

CLIFFORD ODETS

Dead Souls, for all its earthy laughter and fun, is essentially a tragic poem. Gogol himself titled the work "a poem" and it was his friend Pushkin who said of it, between laughter, "Oh, God, how sad our Russia is!"

—from his introduction to *Dead Souls* (1936)

VLADIMIR NABOKOV

The main lyrical note of *Dead Souls* bursts into existence when the idea of Russia as Gogol saw Russia (a peculiar landscape, a special atmosphere, a symbol, a long, long road) looms in all its strange loveliness through the tremendous dream of the book.

—from *Nikolai Gogol* (1944)

D. S. MIRSKY

Gógol's work was satirical, but not in the ordinary sense. It was not objective, but subjective, satire. His characters were not realistic caricatures of the world without, but introspective caricatures of the fauna of his own mind. They were exteriorizations of his own "ugliness" and "vices"; *Revizór* [*The Inspector General*] and *Dead Souls* were satires of self, and Russia and mankind only in so far as Russia and mankind reflected that self.

—edited by Francis J. Whitfield,
from *A History of Russian Literature* (1949)

EDMUND WILSON

Gogol wallows, like his characters, in the paragraphs of a cluttered, apparently phlegmatic style that has [in *Dead Souls*] been brought to perfection; yet this style has a persistent undercurrent of sadness, of disgust, of chagrin; it condemns and it undermines.

—from *The Nation* (December 6, 1952)

Questions

1. Can one tell from reading *Dead Souls* whether Gogol was, culturally speaking, more like a current American conservative or more like a current American liberal?

2. Simon Karlinsky wrote of Gogol: "His erotic imagination was primarily homosexual and his fear of his homosexual inclinations and his suppression of them is one of the principal themes of his writing, one of the main causes of his personal tragedy." One doesn't have to agree with Karlinsky's thesis to feel there is something "interesting" about sexuality in *Dead Souls*. How would you formulate Gogol's conception of human sexuality, his attitude toward it, his fear or longing or repulsion?

3. Is there a unifying theme, or idea, or argument, or ideology that holds the disparate components of *Dead Souls* together, especially as they concern the differences between parts I and II?

4. Gogol has often been championed as a realist, as even the founder of realism in the Russian novel. Would you describe *Dead Souls* as a realistic novel? Would you describe it as a Kafkaesque novel—as psychologically realistic but realistically distorted?

5. What is the main source of Gogol's humor? What do the butts of his jokes have in common?

FOR FURTHER READING

Biography

Karlinsky, Simon. *The Sexual Labyrinth of Nikolai Gogol*. Cambridge, MA: Harvard University Press, 1976. "His erotic imagination was primarily homosexual and his fear of his homosexual inclinations and his suppression of them is one of the principal themes of his writings, one of the main causes of his personal tragedy."

Magarshack, David. *Gogol: A Life*. 1957. New York: Grove Press, 1969. "Now, over a hundred years after his death, a careful study of all the available material of his life may provide a solution to this fascinating literary and human problem."

Setchkarev, Vsevolod. *Gogol: His Life and Works*. Translated by Robert Kramer. 1953. New York: New York University Press, 1965. "The intellectual and spiritual limitations of human life are Gogol's theme."

Turgenev, Ivan. "Gogol." In *Literary Reminiscences and Autobiographical Fragments* (1869), translated with an introduction by David Magarshack and an essay on Turgenev by Edmund Wilson. New York: Grove Press, 1959, pp. 160–171. A vivid description, based on personal acquaintance, by a major Russian novelist.

Criticism

Adams, Robert. "Mirrors and Windows: Poe, Gogol." In *Nil: Episodes in the Literary Conquest of Void during the Nineteenth Century*. New York: Oxford University Press, 1966, pp. 50–60. "The landowners encountered by Chichikov are at the roots of their characters so many responses to the void that surrounds, invades and threatens to supplant them."

Baring, Maurice. "Gogol and the Cheerfulness of the Russian People." In *Landmarks in Russian Literature*. 1910. London: Methuen, 1960, pp. 26–49. "The greatest humorist of Russian literature, the Russian Dickens, is Gogol."

Bayley, John. "The Secrets of Gogol." In *Selected Essays*. Cambridge, England: Cambridge University Press, 1984, pp. 124–137. "Gogol's admirers expected a sort of Russian Schiller, and they got something more like a Ukrainian Groucho Marx."

Bowra, Maurice. "Introduction" to *Dead Souls*, translated by George Reavey. Oxford: Oxford University Press, 1957, pp. v–ix. Gogol writes in the comic tradition of Aristophanes, *Don Quixote*, and *The Pickwick Papers*.

De Jonge, Alex. "Gogol." In *Nineteenth-Century Russian Literature: Studies of Ten Russian Writers*, edited by John Fennell. London: Faber, 1973, pp. 69–129. "The souls are perhaps the most important image that Gogol ever created. They act as a focus for the subtle confusion of real and unreal that occurs on every level, from the level of language . . . to the level of metaphysics."

Erlich, Victor. *Gogol*. New Haven, CT: Yale University Press, 1969. "This relative lack of concern with the way things actually happen, this whimsical or cavalier attitude toward reality, permeates much of Gogol's world."

Fanger, Donald. *The Creation of Nikolai Gogol*. Cambridge, MA: Harvard University Press, 1979. "Living people and dead ones may be clearly distinguished in the action, but the cumulative sense of the text denies this distinction."

Freeborn, Richard. "*Dead Souls*." In *The Rise of the Russian Novel: Studies in the Russian Novel from "Eugene Onegin" to "War and Peace."* Cambridge, England: Cambridge University Press, 1973, pp. 74–114. "*Dead Souls* can clearly be seen to fit Gogol's own definition of a novel as a highly poetic work which resembles not an epic so much as a drama."

Fusso, Susanne. *Designing "Dead Souls": An Anatomy of Disorder in Gogol*. Stanford, CA: Stanford University Press, 1993. The book "seeks to make a system, an anatomy, of Gogol's impulses toward disorder and disruption in *Dead Souls* in all their various and distinctive aspects."

Gibian, George, ed. *"Dead Souls": The Reavey Translation, Backgrounds and Sources, Essays in Criticism*. New York: W. W. Norton, 1985. Includes Gogol's letters and essays by Maguire, Herzen, Fanger, Gippius, Bely, Nabokov, Wilson, Karlinsky, and Bakhtin.

Griffiths, Frederick, and Stanley Rabinowitz. *Novel Epics: Gogol, Dostoevsky, and National Narrative*. Evanston, IL: Northwestern University Press, 1990, pp. 60–105. "The narrating voice of *Dead Souls* recurrently invites the audience to attend to his tale as the 'epic' that it seems so obviously not to be."

Maguire, Robert. *Exploring Gogol*. Stanford, CA: Stanford University Press,

1994. Emphasizes Gogol's language: "Theological issues pale before linguistic ones."

————. "Introduction" to Dead Souls, translated and edited by Christopher English. Oxford: Oxford University Press, 1998, pp. xiii–xxxvi, 412–448. "With Russia as hero, or heroine, Dead Souls attains the capaciousness, high seriousness and magnitude that are essential marks of the epic spirit."

Mirsky, D. S. "Gogol." In A History of Russian Literature From Its Beginnings to 1900, edited by Francis J. Whitfield. 1926. New York: Vintage, 1958, pp. 149–162. Concise, perceptive account of Gogol's life and works.

Nabokov, Vladimir. Nikolai Gogol. 1944. New York: New Directions, 1961. A brilliant, idiosyncratic interpretation, with emphasis on Gogol's grotesque characteristics, by a masterful modern Russian novelist.

Orwell, George. "Review of Gogol by Boris de Schloezer." 1933. In The Complete Works of George Orwell, edited by Peter Davison. London: Secker and Warburg, 1998. Vol. 10, pp. 310–311. "All the characters in the book were not merely base, they were also extraordinarily void of any kind of spiritual awareness—briefly, they were dead souls."

Peace, Richard. The Enigma of Gogol: An Examination of the Writings of N.V. Gogol and Their Place in the Russian Literary Tradition. Cambridge, England: Cambridge University Press, 1981. Gogol defines his characters by "physical appearance, style of speech, ambience (house, estate, etc.), family relationships, hospitality (especially food) and reaction to Chichikov's strange proposition."

Pevear, Richard. "Introduction" to Dead Souls, translated by Richard Pevear and Larissa Volokhonsky. New York: Pantheon, 1996, pp. vii–xxiv, 395–402. "The tremendous paradox of the title—Dead Souls—is fraught with all the ambiguities of this inverted idealism."

Rahv, Philip. "Gogol as a Modern Instance." In Image and Idea: Twenty Essays on Literary Themes. Revised and enlarged edition. New York: New Directions, 1957, pp. 203–209. "His creative psychology is so tortuous and obsessive, so given over to moods of self-estrangement and self-loathing, so marked by abrupt turns from levity to despair."

Reeve, F. D. "Dead Souls." In The Russian Novel. New York: McGraw-Hill, 1966, pp. 64–102. "We can ask if Chichikov is traveling among the damned in Hell or if he is himself the Devil."

Todd, William Mills III. "Dead Souls: 'Charmed by a Phrase.'" In Fiction and Society in the Age of Pushkin: Ideology, Institutions, and Narrative. Cambridge, MA:

Harvard University Press, 1986, pp. 164–200. "*Dead Souls* becomes a picaresque collection of interwoven picaresques, with the biographies of the dead and runaway serfs and the tale of the outlaw Kopeikin casting Chichikov's journeys in sharper relief."

Wellek, René. "Introduction" to *Dead Souls*, translated by B. G. Guerney. New York: Holt, Rinehart and Winston, 1948, pp. v–x. "Here is a comic epic, a gallery of portraits, a loosely assembled travel story."

Wilson, Edmund. "Gogol: The Demon in the Overgrown Garden." *The Nation*, 175 (December 6, 1952), pp. 520–524. Reprinted in *A Window on Russia, For the Use of Foreign Readers*. New York: Farrar, Straus and Giroux, 1972, pp. 38–51. "Gogol presents an unusual case of a frustrating impasse of the spirit, a hopeless neurotic deadlock, combined with a gusto for life, an enormous artistic vitality."

Woodward, James. *Gogol's "Dead Souls."* Princeton, NJ: Princeton University Press, 1978. *Dead Souls* is "the most complex and aesthetically compelling moral allegory in the Russian language. . . . [It] harks back to . . . the tradition of the allegorical journey through the underworld, which was a staple ingredient of the classical epic."

Look for the following titles, available now and forthcoming from
BARNES & NOBLE CLASSICS.

Visit your local bookstore for these fine titles.
Or to order online go to: WWW.BN.COM/CLASSICS

Adventures of Huckleberry Finn	Mark Twain	1-59308-000-X	$4.95
The Adventures of Tom Sawyer	Mark Twain	1-59308-068-9	$4.95
The Age of Innocence	Edith Wharton	1-59308-143-X	$5.95
Alice's Adventures in Wonderland and Through the Looking-Glass	Lewis Carroll	1-59308-015-8	$5.95
Anna Karenina	Leo Tolstoy	1-59308-027-1	$8.95
The Art of War	Sun Tzu	1-59308-017-4	$7.95
The Awakening and Selected Short Fiction	Kate Chopin	1-59308-001-8	$4.95
The Brothers Karamazov	Fyodor Dostoevsky	1-59308-045-X	$9.95
The Call of the Wild and White Fang	Jack London	1-59308-200-2	$5.95
Candide	Voltaire	1-59308-028-X	$4.95
A Christmas Carol, The Chimes and The Cricket on the Hearth	Charles Dickens	1-59308-033-6	$5.95
The Collected Poems of Emily Dickinson		1-59308-050-6	$5.95
The Complete Sherlock Holmes, Vol. I	Sir Arthur Conan Doyle	1-59308-034-4	$7.95
The Complete Sherlock Holmes, Vol. II	Sir Arthur Conan Doyle	1-59308-040-9	$7.95
The Count of Monte Cristo	Alexandre Dumas	1-59308-151-0	$7.95
Daniel Deronda	George Eliot	1-59308-290-8	$8.95
David Copperfield	Charles Dickens	1-59308-063-8	$7.95
The Death of Ivan Ilych and Other Stories	Leo Tolstoy	1-59308-069-7	$7.95
Don Quixote	Miguel de Cervantes	1-59308-046-8	$9.95
Dracula	Bram Stoker	1-59308-114-6	$6.95
Emma	Jane Austen	1-59308-089-1	$4.95
Essays and Poems by Ralph Waldo Emerson		1-59308-076-X	$6.95
The Essential Tales and Poems of Edgar Allan Poe		1-59308-064-6	$7.95
Frankenstein	Mary Shelley	1-59308-115-4	$4.95
Great American Short Stories: from Hawthorne to Hemingway		1-59308-086-7	$7.95
Great Expectations	Charles Dickens	1-59308-006-9	$4.95
Gulliver's Travels	Jonathan Swift	1-59308-132-4	$5.95
Hard Times	Charles Dickens	1-59308-156-1	$5.95
Heart of Darkness and Selected Short Fiction	Joseph Conrad	1-59308-021-2	$4.95
The Histories	Herodotus	1-59308-102-2	$6.95
The House of Mirth	Edith Wharton	1-59308-153-7	$6.95
Howards End	E. M. Forster	1-59308-022-0	$6.95
The Hunchback of Notre Dame	Victor Hugo	1-59308-047-6	$5.95
The Idiot	Fyodor Dostoevsky	1-59308-058-1	$7.95
The Importance of Being Earnest and Four Other Plays	Oscar Wilde	1-59308-059-X	$6.95
The Inferno	Dante Alighieri	1-59308-051-4	$6.95
Jane Eyre	Charlotte Brontë	1-59308-007-7	$4.95
Jude the Obscure	Thomas Hardy	1-59308-035-2	$6.95
The Jungle Books	Rudyard Kipling	1-59308-109-X	$5.95
The Jungle	Upton Sinclair	1-59308-008-5	$4.95
The Last of the Mohicans	James Fenimore Cooper	1-59308-137-5	$5.95
Leaves of Grass: First and "Death-bed" Editions	Walt Whitman	1-59308-083-2	$9.95
Les Misérables	Victor Hugo	1-59308-066-2	$9.95
Little Women	Louisa May Alcott	1-59308-108-1	$6.95

(continued)

𝒥𝔅

BARNES & NOBLE CLASSICS

If you are an educator and would like to receive an
Examination or Desk Copy of a Barnes & Noble Classic edition,
please refer to Academic Resources on our website at
WWW.BN.COM/CLASSICS
or contact us at
B&NCLASSICS@BN.COM.

All prices are subject to change.